BATTLE STATIONS!

The USS HERCULES:

"We have radar contact! Incoming aircraft at 348 degrees. Sixty miles out at fifteen thousand feet. Coming fast at five hundred knots." The voice came in over the intercom from the radar operator at control center.

Commander Gus Jones was standing on the deck of the pilot house. "Is it ours?" he demanded, speaking into his intercom mike.

"Not unless they've changed the ID codes on us, sir."

"Take her to foil speed. Set course at ninety degrees," he ordered quickly. "Fire control, lock the Mk 75 on him. Fire on my order."

"She's at ten miles and ten thousand feet, sir. I have a visual. Looks like an F-5. Standard armament. Philippine markings."

Gus raised his binoculars and watched as the plane crossed directly over his ship, pulled into a wide turn and headed back toward them. "Stupid kid is going to try a strafing attack out of the sun. He's been watching too many old war movies."

"He's at five miles and five thousand feet and coming fast!"

Gus didn't hesitate. "Open fire!"

The Mk started barking, its muzzle flashing. Almost simultaneously, the enemy plane let go four rockets that tore up the sky, but missed their mark. Seconds later, the sound of a midair explosion rolled out across the ocean. Pieces of aircraft floated out of the sunlight as they fell toward the water.

"Keep her on course. Bring her to hull speed," he ordered the helmsman. "It's not over."

TARGET: SUBIC BAY

MACK TANNER

ZEBRA BOOKS
KENSINGTON PUBLISHING CORP.

ZEBRA BOOKS

are published by

Kensington Publishing Corp.
475 Park Avenue South
New York, NY 10016

First printing: October, 1992

Printed in the United States of America

Chapter One

The submarine Kyong Ki.

Captain Kang Ae Kyong stared through the periscope into almost total blackness. He switched on the light amplification mode, and the world beyond the scope burst into greenish light. Now he could see the sand beaches backed by dark jungle. Three fishing boats floated in the bay about a thousand meters from where the slowly moving sub's scope had poked above the water.

Captain Kang watched the fishing boats for almost three minutes before he saw a light start blinking on the bow of the lead boat. He counted the blinks: four, a pause, then three, another pause, and then a single blink. He spun around and checked the open mouth of the bay. All was clear and the sub's sonar was reporting only the idling sounds of the fishing boat engines.

He swung the scope back to look at the fishing boats again. The boats started moving slowly through the waters of the bay, coming in the direction of the *Kyong Ki*. His sonar man reported the sound of the the small screws.

"Down periscope! Take her up!"

He stepped back as the periscope slid down and turned to one of the crew. "Tell Colonel Cho Chae-Jin that we have arrived and his friends are here to meet us."

Colonel Cho Chae-Jin entered the conn as the sail of the *Kyong Ki* was breaking surface. The colonel wore black cloth pants, a pullover shirt and rubber thongs on his feet instead of the fatigue uniform of the Army of the Democratic People's Republic of Korea that he had worn during the voyage. He followed the captain up the ladder and into the cockpit of the sail.

Outside, Colonel Cho took a long, deep breath of the salty, warm air. He held it a moment and took another, trying to wash out of his throat the smell of diesel and *kimchi*-flavored sweat. The colonel took a position to one side of the cockpit and stood silently watching while Captain Kang gave the orders to man the deck guns, elevate the defense missiles, and to put the crew to the difficult job at hand.

Colonel Cho could barely make out the outline of the captain in the faint starlight, but he knew the captain was wearing a set of night vision goggles. There were no goggles for Colonel Cho because the People's Navy had only a few of the magic instruments that turned night into day. The men doing the critical work below were wearing all the other sets on board.

Colonel Cho could tell by the faint sounds that the crew had opened the deck hatches so they could unload the cargo he was responsible for delivering.

This wasn't the first time he had stood on the deck while sailors unloaded cargo of the Philippine coast. He had made four previous trips into the silent bay on surface ships. This was the first time he had come in a submarine. This time the cargo was too important to risk a chance encounter with some Philippine naval vessel, or worse, one of the hated American ships that sailed through Philippine waters like a conquering hoard.

He had expected the fear he'd fought once he first boarded the sub would leave him, now that he was breathing clean air again, but it still twisted his stomach in a tight knot. He thought about it and realized it wasn't the same kind of fear.

Fear of failure had stolen the place of fear of closed space and cramped quarters. That kind of fear was to be expected when victory was almost in the grasp, the closer the chance of victory, the greater the fear of failure.

He heard the sound and felt the thud as the first of the fishing boats touched the hull of the submarine. Five other boats quickly lined up alongside the first boat.

"Your friends are here," Captain Kang announced, still keeping his voice a whisper.

"I will go down and meet them," Colonel Cho announced. "You understand your orders?"

"Of course," the sub skipper assured him. "We will stay hidden until you have bitten the enemy and stolen his meal. When you have the victory, I will put out to sea, surface, and send the news home. We will then stand by to make sure the enemy stays in his cage."

"If all goes well, the next time you come calling here, you will not have to sneak in like a thief in the night," Colonel Cho said. "You can come in during the day, and through the front door."

"I wish you luck," the captain said.

"Our Great Leader tells us that luck is for fools," Colonel Cho reminded the captain. "Victory belongs to those with knowledge, courage, will, and political understanding."

On the deck below, Colonel Cho worked his way to a group of three men who had boarded the sub from one of the five fishing boats now tied to the hull of the submarine.

"Major Kim," Cho whispered as he approached the group.

"Colonel, sir!" a voice replied in Korean, letting the Colonel know he had found the right group.

Too dark to make out features, Cho identified Major Kim Chun-Hwa by his height. He was several inches shorter than one of the three men, but a bit taller than the other. Cho could see enough to tell that all three of the men were wearing clothing very similar to what he was wearing.

"Colonel Cho, it's good to see you again," the tall, thin man said, speaking the words in English. He was stretching his hand out and Cho took it for a shake.

"Hello Aguila," Cho answered. "I bring you greetings from the Korean people and the tools you need for your glorious victory. I met personally with our Dear Leader the night before I left Pyongyang." Dear Leader was the title of respect given to Kim Jung Il, the son and the heir of Kim Il-Sung, the Great Leader of the Democratic People's Republic of Korea.

"The Dear Leader and the Great Leader both send their greetings and the treasures I bring to the soldiers of the New People's Army and to their leader."

Colonel Cho turned to Major Kim without waiting for an answer or comment from the tall man. "How has the work gone during my absence?" he asked switching back into Korean. "Have these pretend Marxists developed any better work habits?"

"Without our constant supervision, our previous shipments would still be sitting in their crates." Neither man feared that the two Filipinos would understand what they were saying. While Aguila Sorreno had gone to North Korea in 1988 for special training, he spoke no Korean.

"Everything is unpacked and distributed to the proper places?" Colonel Cho asked.

"Of course Comrade Colonel. Everything is ready for the final phase of *Operation Strike Back* to begin. All we need are what you bring with you."

"What are the plans for delivering the five crates I bring?" Colonel Cho asked.

"We will load each crate on a separate fishing boat. Each boat will take its load to a different unloading dock. A truck is waiting at each spot. If something goes wrong, we will lose only one piece of the shipment."

"I approve of your planning," Cho whispered. "But we must not lose even one piece of the shipment."

"I understand, Comrade Colonel. I can't tell you how eager

8

I am to get on with the next phase," Kim said.

Major Kim seemed almost anxious to keep the conversation going. Colonel Cho could understand why. It had been many weeks since Major Kim had spoken his native language. The orders stated that none of the Korean officers participating in the operation were to speak their mother tongue at any time while they were on Philippine territory. In the unfortunate event that any one of them was ever captured alive, and kept alive, they were to speak only English or Japanese. If they lived to suffer torture, they were to confess to being members of the Red Army.

"What about security for the operation?"

"We still have total secrecy. There was one close call. Some police thugs caught Comrade Lt. Pak Pyong-ho at a checkpoint. Fortunately, he did his duty. He lived in captivity for only a few minutes. They never got a chance to interrogate him."

"His political being will survive forever because of his sacrifice," Cho said, repeating the quote of the Great Leader. "Now, let's get these presents unloaded and on to shore."

Colonel Cho turned back to the tall Filipino. "Comrade Sorreno," he said, switching back to English. "I suggest that you and I go with the first launch which is loaded. We need to find someplace where we can use a bit of light. I have much to discuss and show you. Now that we have everything you will need to defeat the enemy, we want to move immediately to the next stage."

"It can't be too soon for me. I want to get out of the jungle and live like the leader of a revolution should live."

"That will come, my friend," the Korean answered. "But first we must spring our little surprises."

Chapter Two

Subic Bay, The Philippines.

"Is it a boat or a ship?"

Rear Admiral Augustus Jones glanced at Captain Tim Reilly who was standing beside him on the dock. The vessel they were looking at was the *Hercules,* the last production model of the *Pegasus*-class of hydrofoil patrol boats.

"She's a ship because the Navy says she is," Admiral Jones answered. "I commanded something like her for a while."

"I thought you did all your sea time with the Seventh Fleet. Haven't these things all been assigned down to Key West?"

"I commanded the first hydrofoil the Navy tried, the *Tucum-cari,*" Jones answered. "She was only about a third the size of this one and she had an 81-mm mortar on the fantail instead of missiles. They ran her through a few months of combat evaluation in Viet Nam. I extended a tour for several months to skipper her."

"I forgot you were brown water Navy in Nam," Reilly said, a bit of embarrassment in his voice. "No wonder you wanted to come down and look her over. I still think that this is something the Coast Guard should be sailing, not the Navy."

"I don't think the Coast Guard needs the kind of equipment she's got on the fantail," the Admiral suggested, pointing with his chin toward the stern of the *Hercules.*

The fantail equipment he was referring to was a double set of MK 141 rocket launchers that pointed up and forward from each side of the stern deck. Each set consisted of four tubes and each tube normally held one Harpoon missile. On the fore deck, an Mk 75-OTO Malera antiaircraft gun pointed forward across the bow. The *Hercules* was a small girl with big teeth. The only thing the ship didn't have was an ASW (antisubmarine warfare) capacity. The *Hercules*'s foilborne speed of over fifty knots would allow her to outrun any torpedo.

While Gus still looked back on his brown water Navy time as the high point in his career, most naval line officers would agree with Reilly. The hydrofoil was an orphan class ship that had been shoved on the Navy by a group of congressmen convinced that a NATO fleet of hydrofoils stationed at navigation choke points around the world was a cheap answer to the growing costs of building naval ships.

While the original proposal called for the construction of dozens of the small, lightning-fast craft as part of Admiral Zumwalt's Project 60, that idea sunk out of the budget soon after Zumwalt retired.

They built only six of them. All six were assigned to the Atlantic Fleet and stationed at Key West, Florida where they mostly chased drug smugglers.

A merchant marine container ship had brought the *Hercules* as desk cargo from Florida to Subic Bay. She had been unloaded two days ago. Several American enlisted men and a dozen Filipino workers were working on her, trying to get her ready for sea duty.

"I can't think of any situation where the Navy could use something like that in a modern combat situation," Reilly added to his previous remarks. "I'm betting the only reason they shipped it out here is so we can give it to the Philippine Navy once they finish with those firing tests."

"You're probably right," Admiral Jones admitted. "But I'm not so sure our Navy couldn't be putting these babies to better

11

use than what's been done with them."

"I know some congressmen who agree with you. But, with apologies, I don't," Reilly stated, still sticking with his position. "Why did they have to haul her all the way around the world for some weapons testing anyway? We still have a couple of islands off the Florida coast we use for practice firing ranges."

"Read the GAO report," the Admiral said. "I've got a copy in my office. You know how it works. Congress criticizes the Navy for not spending the money the way Congress said it was supposed to be spent. The Navy's answer is to spend a whole lot more money making it look like the Navy wants to do what Congress thinks it should be doing, but can't. When are the tests scheduled to start?"

"It will be a week or so before they get to the actual live fire tests. They are going to run her through some sea trials first so the officers can familiarize themselves with the waters around the islands."

"We came here to look her over," Admiral Jones announced, "let's go aboard." Jones led the way toward the gangplank that led from the dock to the single outside deck of the small ship.

Lt. Commander Reggie Mundt, the commanding officer of the *Hercules,* stood watching the two officers walk up his gangplank. He had already been warned that the admiral was on his way over for a visit. Mundt hadn't been on base long enough to learn much about the admiral who commanded the largest U.S. Naval facility outside the United States.

The senior officer coming up the gangplank was a big man, at least 6'2". He weighed a good two hundred pounds, all of it muscle and bone. He looked young for the rank he carried; he was somewhere in his late forties. The second officer was shorter by six inches and had a complexion that almost glowed red in the tropical sun.

Admiral Jones arrived at the top of the plank, threw a salute to the flag, and requested permission to come aboard.

Mundt gave the permission and asked whether the admiral would prefer to start with coffee in the ward room, or see the equipment first.

Mundt was nervous and Admiral Gus Jones could understand why. As the base facility commander, Gus had no command control over any of the ships berthed at Subic Bay. He was more like a hotel manager or a gas station attendant who offered all the ships in port protection, repair, and replenishment.

The admiral occasionally accepted a social invitation to dine on board one of the ships in port. He did not make it a practice of boarding every ship that docked in his facilities for a courtesy call.

"Why don't we skip the coffee," Gus told the officer. "I used to skipper a patrol boat on the Mekong. Small boats have fascinated me ever since. I'd like to look her over, see what she's made of."

Lt. Commander Mundt, now smiling with understanding, led the way with Admiral Jones and Captain Reilly following behind. He started with the crew mess room on the only deck that was below the main deck level. They walked from there back through the crew quarters to the engine room where Mundt described the functions of the foilborne propulsion system, a two-speed water jet driven by a single General Electric marine gas turbine engine. Further aft, Mundt pointed out the twin Aerojet water jet pumps powered by two Mercedes-Benz diesels which drove the vessel while she was hullborne.

Next, they climbed up to the main deck and walked forward through the superstructure to the communications and fire control center. From there they climbed a short ladder up to the bridge deck which consisted of a small wheelhouse. Because the wheelhouse sat above the superstructure, it provided a 360 degree field of vision. While much more spacious, the wheelhouse looked more like the cockpit of a jet liner than the bridge of a naval ship.

There were two armchairs that looked out the front ports with an instrument panel below the port. An airplane-style wheel projected from the panel in front of one of the chairs.

Admiral Jones looked around the wheelhhouse while Lt. Commander Mundt described the dual control steering system. The ship was controlled by the wheel while hullborne. A second system, an automatic computer monitor, controlled both steering and the height the foils lifted the hull out of the water while the ship was foilborne.

Jones was about to call his tour over when another officer entered the bridge area, climbing up the ladder from the control center below. The officer wore work khakis and the brass oak leaves of a lieutenant commander. She apparently wasn't aware that the ship had visitors. She saw the admiral as she stepped away from the well, snapped to attention, and gave a crisp salute. The salute given, she stayed standing at attention.

"This is Lt. Commander Kathy Melendez," Lt. Commander Mundt explained to his two visitors. "Commander, this is Admiral Augustus Jones, the facility commander."

Lt. Commander Melendez's looks fit her Spanish name. Her hair was inky black and her eyes almost the same color. Her cinnamon bark skin and her facial features suggested a Mexican-American background with more than a touch of Indian rather than Puerto Rican ancestry. Her rank meant she had to be near forty, but she appeared to be in her early thirties. She stood only about 5'4". If pressed, Gus would have described her as cute more than pretty, although it was hard to think of anyone wearing a lt. commander's khakis as cute. Gus had to admit she did give the uniform a shape he wasn't used to seeing on board a fighting ship.

"At ease!" Gus said, but not feeling at ease himself. It wasn't that he was opposed to women in uniforms, and he didn't consider himself a male chauvinist. But Gus had graduated from the Academy long before women had been admitted. For the men serving on ships of war, the Navy was still a small world in which women appeared as wives, lovers, secretaries, teachers, doctors, but seldomly as professional colleagues. As a result, every time he dealt with a woman as a colleague in arms, he was never sure quite how to act and always very much aware of the dangers of a wrong step. He knew two personal friends who had taken a wrong step and beached their careers on the shoals of a sexual discrimination complaint.

"You're not assigned to the *Hercules*, are you?" Captain Reilly asked.

"Of course not, Captain," she answered. "The *Hercules* is a war ship. I've been assigned TDY to the Subic Naval Magazine so I can be here for these tests."

"Commander Melendez is a weapons guidance system specialist," Commander Mundt explained.

"So you're the expert who is supposed to decide whether or not the Navy could use these as launch platforms for attacks against inland surface targets," Gus said.

"Not exactly," Commander Melendez answered. "My job is to make sure the weapon technical equipment and computer software function as they are supposed to during the test. But I do think that the *Pegasus*-class hydrofoil is an excellent platform for the new SLAMs."

The SLAM AGM-84E (Standoff Land-Attack Missile) was one of the newer missiles in the American arsenal. Built on a Harpoon air frame, the missile used an imaging infrared seeker guidance system and had a range of sixty miles.

"It's not so much a question of can you use them but does the Navy want to use them in low intensity conflicts," Melendez added.

Her English was accent-free with hard As and Es where they should be, instead of the softer Spanish sounds. She had either been raised in a home where English was the native tongue or she had worked very hard at perfecting an Anglo-Saxon-style English.

"Why take a boat to a war when you can take a ship or task

15

force?" Captain Reilly asked, sticking with his own belief that patrol boats were of no tactical nor strategic use for the blue water American Navy.

"If you need a task force, it's not a low intensity conflict," Melendez snapped back, obviously not intimidated by superior rank. "As the GAO report suggested, by positioning these vessels at strategic points around the globe, we could respond within a couple of days, or even a few hours to situations that now require weeks of build-up and positioning of ships, supplies, and men before we dare act. Right now, our response to a given situation is a choice between doing nothing, or an all out war. The *Pegasus*-class hydrofoil, with the firepower that even a destroyer didn't have twenty-five years ago, offers an expanded response option."

"Give me an example where the U.S. would want to start shooting from the deck of a pleasure boat instead of an aircraft carrier," Reilly challenged her.

"The attack on Qaddafi was one example where we could have used one or two hydrofoils instead of flying F-111s all the way from England. Who knows what we could have done in Iraq with something like this on the day Saddam Hussein first invaded Kuwait? Maybe we could have caught him in his command headquarters, not safely hunkered down in his bunker. If the United States is going to play world policeman in this new world order, we've got to put a few policemen on each block with the firepower to stop a low intensity situation before it explodes into war. The American budget can't stand many more Gulf Wars."

The quick way she laid out the arguments suggested it was a speech she had given before. Listening to her, Admiral Jones wondered how much input she had made in the GAO report. As soon as he got back to his office, he would check the report again to see if her name appeared on the list of people interviewed by the GAO (General Accounting Office) team.

"If you're arguing this is an assassin's weapon, I'll agree,"

16

Reilly countered. "But assassination is not the Navy's business."

"I thought killing was the whole purpose of war," she snapped back. "This technology lets us kill the right targets and destroy the right equipment. American forces proved how effective SLAMs can be in Iraq when delivered from the air. We want to demonstrate that delivery from ships can work just as well. We expect to demonstrate that ship-launched SLAMs can effectively destroy specified inland targets such as an insurgent command headquarters, concentration of irregular troops, or even something like a nuclear facility or a chemical plant producing weapon material."

The emphasis that Melendez kept putting on the word *we* sounded almost like a suggestion that she owned the system. Gus wondered how much she had been directly involved in the system's development: probably quite a lot.

"But the IIR (imaging infrared) guidance system is a video system," Reilly argued. "You get the missile to the target area with GPS navigation, then a pilot in a plane above the area has to take over the system for the final minute of flight. I don't see a helicopter landing pad on this patrol boat. But you still need that aircraft in the air for the final sixty seconds. That means you have to have a bigger ship standing by to provide the aircraft. That doesn't make sense."

"We have an aircraft on board." Melendez's voice had taken on the tone of a college professor rather than a military briefing officer. "We're testing the first production model of the new MRPV."

"You've got a drone?" Reilly asked, giving the popular name to what the military called a Medium Range Remotely Piloted Vehicle.

"A very fancy drone. It carries a 100-pound payload which includes a low-light television camera, a forward looking infrared system, thermo spotting capacity and EMS capability. She's launched from a catapult and recovered with a net. We can use her to first spot the target, and then relay signals back to the ship for those final sixty seconds."

Gus smiled. He was enjoying watching the feisty female handle Tim's challenges.

"We are also trying another modification of the guidance system in these tests," she continued, "a laser guidance variation. This would cover a situation in which you had someone on the ground, but you couldn't get a plane in the air. The human source would be able to take an elevated position and shine a laser beam to guide the missile to the target."

"How many missiles are you going to fire during the tests?" Admiral Jones asked.

"We're supposed to test fire four missiles," Lt. Commander Mundt answered. "Two of them with the production IIR guidance system and two with the infrared guidance system."

"I can predict the results," Reilly said. "The Navy will take six months writing a report that will describe why the results prove it's an impractical weapon system, the naval docks here will be ordered to strip off the launch system, and we'll sign her over to the Philippine Navy to use as a patrol boat."

Admiral Jones watched the anger play in the eyes of Commander Melendez, but she held her tongue. She was smart enough to recognize that Reilly was telling the probable truth, even if she didn't like it.

Jones raised his left hand, turning it over so he could look at the watch face he wore on the bottom side of his wrist. "I guess we'd better be on the way," he said to Reilly. "Our meeting with Admiral Rimaldo is in fifteen minutes."

The admiral thanked Mundt for his courtesy and the weapons officer for her explanations.

"If you would like to take a ride with us, we're taking her out for a trial run tomorrow," Mundt said.

"Thanks," Admiral Jones answered, "but I don't think I have the time."

Back in his car, Gus Jones took one last look out the window at the *Hercules* sitting by the dock. He would have liked to have taken the offered ride.

Under the treaty that allows the U.S. Navy to use the facilities of Subic Naval Base, the legal base commander is an officer of the Philippine Navy. Gus Jones had three official titles: Commander U. S. Facility, Subic Bay; Commander U.S. Naval Forces Philippines; and Representative of the Commander in Chief, U.S. Pacific Command in the Philippines.

As far as the day-to-day operations of the naval base were concerned, Rear Admiral Ramon Rimaldo held down one of the easiest jobs in anyone's navy. It was well paid too, but not in the salary and the perks of rank in the Philippine Navy. The navy part of Admiral Rimaldo's job was ceremonial, but all the economic relations between the U.S. Navy and the country of 67 million people, who lived outside the gates, funneled through the office of the Philippine base commander.

Every time a contract was let to a Philippine firm, every time a Filipino was hired for one of the twenty-three thousand jobs for Philippine workers on the base, and every time a naked, brown ass slipped between the sheet with an American sailor on shore leave, Admiral Rimaldo and his friends and relatives in Malacañang Palace or AFP headquarters at Fort Bonifacio collected a piece of the take.

Admiral Jones put on his best false smile as he walked into Admiral Rimaldo's office. His superiors had made it clear during his Washington briefings that he was to get along with his Philippine counterpart, no matter what. The recent negotiations for the continued use of the base had not gone the way either Washington or Philippine politicians had wanted them to go. The eruption of the volcano Mt. Pinatubo had both demonstrated how much the United States needed Subic Bay and at the same time significantly reduced the value of the base from an economic standpoint. As a result, the Americans thought they had paid too much for damaged merchandise while most Philippine politicians believed the Americans had taken advantage of the volcanic damage to knock down the price. But the Navy did have a deal and no one on the American side wanted the negotiations reopened, something that several Philippine senators kept demanding be done. While the base operation pumped millions of dollars into the Philippine economy, it would not be the two hundred thousand ordinary Filipinos who depended on the base for jobs who would decide if the Americans stayed. It would be men like Admiral Rimaldo and the landowner families he represented.

"Admiral Rimaldo, how are you today?" Gus asked as he walked across the room to where Rimaldo stood waiting. "Did you break eighty yesterday?"

"I missed it by two. When do we play again?"

Gus Jones hated golf. He'd taken the game up because he had been ordered to do so by the same people who picked him for Subic Bay instead of giving him the sea command he had hoped for. He'd spent four weeks and five hundred dollars on lessons. Because he refused to do anything badly, he'd arrived in the Philippines with a ten handicap.

In the six months that he'd been playing Sunday golf with Admiral Rimaldo, he'd brought his handicap down to six and lost five hundred dollars in bets to Admiral Rimaldo. It was money that the Navy wouldn't cover, nor could he even claim it as an income tax deduction. He didn't lose deliberately, he lost because Admiral Rimaldo and his caddy cheated.

Rimaldo invited Admiral Jones and Captain Reilly to sit down, and a Philippine orderly came in with coffee to serve.

"I understand you want to talk about the Russian who's coming to visit," Gus began. "The way I understand it, he's your guest, not ours."

"I think it's in both our interests to make sure it's a successful visit," Rimaldo answered. His voice sounding like he was trying to coax a virgin out of her pants. "Your State Department thought up the whole idea. We both know that he's not coming here to see me. He wants to see your facilities."

20

Rimaldo was right about who had originated the idea of exchange visits between the American Commander of U.S. Naval Forces in the Philippines and his Russian counterpart at Cam Rahn Bay in Viet Nam. But the Philippine Navy had welcomed the idea, perhaps as a way of suggesting that if the American Congress would only approve enough money, the Americans could stay for as long as they wanted. If not, there were others who might be willing to rent the property, even if it was covered with tons of new volcanic ash.

"Okay, I'll give him a tour, but only of the base areas that we would let any journalists see. When's he due in?"

"Admiral Yegorov Semenkov will be arriving at Manila Airport in exactly one week. We plan on bringing him by air to Subic."

As the admiral gave the details, Captain Reilly took out the notebook he always carried and jotted down the information.

"I will need tail numbers and precise times," Reilly reminded the Philippine admiral.

"I will host a luncheon for him," Rimaldo explained. "We thought a tour of the base facilities in the afternoon would be appropriate. I would like to suggest that you host a dinner, and we were hoping you could put him up in your guest quarters."

Gus turned to Captain Reilly. "You set it up like that. I suppose I'll have to go everywhere he goes."

"Admiral Semenkov's schedule calls for him being here over the weekend," Rimaldo added. "Perhaps we can all play a game of golf."

"I'll be surprised if the Russian golfs," Gus answered, envying for the first time life in the Russian Navy. "If you like, we can give him a tour of the bay, maybe send him out to Grand Island for the day." Grand Island was an island in the middle of the bay. An old fort on the island had been converted into a resort and recreation center for U.S. military personnel and their families. As most of the families had still not been brought back to the base since the eruption of Pinatubo,

Grand Island had lots of space for visitors.

With the Russian admiral taken care of, they spent the next two hours discussing base hiring practices, off-limit procedures, joint AFP/USN shore patrol units, Base Exchange diversion problems, and the current VD rate in the Olongapo bars. Reilly had the answers to most of the questions the Philippine admiral asked. Gus sat sipping the heavy, sweet coffee and watched the geckos chase mosquitoes on the admiral's walls.

Rimaldo saw the men out to the steps where the two Americans told him goodbye. Gus and Reilly walked down the steps to where their car sat waiting. The bored enlisted driver was sitting in the front seat with all the windows closed and the motor running to keep the air conditioning on. It was against regulations for the drivers to do that, but Gus was just as happy to slip into the cool interior of the car.

"I want tight security for the Russian while he's on our hands," Gus said to Reilly once they were moving down the road. "Don't make it obvious, but we want him seeing only what we don't care about."

"It's a good time for the visit from that perspective," Reilly answered. "There won't be much in port. Just about every ship stationed here will be up north participating in *Team Spirit*."

Team Spirit was the annual joint military exercise that the United States military held with the South Korean military every year in the early spring.

"That solves some of the protocol problems, too," Gus said. "We won't have so many officers on base to invite to dinner. You draw up the list of people for the dinner at my place. Put Rimaldo on it and the Mayor of Olongapo. Keep the numbers down."

Back in his own office, Admiral Jones walked to a bookcase that covered part of one wall. He pulled down the copy of the GAO report that had come in the mail three weeks before. It was a two-inch thick paperback with a green paper cover titled *U.S. Navy Utilization and Deployment of Hydrofoil Surface Ships*. He opened the book to the back pages and found the appendix that listed the sources the three GAO investigators had talked with while gathering material for their criticisms of the Navy for its failure to effectively develop and utilize low-end equipment such as the hydrofoil.

Commander Katherine Melendez was listed there along with a description of her position in the Research and Advanced Technology Division in the Office of Research and Engineering. The entry described her academic credentials, including a PhD in physics from the California Institute of Technology. Kathy Melendez knew more than physics, she had also learned how to manipulate the system. She hadn't come to the Philippines to prove that the *Pegasus*-class hydrofoil had a use in a modern navy. The congressional demand that the hydrofoil be given a fair test had offered her a piggyback ride to test a collection of new guidance systems for short-range cruise missiles.

Chapter Three

Subic Bay, the Philippines.

"Checkmate!"

Chagrined, Admiral Jones looked across the table at his opponent. He'd seen it coming four moves back, but he'd continued playing on the chance his opponent hadn't seen the same thing. The man had not only seen it, he had set it up.

The Russian was looking him straight in the eye and laughed. It wasn't a laugh that claimed victory, but the laugh of an overgrown boy marking a score as he wrestled for the fun and the exercise it offered.

"So, my new friend, do we play again?" As the Russian asked the question he reached for the bottle of Hennessy that the Philippine steward had left sitting beside the onyx chess table. The Russian admiral popped the cork and poured in a splash that suggested he wasn't ready to call it a night.

"You already beat me two out of three. I'll admit you're better than I am," Gus answered.

The Russian grinned and took a long sip of the brandy. "Maybe tonight, but I'm not so sure I will be the best the next time we try. I think you are a man who learns by his losses."

The Russian's English was uncannily perfect. He'd been a surprise from the moment they had met at plane side. The man stood as tall as Gus and weighed maybe twenty pounds

24

heavier. As they had toured the base together, Gus had felt something akin to déjà vu. There was an eerie sense that he was looking into a mirror every time he looked at the Russian.

The Russian was the one who suggested they play a game of chess. He had proposed it as soon as he spotted the small display case where Gus kept his chess sets. While Gus only had four sets in the case, they were all antique, unique, and valuable. They represented the only private thing that Gus had left in his life. The rest of him belonged to the Navy. It had been that way ever since his wife had suddenly demanded her divorce, claiming the life of a navy wife was stifling her creativity. So, she took herself and his two teenage children out of his life. He also let her take without argument everything they had collected over almost twenty years of marriage . . . everything but the chess sets.

It was almost midnight and the rest of the guests had long gone home.

"So," the Russian suddenly asked, "what would have happened if we had played the game for real, instead of on a board?"

"Interesting question. We both spent our lives preparing to kill each other. Instead we meet over a chessboard."

"I think that's as close to war as either one of us will ever come," the Russian answered. "The Soviet Union I was sworn to defend no longer exists, and the Russian Republic has no desire to reconquer the empire we so recently dismantled. You weren't in the Gulf, were you?"

Gus knew the Russian already had the answer to that one. It would have been in the briefing material his staff had prepared for him. It was the same in the American Navy. Before the Russian arrived, Captain Babb had handed Gus a folder telling him everything that the American intelligence services knew about Admiral First Class Yegorov Semenkov.

"I'm not sure I would call that a war," Gus said, "at least as far as our Navy was concerned. It was more a turkey shoot.

Our pilots killed thousands, and some of our men died. But for the rest of the Navy, the closest they came to real war was a couple of mine hits. Our fleet officers faced about the same danger as any oil tanker captain moving a ship through those waters. Our modern navy is no longer composed of sea warriors. Instead, we play video games."

"A remarkably honest appraisal," Yegorov said with a chuckle. "It's what war has become for both our navies. Even if we had fought that last great war, it wouldn't have been war as it was fought in the days of these kinds of ships." As he said it, he waved a finger of his right hand toward the chess pieces designed to look like seventeenth century fighting ships. The pawns were small corvettes; the knights were frigates; the castles round shore fortifications, and the bishops, queens, and kings were increasingly larger ships of the line.

"You're right," Gus conceded, "naval warfare is no longer a war in which daring and bravery determine the outcome. It's all machines, computers, and technology. Nowadays, when the shooting starts, our ship captains don't go to the bridge to command the battle. They send the second in command to the bridge while the captain goes to an enclosed, air conditioned room where all he can see are computer screens."

"Russian admirals still stand on the bridge. I'm not sure whether that's because our technology is inferior or because we never learn to trust others enough to leave them in charge of a bridge."

"Now you're the honest one," Gus said.

"In our new Russian Navy, honest assessments are encouraged. There is no KGB to send reports that ruin careers." The Russian smiled and again lifted his glass to his lips.

Gus lifted his own glass. It had been years since he had drunk so much in one evening.

"So we both followed the ancient career of sea warrior, and neither one ever got a chance to fight," the Russian added.

"I'm afraid I have you there," Gus said with a smile. "Once, I did stand on a deck and listen to whistling lead. I had a boat

26

sunk out from under me, too. It happened about a hundred miles from where you call home these days."

"You were in your brown water Navy?" The Russian saw Gus's nod and added, "I guess we didn't get that in your file. I'll have to rag my G-2 when I get back to base. Tell me about it, I envy you."

It had been a long time since Gus had told war stories. Because the Russian listened, he told a series of anecdotes, encouraged by the questions Semenkov asked. After he finished, they moved into a discussion of why Viet Nam had been a disaster for American military pride and why the Soviet Union had turned around and made all the same mistakes in Afghanistan. The Russian admiral was convinced that the Afghanistan debacle had as much to do with the sudden collapse of the Soviet Union as anything that followed.

Gus asked about the Russian's current situation in Cam Rahn Bay. He got a frank assessment of the economic problems the Vietnamese government was facing, problems that the Russian Republic was in no position to help them solve.

"There are those who argue that the Russian Republic shouldn't keep a piece of its navy in Viet Nam," Admiral Semenkov explained. "Others, including myself, think Russia must protect its own interests in Asia, and that means we have to counterbalance both China and North Korea. We stay in Cam Rahn because we fear the North Koreans will move in if we move out."

"The North Koreans?" Gus asked. "I would have thought you would worry more about the Chinese moving in."

"Beijing has too many problems of their own to worry about Viet Nam," Semenkov explained. "Besides, the Vietnamese will never trust the Chinese, not after that border war they fought. Kim Il-Song claims to be a better communist than anyone, and he's far enough away from Viet Nam that he makes an attractive balance to us. Is Kim giving you any problems here in the Philippines?"

"We have reports he's got contacts with the New People's

Army. But we don't have information on anything more than that. I can't imagine what he could offer them, unless he starts shipping arms, but the NPA's problem isn't lack of weapons as much as a political agenda."

"What's the future of the NPA? They can't still believe in the certainty of a socialist victory, not after what's happened in my own country."

"The NPA has had hard times since the Aquino government took over from Marcos," Gus explained. "They had been telling people for years that they would lead the mobs that threw Marcos from the palace. It didn't happen that way. The volcano and its aftermath didn't help them either. Then when the government arrested their top leaders a few months ago, most people thought that was the end of the NPA."

"But it wasn't," the Russian commented. "Arresting leaders never does seem to work."

"Now they've got a new leader, Aguila Sorreno," Gus continued. "He's promising all the usual things, but they don't have a real issue with the average, middle-class Filipino. Their sparrow teams knock off a local official once in a while, and sometimes they kill one of our sailors, but that's harassment, not a revolution. They suffer the problem all insurgencies suffer. If they get big enough to represent a real threat, they also get big enough to find and take out."

"Again, technology wins."

"I'm afraid so. They have considerable support in the rural countryside, but not the kind of support that will fill the streets like Corazon Aquino did. If they could decisively defeat the AFP (Armed Forces of the Philippines) in a few battles, they might get the popular support. But to beat the AFP, they must have heavy weapons which they don't have."

The Russian admiral looked at his watch. "As you Americans say, I had better call it a night. My Philippine host has planned a full day for me tomorrow, and he is trying to convince me to play golf on Sunday morning."

"You play that game?"

"Unfortunately, I do," the Russian admiral said. "I learned the game while I was doing attaché-duty in Singapore. I'm quite good, but I think it's the silliest game men ever invented."

Gus laughed out loud. "Why don't we spend Sunday morning with a chess rematch instead?"

"That I would enjoy," the gruff Russian agreed. "I will tell my Philippine host you and I have important matters to discuss. Let him worry about what we are up to."

Gus was still laughing as he escorted the visiting Russian to the car waiting to take him to his guest quarters.

Like always, Gus worked in his headquarter's office through Saturday morning. It was an easier day than most Saturday mornings because so many people were away with *Team Spirit*. At 12:15 P.M., he knocked off and headed for the Officer's Club on Waterfront Drive for some lunch. He walked the distance rather than riding in his car. A quick morning thundershower had broken the hot season, making it as pleasant as a March day could get in the Philippines.

As he entered the Officer's Club's dining room he saw Lt. Commander Mundt, the skipper of the *Hercules,* and two women standing at the entryway, waiting for a table for three. All were wearing white tennis outfits. The woman standing right beside Mundt was almost as tall as the lt. commander. She was blond and thin; she had navy wife stamped all over her. When he first spotted them, Gus had thought the second woman was a Philippine civilian. As he walked up to where they stood, he recognized her as a navy officer, the weapons specialist, Lt. Commander Katherine Melendez.

Gus stopped as he reached the spot where the three people were standing. "Hello there, Commanders. How's your firing exercise going?"

"We're finished with dry runs," Lt. Commander Mundt answered. "We do the real fire tests on Monday."

"I'd like to hear more about it. Would you and the ladies join me? I've got a table we don't have to wait for."

"Thank you, sir," the man said. "This is my wife, Susan. You know Commander Melendez."

As he nodded in recognition of Commander Melendez, Gus wondered if he'd committed a faux pas by including Commander Melendez with the ladies instead of the officers. He didn't see any clouds of anger, just a smile that made it look like she was happy to see him.

The four of them walked across the dining room to where the admiral's table waited with its small reserved sign sitting on top. As soon as they sat down, a Philippine waitress appeared, handed out menus, and offered to take bar orders.

"When did you arrive?" Gus asked Susan after they gave their orders to the waitress.

"Two days ago," she answered. She was beaming like most navy wives whenever they find themselves talking with an officer who outranks their husbands by more than two grades. Gus's ex-wife used to display her own charade of the beam, pretending to put on the false face with the same grace of a three-hundred-pound gorilla putting on a girdle. In the last two years of their marriage, she had done her little act for Gus's benefit every time they fought about how the Navy was ruining their life together.

"It's a fascinating place," Susan Mundt continued, still showing enough teeth to advertise fluoride toothpaste. "I expected that the base would be in much worse condition. I saw the news on TV after that horrible volcano blew up."

"It's been a lot of work, but we've got most of it cleaned up," the admiral answered. "We've still got mountains of grey ash, but at least it's all in neat piles. We've been able to let most of the families come back. Having the families here has done a lot for base morale."

"I know," Mrs. Mundt said. "I've got a good friend who just moved in. Holly's husband is Lt. Commander Kevin Dale." She gave the officer's name like she was asking a question, giving the admiral a chance to confirm if he knew the officer in question. Gus didn't know the officer and he kept silent, knowing that the next time Susan Mundt saw her friend Holly she would be claiming points for a lunch with the base commander.

"They invited us for dinner last night," Susan continued, her smile broad with the knowledge she'd just counted coup on a rival. "She's got two servants. I mean Key West, Florida is nice and we don't have volcano ash piled in our front yard, but I do have to wash my clothes and cook the meals."

"You should attend one of our wives' meetings," Gus said, smiling. "The major complaints are always the problems of servants. Good ones are hard to find, hard to train, and hard to keep. The bad ones steal, lie, and never do the work, or at least that's the way the wives tell it."

"I could use the kind of problems they have," Susan Mundt answered. "You can't imagine the problems we have finding someone to help out when we give a party or something, and how much it costs. What about your family, Admiral? Do you have a wife here?"

"No, I'm not married," Gus answered. He turned to Lt. Commander Mundt. "So everything is ready to go on Monday morning?"

"Actually, Monday night," Mundt answered. "We'll do it in the dark before the moon comes up. We'll run up along the coast about forty miles out to sea, launch the MRPV, locate the targets, and see if we can take them out. We've got four different targets. We hope for four direct hits."

"I understand that the four missiles in your starboard launcher are the old Harpoons. I'm surprised you're carrying them."

"That was the subject of some debate," Mundt answered. "The decision was that we should carry one set of weapons to defend the ship in case war suddenly breaks out. I'm not sure who it is we might go to war with, but you know the Navy. It's SOP and it'd take a meeting of the Joint Chiefs to change it."

31

"And you are using standard explosive warheads in the tests, instead of practice heads," Gus added, letting them know he had read his copies of reports on the tests.

"Part of my evaluation will be a damage assessment of near misses," Lt. Melendez answered the question, speaking for the first time since giving her order to the waitress. "We believe we can launch missiles from the hydrofoil with the same accuracy of an aircraft delivery. Close does count in bombing as well as horseshoes, but we want to make sure we can deliver close enough. The targets will be set up with instrumentation that will give us readings, but we need full explosions to get the best data."

Gus turned toward Lt. Melendez. "How long will you be staying with us?"

"My orders say no longer than the tests. I'll take the data back to Washington to analyze. I wish I could stay longer. I've always wanted to visit the Philippines."

"You going to have any time to travel around?" Gus asked.

"I've done some traveling already. I spent last weekend in Manila. I stayed in the new Makati International. What luxury. You can't get that kind of treatment in any American hotel. I'll have to go back and see more of the city."

"Manila's the worst part of the Philippines," Gus said. "If you have any chance, get out in the countryside."

"What about security?" Susan Mundt asked. "Aren't there some pretty severe travel restrictions for people assigned to the base? I mean those awful communists are still killing Americans, aren't they? Holly Dale tells me that she and her children never leave the base. She says they have everything they need right here, so why risk getting killed by some terrorist."

"Security is a problem, and I'm the one who makes the rules about travel," Gus said. "But we try to balance good sense against the risks. We ask that base personnel avoid areas where the NPA is active. We also suggest that when base personnel travel in the safe areas, they dress like tourists and avoid looking typically American, especially not Navy. That's one of the reasons I've relaxed the dress code when it comes to haircuts. When I arrived, you could spot an American sailor on the streets of Manila by his haircut, no matter what he wore. So go, but don't wear your college sweatshirt."

"From what I've seen so far, putting on an American college sweatshirt would make me blend in with the local population, not stand apart," Kathy Melendez said with a laugh. "I took a walk through Olongapo City along Magsaysay Street yesterday evening. I could have been right back in the barrio where I grew up in Houston. Most of the women I saw were wearing American T-shirts advertising everything from Winstons to Jack Daniels. I felt positively overdressed in slacks and a blouse with buttons."

"I don't think you want to look like the local female population on Magsaysay Street," the admiral said, looking at the woman. "Some enlisted man might try to date you and I'd have another personnel problem to deal with."

"One did. I didn't know whether to take it as a compliment or an insult. He couldn't have been more than nineteen years old. I was sitting in a little street stall, eating some pork satay when he came up and asked me if I would like to have a beer with him. I'm no young chick. I guess he was looking for a mother figure, or something."

Gus smiled. Kathy Melendez didn't look like what he would consider a mother figure. "How did you handle it?" Gus asked, curious about why she would even be telling the story.

"I have to admit, that for a second, I had this terrible urge to play him along. I wondered how far it would go. I found it an exciting fantasy."

"With an enlisted man?" Susan asked, her voice tone rising on the question mark like an F-14 climbing after a takeoff.

"Hey! I said I was fantasizing, and only for a minute. He was young and good-looking. I told him I was waiting for a friend, a very big friend who was an officer. He walked

33

off, I finished my satay, and came back to the base."

She looked back at Gus, saw a smile on his lips, and gave him one of her own. Before anyone could say anything else, the waitress came back with the meals they had ordered.

Chapter Four

Zambales Province, the Philippines.

AFP Major Hoppy Yarcia stood beside the jeep and watched the two armored vehicles climbing up the mountain road behind him. Standard patrol procedures demanded that Hoppy keep one of the APCs (armed personnel carriers) in front of his command jeep, but he hadn't been doing that. Hoppy had been trying something he knew could be stupid, putting himself out in front like the bait on a hook.

But that hadn't worked either. Nothing he had done for the last three weeks had worked. That was the problem with fighting insurgents: you always fought them on their terms, not yours. He lifted the hand transceiver to his lips and barked the call signal of the lead APC.

Captain Ramon Torres answered back.

"A half day's work is enough for a Saturday," Hoppy said. "Let's head back to base. Pass me on by. I'll follow along behind. Maybe riding behind the APCs will work better than riding in front."

"Okay if I get out and ride with you?" Torres asked. "I'm fucking boiling inside here!"

"Fine with me," Garcia barked before hanging the transceiver back on his belt.

He watched as the two APCs pulled up and parked. The APCs were M113s, a full-tracked vehicle armed with one .50 caliber and two .30 caliber machine guns perched on top behind armor shields.

The eight men in each of the vehicles piled out, their jungle fatigues soaked with sweat. No one stayed on top manning one of the machine guns. Most of the men climbing off the vehicle left their personal weapons in the vehicles. Only one of them, Captain Torres, spent a second or two checking out the terrain. Several of them quickly stepped over to the side of the road and unzipped to take a piss. Those who weren't pissing were sucking on their canteens.

Disgusted, Hoppy dropped the butt he'd been smoking into the road gravel and ground it out with the toe of his jungle boot. He thought about reaming a bit of ass and decided it wasn't worth the trouble. They were mad at him already because he'd insisted they go on patrol on a Saturday morning.

The scouts he had once commanded would have jumped out of the vehicle with their weapons at the ready and spread out into defense parameter around the three vehicles. Only when the noncoms were sure they were safe from immediate attack, would they release half the men for latrine duty. All four machine guns would have been continually manned through the rest stop.

But Hoppy wasn't commanding a scout ranger unit any more. The First Scout Ranger Regiment, the crack counter-insurgency force that had fought and bloodied the NPA for twenty years, no longer existed because a couple of the senior officers had followed orders in one of the seven military coups launched against the Aquino government. Now the officers were in jail and Hoppy was in charge of a company of Illicano misfits assigned to weed out the insurgents still operating in the mountains of the Zambales province. He was filling a captain's slot, too, and Ramon was suddenly back to being a platoon leader.

Fucking politics he thought to himself. No wonder the

damn communists got stronger while the Philippine Army kept shooting itself in the foot.

"Saddle up!" the major ordered. "Let's go home."

Captain Torres climbed into the backseat of the jeep, and Hoppy took the seat beside the driver. One of the noncoms who had been riding in the back of the jeep climbed into the first APC to take the captain's place. A second sergeant climbed in beside Captain Torres.

"Let the APCs get a couple of hundred yards in front of us," Hoppy told the driver, a short, dark corporal of Negrito descent. "No reason to eat dust all the way back to the camp."

The dirt road climbed slowly for another ten miles before starting a series of steep switchbacks heading up over the pass. On the other side of the mountain, the road wound down the eastern slope into the armored battalion's temporary headquarters near the small town of O'Donnel.

The jeep was about a hundred yards short of the top that the two APCs had already crossed over when the right front tire went flat. It didn't go with a bang, but with a slushing noise that sounded like the fart of a carabao. They were going slow enough that the driver had no problems controlling the vehicle. The driver didn't pull to the side of the road, but stopped in the middle. He climbed out to take a look.

"Ramon, radio the APCs and tell them to hold until we can catch up," the major told his captain. He climbed down from the passenger side to take his own look at the wounded tire. The flat tire was almost bald as were the other three tires, as well as the spare hanging on the back of the jeep. The driver and the sergeant who had been riding in the back with Captain Torres didn't need orders to start changing the tire.

"The fucking generals get the new tires for driving around Manila while we risk our lives on worn out retreads," Hoppy muttered as he walked away from the jeep. He jerked a smoke out of a pack of Winstons, and offered a second butt to Ramon. The American cigarettes were a luxury that Hoppy enjoyed because an American Military Advisory officer assigned as an advisor to Hoppy's battalion didn't smoke but gave away his PX ration.

Both men walked across the dirt road and stood on the edge, looking back toward the west while they lit their smokes. While the hillsides were green, the valley below and its rice paddies were yellow-brown. The two months of the hot dry season had ended. While the thunderstorms had started, there hadn't been enough rain to green up the valley floor or start the rice seed beds growing. Thunderclouds were building up in the west and the south and were already high enough to cover the noonday sun.

"So what do you think about the grand new tactic of concentrating all our armor in one province, beating the bush for a few days, then moving on to the next place?" Major Yarcia asked the captain.

"We must have got them scared to death," Captain Torres answered with a twisted grin. "None of them dare shoot at us. They just hide and wait until we move on to the next place."

"It's a good thing the NPA doesn't have crew-served weapons," Yarcia said. "What a fucking target that temporary base would be. We've got so much armor parked there it looks like a fucking supermarket parking lot."

"Speaking of fucking, you got plans tonight?" Torres asked the major.

"Let's drive into Tarlac and get laid. If we can't fight, we might as well fuck."

The two men were old friends. They had studied a year apart in the Philippine Military Academy and both came from the same town in Quezon. Torres was the only officer in their new regiment except for the paymaster who knew that Hoppy wasn't a nickname. Hoppy's father had been a fan of an American movie cowboy as popular with the children of the Philippines as he was with American kids.

"I hope my luck at finding pussy is better than my luck at finding commie insur—"

The flash behind them lit up the dark thunderhead in front

38

of them with a brilliance that hurt the eyes.

Both men man acted with the instinct of a soldier who's been shot at before. They dove to the ground off the edge of the road, pressing their bodies as tight to the dirt as possible. They waited, frozen in time and space for five full seconds and then the shock wave and the sound rolled down from the top of the mountain, pounding on them, trying to pop their eardrums open, and shaking them like loose rocks in an earthquake.

They waited a full two minutes more before either man tried to raise his head. Then they crawled out from under the several inches of dirt, dust, small pebbles, leaves, and sticks that covered them both. As Hoppy painfully stood to his feet, he looked at a silent world around him.

The Negrito driver was getting back to his feet beside the jeep. He was naked. He had both hands over his eyes and his mouth was open like he was screaming. It took a second for Hoppy to figure out that he couldn't hear the man screaming because he couldn't hear anything. He looked up, toward the top of the hill. Every tree along the ridge line was down, blown over by the force of the blast of air that had followed the flash of light. Above the hill in the distance, a new cloud rose in the sky, a white mushroom reaching for the upper atmosphere.

Hoppy looked back at Ramon who was getting to his own feet, a confused and dazed expression on his face. Ramon's mouth moved like he was trying to say something. Hoppy pointed to his ear and shook his head. Both men climbed up to the road and walked over to the jeep. As Hoppy got closer to the naked Negrito he could hear what sounded like the sound of screaming from a distance. It was the Negrito he could hear. His hearing loss wasn't permanent, it was coming back.

The Negrito corporal had been looking in the direction of the flash. Instantly blinded and dazed, he had stood there waiting until the shock wave stripped him naked and pushed him backward to the ground. The backside of his body was a mass of scrapes, cuts and abrasions, the red blood etched a sharp contrast with his chocolate-brown skin.

Hoppy found the sergeant lying beside the jeep near the flat tire. He was dead. Hoppy could see no evidence of a fatal wound. It could have been a flying rock, or perhaps the rupture of an internal organ.

He turned his attention back to the corporal. Ramon was leading the corporal to the front seat of the jeep. He helped the blinded man lean over the side of the jeep, exposing his lacerated back. Ramon found the first aid kit and washed the worst of the wounds with a peroxide solution. Hoppy made an injection motion into his own arm. Ramon saw it and pulled out the morphine kit. He opened it, looked in it, and moved his lips like he was swearing. He held it up to show Hoppy that someone had stolen the morphine.

Hoppy inspected the jeep while Ramon treated the corporal. The two enlisted men had taken off the tire before the blast. The shock wave had knocked the vehicle off the jack. Hoppy dug the jack out from under the car, put it back under the axle, and jacked the car back up. He worked frantically. In five minutes he had the spare tire on. He climbed into the driver's seat and tried the key. The engine caught. He left the engine running and helped Ramon boost the terrified, blinded corporal into the backseat of the jeep.

Hoppy got back behind the wheel and Ramon jumped into the other front seat. Hoppy put the jeep into gear and backed it up to turn it around so they could head back the way they had come. Ramon grabbed at his arm and motioned with his other hand in the direction they had been heading, up over the pass of the hill. Ramon wanted to check on the men in the APCs. Hoppy stopped trying to turn the jeep around and looked at Ramon.

"All dead!" he shouted, hearing his own voice like it was a whisper. "All dead!" he said again. If it had been easier for him to talk he would have added that they were as dead as

40

everyone in their headquarters camp would be. The blast must have been right over the camp.

"Not sure! We check!" Ramon shouted back at him. Hoppy could barely hear him.

"Too dangerous!" Hoppy said. "Ra . . . di . . . a . . . tion! Will kill us too!"

He saw the anger fade to sudden fear on Ramon's face. Ramon must have thought the explosion had been Mt. Pinatubo blowing up again. Hoppy pointed to the mushroom cloud on the other side of the mountain. It held a perfect shape that didn't look anything like the plumes that the volcano had sent into the air. Ramon made no further effort to stop him as Hoppy finished turning the jeep around. He headed down the hill as fast as he could drive.

A half mile down the mountain, they drove around a curve that gave them a view to the south. Hoppy suddenly pulled up. He pointed to the south. Far in the distance they could see another one of the mushroom clouds climbing into the sky.

He shoved the jeep back into gear and peeled rubber as he pulled away. He was running, and he knew what he was running from, but he had no idea where he should run to. When he hit the coastline, he turned left and headed south. It was another forty miles to Subic Bay. He could see no mushroom clouds in that direction. Maybe the Americans could tell him who had attacked his country with nuclear weapons.

As he drove he wondered about that. Why had someone dropped an atomic bomb on the Armed Forces of the Philippines, but not on Subic Bay. If the world was at war, why would they spare the American base?

Chapter Five

Malacañang Palace, Manila.

Large tears rolled down the cheeks of the President of the Philippines as he stood staring out the window of his office in the Malacañang Palace. He was looking to the southeast at the mushroom cloud rising high in the sky over Manila Bay. General Primo Abadia, his military aide had told him that the cloud hung above the Philippine naval and air bases at Sangley Point. Looking out another window to the north, he could see another mushroom cloud in the distance.

He turned away from the window and looked at the crowd of a dozen people in the room with him. Most of them had tears rolling down their own cheeks. None of them knew any more than the President did about what had happened or why. The phones and the palace's radio communication system had stopped working the instant the blinding flashes lit up the noonday sky. All any of them knew was what they could see out the window.

"Who?" he asked. "Who's responsible? It can't be our own armed forces, can it?" The President, who had only been in office for a little over a year, had already survived one attempt at overthrowing him by soldiers in the army he was supposed to command.

"It can't be the Armed Forces of the Philippines who did this," the general standing behind him said, his voice low. "Thousands of our own soldiers have died. God knows how many more civilians. It's got to be the New People's Army, the communists. They're the only ones who would slaughter people like this with no warning, no reason."

"But where did they get atom bombs? Why did they do it this way? We've been willing to talk to them. I turned the leaders we had in jail loose. I've pleaded with them to sit down and talk to us. Why did they start such a slaughter without warning?"

General Abadia didn't answer the questions. While he owed his current position in Malacañang Palace to his loyalty to the President, he was painfully aware that the officers within the AFP who opposed the President justified their disloyalty by their disgust with his unwillingness to get tough with the communists. As far as the military was concerned, the new President was no better than President Aquino had been.

"Where did they get the bombs?" the President asked again.

"Maybe the Chinese, possibly the Russians, I don't know," the General answered. "We still can't talk to anyone and ask the question. The phones don't work, nothing works."

Another military aide, a major, entered the room.

"Mr. President, General," he said, forcing the crisp, military style with effort. "There's a helicopter coming in. It looks like the Puma General Batac uses. It's going to land. Do we let it?"

"I think we better," the President said.

The major spun on his heels in a military about-face and disappeared back through the door he had come in.

The President and his staff waited, no one talking, no one knowing what to say. Outside they could hear the sound of the chopper landing. Five minutes later, General Oscar Batac, the Chief of Staff of the Armed Forces of the Philippines, walked into the room. Three more soldiers, all wearing officer insignia, followed him.

The general was wearing civilian clothes, a yellow knitted polo shirt and orange plaid pants. He had been on the golf course at Fort Bonifacio when the flashes came. The general was short and overweight. Like most of the military officers currently in command of the AFP, he had been in his current position for only a short time and had won his promotions by remaining loyal to the civilian government while others tried to overthrow it.

"What can you tell us, General?" the President demanded.

"The Armed Forces of the Philippines has been attacked in several places by nuclear weapons," the general began, stating the obvious. The general's voice sounded dull and emotionless. It was the voice of a man suffering from severe shock. "There have been at least three explosions on the Island of Luzon, maybe more. We have no idea what has happened elsewhere. Our radio communications are all out. So's the telephone system. The only things that work are some of the hand-held transceivers. The commercial TV and radio stations are also out. From what little I could see from the air, the targets were troop, armor, and aircraft concentrations, not command centers. They didn't attack Fort Bonifacio or the headquarters of the Navy or the Air Force."

"How many have been killed?"

"I have no idea, but there must be thousands. I flew over the city on the way here. People are panicking in the streets. The highways out of the city are clogged. We've had reports on the small radios from a few small units of both the army and the constabulary. Several of them are under attack by armed NPA units. Others have stopped reporting in."

"How do we find out what is going on? Who is doing this to us?" the President demanded, his small frame shaking with emotion.

"It's obvious who is doing it to us," the general answered, his voice weary. "It's the communists, the New People's Army, but I don't know where they got missiles with nuclear warheads. The Americans don't know either. I was playing golf with General Malawitz from JUSMAG. He was looking up at a shot he had just hit when the flash went off. He was blinded. He's in our base hospital. We still haven't been able to contact the embassy or his office."

"What about Subic Base?" General Abadia asked.

"I don't know," General Batac answered. "From the air I couldn't see any mushroom clouds over that way. But I hope they do hit the American base."

"Why?" several voices including the voice of the President asked.

"If the NPA kills a lot of Americans, then they will have to help us. I don't have an army or an air force to fight with anymore. The only way we can save our country is with the help of the Americans."

"The Americans will help us," the President said, his voice firm. "They have to help us, I have to get hold of the American ambassador immediately. How can I do that?"

"The embassy has a helicopter pad on the roof. I'll fly over there. I assume the ambassador is at his office. I'll bring him back here. Maybe by now the Americans will know more than we know about what has happened."

"Look!" one of the secretaries in the room shouted.

She was pointing at a television set. It had been turned on right after the flashes and left on with the sound turned down, the screen lit but blank. A picture had just appeared on the screen. There was a red banner with the words "The New People's Army" flashing in black letters.

Someone reached over and turned the sound up.

"Please stay tuned for an important announcement from the President of the New People's Democratic Republic of the Philippines," an invisible announcer said. He repeated the announcement and continued to repeat it for two more minutes.

The picture on the screen faded and they were looking at a

man standing in front of a draped flag. The man was dressed in combat jungle-green fatigues. He stood tall for a Filipino. His face was long and thin. He wore a small goatee and a thin mustache under a hook nose. Everyone in the room with the President recognized the man on the TV screen. The President had pardoned him and had spent an hour talking with him shortly after he had become the President. He had thought when they parted company that he would be the one who would make a permanent peace between his government and the NPA.

"People of the Philippines," a voice announced. "We are honored to present the President of the New People's Republic of the Philippines, Aguila Sorreno!"

"People of the Philippines," the man on the screen spoke as the camera moved in to fill the screen with his face. "Today will live forever in our history as Liberation Day. Today, units of the New People's Army have struck a decisive blow against the forces of those who have held us in bondage. We have destroyed the ability and the will of the army of the oppressors to fight. The Philippines now belongs to the people.

"As I speak, units of the New People's Army under my command are taking possession of all government buildings, all military bases, and all police facilities. Those who served the oppressors who lay down their arms and surrender with no further resistance can expect forgiveness and reeducation. Those who resist will face the same death that rained down on others.

"Our great victory has been made possible because we have taken command of the very weapons the imperialists have used to frighten and control the free peoples of the world. We have many more of those weapons in our arsenal which we will use to crush any force so foolish as to oppose the will of the people."

The self-declared new leader slipped into a long explanation regretting the death of some civilians who lived near what he called the centers of tyranny.

"Because we did not want to see more innocent lives lost," he continued, "we have not yet wiped off the face of the earth the nests of those who have so cruelly oppressed us. We will do so if they do not immediately surrender. Even as I speak, our urban watch commands are evacuating those areas close to such obscenities as the palace at Malacañang and the headquarters of the Army of the oppressor at Fort Bonifacio. Their destruction is scheduled for exactly thirty minutes from now.

"However, in hopes that the dens of iniquity can be preserved for their value in teaching our children the history of this glorious day, I would like to spare the structures and the people now in them. But I can do that only if everyone in those places immediately leave the buildings and the grounds, walk out to the street, and surrender themselves to the first unit of my men they encounter.

"I repeat. This surrender must be effected immediately. We have our eyes on Malacañang. We know that the chief lackey of the foreign aggressors is at this moment meeting with the chief of his armed forces. They are planning how they will defeat the people's revolution and how they will give away even more of our sovereignty if their imperialistic friends will help them snatch victory from defeat. If the people in Malacañang do not surrender, we will launch more of our weapons. It will take less than a minute to arrive at its target."

"He wants us to surrender. He wants us to walk out of here and give ourselves up," the President whispered.

"We can't do it," the general said, speaking directly to the President. "He'll put us up against the wall and shoot us. You and I, we have to get away."

He looked around the room. "Everyone else do what he says, walk out and head for the gates." He turned back to the President. "You and I will take the chopper. We can fly to Subic. He won't dare attack the Americans. They have weapons that can fight back against his."

47

"Listen!" someone said, drawing the attention back to the screen.

"I repeat, all operations by any unit of the AFP must halt immediately. That includes all air operations, all ground troop movement, all radio transmissions, and all naval movements. From this moment, if any aircraft attempts to take off, if any land vehicle moves out from any base, or if any ship leaves port, that facility will be immediately destroyed."

"We have no choice," the President said. "We must do as he said. If we don't, we will die and thousands more will die with us." He turned and walked toward the door. No one tried to stop him.

Chapter Six

Subic Bay, the Philippines.

Admiral Jones stood in the headquarters command center watching the screen on the television set. The TV and some hand-held transceivers were the only pieces of communications equipment that worked. Two dozen other officers stood in the room. All but three or four of them watched the harangue on the TV. The man had been speaking for more than thirty minutes.

First, he had levied his demands for the immediate surrender of the elected government of the Philippines and all units of the Armed Forces of the Philippines. Then, Aguila Sorreno launched into a long, lengthy description of the new communist paradise he intended to impose on the Philippines.

"The son of a bitch has been taking speech lessons from Fidel Castro," Tim Reilly muttered. "This could go on for the next four hours."

"Make sure someone keeps watching it in case he starts talking about us," Admiral Jones said. "The rest of us have to decide what we do next."

The mountains that surround Subic Bay on the land side had blocked a view of the nuclear flashes so no one on the base has seen them.

Captain Reilly was talking to a CINCPAC (Commander in

49

Chief, Pacific) duty officer on the AUTOSECVOCAM, the worldwide military secure phone communication link, when the line suddenly went dead. Within five minutes, Reilly confirmed that Subic was suddenly off-line with every military communication link to the outside world. The nonsecure AUTOVON and AUTODIN and the secure digital message system were down.

Commercial phone communications with the other American facilities in the Philippines had also been cut. Even the base telephone exchange was down. Some hand-held radio equipment was working and the control tower at Cubi Point Air Station had gone back on the air using backup equipment. As all the base radar facilities were out, the control tower had no idea what had happened to the six planes that had been under the tower's control at flash time.

Fifteen minutes after the communication breakdown, a P-3 Orion that had been on an antisubmarine warfare patrol over the waters around the island of Luzon came in for a landing.

On the ground, the Orion crew reported they had spotted three nuclear detonations and subsequent mushroom clouds over the island of Luzon. Three of the crew, including the pilot, had been blinded by one of the flashes.

Admiral Jones left his hamburger with three bites missing on his plate and headed straight for the base operations center. Lt. Commander Melendez asked if she could ride back with the admiral, suggesting that an extra pair of hands and eyes might be useful. Her unique situation made her one of the few officers on the base who would not have a battle command station. On the admiral's advice, Commander Mundt had taken his wife to the quarters of their friends on the base and then reported to his ship.

The word spread by hand radio sets, messenger cars, and word of mouth ordering every officer to report to his duty station and every family member to go to quarters, close the doors and windows and hunker down.

Admiral Rimaldo came into the operations room as Sorreno started his speech. He stood on the other side of Admiral Jones, still wearing his brightly colored golfing togs, and staring at the TV set like a rabbit looking at a snake.

Commander Ted McBride, the base's communications officer, walked over to Admiral Jones. "It's the electromagnetic pulse effect," he said. "It knocked out all the communication equipment and radar. The electromagnetic waves generated by the nuclear explosions burned out the circuits on almost every piece of on-line communications equipment. The more sophisticated the equipment, the better the chance it's out of operation."

"If we knew it could happen, why in hell didn't we prepare for it?" Gus asked.

"We were trying to," McBride answered. "The MILSTAR satellite system is scheduled to go into operation in a few months. That would have kept us on-line with CINCPAC, but the whole damn system got delayed when the *Challenger* blew-up. With the Soviet Union falling apart, no one thought there was any hurry to catch up on the schedule. We were expecting to get hardened ground equipment next year."

"Why the fuck can we watch this clown describe his victory," Tim Reilly asked.

"He must have had his equipment stored somewhere, ready to use, but turned off and protected. He waited until the background radiation died down, then he plugged in his equipment. People lost their TV sets if they were turned on. He picked noon on a Saturday since there were no big sports events this time of the year so a lot of sets would have been turned off. There will be a lot of people out there picking up what he says."

"He's got the airwaves to himself," Reilly said. "All the commercial Philippine TV stations are off the air. The base AFPN TV station and the two base radio station are down, too."

"How long will it take to get our radar and communications network operational?" Gus asked the expert.

51

"We should get some of the radar back on-line in a couple of hours. The same with on-base communications. The more sophisticated stuff depends upon what this has done to the communications satellites. We may be talking weeks. I have no idea what they have in spares at San Miguel. I'm betting everything they have is down, including the submarine worldwide communication system. San Miguel is our satellite link, too. Even if I can reestablish the link between them and us, there's still no guarantee we'll be able to talk to CINCPAC if they don't have replacement parts for their up and down-link systems."

"We've got to get the information out," the admiral said. "We have to tell CINCPAC and everyone on the other side of CINCPAC what's happening here. I want to set up an air courier operation immediately."

He turned to Captain Reilly. "Singapore is the closest place where we have landing rights without too much hassle. Find out what we have that will fly from here to Singapore without refueling. I want a plane off the ground in fifteen minutes with all the information we have. I want another plane standing by every hour ready to take out update information."

He thought a second then added, "They may attack us here. Let's clear the bay. If we need anything in the bay to defend the base from a ground attack, keep it. Otherwise, every other ship fit to sail should make a run for open sea. They should disperse and follow nuclear war defense SOP. The first ship we've got to get out is the *Mauna Loa*. There is no way we can let her fall into the hands of anyone unfriendly."

"We may have a problem." The officer speaking was Captain Melvin Babb, the G-2. "The Orion copilot reports they were tracking a submarine just before the crew saw the flashes. The sub was in Philippine waters and heading south toward us. They identified it as a diesel. It's not one of ours. We have to consider it unfriendly."

"What has the best ASW equipment?" Gus asked.

"The *Stump* and the *McCloy* both have ASW," Captain Craig, the G-4, said. "That's about all that's in the bay, except for a few cargo ships and that hydrofoil. Everything else is off with *Team Spirit*. The *McCloy's* got a LAMPS (light airborne multipurpose system) capacity."

"Get her choppers out in front and looking for that sub," Gus ordered. "As soon as they neutralize the sub, get the *Mauna Loa* at sea."

"What else do we know?" the admiral asked the G-2.

"Two other planes landed after the Orion landed; an F-18 that was on a training flight, and a C-12 from JUSMAG. They were headed for Manila, but diverted to here," Reilly reported. "They've both got blinded crewmen aboard. We've debriefed the crews. I've put two more planes in the air with radios that work and they are starting to report back in. There were definitely three different explosions."

"That son of a bitch on the TV has told us what the targets were," Admiral Rimaldo interjected. "He claims they destroyed Sangley Point, an armored brigade base in Tarlac province, and Fort Magsaysay in Nueva Ecija Province. We had major concentrations of forces and equipment in each of those places. They couldn't have picked three targets that would do us more damage."

"It looks like they wiped out the AFP as a fighting force on the island of Luzon," Babb said. "Anyone who survived will surrender or hide out. We don't know if they hit targets on any of the other islands. But even if they didn't, the troops in the Visayas or Mindanao aren't going to come to Luzon to rescue the legal government."

"Do we have any idea how the weapons were delivered?" the Admiral asked. "Were they launched from planes, ships, or land?"

"The C-12 crew saw missile launches up in the direction of the Sierra Madre mountains," Babb answered. "Their radar picked up all three missiles, all coming from the same direction. They were fairly slow moving, subsonic, so I'd bet on something like SCUDs."

"I've got all our defense systems on full alert, including those on board the two fighting ships in the harbor," Reilly reported. "But most of the systems use radar. We think any system not on-line will still function when we turn it on, but we can't be sure until we check them out."

"Who gave these beasts nuclear weapons?" Admiral Rimaldo said, his voice shaking with emotion. "I don't believe that they made them themselves in jungle laboratories like that man is bragging they did. Someone had to give them the weapons."

"I wish I knew," Admiral Jones answered. "I agree they didn't make them on their own. I'll bet whoever owns that sub had a hand in it. I can't imagine either the Russians or the Chinese doing something so irresponsible. Maybe Qaddafi did it, or someone else in the Middle East. Maybe this is some kind of revenge by Saddam."

"Can we be sure this is just happening here, and not all over the world?" The man asking the question was Commander Philip Baker, the base chaplain. It was the first time Gus Jones had seen the chaplain in the command center. He probably didn't have the clearance to be there, but the possible end of the world made it a special occasion.

"I don't think so," Admiral Jones answered. "If this had been a worldwide attack, we would have been hit, not just the AFP. It's exactly what that clown on the tube is claiming, a strike against the Philippine government."

"What are we going to do?" the Philippine admiral pleaded. "How do we save my country from this horror? You Americans are going to help us, aren't you? We have to attack back at these beasts and immediately."

"No American facilities have been hit yet?" Admiral Jones asked, looking at Captain Babb.

"Not that we know about," Babb answered. "I'm assuming we lost the three planes that haven't shown up, but that was

54

collateral damage not targeting. There have to be some American losses near the target areas, too. JUSMAG advisors, someone on leave . . ."

"If we haven't been directly attacked, we can't attack them, not without command approval," Jones said, looking over at Admiral Rimaldo.

"You can't wait!" Rimaldo insisted. "This is a Philippine base. I can order the attack. I do so now. I order you to attack and defend my country from this beast who is talking on the TV."

"Admiral, I wish I could do exactly that," Gus said. "If it was possible, I might do it without waiting for orders from my command. But I can't attack people unless I know where they are."

Jones turned and looked at Captain Reilly. "What's the current base security situation?"

Reilly gave a quick rundown on the security situation.

"What about radiation fallout?" Gus asked.

"The prevailing winds should blow the clouds eastward," a commander wearing a khaki work uniform with a medical insignia on the collar answered. "We're monitoring it, but we don't think base personnel have to worry about radiation, at least not yet."

"We've got some Filipino troops who are starting to show up at the base gates, too," Reilly reported. "Mostly stragglers and small units. They all want in."

"We have to let them in," Admiral Rimaldo insisted. "Right now, this may be the only place they can run to."

"Then you provide the troops to look them over," Jones snapped. "I want them disarmed until loyalty is verified, and I want to make damn sure none of them carry in anything that threatens the security of the base."

"Admiral!" The voice belonged to Lt. Commander Kathy Melendez. She had been monitoring the speech on the TV set. "He's talking about us."

Gus turned his attention back to the television screen.

Kathy stepped forward and turned the sound up higher. Aguila Sorreno was telling his audience that the New People's Republic wanted the friendship of all peace-loving people in the world including the peace-loving people in the United States.

He was shouting like he was trying to speak above the roar of an invisible crowd as he announced that he was renouncing and abrogating all treaties which granted the use of Philippine sovereign territory to the military of the United States of America.

"We can no longer tolerate the United States military using our territory to launch planes and ships of war which suppress the aspirations of freedom-loving people in our own country and in other friendly countries," he continued.

"We order all U.S. Military personnel stationed anywhere in the Philippines to halt all military operations immediately. This includes all movements on land, on sea, or in the air and all communications using any radio waves that pass through Philippine air space. No American military planes are to take off or land, no ships in Philippine waters are to sail, and no vehicles nor troops may leave base areas which they now occupy. The planes that are flying over our head, threatening us with destruction, must immediately return to their base."

Sorreno talked for another five minutes about the friendly intention of his government toward the United States. He said he hoped that the United States would allow his new government to seek a new beginning for the Philippine people without interference before he got to the kicker.

"Let it be clear," he added. "We will defend ourselves. As we have demonstrated on this day of liberation, we have weapons of power and might which we will employ in our defense. If any American military commander chooses to ignore my order, if one plane takes off, if one ship tries to sail from port, if one armed soldier of the United States is seen moving through our territory, we will consider that an act of war. We will not only destroy the plane, the ship, or the man, we will destroy the base which launched the weapon. We already have our weapons targeted at the American base. Do not give us an excuse to attack you."

He paused and smiled. He had to know that the American base commander at Subic Bay would be watching him.

"Many of the ships that use Subic Bay and the men who manned them have now formed a giant task force called *Team Spirit* which threatens a country friendly to the Philippines," he continued. "The ships in that task force must sail back to the United States, not back to the Philippines. If we learn that the task force is sailing back toward the Philippines, we will consider that as evidence that the United States military leaders intend to attack us. As soon as we learn that any American ship has entered waters within two hundred miles of any territory of the Philippines, we will react as swiftly as we will act if an American unit attacks us from within our own territory."

"Jesus Christ," several people whispered, almost as a chorus. Then Sorreno moved on to his next subject, what was going to happen to the banking industry of the Philippines.

"What's the status of that courier plane?" Gus asked.

"She's ready to go," Reilly answered. "We picked a P-3. Her motors are spinning and she's ready to taxi. We've got one ship ready to sail, too. The *Hercules.*"

Gus hesitated and looked around the room. He saw the question in every eye, then gave his order. "Tell them both to stand down. All the other ships, too. Call the planes we've got up in the air back to base. I've got to believe the man has what he claims to have. If I'm going to risk getting nuked, I want to make sure I can shoot back with the same kind of weapon."

Captain Jarvis, the Commander of Naval Magazine Facility, stepped forward to say something. "We can turn this whole base facility over to them, but we can't let them have the *Mauna Loa.*"

"I know," Gus answered, his voice firm. "Order the skipper to keep a head of steam and be ready to sail. He sails immediately if the base comes under attack, either from the ground or from the air. Give the same orders to the *Stump* and the *Mc-Cloy*. They should get out in front and try to handle that sub. Even if the *Mauna Loa* is sunk, I'd rather have her cargo on the bottom than in the hands of this clown and whoever is pulling his strings."

He turned to the communications officer, Commander McBride. "Ted, get us some kind of communications link with CINCPAC. I don't care if it's an open voice single side band or some ham radio operator. I want to get some orders, and maybe some codes."

He looked back around the room. "Until I get those, we have to consider ourselves as trapped behind enemy lines."

"What do we do if they show up at the gates to take things over?" Reilly asked.

"I'm not ordering offensive action, but I'm damn well not going to surrender either. This base is sealed. We let friends in. That includes Philippine workers with the proper ID and members of the AFP fleeing attack. Anyone else will have to fight their way in. If they want to nuke us for that, let it happen."

There were no cheers for his bit of bravado. Gus could understand why. Most of the officers in the room had family with them who lived on the base. The families were as much trapped behind enemy lines as the men were.

Chapter Seven

Pyongyang, North Korea.

Major General Bae Bong-Soo had gas. His stomach was churning up the smell of the *Bulkoki,* rice, bean curd soup, and *kimchi* he'd had for lunch. He always had gas when he sat waiting to be called for a meeting with the Dear Leader, Kim Jung Il.

Once, when the Dear Leader had been very angry with him, he'd sat waiting for almost five hours before he had been ushered in to confess his shame of failure. But why the gas today? Why, when all he carried was good news of a great victory?

He had implemented *Strike Back* as the perfect operation with total security, something he didn't think would be possible when the operation had begun three years previously. The Korean Democratic People's Navy had smuggled into the Philippines five SCUD-C missiles. North Korea technicians and their Philippine helpers had fabricated three fixed launch platforms and two mobile launch vehicles with only minimum requirements for additional imports. While they had made elaborate preparations to blame the missiles on the Chinese, if one of them had been discovered by the Armed Forces of the Philippines, that hadn't happened.

The five warheads, the last items delivered, represented the entire production of his country's fledgling nuclear weapon's industry. It had been a high risk gamble. As the Korean scientists had not been able to test even one weapon without giving away the secret, they hadn't known how efficient the bombs would be, or even if they would go off at all.

It had gone so well that the two missiles mounted on a mobile launch vehicle still waited in reserve. The reserve weapons could be moved and aimed at any target anywhere on the island of Luzon or at a target more than two hundred miles out to sea in any direction. No enemy invasion force could undo what General Bae and his team had achieved unless they were willing to risk tens of thousands of casualties.

All that remained was the implementation of one last phase. The remaining SCUDs guaranteed either the success of the last phase or the decimation of the American fighting force in the Pacific and the embarrassment of the American government around the world. Best of all, there was no way that the Americans could know who was responsible for doing such a terrible thing to them.

A woman wearing the crisp uniform of a major appeared at the end of the hall, looked his way and nodded her chin. He had been waiting only three minutes. He rose from the stiff back, wooden chair and followed her into the second largest office in the entire city of Pyongyang, his gas attack suddenly cured.

The Dear Leader sat at a desk in the middle of the large room. There were windows on three sides of the office and the early morning spring sun was shining through the window behind the Dear Leader. The light cast a long shadow that made the small man look like a giant.

"So my friend," the Dear Leader announced as the general approached the desk. "You bring me news of a pending great victory for our revolution."

"The *Strike Back* victory is only possible because of the leadership of our Dear Leader and the guidance of the Great Leader," General Bae answered.

The Dear Leader rose to his feet. "Yes," he agreed. "But even a brilliant idea demands a brilliant execution, don't you agree?"

"The Dear Leader is too kind."

"No, excellence must be recognized just as failure must be confessed. Come let us sit together while we talk." The Dear Leader motioned toward a set of twin chairs and a sofa that sat in one corner of the spacious office. General Bae walked to one of the chairs. He turned and waited until Kim Jung Il stood in front of the second chair. The Dear Leader sat down, then motioned for his Chief of State Security to take a seat.

"So we have a new government in the Philippines and all those American ships that play war games off our coast have no home to return to? We will have a new world order, but not the one the American President expects."

"The country fell like an overripe mango that has hung too long from the limb," the general answered.

"I am not sure I agree with your simile. This mango would have never fallen were it not for the pruning shears which we gave our allies. I hope the new government of the Philippines is appropriately appreciative."

"I have a full report from Colonel Cho Chae-Jin. The new President of the Philippines is not only grateful, he knows that he can only remain in power for as long as he wears the teeth we provide."

"I am still not convinced that we should have entrusted such a responsibility to manage this operation to a person with so little rank as a colonel. Perhaps, now that victory is ours we should replace Colonel Cho with someone of more appropriate rank."

"I would suggest we leave him for the moment, at least until we have completed the second phase of the operation," the general suggested. "Colonel Cho combines both intelligence and loyalty to our revolution and our Great Leader. He also understands our new allies, and that is no easy task. They are a lazy, contentious, superstitious people with no sense of will,

61

discipline, or dedication. They played at revolution for twenty years with no progress."

"How embarrassed the Americans must be." The Dear Leader was beaming with happiness as he spoke the words. "They have thought that the world was theirs because those idiots who ruled the Kremlin self-destructed. Now their pearl in the Pacific has been plucked from their grasp, and they have no idea how it happened. Are we sure that the Americans do not know how the New People's Army obtained nuclear weapons?"

"How could they suspect us? They think we are not clever enough to manufacture our own weapons of destruction? We have hidden our factories so that they can not find them with their satellites. We collected our payment of uranium ore from Saddam Hussein for the missiles we gave him long before he made his stupid move in Kuwait. The Americans can not suspect us."

"It matters not whether they suspect us, as long as they can not prove it. When do you implement the final stage?"

"Very soon," General Bae answered.

"Do not delay too long. We must not give the Americans a chance to hide the material we seek nor to sneak it out of the Philippines some way."

"I don't see how they could sneak it out," General Bae assured his Dear Leader. "They are obeying the order of the new Philippine government to cease all operations. No planes are taking off and no ships have sailed since we made the strike. Our submarine is in place at the mouth of the bay and will sink any ship that tries to sail. Other subs are in position at key points to listen and insure that the Americans are not trying any tricks. Our subs are backed up by our frigate further out to sea. Our cargo ships wait in the South China Sea, ready to move in and collect the material as soon as we take possession of the base."

"Still, I am nervous. We have developed at great expense some powerful weapons that make us the equal of any country. They also gave us the potential to insure that no enemy could attack us without paying a terrible price. Instead of using those weapons in the defense of the homeland, we have opted to use them in this operation, but only because we expect to gain even greater weapons through this clever plan.

"We know that the Americans have nuclear weapons stored in Subic, many more nuclear weapons than we could produce in many years. It is not only the weapon material we need. When we have their weapons, our scientists can dismantle them so we can learn the secrets that have eluded us. We must take possession of those weapons. We can not fail!"

General Bae felt his gas pains again. He did not argue. Those who survived the politics of the Central Committee of the Party did so by always agreeing with the Dear Leader. The original plan had not measured the success or failure of the operation by whether or not the stores of nuclear weapons at Subic could be collected and shipped to North Korea. Indeed, they had recognized that such weapons might not even be stored at Subic, or if they were, that the Americans would never turn them over without a fight.

The operation was to be considered a success if all that was achieved was the establishment of a socialist government in the Philippines and removal of the American base. The missiles still held in reserve were originally to be used against Malacañang Palace and the AFP headquarters at Fort Bonifacio if the Philippine government had refused to surrender immediately.

Only after the standing government surrendered, was one of the remaining missiles to be retargeted at the American base. The chance of getting a new supply of nuclear weapons was to be a bonus, not the goal of the operation.

Now the Dear Leader had changed the rules of the game. General Bae and his men in the Philippines had to present the Dear Leader with a supply of American nuclear weapons equal to what was invested in the project. If not, the project and General Bae would be considered failures. It was not the first time that such a thing had happened in General Bae's career.

"We will move quickly," General Bae assured his leader. "The people who command the American base will have no choice. They all have their families with them. American soldiers are ready to die for their country, but they have this delusion that their families are not soldiers, too. If they refuse to give us what we want, we will destroy them."

"If you destroy the base, do it in a way that still allows us to collect the material we want," the Dear Leader warned.

"We plan on aiming one of the remaining weapons so that we can," the general answered.

"Are you saying that you know where the nuclear material is stored?"

"We assume that the nuclear material is stored somewhere in the ammunition dump the Americans maintain at Subic." Bong-Soo saw the frown instantly appear on the face of the Dear Leader. "But we know where the material is not stored," he spoke before the Dear Leader could object to the use of the word assume. "We know it is not stored where they live, nor where they work in their offices and their repair docks. But the living area makes a perfect target for the kind of weapon we have. If we use a nuclear weapon, we will aim to effect maximum casualties. Thus we will not damage the weapon material which will be stored far from the living areas. With the Americans and their families all dead, we can take our time looking for their nuclear weapons."

Kim Jung Il's face broke into a sudden smile, and General Bae continued quickly with his explanation.

"Whichever way it goes, our frigate, the *Najin,* will enter the bay immediately. Our experts on board should have no problems finding where the weapons are stored. We will bring in our two cargo ships when we locate the nuclear material. We expect to load our ships in no more than eight hours. Even if the Americans launch a counterattack against our allies, it will take them longer than that to get their own ships into position. And we will have the final weapon still in reserve to use against any American invasion force. The plan can not fail. We will be gone, and our Philippine allies will be the ones who answer to the anger of the Americans."

"Excellent planning," the Dear Leader said, a smile on his face spreading in a broader pattern. He thought a moment, his face a broad smile. "If you are sure we can collect the material even if we drop an atom bomb on the base, then we don't have to bargain so long trying to scare them into surrendering. I would suggest a quick one-two punch. Demand that they immediately surrender the base or suffer instant annihilation. If they refuse, back down and talk for a day or two while they worry about their families and learn to fear for their lives. Then deliver the second ultimatum, this time backed up by troops ready to fight. If they choose to fight instead of delivering the base, kill them all and take the weapons as you propose."

He sat thinking a moment, then added, "If you fail in getting those weapons for any reason, you must not let a single American at Subic Bay survive. If they are unwilling to share their treasures with us, that is what must happen. They all must die." Kim Jung Il paused and then repeated the sentence, slamming his hand on his desk as he pronounced, "They must all die!" He smiled again, took a deep breath, and added, "But do make sure that the world thinks that this Aguila Sorreno ordered the killing, not us."

"If they surrender the base, they will know we are the ones taking the material," General Bae pointed out.

"I don't think the Americans will do that," the Dear Leader answered. "They will think that they can talk and that we will do nothing while they talk. But if they surprise us and do surrender the base to our allies, we must do what any smart thief does. We must leave no witnesses. If they surrender, collect the material we want. After our ships are out of the bay, destroy the base."

The Dear Leader got to his feet. The meeting was over.

General Bae jumped to his own feet and accepted again the thanks of the Dear Leader. Dismissed, General Bae turned and walked toward the door.

He left the presence of the Dear Leader with new understanding. For more than forty years, everything that Kim Jung Il's father had done had been done with the purpose of reuniting the two halves of Korea into one country, a country ruled by Kim Il-Sung until he died and then by his son and heir Kim Jung Il.

For the son, it had turned into a lifetime frustration that was twisting into a flaming hatred for the country he held responsible for his father's failure. While Kim Jung Il wanted the nuclear material stored at Subic Bay, there was something he wanted even more. He wanted to kill as many American soldiers as possible in one grand gesture, and he wanted it done in a way in which he could avoid the blame. The Dear Leader would let the Filipinos play with the Americans. He would let the talk of peace and surrender go on for a short while, but it would only be the game a cat plays with a mouse.

While the Dear Leader would not say it out loud, the only thing he would demand he be given, at all cost, was the nuclear destruction of the American base in the Philippines.

General Bae smiled to himself. Now that he understood exactly what it was the Dear Leader wanted, it would be easy to give it to him. He and his team would destroy Subic Bay. But first, they would teach the Americans to be afraid.

Chapter Eight

The White House.

Tabor Carol sat at his desk in a small office in the basement of the White House. As the National Security Advisor to the President of the United States, Tabor had another larger office, right next to the Oval Office. However, he liked working in the basement because the Sit Room offered greater security for the sensitive material he handled so much of the time.

Tabor was going over the Philippine hourly situation reports which read like some Hollywood horror story. For the first several hours, all they had known was that the Philippines was off-line and that there had been several nuclear explosions in Philippine air space. During those hours, the U.S. Military had gone to DEFCON Three: all military forces on alert, awaiting further orders.

The geosynchronous communications and navigation satellites hanging suspended in space twenty-six thousand miles above the Pacific Ocean had survived the electromagnetic pulse effect of the multiple nuclear explosions. However, the energy blast had put the surveillance satellites flying over the area in lower orbits out of commission.

CINCPAC had reestablished unclassified communications

with the Naval Command Headquarters at Subic Bay. The State Department also had an unsecure link with its embassy in Manila.

High altitude, oblique angled, air recon photos taken from off the Philippine coast confirmed that all the American facilities were still physically intact. Likewise, they provided detailed evidence of the destruction of three Armed Forces of the Philippines facilities on the island of Luzon. Intelligence satellites that had been on the other side of the globe had been reprogrammed to overfly the Philippines and provide more detailed intelligence.

The intel photos analysts all agreed that the three detonations had ranged in power from ten to fifteen kilotons, about the size of the Hiroshima Little Boy bomb. While the bomb that hit the Sangley airfield and Philippine naval port combination was the right size for the job, the two other bombs had been much bigger explosions than the target required. That suggested the manufacturer of the bomb had not yet mastered the science of reducing bomb yield to produce a true tactical weapon.

No one had any idea of the scope of casualties, except that they were horrendous, estimated at somewhere between fifty thousand and two hundred thousand dead. While the targets were military, civilians always lived close to military bases in the Philippines and thousands of them must have died. Thousands more would be dying over the next twenty years from radiation burns.

It had not been just a nuclear attack. The New People's Army had launched an all-out attack against Philippine government installations around the island. Besides the fifteen thousand or so armed insurgents, an estimated two hundred thousand NPA sympathizers from the countryside had flooded into urban centers, giving the impression that mobs of thousands supported the new Socialist Republic of the Philippines.

The Philippine President, his cabinet, most members of

the Philippine Parliament, and most of the military leadership who were not killed at one of the target sites were under arrest.

NPA armed units, posed at key points around the island, had moved quickly to round up any resistance. NPA cadre had entered all of the government ministries and taken control. While NPA officials held control of the country's command center, no one knew where Aguila Sorreno, the new president, had his headquarters. The best guess was that he was directing it all from a secret headquarters somewhere in the jungles of Luzon, probably near the spot from where the missiles had been launched.

The NPA only controlled the island of Luzon. The Moro National Liberation Force, a Muslim separatist revolt in the southern islands, was engaging the AFP forces in an all-out war that appeared to have the AFP on the ropes in the southern islands.

The regional AFP forces in the Visayas were holding their own, but there was no hope the troops could move to Luzon and attempt to recapture the center of government. The Philippines had been cut into three pieces.

From the American point of view, the one piece of the country that counted was Luzon where all the American military facilities were located and where fifty percent of the Philippine population lived.

The immediate losses to the ability of the United States to operate in the Far East were horrendous. Besides the loss of the use of Subic Bay, a major link with the communications system serving American nuclear submarines was out. All American diplomatic radio communications in South East Asia had funneled through a repeater station in the Philippines that was off the air. The Voice of America's Asian broadcasting transmission system was shut down. The Federal Broadcasting Information Service that listened to commercial broadcasts around the world was no longer reporting what the governments of Asia were telling the people of Asia.

More than ten thousand American military personnel, civilian employees, and their families were trapped behind what had to be considered enemy lines. So were another three thousand or so employees and family members belonging to the State Department, the Agency for International Development, and other government departments. Additionally, thousands of American businessmen, missionaries, and tourists were at the mercy of the new communist government.

So far, there were no reports of major threats against American life. The only American casualties were those unlucky enough to be caught near one of the targets.

The embassy had established contact with representatives of the new government who were promising that all Americans would be safe as long as no Americans took any military action against the new government. But the new NPA government insisted it would consider any attempt to operate American military equipment an attack against the new government. The new government was also promising that all Americans would be able to leave the Philippines in peace as soon as commercial flights could be arranged. However, they would only be able to carry hand luggage, nothing more.

The intelligence community agreed that North Korea had to be the source of the nuclear warheads, but lacked the hard proof that might be given to the press.

There was considerable argument about whether or not it had been a brilliant move to launch the attack while the *Team Spirit* exercise was in progress. Ships and troops that might have been caught at Subic Bay were on the high seas and available for operations instead of locked up at Subic. But the absence of those same forces made it much more difficult to defend the base if that became necessary. For the moment, the ships of the task force had been ordered to hold their position while CINCPAC and the President decided what to do next.

Tabor gathered the situation reports and put them into a brown leather briefcase. He turned to a second leather file holder. This one held a sample of press clippings and editorial writings on the situation in the Philippines.

While the more conservative newspapers in the South and the West were demanding some kind of immediate action, the liberal press on the East Coast counseled caution and prudence while condemning the indiscriminate use of nuclear weapons. The lead editorial in the *Washington Dispatch* bemoaned at length the fact that an insurgent group had nuclear weapons. The editorial argued, however, that the United States, a country that began with a revolution, could not too loudly condemn a revolutionary army for the weapons it used, provided the rebel government didn't use those weapons against civilian populations nor a neighboring country.

The editorial argued that the American military should have closed down the Philippines base long ago and that the United States now had no choice but to respect the demands of the new Philippine government. The editor added that nothing the United States had in the Philippines was worth a heavy loss of American life. Indeed, the American military should do nothing to give the new Philippine government a justification for an attack on American personnel with nuclear weapons.

The beeping tone on Tabor's Seiko watch sounded, reminding him to head upstairs for a meeting of the full National Security Council which the President had called. He punched the alarm off, picked up the classified and the unclassified folders, and walked out of the Sit Room.

The men filed into the meeting room silently. The greetings, when given, were quick, short recognitions and nothing more. No one started the chatter and joking that usually occurred as they gathered around the heavy, natural walnut table. Each man had brought his own copy of the National Policy Decision Memorandum (NPDM) scheduled for discussion. Most of the men laid their copies on top of the table as they sat down. Several of them started paging through papers while they waited, reviewing arguments or collecting their thoughts.

The President's secretary, Jane Teague, stuck her head in the door to check that everyone was there. Thirty seconds later the President walked into the room as all the men in the room jumped to their feet. The President took his own chair, and the others sat back down.

"I don't like it," the President began, slapping his own copy of the NPDM down on the table in front of him. "You haven't explained how this happened, and why we didn't see it coming. You've given me the worst intelligence failure we've had since Pearl Harbor. The press is demanding answers, and I don't have any. I've got a bookcase full of contingency papers dealing with the possible uses of nuclear explosives against us or a friendly power and not one of them addresses what just happened. It's happened in the worst possible place it could have happened."

The President looked around the room, his face glowing red. "You haven't offered a single suggestion for action that will put America back out in front on this. And what about the North Koreans? You don't give me a single policy option about what we should do to them. Aren't they the international criminals we should be focusing our attention on?"

"We don't have any proof they're the ones who provided the nuclear warheads," Kyle Swenson, the Director of Intelligence, pointed out. "We don't have satellite photos, no human resources reports, nothing we can show to the press and the TV. We know they did it more through the process of elimination than hard evidence. We're damn sure it wasn't the Russians, the Chinese, or any of our allies. It wasn't the Paks, the Israelis, the Indians, or the Brazilians, or even Qaddafi. So it has to be the North Koreans."

"There's no chance for a quick, surgical strike to take out all the nuclear weapons the NPA still holds, before they shoot one at Subic?" the President asked.

"We have only a general idea where the weapons were fired from," Swenson answered. "We might try some carpet bombing over the area, but we would have no guarantee we would take them all out. If we try to take them out and we miss, ten thousand Americans at Subic die."

"We can't let that happen," the President said. "The American people won't tolerate those kind of losses, not when they were all convinced that socialism was dead and peace guaranteed. Our first priority is to get those Americans out of the danger zone, then we deal with how we handle the NPA and the North Koreans."

"We have to get more than our troops out of there," the Secretary of Defense interjected. "We've got to get a ship loaded with nuclear weapons out of there. We can't let that ship fall into the enemy's hands. If we have to leave our men there to protect it, we will. If State can convince the new Philippine government to let the families come home, so much the better, but the Navy won't leave Subic Bay until we can take what we want with us."

"So, we make that a bargaining chip," Crandall Kelly, the Secretary of State, suggested. "We demand the right to take a few things with us when we take the families out."

"It's a damn good thing those weapons are on a ship and not stored in an ammo dump," the President said. "Is that why we did it that way, so we could get them out in a hurry?"

"Not really," Crandall Kelly answered. "We kept the nuclear weapons stockpile on that cargo ship to avoid the question of whether or not we had nuclear weapons stored in Subic. As long as they were in the harbor and not stored on land, we could tell the Philippine government we didn't store nuclear weapons at Subic. The new treaty does give us permission to transit nuclear weapons through Subic. As long as they are loaded on a ship, we can claim they are in transit. That works to our advantage now. The new Philippine government will have no reason to suspect that we have nuclear weapons

73

stored at Subic when they go through the old government's papers on the base situation."

"I want it understood," the President said. "I don't want to lose ten thousand American lives. I don't want the Navy or the Air Force to do anything, *repeat, anything*, that gives the NPA an excuse to bomb an American facility while we figure out how to get them out."

"What about communications?" the Secretary of Defense asked. "All we have with Subic right now is an unclassified communication link, but my technicians tell me we can hook up a secure tactical link using our tactical satellite communications systems in another day or so."

"The NPA foreign minister is telling our ambassador that their order to terminate all military operations includes all military communications," the Secretary of State pointed out.

"Then let's not risk it," the President decided.

"That keeps our commander there in the dark," the Secretary of Defense said. "We don't dare share any of our intelligence or information over an unclassified link."

"We can't help that," the President said. "There is nothing he can do to get himself out of this mess anyway. He'll have to sit tight and wait it out while we talk with the new government."

"Time should be on our side," the Secretary of State added. "The New Philippine government has to understand that if they nuke our forces, we'll retaliate in a big way. We'll play the diplomatic card and play it hard. We'll tell the world we are perfectly willing to abandon our base, but that we have to take all war and weapon material with us to keep them out of the hands of the NPA. We shouldn't have any trouble painting this Sorreno character as black as Saddam Hussein. Right now, he's not letting the international press get anywhere near those nuclear blast sites. But when the international community begins to understand the tragedy, international public opinion will rally to our side."

"The longer we stretch this out, the better our chance will

be for collecting the intelligence we need for a preemptive strike," Kyle Swenson pointed out. "If we can pinpoint where they keep the nuclear weapons they still have, we're back in the driver's seat."

"Make that a top priority," the President ordered. "I don't want this to drag on like the Iran hostage situation did."

"What about our ships in the Seventh Fleet?" the Secretary of Defense asked. "CINCPAC wants to move them as close to the Philippines as he can."

The President looked over at the map of the world that hung on the wall. "Let's keep part of the fleet right where they are, off the coast of Korea. I want the Kims to know we have them in our sights. Order the rest of the Seventh Fleet into position somewhere west of Guam. Keep them on this side of the Marianas Trench line, no closer than three hundred miles from the Philippine coastline."

The President looked around the room. "I want good contingency planning for what we do, once we get our people out of there. I want even better planning for what we do if this thing starts to drag on for months."

"My bet is that's exactly what's going to happen," Swenson suggested. "We'll talk and talk, and eventually we will have to act. But as long as we don't initiate force, it will make no sense for the new Philippine government to attack our base. It will be a bargaining game over how much stuff we leave behind. It will be a bad time for the men and their families, but if we play this carefully, they'll all survive."

The Chairman of the Joint Chiefs rode back to Pentagon with Admiral John Miller, the Chief of Naval Operations. The two men sat together in the backseat of one of the Chairman's official limousines.

"What kind of man is Gus Jones?" the Chairman asked Admiral Miller as the car drove across Memorial Bridge.

"He won the Medal of Honor in Nam," Admiral Miller answered. "Not many Navy officers who weren't flyers got the chance to get that close to the real shooting. He comes from an old Navy family. His father died in the Pacific in the "Big War." There was a rumor for a while his family line went back to John Paul Jones, but I don't think it's true. His name Augustus comes from Octavian Augustus, the Roman naval leader. Apparently, the family tradition is to give all the males names of famous admirals. He's popular with his men, but he doesn't fit very well in a modern navy. He never did enough Pentagon time, and he doesn't understand the politics it takes to go all the way up the ladder. He made rear admiral because he's academy, he never made a mistake and he wears the medal, but he won't go any farther."

"He doesn't sound like the kind of man who will take to being a hostage very well."

"He won't. If he could think of some way to solve this himself, he'd do it."

"There's not a chance for that, not unless he wants to get the whole fucking base blown off the map."

Chapter Nine

Subic Bay, the Philippines.

At least some of the damn phones were working again. The AUTOVON and AUTOSECVOCAM connections were still down, but Admiral Jones could talk to the Embassy's attaché office in Manila, the JUSMAG headquarters, Cubi Point, and the offices around the base. He still couldn't make an international long-distance call, but he did have radio communications of a sort with CINCPAC.

None of the communication links that did work had brought him any good news. CINCPAC had told him to sit tight, maintain the integrity and security of the base, and wait while the diplomats negotiated the next step.

The base remained on full alert. Base stores had distributed nuclear protection and defense gear to the troops and the families. Dependents were being taught self-defense measures they should take in the event of a nuclear attack on the base.

While the base and the ships in the harbor had considerable defense capability including SAM missiles, and a battery of Patriot missiles, none of the defense measures had ever been combat tested against missiles carrying nuclear payloads. The weapons and communications people were frantically checking out all the systems. Most of the electronic defense equipment turned on at the time of the nuclear blasts required major repairs or total replacements.

Even when they got all systems working, the systems would be most effective against an attack from the sea. Geography worked against defense from a land-based nuclear attack. There was no way to stop a nuclear tipped shell fired from the other side of the mountains as it crossed the ridge line and headed down into the base area. It would be almost as difficult to stop a SCUD crossing that geographic profile.

The base security forces had spotted armed men patrolling through the areas outside the gates and the fence, but there had been no attempt to penetrate the base defenses. About three hundred Philippine soldiers had come in to seek sanctuary on the base territory. Admiral Rimaldo's security guards had processed the AFP men through the gates to insure none were enemy infiltrators. Marines from the base's Marine barracks had manned defensive positions around the base perimeter backed up by men normally assigned noncombat duties and the Philippine forces that had entered the base area.

For a few hours, hundreds of Philippine citizens had crowded at the gates begging for permission to enter. They had disappeared suddenly. One of the Philippine military officers who came in a while later reported there were rumors circulating in Olongapo City that the NPA was going to drop an atom bomb on the base. The residences of the entire town had fled over the roads that crossed the mountains out of the Subic Bay area. The Philippine officer had come in anyway because there was another rumor that NPA gangs were executing all AFP officers above the rank of captain whom they could identify.

Gus had been back to his quarters just once in the twenty-four hours since it had all started. He'd bathed, changed into a clean set of whites, and come right back to his office in the base administration building. What little sleep he'd found had been taken on the leather covered couch in his office. But the lack of sleep wasn't the results of demands on his time and the requirements to take immediate action. It was the frustration of being able to do nothing while the world collapsed around him.

The only one more frustrated on the base than Gus was Admiral Ramon Rimaldo. A dozen different times since the destruction of the AFP, Ramon had walked in on Gus with a new idea of how the Americans could take back the Philippines. As far as they knew, Rimaldo was the only AFP officer of flag rank on the island of Luzon who was not either dead or under arrest. Ramon claimed that made him the acting commander of the Armed Forces of the Philippines and that any action he might take to defeat the NPA would be a legal action, including enlisting the aid of the American military forces.

Ramon repeatedly insisted that he and Admiral Jones launch a joint Philippine/American counterattack on the NPA. Gus had been initially surprised at Rimaldo's enthusiasm for action, given the man's previous dedication to politics, business, and golf. But it wasn't hard to figure out why the Philippine admiral was so anxious to attack. The new order in the Philippines would have no place for men like Ramon Rimaldo. There would be no plush officer clubs, no manicured golf course, no cuts on government contracts, no bloated bank accounts, and no income from family lands farmed by tenants. Rimaldo knew he was already a dead man. The only way to climb out of his grave was to fight the NPA.

Even though much of the equipment and the fighting men normally stationed at Subic were away participating in *Team Spirit*, Admiral Jones still had enough weaponry at his disposal to destroy the armed forces of any third world country, especially if they could use the tactical nuclear weapons stored aboard the *Mauna Loa*.

The problem was that there had been no targets to hit with all that firepower. Aguila Sorreno was commanding his new government from some secret hideout. His nuclear weapons were as well hidden as he was. For all Gus knew, there might even be a couple of nuclear warheads hidden in some truck parked on a street in Olongapo City outside the base gates. Unless an attack could take out Sorreno and all the weapons he controlled, any use of military force would result in the slaughter of a lot of innocents with no danger to the guilty.

A light blinked and buzzed on his telephone. He picked it up. Karla Forsman, the warrant officer who worked as his secretary, told him the embassy was on the line. Gus told her to put the caller on, expecting to hear the voice of Captain James, the Naval attaché. Instead, he heard the voice of the American ambassador on the other end of the line.

"It's a bad time isn't it, Gus?" Ambassador Black asked.

As the CINCPAC representative in the Philippines, Gus had sat on the ambassador's country team and attended the weekly meetings held at the embassy.

Ambassador Peter Black was a tall, thin man with a head full of carefully trimmed white hair, an aquiline nose, and bright blue eyes. He looked like he could have been cast for a movie role for the same part he played in real life. While Gus didn't have much more use for most professional diplomats than he had for politicians, he liked Black. He had decided he liked him even before one of Black's staffers had told him that the ambassador, as a very young man, had flown a torpedo plane off a carrier deck during the Battle of Midway.

"From what I hear from the bastard on the TV, you've been negotiating the terms of surrender," Gus answered, his voice tinged not with anger as much as frustration.

"What I have gone through the last four hours, I wouldn't call negotiating," the ambassador answered. "Listening to an ultimatum isn't negotiating. I've been ordered to immediately abandon all U.S. facilities, to order all American government employees into central locations, and to cease all communications with my government except for those carried over commercial channels."

Gus didn't comment on the obvious. The new Philippine rulers would be listening to everything being said over any commercial telephone line including the one he and the ambassador were using.

"I've been ordered to make this phone call," the ambassador continued. "The new masters of the Philippines obviously don't understand how our government works. They believe

80

that I can order you to do something, even if it goes against orders you've received from your own command headquarters, and that you will obey my command."

"What are the orders you are supposed to give me?"

"You are ordered to surrender immediately the facilities you command to representatives of the New People's Republic. All military personnel will lay down any weapons and move to central locations and parade grounds. They are to form up in ranks and wait. Civilian personnel will return to their quarters and remain inside until further notice. In one hour, a plane will overfly the base to observe if you are complying with this order. If the troops have assembled on parade as ordered, an NPA detail will enter the base to take the surrender of the facilities."

The ambassador was speaking as if he were reading from a paper. His words were spaced and spoken with no emotion nor inflection. He sounded like one of the prisoners of war that Saddam Hussein had displayed on TV.

"Once the NPA forces take control, they will inspect the base, make sure that everything is intact, and that there has been no sabotage. When they have verified that, your troops will be permitted to return to their quarters," the ambassador continued. "There will be a twenty-hour curfew, except that the base commissaries will be permitted to operate during a four-hour period. All food supplies currently stored on the base can be used for base personnel until arrangements can be made with commercial air line companies to fly all personnel out of the Philippines."

"What's the chances that the NPA won't do us any harm, once we've laid our guns down?"

"I have already done exactly the same thing they are asking you to do. I had no choice. I don't have the kinds of weapons you have at your disposal. They have occupied the embassy compound, JUSMAG, and the AID (Agency for International Development) building. Fortunately, we started destroying our classified material as soon as we learned about the nuclear attacks. So they didn't get anything of intelligence value. So far, no Americans have been deliberately hurt. Most of the embassy staff are staying in their own apartments until flights can be arranged out of the country."

"What's the threat if I don't surrender?"

"I have been ordered to tell you if you do not surrender the base within the hour, the NPA will consider that as an act of open aggression against the new government of the Philippines. Acting in the defense of their own territory, they will immediately destroy your war-making capability with nuclear weapons already aimed at the base."

"If I refuse to give up the base, is there any chance they will allow civilians and families to abandon the base before they nuke us?" Gus asked.

"I don't think so. The orders were very specific. If you and your men aren't in parade formations in exactly one hour, they will launch a nuclear attack."

"I understand what you are saying," Gus answered. "You understand that I will have to make the decision based on military considerations? Those considerations will include concerns over what might fall into the hands of the NPA if we surrender the base, and what impact that would have on the future of peace in this area."

"I think you are telling me you'll fight before you will surrender. That might be a hopeless gesture and very expensive in human life."

The line suddenly went dead.

The ambassador had either hung up without saying goodbye, or he had been disconnected. Gus tried to get a dial tone. He couldn't. The commercial phone line was dead.

Gus didn't put the phone back onto the hook. Instead, he punched the button that put him back into the base communication system which was working. He punched the call button for WO Forsman.

"Get all available staff members into my office immediately!" he barked as soon as Forsman answered.

While he waited for the staff to gather, Gus dictated a quick message to CINCPAC describing the threat and how he intended to respond. He worded it carefully. As he had no secure communication link to CINCPAC, he assumed that the enemy would be reading the message as soon as he sent it. As he finished it, a dozen different men and women came through his office door one or two at a time. Most of them were wearing eagles on the collars of their khaki work uniforms. There weren't enough chairs in the office for all, but as Gus was standing in front of his desk, no one else looked for a place to sit down.

Gus handed the tape he had just dictated to WO Forsman as Admiral Rimaldo walked through the door. A few key staff members were still missing, but Gus had no time to wait.

Using five quick and brutal sentences, Gus summarized his conversation with the American ambassador.

"We will not surrender this base," Gus said at the end of his summary. "I want the air raid alarms sounded and everyone not manning one of the air defense systems taking whatever cover they can. There's a chance we may shoot down whatever they throw at us. If we don't, some of the units on the base may survive the attack. The standing orders for any ships in the harbor which survive are that they should make a run for the open sea if possible."

"Admiral!" The speaker was Captain Raymond Johnson, the commander of the Naval Hospital complex. "We're talking a minimum of five to ten thousand casualties, probably many more. That's insane! We have no choice. You have to surrender the base."

Gus looked around the room at the faces. The doctor was speaking for others as well as himself. Gus knew that it was not that they were afraid of dying themselves. Everyone who was nodding his head in agreement with the doctor had a family somewhere in the base housing. Most of them had only recently arrived now that families were being brought back in. Many of the younger men and women had their children with them. They would be sacrificing not just their own lives, but their hope of future generations.

"Doctor, we have things stored on this base that can not fall into the hands of our enemy. If they do, we can expect many more thousands of people to die, many times more than those of us on this base."

"If we are going to defy the NPA, let's order the *Mauna Loa* out of the harbor right now," Captain Reilly interrupted. Captain Johnson looked puzzled by Reilly's comments. As the commander of the base hospital, Johnson had no need to know about the cargo on board the *Mauna Loa*. He didn't know what Tim Reilly was talking about.

"If I thought that would save us, I would," Gus answered. "But I think that keeping the *Mauna Loa* right where she is in the bay may be what will save us. I think that's what they want. If it is, dropping a few nukes on us is a damn good way of guaranteeing that they won't get it."

"You think they are bluffing?" Reilly asked.

"I hope they are bluffing. It's not just the *Mauna Loa*. This base has got all sorts of things the NPA must want: planes, ships, supplies, weapons. They are trying to scare us so they don't have to negotiate with the diplomats about what they get and what we can take away."

That time had come to end the discussion. Gus wasn't too sure that if he let it go on, he might have an immediate mutiny on his hands.

"So get to your battle stations. If I'm wrong, I'll take your complaints in Hell."

"What about the plane they are going to send over to check out our surrender?" Reilly asked.

"I would like to shoot the fucker down, but the orders stand that we don't shoot first. I want the weapon systems tracking him the minute we get him on radar. But no one shoots unless he drops a bomb or opens fire."

"Admiral!" Commander Ted McBride, the communications officer, called out. He saw Gus's eyes give him permission to talk.

"That plane that is going to do a fly over. They will have to be

84

talking by radio to someone, telling them what they see. Anyone who talks back to the plane will give us an identified position. That might give us a target to shoot back at, if any of our weapon systems survive their first shot. I won't guarantee a hit, though. If they are smart, they'll have their antenna field several miles from their headquarters."

"It's still worth trying. If you get a radio fix on any station talking to the plane, I want those coordinates fed into every weapons system we have, the Tomahawks on the ships in the bay, too. If we are attacked, all surviving weapons systems will fire on that target."

Gus turned to Admiral Rimaldo. Before the sudden NPA destruction of the AFP, Gus would have predicted that Rimaldo would be leading the chorus demanding surrender instead of facing death. But, Rimaldo had stood quietly during Gus's explanations, letting a smile break out when Gus announced his intention not to surrender. Gus knew from his own sources that Rimaldo was already in contact with small resistance groups around the island of Luzon through a group of runners that snuck on and off the base.

What Rimaldo was doing was more a futile gesture than anything with hopes of success, but he didn't blame the man. The Americans could hope for repatriation back to the States. Rimaldo and his men would be imprisoned and probably executed.

"I suggest that you pass the word to the Philippine soldiers on the base that if we get nuked, the survivors take to the jungle and start organizing resistance movements," Gus told his Philippine counterpart. "I can not imagine my country not coming in on your side if the NPA deliberately slaughters several thousand of us."

"For the sake of your families, I hope Sorreno is bluffing," Rimaldo answered. "But as soon as I leave here, I'm doing exactly what you suggest."

Chapter Ten

The Sierra Madre Mountains, the Philippines.

Colonel Cho Chae-Jin looked at his Seiko wristwatch again. Chae-Jin liked the watch. It told the time in real numbers, and it served as a stopwatch, a timer, and an alarm clock. It would be the one souvenir that he would take back home once the ultimate success had been achieved. He wore a Japanese watch for the same reason he was wearing rubber thongs, black cotton pants, and a dirty T-shirt. It was part of a disguise to make him look like he belonged in the Philippines. The printed design on the shirt talked about God, pussy, and an oyster. For reasons Cho didn't understand, the Filipinos found some kind of strange humor in a nonsense phrase that combined cats, religion, and seafood.

Not only did he and all the other North Koreans working on the project dress like the natives, none of them carried anything in their pockets that came from home, except for the small cyanide capsules sewed into the linings of shirts or pants to guarantee that no interrogation would ever force secrets out of lips.

He looked at the watch again. The timer function was telling him there was only five minutes left in the event being timed. Was it five minutes to quick victory? Was it five minutes closer to the time when he could walk away from hot tropical weather, mosquitoes, stomach trouble, and idiots who perceived themselves to be great revolutionaries? He didn't think it would be. Success never came that quickly and easily.

He looked around the small shack. They had taken it from a local peasant. NPA workers had put in a new floor to hold all the equipment the room held, but other than that, it was original material. The roof was old thatch that leaked when it rained and the walls had cracks that showed daylight.

Sorreno's men had converted one corner of the shack into a small television studio. A television camera on a tripod pointed at a red banner, which covered part of one wall. A wooden podium stood in front of the banner and several microphones waited in front of the podium. Only one of the mikes was connected to the video tape machine that recorded the daily speeches of Sorreno, but Aguila wanted to give his people the impression he was speaking to the international press. In fact, he was. Copies of the tapes Sorreno made were shipped to Manila and distributed to all the news services that still had offices there.

The opposite corner of the shack held the radio and communication equipment that Sorreno used to direct his new regime and command his many different units scattered through the Philippines. All of the communication equipment was good Japanese technology bought on the commercial market.

In order to insure the secrecy of the base, only a small number of people knew its location. Even the cabinet members of the new government didn't know where the president was hiding. With only a few exceptions, the cadre, workers, and security forces assigned to the base were never allowed to leave the base area. The base buildings had no radio antennas either. The antenna farm sat on top of a mountain peak five miles away.

Aguila Sorreno didn't like hiding in the jungle now that he ruled the Philippines. He had wanted to march into Manila in front of the mob he led on the first day of his victory. Colonel Cho was the one who had argued that Sorreno should stay in the jungle for a while for his own safety. Sorreno suggested that if the Americans couldn't find Hussein with their smart bombs, they wouldn't be able to find him either. Colonel Cho pointed out that Saddam had secret concrete bunkers. Any bunkers in Manila belonged to the puppets of the Americans and the puppet masters would know where they were and how to destroy them.

Sorreno, with his stupid pride, had accepted Cho's arguments that he was too important as a leader and a symbol to risk death by surprise attack. He had finally agreed that they would stay hidden in the Sierra Madre jungle until they were sure they were safe from American attack.

As far as the Korean government was concerned, it was not Sorreno who was of critical importance to the success of the mission. Without Colonel Cho Chae-Jin and the knowledge he carried in his head, the venture could go no further. The weapons would never be fired, and the Americans would sit fat and happy in their giant base in Subic Bay, planning how they would impose their own new world order and halt the march of socialism.

Cho had been tempted to let Aguila Sorreno go to Manila where he could listen to the crowds cheer him on while Cho stayed safely in the jungle with his weapons of destruction. If Sorreno died suddenly, there were a dozen others who could be quickly slipped into his shoes. But the kind of control that Colonel Cho wanted over Sorreno demanded constant daily attention. He had to feed Sorreno's stupid ego and direct his thinking on a regular basis. So Cho Chae-Jin kept Sorreno with him in the hideout; he intended to do so until his government had everything they wanted.

The watch on his wrist beeped its tone. Colonel Cho stood up and walked across the reddish colored, new lumber floor to where a radio operator sat in front of the bank of radio communication equipment. Aguila Sorreno was standing beside the radio operator who was fine-tuning the equipment.

Sorreno wore a jungle-green fatigue uniform. He had given himself the rank of general and someone had sewn two red stars on each of the shoulders. He wore a tooled leather gun belt strapped around his waist. A U.S. military issue 9-mm automatic pistol rode in the gun belt's holster.

"I am now approaching the base, flying at twelve hundred feet." The words came in over the loud speaker.

The pilot, Chuey Drilon, had been in the Philippine Air Force and had reached the rank of captain. He had defected to the jungle instead of surrendering after flying against Aquino in the attempted coup in which American fighter planes had chased the rebels out of the sky. He was now a colonel in the NPA's new air force. This day he was flying a Cessna 310 observation plane, one of the Philippine Air Force planes that had not been sitting on the runway at the Sangley Point Air Base.

"I can see no troops assembling!" Chuey shouted over the radio. "I see men in many defense positions. They are all still armed. They are pointing their weapons at me, but not firing."

"The Americans are defying me!" Sorreno announced, his voice loud and angry. He reached forward and grabbed the mike from where it hung on the front of the radio console.

"Bird Dog!" he called. "This is The Eagle. Make sure they are not surrendering. Fly one more circle. They have to give up! If they have not shot you down, that must mean they are going to surrender. Maybe they are still walking to the parade grounds."

"No they are not surrendering," Chuey answered. "Give me fifteen minutes to clear the area, then let them have it. Destroy them!"

Sorreno turned to face Colonel Cho. "You said they would surrender, that the base would be ours, that they would give up. You said they would do so because they would want to save their families. So why have the Americans not laid down their weapons?"

"The American commander must realize that you would prefer to get all he possesses rather than allowing him to take his weapons to Hell when he goes," Cho said.

"They are fools and they will die," Sorreno proclaimed as he handed the mike back to the radio operator. "The Americans must learn that they can not defy me. Respect is more important than the toys we might steal from them."

Sorreno stood up and paced back and forth across the small room for a moment. He stopped and turned to Colonel Cho. "We will order the attack immediately. I'll give our teams thirty minutes to get away from the area, then we will launch the weapon. You must give Major Estuar and Comrade Jose the codes so they can arm one of the warheads."

Comrade Jose was the code name for Major Kye Dae Jung, the Korean weapons expert assigned to the project. Antonio Estuar was the Filipino trained by Major Kye.

Six years earlier Antonio Estuar had been an electronics engineering major at Manila University when AFP troops fired on a crowd of students protesting the Marcos government. The soldiers wounded several people and killed one young girl. The girl hadn't been part of the protest. She had been walking to the university to visit her brother, Antonio. Antonio had gone into the jungles, and Colonel Cho had personally selected him for two years of special education in Pyongyang. He was now the senior NPA officer in command of the missile team. He had all the knowledge he needed to aim the SCUD guidance systems and fire them. The only thing that neither he nor Major Kye had were the unlocking codes that would arm the remaining warheads of the five that the North Korean government had given the NPA.

"I decide when we fire a weapon and what we aim at," Cho answered, his voice cold.

"It was not my idea that we threaten the Americans so soon," Sorreno said, his voice louder. "You were the one who insisted that we must either force the Americans to surrender or we must destroy the Americans."

"And so we must, but we must do it a step at a time. They are brave now, but they will wear down. What we want to do is scare them into shooting first. We want the opinion of the world on your side. When you destroy the Americans, it must look like you did it in self-defense. If they had shot at us today, or launched one of their missiles at your government in Manila, or even shot down Colonel Chuey Drilon, then we could have attacked. That is why we sent those press people with our team to collect the surrender, so that they could witness to the world our peaceful intent. But now we must wait while we scare them some more."

"I was in no hurry to push the Americans out of Subic," Sorreno said. "I only played this game because you insisted. But I am not a man to make empty threats. Now that I have made the threat and they have defied me, why not use one of the weapons we have left to destroy the American base? What will the Americans do? Destroy Manila? It would be best for the revolution if that happened."

"I agree it would. But that is not what the Americans will do. If you give them the right excuse, they will invade your country. If you use one of the weapons that you have left to destroy the base, how strong will you be when the Americans come storming onto your shores to collect their vengeance? Your army is still a mob, you have no navy, and while you have planes you have captured, you have only one pilot to fly them. You must take over the naval base so you can grow strong and build a navy of your own, but you must do it smartly."

Cho looked for a moment into the face of Sorreno to make sure he was listening and not just thinking about what he would argue back. Certain he had the man's attention, Cho continued. "All wars are won politically. The American public is an easy mob to lead. They do not trust their own leaders and they fear death. They believe in the stupidity of fair play. If you can make it look like the American Navy hit you first, they will not permit their president to risk more lives. But if they think you struck the first blow, then they will pay any price to take their revenge."

"If you had provided us with what we needed before we launched this operation, I would not have these problems. I told you many times that we should have as many weapons in reserve as we used in the initial attack. If I had more weapons

I could handle this easily. They would not dare attack me."

"We gave you everything we had!" Cho shouted, his voice rising in anger. "That is why you can not waste what you have."

"If we don't use one of the bombs right now, the Americans may think we have none. They will attack us immediately anyway."

"I think not. They can not be sure of that. They still fear you. We have worked on that fear today, but their will was still strong enough to resist. That disappoints us, but it does not defeat us. Now we must begin to wear that will down. The Americans fight well for a while, but they tire quickly. For now we will show both passion, and the will to stay. We will tell them we spare them for a while, but only because of pity for their women and children. We will continue to bargain, telling them we will let their women and children go, but never doing so, and each day we will build on that fear."

Cho watched the anger play across the face of Sorreno. The man wanted to lash out, but he had enough brains to know he would be nothing without the Korean, not as long as the Korean kept the secret of the weapon codes. Cho had no doubt that he would eventually fire the weapons and kill the hated Americans, but Cho would make the decision when it would be done.

"You must talk to your foreign minister in Manila," Cho added, working hard to keep the smirk off his face. "Tell Comrade Peralta to meet immediately with the American ambassador. Have him tell the American how compassionate you are, but make sure he understands that compassion has its limits."

Colonel Cho walked out of the shack and across a small clearing to another shack he used as his own office. Inside, he sat down behind an old wooden desk. He reached for a piece of notepaper and wrote out the message he would send to Pyongyang. It would take very careful wording. He would have to describe how the day's failure had been the first small victory in a long campaign that would result in a final victory. Things were proceeding exactly as Pyongyang had told him they would.

Chapter Eleven

Subic Bay, the Philippines.

Gus Jones and everyone else in the operation center took a deep breath. They had all heard his side of the conversation with the naval attaché from the embassy in Manila. Captain James had called on a line that was suddenly working again to report what the NPA foreign minister had told the ambassador. The NPA was delaying the destruction of Subic Bay to give the base commander more time to consider his responsibilities to his men and their families. Captain James added that NPA had denied a request that all dependents be permitted to depart the base and had again repeated the warning that should any American engage in any overt military activity, the response would be immediate and deadly.

Subic Bay had a delay of execution, not a reprieve. Gus was sure of that and he wanted to be better prepared to shoot back when the threat was made again. He hung up the phone, which had gone dead again, and walked over to a large scale map of Luzon.

Ted McBride pointed to a spot on the map. "We have a good direction bearing from the control tower at Cubi on the station talking to that pilot," he said. "We locate the source of the signal right here. They are not just talking to that plane either. There's a whole lot of radio traffic coming out of there on enough different frequencies to suggest a small antenna farm. It's got to be the main NPA command post."

His finger pointed to a mountain valley in the southern part of the Sierra Madre mountains. "It's about twenty air miles north of the town of Maria Aurora. That's 120 miles from here, well within Tomahawk range."

"We've gone over the tapes several times," Captain Babb, the base intelligence officer, added. "We're positive the voice talking to the airplane was the voice of the man on the TV, the so-called new president of the People's Republic. That's his headquarters. We take that out, we've cut off the head."

"We can get him," Admiral Rimaldo stated. "We take him out, and the country belongs to us again."

"Only if we get the weapons, too, however many of them he has," Gus stated. "If we shoot and we don't get those, we're right back to where we were thirty minutes ago, waiting for the bomb to come at us from over the mountains."

"I still think we should go for this bastard," Rimaldo insisted. "You should use the same kind of weapons he used. You have tactical nuclear weapons. You never admit you do, and you told our government that you don't keep them at Subic, but I know you have them."

"If I had them and I had the key to unlock them, I'd use them, if I had a target," Gus said, still taking care not to confirm or deny the presence of nuclear weapons on his base. "But all I've got to use are conventional warhead weapons."

That was the truth. He didn't have the presidential codes necessary to arm the tactical nuclear warheads stored on board the *Mauna Loa*.

"So the question is, if we blanket this area with several Tomahawks carrying conventional warheads, what's the chance we'll get him and his weapons?" Gus asked.

"Not good at all," Lt. Commander Melendez answered. Melendez had worked all night checking out weapons systems, deciding what had been damaged by the pulse effect, what could be fixed, and what had to be junked. She had quickly established herself as the expert on the entire range of high tech weapons delivery systems. Gus was the one who had suggested her participation in the current discussion of response options.

"Our first problem is that we have to feed the map data into the Tomahawk guidance computers for this kind of shot," Melendez continued. "I'm not sure we even have all the ground data we need, but I could get around that by programming a high altitude flight pattern. The NPA doesn't have Patriots to shoot them down. But we don't have the accurate coordinates I would need to guarantee a direct hit. Visual guidance systems wouldn't do us any good because we don't know what the target looks like. That dot on the map covers a couple of square miles. We don't know how far away the antenna farm is from the headquarters. We could blow apart a mountain peak and not come close to hitting the target we want. We don't know how many warheads they still have and how far the launchpads are from the headquarters."

"Let's go ahead and program a few missiles to hit in that target circle anyway," Gus said. "We won't shoot them unless they shoot at us, but that gives us at least one shot at getting even if the bomb comes in."

"We would have to put men on the ground to get the intelligence we need," Captain Babb answered. "With the jungle cover, we can't count on satellite or air surveillance. If we could find out where they keep their weapons, we could take those out. That would be much more important than taking out the leadership."

"For all we know, they could have weapons stored all over the island," Reilly said.

"I don't think so," Babb answered. "They can't have that many weapons in reserve, maybe three or four warheads at the most, maybe not that many. I don't buy that shit Sorreno is spouting how they made the bombs in jungle laboratories. Someone gave them the weapons, probably a country that's recently developed a nuclear capability. My bet would be the North Koreans. A new member of the nuclear club won't have produced much weapon material. Remember, we spent the whole Second World War producing enough material to make just three bombs."

"Then it's even more important that we keep any nuclear warheads we have on the base out of their hands," Reilly said, forgetting he wasn't supposed to admit in front of Admiral Rimaldo the presence of nuclear weapons on the base.

No one called him on it.

"I know this makes Admiral Rimaldo unhappy, but I think the decision has been made in Washington to give up the Philippines, if they can get us out of here," Babb continued. "I can't blame Washington either. The Philippine government was going to kick us out sooner or later, so why should we risk nuclear casualties to help them take their country back. There are still people in Washington who think we should have left after Mount Pinatubo blew up."

Gus looked over at Admiral Rimaldo. There was no longer any reason for him to play the politician when he dealt with the fat crook. But getting out of the Philippines wasn't the only problem the Navy faced. "Frankly I could care less if the crooks who have been running this country are thrown in jail and left to rot," he said. "But this is more than just the Philippines. If we let the NPA win this and stay in power, every two-bit thug who can stomach calling himself a socialist revolutionary is going to be looking for his own supplier of nuclear weapons.

"We taught Saddam that having the military power doesn't give one the right to stomp on a neighbor. Now we have to teach people like Sorreno that nuclear weapons aren't going to win any revolutions, no matter how many people you kill. If we don't stop this Sorreno, we'll have to deal with more like him, especially if they get their hands on the stock of weapons we have stored at the base. I'm convinced that what Sorreno wants is to collect the nuclear weapons he thinks we have."

"Admiral, it's a good speech, but what can we do about it?" Reilly asked.

"The only way we can win is to take out the new government

of the Philippines along with their nasty toys and put the old government back in," Gus said. He saw Rimaldo's smile as he made the suggestion.

"To do that, we can't wait for the enemy to call the next play," Tim Reilly interjected. "We've got to take the initiative away from them."

"Agreed," Gus said. "But we can't do it from here. I hope that's what CINCPAC and Washington are planning to do."

"Don't count on it," Reilly said.

Gus turned and looked back at the map. "We know that both their headquarters, and the missiles are somewhere inside this circle," he said as he drew a quick circle with his finger on the map. "What would it take to narrow down the area where they are hiding to the point where a recon team might find it?"

"It shouldn't be that difficult." Captain Babb answered. "This is the most remote part of Aurora Province. There's a coast road, but not much that goes into the mountains. They must have brought the SCUDs in along that coast, close to the road. Those babies weigh almost seven tons. While they could be broken down and the fuel shipped separately, there is no way they carried them up the mountain on backs or by mules. They used trucks, big trucks, so there's some kind of road leading into where they are. Find the road and you can follow it right to the base."

"It's exactly the job for a SEAL team," Reilly interjected. "The SEALs assigned here are at sea with *Team Spirit*. The team members are already familiar with the general area, the terrain and the people. Three or four SEAL teams could land along the coast and run intel recons into the Sierra Madres. Some of the peasants in the area must have seen something, but a good team could probably locate the targets without making contact with the local population. High altitude, nighttime aerial recon with thermo imaging cameras could pick up concentrations of people and machines under the canopy."

"Add in good satellite SIGINT (signal intelligence) information and you could narrow that circle the SEAL teams would have to search," Ted McBride threw in. "If the NPA leaders are smart, they'll have an antenna field located a long way from their headquarters, but that still narrows the search."

"Once NSA gets good satellite photos the PIs might pick up something too, even if it is jungle," Mel Babb added. "There has to be some blast evidence where they shot off those three missiles."

"The SEAL team could take out both the headquarters and the weapons with a commando attack," Tim Reilly added.

"I think I'd go with Tomahawk missiles with conventional warheads instead of a commando attack," Gus suggested. "Let the SEAL teams point at the target, then go in and mop up the scene after the Tomahawks land. If we did it right, we could do it and not tell anyone we did it. Let Rimaldo here take the credit."

Rimaldo smiled at Gus. "Are you going to recommend that to CINCPAC?" he asked.

"I can't," Gus answered. "All I have is an open line to CINC-PAC, and I'm not supposed to use even that. If I had a secure communications link, I'd be on the line right now, trying to sell it. I hope that CINCPAC is thinking along these lines."

"They'd better be doing more than thinking about it," Captain Reilly said. "The fleet and the SEAL teams are over a thousand miles away. It will take them several days to move into an area close enough that the SEALs can sneak ashore."

"We won't know if they are doing that, or not," Captain Babb said. "We're like prisoners of war. We don't know what's going on."

"If not like prisoners of war, like hostages," Gus said. "As much as it galls me to say it, we'll have to wait for someone to rescue us. At least we have some freedom on the base. I want to establish as normal an existence as we can for the families. We keep the commissaries open, the schools going, the clubs, the theaters, and the swimming pools."

"What do we do for workers?" one officer asked. "Almost none of the Filipinos showed up this morning for work."

"Being as we didn't get blown up, maybe they will start coming in tomorrow."

"If they do, some of them are going to be working for the new government as spies and saboteurs," Captain Babb pointed out.

"I know that," Gus answered, "but they could be our early warning system, too. If they leave again, we know the word is out that we're in trouble."

"What about our local communications systems?" Commander Ted McBride asked. "The Naval attaché told us the NPA forbids the use of all frequencies on all communication bands. Do we comply or not? The last message from CINC-PAC told us to comply with any requirements levied by the new government as long as it didn't compromise the security and safety of the base."

"We keep using *all* of the equipment we need to use for the security, safety, and morale of the base," Gus answered. "I want to establish a daily routine that is as normal as possible while maintaining battle ready condition. Battle ready condition means we will use tactical communications, just like we will keep our weapons ready and targeted." He paused, thought a moment and added. "If you can get the AFN TV station back on the air, do it. I've got enough problems without denying the families the joys of CNN news and reruns of 'The Cosby Show' if we can give it to them."

Karla buzzed Gus on the intercom. Gus picked up the phone and asked what she wanted.

"I've got a very angry Russian general here in your office," she said. "He insists he talk to either you or Admiral Rimaldo immediately."

"Shit!" Gus swore. "I forgot we had him on our hands. I'll handle him. Tell him to wait a minute."

Gus looked around the room. "All of you back to your duty stations. Reilly, walk with me back to the office."

"You think the Russians have anything to do with this?" Reilly asked as they walked down the hall together.

"If this had happened five years ago, I'd be sure they did. Now, I don't think the current Russian government is playing the game. But we can't be sure that our visitor is completely innocent. Everyone who was an officer in the old Soviet military can't be happy with what happened to the Soviet Union. There could be some kind of rebel group who is involved in this in some way. That submarine standing off the mouth of the bay bothers me. If it's not Russian, I'd like to know who it does belong to. In the old days, I would have thought the sub was here to pick up the Russian admiral so they can blow us off the map without killing one of their own."

"You want me to order a security detail to arrest him?"

"I want to talk to him first, see what he has to say. I want to know if he had any idea that this was going to happen."

"You don't think he'll tell the truth if he did, do you?" Gus asked.

"Of course not," Gus answered. "But if he says one thing that makes me think he's lying, I might not just arrest him, I might try him as a spy and shoot him."

"You want me to come in, too," Reilly asked as they reached the private, backdoor entrance into the admiral's office.

"No, let me handle him. I'll call for help if I need it."

"I demand you allow me to contact my embassy," Admiral Semenkov announced as soon as Karla ushered him into Admiral Jones's office. The Russian admiral was wearing a heavy dress uniform that made Gus think for some reason of how American missionaries used to dress in the Philippines, covering their bodies, arms, and legs with layers of cloth that were constantly soaked with sweat.

Gus had sat down in the chair behind his desk for the first time in several hours just before the Russian came in. He didn't bother getting up. He waved one hand in the direction of one of the three phones sitting on his desk. "Be my guest," he said. "That's the phone that's connected to the Philippine phone system. No one else on this base has been able to get a dial tone for the last thirty minutes. But people do call us once in a while. If you can get out, more power to you. I would love to hear what your embassy will tell you."

"The phones don't work?" the Russian asked, standing still, but not reaching out for the phone.

"Sometimes they do, when your new ally wants to tell us something."

"My ally? I have a small Sony shortwave radio. I've listened to the news. My country has not yet recognized the new government of the Philippines and has sided with the Americans at the UN in denouncing the use of nuclear weapons. There is no way the people who now govern Russia can be happy with this. We want American food to feed us through another winter, not American bases."

Gus motioned the Russian admiral to take one of the chairs that sat in front of his desk.

"What the news hasn't reported is that we are being threatened with nuclear attack if we don't immediately surrender the base. I'm sorry that you must share our fate. I will tell you in all frankness that I do not have high expectations that any of us will survive this experience."

"You think that the base will be attacked?" the Russian asked. "That makes no sense? The new Philippine government can't be that stupid. If they kill thousands of Americans, your government will surely declare war on them."

"You're the chess player, you know the importance of figuring what an opponent sees on the board. Tell me why I believe they will attack the base? And while you're at it, tell me what you know about this."

"I know nothing," the Russian insisted. "But I refuse to believe my government gave these thugs nuclear weapons."

"But your country is observing events from close at hand. You have a sub patrolling the waters outside my base."

"I know of no Soviet subs assigned to patrol so close to the Philippines. I would assure you, if it was a Russian sub, you wouldn't know where it is. We have learned how to stay hidden, too."

"It's a diesel sub. At night it sails on the surface. We have it on radar and under night vision observation. My intelligence people tell me it is Russian made, probably what we label a *Romeo*-class."

"Then it can't be a Soviet sub, even if we did make it. We've got lots of diesel subs still in operation, but we don't send them this far away from home. If it is what you call a *Romeo,* then it must be either Chinese or North Korean. Both have such subs in their inventories. The North Koreans have manufactured some of those on their own."

"Then it must be Chinese, because it's got to be the same country who gave the NPA the nuclear warheads. But why would the Chinese hand out nuclear weapons?"

"I don't agree it was the Chinese," the Russian said. "It must be North Korea."

"The North Koreans?" Gus asked, getting the confirmation he had expected. He had already decided who the villains had to be. "Are you telling me that they have gone nuclear?"

"You must know that, too," Admiral Semenkov insisted. "That's the bad news," he added, showing how well he had studied American culture by the idiom he picked. "The good news is that they can't have many nuclear weapons. The Koreans haven't been in the business long enough to build up a stockpile. How many have the rebels already exploded, three or four?"

"Three, all crude Hiroshima-sized explosions."

"Then it's the Koreans for sure. The Chinese have developed smaller tactical weapons which would have been much more appropriate for this kind of operation. The Koreans couldn't have gotten that far in the development process yet. The North Koreans must have shipped most of their production to this part of the world." The Russian started to say something more, stopped, and thought for a moment; his craggy features froze and gave no hint of his emotions. Suddenly the features broke into a wry smile.

"So that's why they demand that you surrender your base immediately," he stated. "They have discovered how difficult and expensive it is to produce nuclear weapon material, and like all criminals they have decided to steal what others have produced. I don't suppose you would tell me how much they might collect if this theft works."

"You know I won't even tell you whether or not they are trying to rob the right store."

"How is your government going to frustrate the robbery?"

"As far as I know, they hope to talk the crooks to death."

"Are they talking to just the NPA, or to the Koreans, too?"

"I don't think the Koreans admit to being part of this," Gus said. "That's why I think talking will do nothing but give us a little more time to live."

"You are right, I am sorry to say. I know too well the minds of both Kims. The chubby-faced boy is a petulant child who throws a tantrum when he is frustrated. He will expect you to give up anything he wants on this base. When he decides you will not give him what he wants, he will attack. It will be nothing but a senseless killing, but we will all die. I guarantee it."

The Russian admiral paused a moment, thinking again.

"I can understand why you might not trust me," he said. "Believe me, what is happening in the Philippines is not good news for my country. The North Korean leaders are ambitious. You Americans are the target right now, but if they succeed here, we will be the next target. The North Koreans have already made friends with the Khmer Rouge in Cambodia. Once they have more nuclear material, they will certainly give some of their new weapons to Pol Pot. With such weapons of mass destruction, Pol Pot will not only take Cambodia back, he'll attack Viet Nam, too. Cam Ranh Bay will soon be in the same noose that is around your neck."

"If you were playing from my side of the chessboard," Gus asked, "what would your move be?"

"One only wins by going for the king," Admiral Semenkov answered. "I would announce to the world that I had proof that it was the North Koreans who provided the weapons, even if I didn't have such proof. I would take out both the Kims, and all of their nuclear production."

"Would you use nuclear weapons?"

"You Americans proved in the Gulf War that nuclear weapons, even tactical nuclear weapons, are no longer required if one has the accuracy of the technical weapons that you have. The only thing you would need is surprise. You must shoot before you tell the world why you are shooting. That might not save us, but it would make sure this never happened again."

"And that's two reasons why my President can not do it that way. He doesn't dare tell lies that big and he won't shoot first."

"If a player can not go after the king, one must try to capture the queen. If you can find the hiding place of the head of this new Philippine government and where he has his remaining weapons, you should destroy both the man and his weapons. Do it right, and we all might live, too."

Gus agreed that was exactly what he would do too, if he was free to operate. "Unfortunately, I suspect the politicians in Washington hope they can talk the new government into some kind of agreement that will let us take our weapons and go home."

"Perhaps they could, if they were dealing with just the Filipinos," Admiral Semenkov said. "But if the North Koreans are behind this, talking will only make them think you are weak. The Kims must see this situation as a perfect opportunity to take vengeance for 1950. If it is the son, Kim Jung Il, who is in charge of this operation, I predict he has already decided to blow this base up, but to let the NPA take the blame."

"I'm afraid you are right," Gus said. He looked at his watch. "I apologize for forgetting about you. I offer the hospitality of the base, for as long as we live. As soon as I have an open communications channel with my embassy again, I'll pass on the word that you are here and safe. Once your embassy knows that, they may be able to arrange a safe conduct for you before they destroy us."

104

"If you have time in an evening, perhaps we might have that rematch we didn't last evening," Admiral Semenkov suggested.

"I am afraid that the longer this goes on, the more free time I am going to have. If we are still alive, why don't we play tomorrow night? Come by my place about 6:30 P.M. You can walk from the guest house where you are staying. I'll also arrange for you to use the base exchange in case there is anything you need to buy. I assume you did not bring the luggage for such a long stay."

"I will need some way to do laundry, too," the Russian answered. "I'm down to my last uniform."

Chapter Twelve

Subic Bay, the Philippines.

It was past seven o'clock when Gus left his office and walked straight to the O'Club. He headed for the bar, slid onto a stool, and ordered a double scotch on the rocks. The surprised bartender, who had never seen the base commander ordering from the bar, let alone drinking by himself, quickly fixed the drink and sat it in front of the admiral.

As he took his first sip, Jones felt exactly like General Halftrack in the *Beetle Bailey* cartoon strip. As the afternoon had worn on, he'd found himself with less and less to do. Most of the base activities had closed down because the Philippine labor was no longer working. Once the base was ready to defend itself, there wasn't much else to do until the next attack came.

With time on his hands, he worried. The attack would come. Gus was sure that the Russian admiral was right about what Kim Jung Il was planning. Subic Bay was going to be North Korea's revenge for the Korean War.

Someone was going to have to do something to stop it from happening. Gus had spent a half hour talking to CINCPAC on the phone. It hadn't been an easy conversation. Admiral Belmont kept reminding Gus that they were talking on an open line everytime Gus tried to say something significant. He had refused to give Gus even a hint about what the U.S. Navy was

106

planning to do. But what bothered Gus most about the phone call was that Admiral Belmont had twice reminded Gus that they had to assume they were dealing with rational minds. There was no rational reason why the NPA should attack the American base without provocation.

But the Russian admiral didn't think they were dealing with a rational mind, and neither did Gus. In his entire career, Gus had never felt so helpless.

"So why are you still here?" he asked the bartender, a short, dark brown Filipino who was somewhere between the ages of thirty-five and fifty. The man, who everyone called Joe, had been behind the bar for more than ten years.

"I think the others come back soon, as long as our new government let us," the bartender said. "They won't find good jobs like Americans give us. Right now everyone is afraid that this Sorreno guy, he will blow up the base. But soon he will understand that my country needs Americans, just like they need this base. Until he figures that out, things are going to be very bad."

"Aren't you afraid of being blown up?" the admiral asked.

"I'm more afraid I watch my children starve. I have eight. I send them and my wife to stay with my brother in Botolan. But I must feed them. The other workers, they get hungry, then they will come back to work."

Botolan was a town a few miles north of Subic, far enough away that his family would be safe if the base was nuked.

The bartender moved away to take an order from another officer sitting at the other end of the bar. It was a lieutenant JG and Gus didn't know who he was or where he worked. Gus turned on his stool, holding his glass in his hand and looked over the lounge. He and the JG were the only customers. The class six stores were selling lots of booze, and most of the officers were drinking it at home, keeping their wives and children company.

As Gus watched, another customer entered the bar, looked around, then headed for one of the tables. It was Lt. Commander Kathy Melendez. Dressed civilian, she was wearing a

107

blue skirt with a white blouse. She saw him and smiled in his direction as one of the enlisted wives, who had been hired to fill the jobs abandoned by the Philippine workers, walked up to her table to take her drink order.

Gus wondered if Melendez was meeting someone. He thought again about her story of how some kid had tried to pick her up in Olongapo. He couldn't blame the boy for trying. Wearing a dress, Kathy Melendez didn't look her age, and she did look worth a try at picking up.

Gus spun back around and put the glass back on the bar and motioned to the bartender to fill him up again. When he had a refill, he turned back around and found that Kathy Melendez was still looking at him. The waitress walked with a tray to her table and set a San Miguel and an empty glass in front of the Lt. Commander.

"Can I join you?" Gus asked, speaking just loud enough for his voice to carry across the space. It was not something he had thought about, but did quite spontaneously. He had surprised himself by doing it, but the woman didn't look surprised at his action.

"I'd like that," she said, giving him a smile with just enough upward twist of her lips to suggest it was real, not something she had put on.

He picked up his glass and joined her.

"I appreciate the way you have helped out," he said as he sat down.

"It helps keeping busy," she answered. "I don't have time to think about how scared I was today, waiting for it all to end. For a moment there I hated you. I thought you were playing one of those macho military games. Damn the torpedoes and who cares who dies? Then I figured out what all that talk about the *Mauna Loa* meant."

"I don't think Dr. Johnson ever did figure it out. Most of the people on the base don't have the foggiest notion why I'm so ready to put all their lives on the line."

"The loneliness of command. I don't envy you the rank. I'm

108

glad I'm a specialist and not a line officer. What's our real chances? Are we going to be alive when this is all over?"

Is that why she seemed so pleased when he invited himself over to her table? Was she only interested in what he knew?

"You don't have to answer that," she said suddenly, like she was sorry she had asked it. "I'm a smart girl. I know the answers. They want the nuclear weapons. If they drop their bombs in the right places, they'll get what they want, after we are all dead. The plutonium will survive an overhead nuclear blast; we won't. Once it's produced, about the only way you can destroy enriched uranium or plutonium is by making a bomb out of it."

"I think that's why we're still alive," Gus answered. "They are trying to figure out where we store the nuclear weapons so they can target away from them when they do bomb us. When they figure out where we keep our weapons, we get the last morning call. The next time they tell us to surrender or die, they won't be bluffing."

"How long will that be?"

"Kim Jung Il is not a patient man. I'd guess no more than a couple of days. They are up in the hills around the base, watching us. They probably hope we will try to move the weapons, maybe even sneak them out of the base. Some people think I made a mistake not trying to sail the *Mauna Loa* out of the bay. But that sub would have sunk her in water shallow enough that they could have salvaged the entire cargo."

"That plan you were all talking about this afternoon. It's so obvious that's what has to be done. Maybe CINCPAC will do exactly that."

"I hope so, but I don't count on it. Nobody will want to believe that the NPA and their Korean bosses might blow us up. The politicians will want to talk, not start a fight."

He wondered why he was talking business to her. It had been a long time since he had talked business to any woman in a one-on-one conversation. In the years they had been married, Lois had never probed about his work. She always wanted to talk

109

about her problems: the kids, school, commissary prices, money, her latest diet, his working hours, and the character of the base commander's wife.

"What about you?" he deliberately asked, shifting the attention to her. "What's the word home mean to you?"

"If you are asking if somebody is tossing nights worrying about me, all I left behind was a rut and an empty condominium in Pentagon City. I was working twelve-hour days, eating breakfast and supper out of microwave boxes and lunch out of sandwich machines. My office at the Navy Annex was one of those interior rooms with no windows and vault lock doors. The only time I saw real sunlight was on Sunday. I hadn't been laid in more than a year."

She dropped the last sentence like it was a dare. She looked at him, watching for a reaction, the same as she had done at lunch when she had described how a sailor had thought she was a Philippine whore waiting for a pickup.

"I jumped at the chance to come out here," she said quickly, like she had changed her mind and decided to retract the challenge she had laid down. "If you want to know all the personal data, I was once married for about five years. I met him at MIT. It was a good marriage as long as we were graduate students. It turned sour in a hurry when I went back to being a naval officer while he worked as a physicist in a private laboratory."

She didn't ask him about his private life. He wondered if she had already asked others on the base about him. Gus wasn't sure what to say to keep the conversation going. He had heard other people talk about it. One problem of getting over a divorce is that you find you have lost all the social skills that go with the dating dance. He was six years into his second single life, but the Navy and command responsibilities kept getting into the way of social reeducation. Society had changed on him too. Kathy's frank speech marked the difference in the dozen or so years that separated them in age.

Her glass was empty and she waved at the waitress. Gus asked the waitress to bring him a glass of wine, too. The scotches had given him all the buzz he wanted. He was feeling comfortable enough that he wanted to keep the buzz he had, but he didn't want to let it slip into the next stage of intoxication.

"I guess we do have to consider ourselves prisoners of war," Kathy said after the new glasses of wine were in front of them. "Even if this is a pretty luxurious prisoner of war camp."

"I like POW better than I like hostage," Gus said. "I guess there's not much difference."

"Maybe we should call it trapped behind enemy lines," she said. "What's the standard orders for officers trapped behind enemy lines anyway? That's one of the manuals I never paid much attention to."

"I agree, trapped behind enemy lines does sound better than POW or hostage," Gus answered, not surprised that she had taken the conversation back to their plight, but still not exactly sure what her game was. "The rules of war are pretty clear. Oath and order obligate us to do everything possible to avoid capture, to return to our own lines, and to harass the enemy in any way possible."

"And we only surrender when death is inevitable," she added. "You already refused to do even that."

"The rules don't require you die in a hopeless situation, but they don't forbid it either," he answered, smiling at the smile she was showing.

"So, your standing orders are to do anything necessary to protect your base, to keep the enemy at bay, and to insure the survival of the personnel on the base."

She was leading up to something. Gus was suddenly positive that she had not just wandered into the O'Club. She must have known he would be there because he had announced in a loud voice that was where he was going as he left his office. What she wanted wasn't to get laid. That cute little remark had been part of the game plan, to keep him interested.

"What are you getting at?" he asked.

"I was thinking," she said. "You've been cut off, trapped behind enemy lines. You have no channels of communication

111

with headquarters, at least not one you can talk on. That's an artificial situation, but it's still real. You have good reason to believe an attack is imminent that will kill several thousand people under your command and protection. Aren't you legally permitted to take any action required to stop that from happening? Doesn't that also put you, as the senior officer, in command of all the forces on the base, even those you normally don't command?"

"That's a good court-martial argument. I don't need it. If there was anything I could do to stop things from happening, I wouldn't give a damn about the legality. Get to the point, what are you trying to say?"

"The plan you all were talking about in the command center . . . find them and their bombs and destroy them with high tech weapons. It's a sound idea. So why don't you implement it?"

"Because that plan needs a task force off the coast, a half dozen intel teams in the Sierra Madre, and I'm stuck here. I've got enough ships in the bay that if I could break them out, I might be able to do it, if I could find out where the NPA is keeping their missiles. But if I tried to sail those ships out of this harbor, they would nuke the base. That is one thing I'm sure of."

"The fact they haven't already blown us up means they don't want to blow us up, at least not yet," she said. "There has to be some kind of trip point. If one of the launches moving around the bay suddenly ran for open water, do you think they would nuke the base, even if the launch made it?"

"If it was just a launch trying to make a break for it, that sub waiting outside the bay would sink it with a deck gun. If it was a single boat a little larger, or a couple of small ships, the sub would use torpedoes. If I sent out a frigate with ASW capability that could handle the sub, we'd be nuked before the ship reached the mouth of the bay. If there was an SSN in port, maybe that might sneak out at night, and get by the *Romeo*. But what would our sub do after it was out? Even if we had it loaded with Tomahawks, there wouldn't be a target to shoot at, not without on-the-ground intelligence. But we don't have one of our own subs in port, so what's the difference anyway?"

The way Gus laid out the alternatives and why he thought none of them were viable was evidence of how much time he'd spent thinking about what he might do.

"The biggest problem is that even if I got something out of the harbor that had weapons that could hit an inland target, I have to have intelligence information with exact coordinates on the target," he continued. "That requires intel teams on the ground. I think we'd have a reasonably good chance of sneaking a couple of LRP (long range patrol) teams out through the base perimeter, but the Sierra Madre mountains are over 125 miles away. And it's all through hostile territory. No Commander, I've thought about doing what I think you're trying to suggest. I don't have what I need to do the job."

"What you need is a weapon's platform system that you can sneak out without bringing down a nuclear attack, a transportation capacity that will allow you to land recon teams along the coastline near the Sierra Madres, some air intelligence to go along with that, and a missile launch platform to strike the targets, right?"

It clicked. He knew what she was leading up to.

"The *Hercules!* he said. He didn't say it in a loud voice. He leaned over toward her, almost close enough for a kiss and whispered it. "You're suggesting we use the *Hercules.*"

Without thinking what he was doing, he pushed the glass of wine in front of him to one side. He looked around to make sure no one was watching. The bartender was stacking glasses but was looking through the mirror behind the bar at them. It was too far for sound to carry as long as they kept talking in a whisper.

"It's got a battle load of four SLAMs with two different guidance systems, and it's already put to sea," she answered, leaning close in and whispering back. "There is a second load of four Harpoons that could keep ships away from us and an antiaircraft gun on the fore deck. That's all the firepower you would need. It's small with a low radar profile and it's got a speed that will outrun any torpedoes that sub might be carrying. It's also the perfect craft for landing a few intel penetration teams along an unfriendly coast."

"And it's got that toy plane with the high tech sensors," Gus said. "What I don't have are the intel teams. Our SEAL detachment is off with the fleet."

"On a base this big, you must have some other people with reconnaissance patrol or training experience. The marine barracks troops are still here. There are a lot of Philippine soldiers, too. They know the territory, the people, and the language. You could recruit the teams you need."

"I'd want at least four teams to land, with at least three men on each team."

"You would want high tech teams," she suggested. "They should carry night vision goggles, personal satellite navigation systems, burst radio transmission capabilities, anything you've got in the supply depot. If one of the teams can find the NPA headquarters and where they are keeping their warheads, I can program those weapons so they can go through a door and find Sorreno sitting on a toilet."

"Let's get out of here," he said suddenly, his voice louder. He looked around again. The bartender was still stacking his glasses. The bored waitress was leaning against the bar, examining her nails. The sole other customer was working himself deeper into his own oblivion from his stool at the end of the bar.

"Let's go back to my office. This is a conversation I don't want to share with strangers." He waved at the waitress using a hand sign to ask for the check.

"You think it might work?" she whispered while they waited for the check to come.

"No, not really," he answered. "It's insane. I'd be court-martialed if I ordered it. I'd give it about one chance in a hundred. But that's better odds than anything else I've got to play with."

"The bartender has been watching us like a hawk," she said, still whispering and positioning her face so Gus was covering it

114

from the bartender's view. "Maybe I'm paranoid, but let's not let him think we're going back to work to do something important. When we get up, do something that suggests you just got lucky. Pat me on the butt or something."

Gus didn't do that, but he did put his arm around her waist as they walked toward the door, his hand resting just above her hip. It was a long time since he had touched a woman like that. He dropped it as soon as they were through the door.

The bartender watched as the base commander and the woman got up from their table and walked out. He smiled. It would be a good report for the men who would be waiting for him when he left the base. It was easy to guess what the base commander had been suggesting to the woman. Joe had seen the way the man leaned over to tell the girl what he wanted from her. It would not be necessary for the NPA to blow up the base. The stupid American base commander was more interested in fucking his help than in worrying about his future. He wouldn't want his new girlfriend to die. Americans were such sentimental fools.

By the time they had walked back to the base headquarters building, Gus and Kathy had worked out the general details of the suddenly planned breakout. The first priority would be to identify the personnel whom Gus would invite to participate in the operation. He would have to find a volunteer crew to man the *Hercules*. Commander Melendez had spent almost two weeks working with the officers and the crew of the hydrofoil. She impressed Gus with her ability to judge the personalities and competency of each of the officers and petty officers.

"Reggie Mundt is competent, but I don't think he's what you want for this," she said. "He doesn't like his assignment to hydrofoils, and he's been trying to get back into regular ships of the line. He's got his wife with him, and I'm not sure he'd agree to go even if we asked him."

"I agree," Gus said. "This has got to be all volunteer, and I mean real volunteers. I know admirals aren't supposed to do this, but I'm going to take command of the expedition. The *Hercules* can't be that different from the *Tucumcari*. I'll need a good XO."

She didn't act surprised at his announcement of his intent to lead the operation. It was as though she had expected it.

"You're in luck there," Kathy said, "the current *Hercules* XO, Lt. Phillips is bright, young, and dedicated. He gets mad easily when other navy officers make fun of his ship. He'll jump at the opportunity to prove she's a real warship. Chief Wozniak is another one you have to take. He can tell us which of the rest of the crew we should take."

"I've got to have the best damn weapons control officer we can find. If the one on the *Hercules* isn't good enough, I'll have to find one from another ship in the harbor."

He saw the instant frown.

"The officer assigned to weapons control on the *Hercules* isn't one I would pick," she said, speaking slowly. "He's been perfectly willing to let me do all the work since I showed up, and he hasn't wanted to learn anything he doesn't have to learn."

She paused, looked Gus straight in the eye, then continued. "You can't find anyone on this base who is familiar with the modifications we've made in the guidance systems on the SLAMs. It would take me three weeks to teach the skills needed to program the final data into those babies once you've got the target. You've only got one choice when it comes to a weapons control officer. You may not like the idea of taking a woman along, but I'm not just the best, I'm the only choice. If you get one good shot, you want to make it count."

"I can't do that. And it's not just that law about no women on warships. That I could ignore. We're going to take that ship out with thirty men on board. There will be no privacy, no place for a woman to use a head or take a bath. I can't guarantee you

116

safety from the men either. I won't worry about the navy men that run the ship. But I want the meanest, toughest bastards I can find for the recon teams. I won't have time to mess around with complaints about sexual harassment or rape prevention programs. We'll find the best damn weapons control officer on the base and you spend the next twenty-four hours working with him. I'm making the decision that's in your best interests."

"Damn it!" she shouted, getting to her feet and walking across the room. She spun and looked back at him. "Don't give me that fatherly shit. You're not old enough to be my father. I can deal with harassment, locker-room jokes, and unwelcome pats on the ass. I can't deal with the fatherly bit. You can treat me like a Naval officer, an airhead, or a whore, but don't treat me like a daughter. Trying to teach someone everything I know about those experimental weapon systems in twenty-four hours would be like trying to soak forty pounds of beans in a five pound crock."

She stood still, her right hand on her hip, staring him straight in the eye, looking like the heroic women of her Mexican heritage who followed their men into battle during Mexico's bloody revolution. Gus remembered for some reason a book he had read about the Indian woman Marina who served Hernan Cortez, the conqueror of the Aztecs, as his translator, his advisor, his confidante, and finally his mistress and the mother of his mestizo children.

"Gus," she said, deliberately using his nickname for the first time. "Either you take me, or those weapons aren't going to fly straight."

Gus got to his own feet. "You want me to treat you like a Naval officer? Fine! Then you will damn well do what I order you to do! You'll do your damndest teaching the weapons control officer I choose everything he needs to know. You do that, and if he can't handle it, then you go, but you better damn well not dog it on the teaching chores."

She stepped back toward the chair at the table where she had been sitting. "I won't dog it," she said. "If you've got some genius

117

on this base who can learn it all in one day, I'll make sure he understands it all. But you are going to have to find someone at least as smart as I am, and I've got an IQ of 175."

Gus sat back down and reached for his phone. He punched a number, got no answer, then tried another. The voice that answered confirmed that Admiral Rimaldo was in his quarters. A moment later the Philippine base commander was on the line.

"Admiral, Gus here. We need to talk and now. I can't explain over the phone. We've got to talk in a secure spot, just the two of us. You want it to be in your office or mine? . . . Okay. I'll wait right here for you."

Gus hung up the phone and looked at Kathy, seeing the puzzled look on her face.

"I have to bring him in on it," he explained. "In the unlikely event that we are successful, I want the legal cover that we are acting under the direction of the Armed Forces of the Philippines. More important, I want the LRP teams to be at least two-thirds Filipino. I'll need his help finding the best among the Philippine officers who are on the base."

Chapter Thirteen

Subic Bay, the Philippines.

Gus walked through the front door of his base house at 6:15 P.M. the next evening, intending to take a quick bath, change into a clean set of work khakis, and pack the few personal items he would be taking with him.

The breakout was scheduled for as soon after dark as possible. The day had started with the news that none of the Philippine employees had shown up for work. Most of those who lived within the base perimeter as housemaids or similar occupations had left during the day as rumors spread of a coming disaster.

Admiral Rimaldo had given his immediate and enthusiastic support for the project. He not only approved of the plan, he wanted to participate. After some argument, Gus convinced Rimaldo that it was more important for the Philippine admiral to remain on the base. Then, if Gus succeeded in destroying the NPA leadership and taking out their nuclear weapons, Admiral Rimaldo could lead a force on an attack into Manila that would seize the center of government and proclaim the restoration of the legitimate Philippine regime.

Gus did agree to take a senior Philippine officer with him, Colonel Orlando Ziga, an officer in the small Philippine marine force. Orlando Ziga was a graduate of the American

Command and General Staff school and a good friend of Colonel David Dorrence, who was in charge of the Subic Bay Marine Barracks.

Colonel Ziga immediately began the work of identifying and recruiting the Philippine officers who would participate as members of the intel teams which Gus hoped to land along the coast of the Sierra Madre. Gus and Colonel Ziga agreed that they would land five teams. Each team would include two Filipinos and one American. Ziga would pick his Filipinos on the basis of their knowledge of the target area and prior combat experience in operations against the NPA. Each American team member would be an officer or noncom trained in LRP operations and familiar with the high tech equipment that each team would be carrying. If possible, each of the American officers would be of Latin or Asian ancestry to avoid easy identification as Americans once they were on the ground.

Captain Tim Reilly argued for a while that he should lead the expedition but reluctantly agreed to take over as acting base commander once the *Hercules* was on its way. He also recommended the name of a possible fire control officer for Lt. Commander Melendez to train.

Colonel Dorrence took over primary responsibility for identifying the Americans who would go as members of the intel teams.

One of the few Filipino employees still on the base was the twenty-year-old houseboy who worked for Gus. Julio Lazaro had high hopes of winning one of the four hundred enlisted slots that the U.S. Navy granted to Philippine nationals each year. He wasn't about to risk losing the chance because of a few rumors of impending death and disaster.

He greeted Admiral Jones at the door and asked if he could prepare the admiral something to eat. Gus told him to fix a sandwich as he headed up the stairs on the run.

Gus had stepped out of the shower and was putting on

120

his khakis, when Julio knocked on the bedroom door.

"Sir," Julio said when he entered into the room. "Your guest for dinner is here?" The frown on the Filipino's face made it clear that he was unhappy the admiral hadn't warned him a guest was coming for dinner.

"Shit!" Gus exploded. He had forgotten about the damn Russian admiral again. He had invited the man for dinner and a game of chess. The Russian was the last person on base Gus wanted getting suspicious that something was up. He decided his best choice was to feed the Russian, play a game of chess, then get rid of him as soon as he could think up a decent excuse for bringing the evening to an end. While he wanted to be at the docks while they finished loading the *Hercules,* his presence wasn't required.

"Put something in the microwave," Gus told the houseboy. "For God's sake, don't let him know I forgot I invited him over. Tell him I'll be right down and serve him a drink."

Gus used his transceiver to call Captain Reilly and tell him about the Russian. He took the khaki uniform pants back off and put on civies, a pair of brown chinos, and a cream-colored, Filipino-style shirt with short sleeves. Downstairs, he found the Russian admiral standing in the reception room, sipping a drink the houseboy had served him. The Russian had taken advantage of the BX. He wore new Levis, a light green sports shirt, and a brand new set of Pumas on his feet.

"Sorry I kept you waiting," Gus said. "Dinner will be ready in a few minutes. It won't be anything fancy."

The houseboy came in, carrying a tray with a scotch and water for Gus.

Gus was playing badly, and he knew it. He had stepped in the same trap that the Russian had laid for him the first night they had played. He wanted to look at his watch, but he forced himself not to do it. As much as he wanted to be at dock side, if there was a problem, someone would have to let him know. The best thing would be to enjoy the game. He reached out, picked up a knight and moved it to the king bishop three position.

He looked up to see the Russian staring at him.

"An interesting move," the Russian said. "I'm not sure whether you have made a feint I can't figure out, or if you are just trying to end the game quickly. Now I can checkmate in two moves, instead of four. I do hope that the plan for your breakout is better conceived than your chess game tonight."

"What are you talking about?" Gus asked, working to keep his poker face in place as he stared across the board at his opponent.

"Come my new friend. Why would a man who had nothing to do but play chess until the world ends, not concentrate all his energy on the game? That's why we invent games, is it not? A good game allows us to pretend that we can control our destinies when we can not. When a man loses interest in playing the game, it means that he thinks he has a chance of regaining control over his destiny."

"I'll admit I'm not playing my best game of chess, but that doesn't mean I have some kind of plan, or something," Gus insisted. "You can't expect me not to be distracted. I've got ten thousand Americans on this base. They expect me to do something to save their lives, and there is not a thing I can do."

"Admiral Jones, you are a kind of man who, when placed in a hopeless situation, will try and do something, even something hopeless. I have been out and about your base today, looking in the faces of the people who live and work here. They are the faces of the lost and the damned. But a couple of times I have seen something that doesn't fit such a sense of hopelessness.

"There are a few people who are moving like they had purpose in their life. I called this morning on Admiral Rimaldo.

He was polite, but he had little time for me. He didn't once suggest we play golf. He was anxious to see me go. I saw your officer, Captain Reilly, riding in the back of a car. He was leaning forward, yelling something at the driver, telling him to hurry. I saw a lady officer and a man eating lunch in the officer's club where you so kindly let me take my meals. They ate in a hurry and left, talking business in whispers, not pleasure. And then there is you, so anxious to make me feel at ease but to get me out of your hair so you can go back to work."

Gus didn't say anything. The Russian was damn smart and Gus had made a mistake. He should have restricted the man to his quarters and sent his meals into him. He thought again about the possibility that the Russian admiral was a member of some military group who wanted to turn the clock back and forge a rebirth of the Soviet Union.

"There is something up on your base and only a very few people know about it," the Russian continued. "So what could be so important? I ask myself. Obviously you cannot try a breakout of everyone on the base, not with the weapons aimed against you. That suggests you are about to launch a small operation, one aimed perhaps at taking out the weapons your enemy has. But you must find where they are. That will require penetration teams, and if it was me, I would land those from the coast, not let them try to move overland."

"You realize of course," Gus interrupted, "that if I was planning something, I would have no choice now but to arrest you and lock you away until it was done."

"If I thought that was the only choice, I would not have opened the subject for discussion. There is one other option, the option I hope you will choose."

Gus didn't ask what. The Russian was going to tell him anyway.

"Let me go with the team," the Russian said.

"Why?" Gus demanded, his voice louder than he meant it to be. "So you can sabotage the mission?"

"Admiral, let me show you something." The Russian reached into his shirt pocket and took out a pen. He laid it on the chessboard between them. "Look at it."

Gus picked it up. It was an old-fashioned fountain pen, one filled from a bottle of ink. Gus tried to unscrew the cap, watching the face of the Russian as he did so. It wouldn't unscrew, but it would pull back, like it was on some kind of a slide. As he pulled it back, Gus heard the distinct click of a cocking action. As it clicked, the fill lever popped out, looking suddenly like a trigger.

"Now that it is cocked, please don't point it at me," the Russian said, a grin covering his broad face. "At this range it's a deadly weapon, and rather quiet, too, not much louder than a cap gun. Your servant might not even hear it."

The Russian deliberately reached for his glass and took a sip of the cognac before continuing. "Before I went to Singapore as an assistant attaché, I went through a rather fascinating six months of training provided by our KGB. That's a little souvenir of that training. If I wanted to sabotage your plan, you would already be dead and I would be looking for those others whom I saw today who had places to go and things to do."

Gus put the pen down beside the playing board, pointing it out to the side. He kept it on his side of the board.

"I want to go with you for two reasons," Admiral Semenkov continued. "First, for me, it could be the only chance I will ever have to play the role of a sea warrior instead of just wearing the uniform of one. And for you, I might be able to help."

"How?"

"Once we are clear of the bay and into open water, I may be able to contact Cam Ranh. I suspect that you are doing this on your own, that your own navy is not going to help you with intelligence photos and SIGINT information. Perhaps I can convince my navy to do so, if I can communicate with them."

Gus said nothing. He still hadn't made up his mind how to

124

play it. Should he arrest the Russian and lock him up, or should he deny it all?

"Let me make one more argument," the Russian said. "I can understand why a commander would never send a team of men out on a dangerous assignment with a potential spy in the group. But I've made another bet with myself. I don't think you will be sending men out on this mission. I think you will be leading them out. If I'm wrong, if you're not going to lead this expedition, call your military policemen right now. I'll go peacefully with them. But if you are going to lead this breakout, take me with you. Once we're out of the bay, you can shoot me anytime you want if you think I threaten the safety of the mission."

"What makes you think I would lead such a foolish endeavor?" Gus asked.

"Because if this was Cam Ranh Bay, that's what I would do."

Gus reached for his radio. He punched the transmit button and called the base operations center.

"Send two SPs to my quarters," he said when he got an acknowledgement. "I'll give them orders when they get here."

He put the radio brick down on the table and looked at the Russian. "I have no choice. As of this moment you are under house arrest. You will stay in your quarters under guard. You will talk to no one except for the guards. You will understand that I must also order the guards to search your room and your belongings to make sure that you are not carrying a radio transmitter of some kind."

There was no break in the blank expression on the Russian's face. His eyes stayed locked with Gus's eyes. He didn't glance down at the cocked weapon lying beside Gus's right hand.

"While I have to put you under arrest, I will make you a promise. If I leave this base for any reason, I'll take you with me."

125

The Russian smiled, just a bit.

"So, while we wait for the SPs, why don't we start another game?" Semenkov suggested.

Gus kept the SPs waiting in his living room while they finished the game. This time he beat the Russian. A few minutes later, he watched the Russian walk down the sidewalk between the two Shore Patrol. Then he turned and hurried up the stairs to put his work khakis back on.

Gus stood in the darkness on the main deck of the *Hercules*, watching twenty men loading the last of the supplies and equipment. It was 10:30 P.M. and moonrise would come at 12:47 A.M.

"How much longer?" he asked the man standing beside him.

"Everything we're taking is on board," Lt. Jack Phillips answered. "We should have it wrapped up in thirty minutes."

The operation was still a secret as far as most of the naval personnel at Subic knew, but a lot more people knew about it than Gus would have liked.

Lt. Commander Reggie Mundt, the skipper of the *Hercules,* had formally objected to being relieved of his command by an officer who was not in his direct command structure, but the objection was more along the line of covering his ass than serious opposition. Mundt had given no indication that he wanted to go on the expedition. Kathy Melendez had told Gus that Mundt was not only worried about his wife, who was three months pregnant, but that she was giving him a full load of shit for bringing her to the Philippines.

The *Hercules* normally carried a crew of twenty-one to twenty-four men, but the number of crew had been cut to the absolute minimum required to operate the vessel. Thirteen members of the original crew had been recruited. They included Jack Phillips, the XO, and Lieutenant JG Bryan

Bradley. On Chief Wozniak's recommendation, only one of the other petty officers assigned to the *Hercules* had been invited. Another petty officer had been selected off the *Stump*.

A figure stepped through the hatch that led into the command and fire control center and walked over to where Gus and Lt. Phillips were standing.

"The fire control and guidance systems all check out," Lt. Commander Melendez said, her voice a whisper. "They're ready to go."

Kathy Melendez had spent the afternoon and evening on the *Hercules,* checking out the weapon systems and the SLAM and Harpoon guidance systems.

Now that she was on board, she would not be leaving the ship. She had been right, her attempt at teaching another officer everything she knew about the systems in twenty-four hours hadn't worked. Gus had checked in often enough to know that she and the officer had tried hard to make it work. Part of the problem was that Gus kept interrupting the teaching process to check out some technical detail with Melendez. After his last conversation with her, Gus decided that there was no way he wanted to sail the *Hercules* out of the mouth of the bay without Lt. Commander Melendez on board to make sure any shots he fired counted.

Kathy had also provided invaluable advice on selecting the high tech equipment that each one of the recon teams would take ashore. Each team member would wear a no-hands UHF tactical radio equipped with an earplug receiver and a needle mouth mike. They would each carry a Trimble navigator, a small hand-held electronic device that received signals from the NAVSTAR Global Positioning System and used its microprocessors to determine the man's exact geographic position with an accuracy of no more than a hundred feet in any direction.

They would all carry M-16A2 rifles, with M9 automatic pistols, and a basic ammo load. The rifles would be mounted with a combined enhanced light, thermo sensor, and laser beam sight and a silencer. All team members would have night vision goggles. Each of the teams would carry a small supply of C-4 plastic explosive and a radio command detonator.

Each of the teams would take along one Enhanced Joint Tactical Information Distribution System, called EPUU for short. Carried as a backpack, the EPUU was a hybrid combination radio transceiver and position location system that utilized the same satellite navigation system as the Trimble navigator. But unlike the Trimble which only told the soldier where he was, the EPUU's advanced satellite telecommunication system would report that position information along with written communications to the *Hercules* in coded, burst transmissions of less than a second. The EPUU used ultra high frequency, line-of-site radio waves that would be relayed by satellite back to the Net Control Station on board the *Hercules*. If any of the teams located either a command headquarters or a nuclear weapons site, Lt. Commander Melendez would have the exact coordinates to feed into her computer guidance systems.

Each team would also be carrying a notebook-style laptop computer that weighed only seven pounds. The high tech computer called a TACCOM had sixteen megabytes of RAM that was retained by the battery even when the machine was turned off. In addition, small three-megabyte RAM cards could be inserted to change programs, add storage or feed in data including screen displayable maps, coding programs, and information on subjects ranging from first aid medicine to edible plants and basic communication words in a dozen different Philippine dialects.

Additional intelligence collection equipment included a fold-up parabolic mike, laser beam listening devices that could be aimed at windows to capture conversations on the other side, a small geiger counter, the wire and tools necessary to tap a phone, miniature battery operated listening devices, and a mini-cassette tape recorder.

The deck of the *Hercules* looked more like the deck of a coastal trader than a warship. A dozen extra drums of fuel stood on the deck and piles of equipment occupied much of the rest of the space. Most of the intel team members would have to sleep on the deck until they were landed. The ship had been stripped of every piece of equipment not needed, but she was still overloaded.

"It looks like we're about ready. Let's go over it again," Gus suggested to Phillips. Both men turned and walked through a hatch into the deckhouse command and fire control center. The chart on the table showed the bay and the surrounding ocean.

"The last radar contact shows the sub right here," Phillips said, pointing to a position about two miles out from the mouth of the bay. "She's on the surface, recharging her batteries like she does every night. She's been doing a figure eight about three miles long and a mile or so wide. If she follows her usual habits, she'll be at the top of the eight pattern that will give her the worst possible torpedo resolution in forty minutes."

Gus wasn't especially concerned about a torpedo attack from the sub waiting outside the bay. On her foils, the *Hercules* would be almost impossible to hit with a torpedo, although a torpedo with a proximity fuse might damage the ship if it blew at exactly the right moment and position.

What did concern him was the possibility of surface-to-surface missiles. If it was a Korean sub, she might be carrying Chinese C801 missiles. The *Hercules* carried chaff cartridges, had radar jamming capability, and the Mk 75 deck gun could theoretically bring down a C801, but none of the defensive equipment had ever been battle tested.

It was after they got away from the submarine blocking the bay that had Gus worried. The North Koreans had the third largest sub fleet in Asia. If a sub could sneak up on the *Hercules* while she was traveling on her hull, she would be vulnerable to torpedo attack. He had therefore ordered a load of sonobuoys usually dropped by LAMP helicopters. They had squeezed sonobuoy monitoring equipment into the *Hercules* command center and recruited a good sonar man off the *Stump*.

"We'll use the cover of Grande Island as we pull out," Gus said, pointing on the map to the island in the mouth of the bay. "We'll keep the island between us and the sub, then sneak around the island so that the island is at our back. We'll bring us to hydrofoil speed, cut a hard turn to starboard, and hug the coast until we know what the sub is going to do."

"Why not launch a Harpoon from behind the island?" Phillips asked. "That sub is a sitting target."

"I want them to think we're a bunch of VIPs trying to escape. We sink that sub and we'll survive, but a lot of the people on the base will die."

The hatch opened and Admiral Rimaldo and Colonel Orlando Ziga came in.

"The teams have got all the equipment on board," Colonel Ziga said. "We're ready to go."

"I want to wish you luck," Admiral Rimaldo said. "I wish I was going with you, too."

"If what we do works," Gus said, "we'll start the ball rolling. You'll have to take it from there. I'll try and give you as much warning as possible if we can get a shot at targets."

Rimaldo held his hand out for a shake. Gus took it and told the admiral he'd see him back to the gangplank.

Outside, they shook hands again and Rimaldo saluted a goodbye. The Philippine admiral walked down the gangway to the dock. He turned to stand and watch the departure.

A car pulled up to the dockside, moving slowly with only the parking lights on. Three men got out and walked to the gangway. Two of the men, both wearing SP armbands, bracketed the man between them who carried a small bag in his right hand. At the gangway the two SPs halted, but the man in the middle proceeded up the gangway.

"Permission to come aboard?" Admiral Semenkov asked.

"Granted," Gus answered. "Now that you see what we're using, are you sure you want to go?"

The Russian admiral turned and looked around the crowded deck, stopping to stare for a moment in the dim lights of the docks at the eight missile launch tubes on the stern deck. There was enough light to see his smile.

"An excellent choice," he said. "I didn't know you had a hydrofoil stationed here in Subic. We have a whole fleet of them in the Soviet Navy. I've often wondered why you Americans didn't include more of them in your own fleet."

"Come!" Jones said. "I'll show you to your quarters. You and I are going to share an upper and lower bunk."

While the *Hercules* did have a single accommodation cabin for the ship's skipper, that cabin had been assigned to the one woman on board despite her rather vocal objections. The officers' staterooms were not much larger than those on a submarine. Gus watched as the Russian quickly stowed his gear.

"Let's climb up to the pilothouse," Gus said. "I'm going to let my XO and the weapons officers man the fire control center down below. You'll have a good view of your first live naval action from there."

Chapter Fourteen

The Kyong Ki *in the South China Sea.*

Captain Kang jumped from his bunk as the seaman touched his shoulder. The red light in his quarters was blinking the signal for general quarters. The captain was instantly awake as he slipped on his shoes. The seaman bent to tie them as the captain stood up, straightened his shirt and tucked in the tail. He had been sleeping in his uniform. The seaman backed out of the way as the captain stepped by him and through the hatch that led to the sub's command center.

Captain Kang could tell by the vibrations of the deck under him that the sub was picking up speed. The ship was still on the surface and the sounds of the diesel engines carried through the compartment.

"We have a contact coming out of the bay," Captain Second Class Ho Ung-to announced, his voice excited. "We have the ship on both sonar and radar. It's heading right at us and moving fast. They have a radar on us, too, but it's not weapon radar."

"How fast she coming?"

"At least fifty knots."

"Impossible! Nothing they have moves that fast."

"It's not very big, so it must be a hovercraft or a hydrofoil. I already have torpedo resolutions, but the fuses are contact. If it is a surface skimmer the fish will go right under it. Do we dive?"

"If they are attacking us, it's too late. Order the torpedo room to change to proximity fuses immediately. Is she in deck gun range?"

"Craft has taken hard turn to port," a crewman manning a radar screen called out before the question could be answered. "Distance is now 9,500 meters. Separation distance is increasing."

"She's making a run for it," Captain Kang announced. "Give me full speed with a course of 320 degrees. Do we have a fire resolution?"

"Computer running a resolution now, sir, but the torpedo room is still changing fuses."

The captain waited a few seconds.

"What's the delay? I want a resolution."

"We have a resolution."

"Are the torpedoes ready?" the captain demanded.

"Thirty more seconds, sir!" someone reported.

It took almost forty-five before the announcement came, "Torpedoes ready and in the tubes."

"Is fire resolution still valid?" the captain demanded.

"Fire resolution is . . . wait, we lost it."

"How can we lose it?" the captain demanded. "Get me a fire resolution."

"Captain," the fire control officer announced. "We can't get a resolution. We lost the angle. She's moving too fast. Our torpedoes won't catch up to the target."

"Prepare to launch missile," the captain shouted, the frustration and anger building in his voice.

The *Kyong Ki* carried Chinese supplied C801 antiship missiles. Unlike American and Russian antiship missiles carried by submarines, the C801s could not be fired from the torpedo tubes but were carried outside the pressure hull in a firing pod that contained six missiles. The sub had to surface and elevate the missile launch mechanism to a forty-five degree angle before the radar guided missiles could be launched. As the sub was already on the surface, the missiles were ready to fire.

"Are deck missile units elevated and cleared for action?" the captain demanded.

"Aye sir," Captain Second Class Ho responded.

"Fire missile!" the captain commanded.

"Missile away," a crewman called out three seconds later. "Seventeen seconds running time . . . fourteen . . . thirteen . . ."

"Target turning hard left, taking evasive action."

"Nine . . . eight . . ."

"Radar screen blank!" the radar operator called out, a signal that the target was using radar jamming equipment.

"Target has opened fire with deck gun at missile." The message came from the watch on the deck.

"Two . . . one . . ."

"Watch deck reports missile missed, no explosion."

"Fire missiles two!" the captain called out, anger and frustration fighting for control of his voice.

The hull of the sub gave a shudder as another surface-to-surface missile launched from the upper deck.

"Missile Away! Eighteen seconds running time . . . seventeen . . . sixteen . . ."

The count continued down, this time without a radar report. Captain Kang could see the radar screen from where he stood. It showed a jumble of gray static.

"Twelve . . . eleven . . . ten . . ."

"Target still running," the sonar operator reported.

"Three . . . two . . . one . . ."

"Target still running," sonar reported again.

It took another five seconds for the sound of a missile exploding in air to come back across the water to the *Kyong Ki*.

"We got a hit," Captain Second Class Ho shouted.

"Target still running," sonar called out.

"Our missile didn't hit the target, the target shot our missile down," Captain Kang said in disgust. "How am I supposed to carry out my assignment with antiquated weapons that don't shoot straight and move so slow they can be shot down like airplanes?"

"Sir!" Ho reported. "Shall we fire another pair of missiles?"

"What for?" Captain Kang said, disgust apparent in his voice. "Why give them more practice with their defense systems. We must save the rest of the missiles for shooting at something big enough to hit."

"Radar is working again, sir," the radar man called out. "Target is turning to starboard and heading to open water."

"They have a weapon radar lock on us!" a crewman sitting in front of another screen called out. "Repeat! Hostile weapon radar lock."

"Dive! I say dive!" the captain shouted, his voice sounding almost like terror. "Have they launched weapon?"

"Not yet," the radar operator answered. "Radar weapon lock is still on us."

The Klaxon horn sounded, warning those above deck to get below. The deck shifted to an angle as the deck watch came pouring down the ladder.

"Captain Kang, you can't let that ship get away. Your orders are to stop anything leaving the harbor." The man reminding Captain Kang of his duty was Captain First Class Pak Nam-Ju, the political officer on board the *Kyong Ki*. He had come into the con shortly after Captain Kang had arrived at his post.

"Tell me how I can put wings on this ship so I can skim over the water and I'll go after that boat," Captain Kang said, his voice angry. "I can't catch them with this tub. If we don't dive, he will sink us."

"I do not envy you, having to report such a failure," Pak said. "Your ship should have been better prepared. If you had

135

shot the torpedoes and the missile sooner, you would have sunk the craft."

"It was not a failure of the mission," Captain Kang insisted. "That was a very small craft. They could not have been taking very much with them. One patrol craft represents no threat to the operation. I think it is nothing but a few of the officers who fled for their own safety and left those they command behind to die."

"But you must report what has happened to Col. Cho and to Pyongyang."

"They will be informed, when it is safe to bring this boat back to the surface."

The radar scan operator was still reporting an active weapons radar loek as the *Kyong Ki* fin slipped below the water. Captain Kang stood at his position in his con, watching the dials and hoping that the only antiship weapons the enemy had were the missiles the watch with the night scope had reported. If the hydrofoil carried either torpedoes, or worse, the dreaded SUBROC depth charges, his ship was still in serious danger.

The USS Hercules *in the South China Sea.*

"Exhilarating", Admiral Semenkov said. He was standing beside Admiral Jones on the deck inside the *Hercules*'s pilot house. Each man was holding a night vision monocular magnification scope to an eye. Although the ship was still moving at a speed in excess of fifty knots, the deck was level with no more bounce or roll than there would be on an aircraft flying in good weather.

The off deck explosion of the incoming missiles had sprayed a haze of shrapnel and sent a shock wave over the deck and upper superstructure of the *Hercules* that had blown out the back ports of the pilothouse. Each step they took on the deck crunched plexiglass slivers under their shoes.

Both Gus and the Russian admiral had avoided injury because they had both hit the deck when they saw the rocket flash of incoming missiles.

Gus took his night scope down from his eye. "What's the casualty and damage report?" he asked one of the crewmen manning the pilothouse. The crewman was wearing a helmet with communications equipment.

"Except for broken glass, there's no serious blast damage, but we have a KIA and wounded on the main deck," the crewman reported. "They were three members of the same intel team. The American is the KIA."

"Damn!" Gus exploded. "Keep me posted."

He turned back and looked at the Russian admiral standing beside him.

"You take two missile shots from them at almost point-blank range, and then you scare them into the deep with your radar," Semenkov said.

"We could have sunk them," Kathy Melendez said from behind the two men. She had just climbed up the ladder well from the command and fire control center. "If we had fired any one of our Harpoons at such close range, it would have broken through any defense system that sub might have had."

"I don't understand why you didn't. Now they will give our position away," Semenkov commented. "Did you fear that if you sunk the sub, the NPA on the land would have nuked your base?"

"I don't think they would have launched a nuclear attack on the base because we got away in this small-sized boat. I'm still betting they still prefer to take over an intact base," Gus answered. "I was more worried about what the people we left back at base might do if that sub wasn't corking the bottle. A couple of ship captains might get tempted to make a run for it without that sub in the bay. I am convinced that if anything much larger than this ship tries to

137

get out, the base will be instantly nuked."

"That was an impressive display of firepower from the deck gun. I assume it's automatically controlled. I'm surprised that it could knock a missile out of the air," Semenkov said.

"I wasn't sure it could," Gus answered. "I hope we don't have to try it against something faster like some of the missiles your ships might carry."

Jack Phillips came up from below. He was followed by Colonel Ziga.

"Except for the broken glass and a couple of antennas knocked down, we got off light on the equipment damage," Phillips reported. "But not on casualties. We've got two more casualties to add to the first three reported."

"How bad are the wounded?" Gus asked.

"We may lose Lt. Moleta," Orlando Ziga reported, his voice dry. "Captain Torres lost some blood, but he'll be ready to go to work after a day or two of rest. But I can't send him in alone. The other two are minor."

"Put Torres with one of the other teams," Gus ordered. "I'd rather have four teams with four men on one team, than send in five teams with only two men on two of the teams."

"I agree," Ziga answered. "I'll put Torres on Hoppy Yarcia's team. He and Hoppy are old friends."

Gus had spent several hours with the fifteen men chosen for the intel teams. Four of the Americans were officers from the Marine Barracks and one was a Navy SEAL. A fifth marine, a tech sergeant, had been brought on board to handle the specialized Net Control Station equipment that would electronically monitor the progress of each of the teams. The dead American, Lt. Howard Sharps, had been a Marine officer.

The other team members were all Filipinos. While Colonel Ziga had personally picked them, Gus had also interviewed each of them. Gus had listened to both Hoppy Yarcia and Captain Torres describe how they had avoided death because of a flat tire. He had asked Major Yarcia a dozen probing questions to determine if his decision not to go over the top of the hill to verify casualties in his APCs had been a wise command decision or the act of a coward. He had decided it was the former.

The American on Yarcia's team was Lt. Commander Wade Hernandez, the Navy SEAL. He had arrived in Subic on a new assignment three days after the team he was to join had left for *Team Spirit*. Hernandez had been waiting for air transportation to the *Nimitz* so he could join his new unit when the Philippines fell.

Gus had started with five teams and he was already down to four teams. They still had over five hundred miles of open water to cover before they could start unloading their teams.

"Let's look at the charts," Gus suggested.

The group moved to the chart table. The Americans and Colonel Ziga already knew what the plan was, but Gus wanted to let his Russian passenger have some idea of what they were in for.

"We'll proceed at foilborne speed for three more hours," Gus explained. "That should take us out of the range of that sub. We'll stay off the coast and head north. Then we'll go back to hullborne speed. That's a lot slower, but we have a fuel problem. We have to go around the northern end of Luzon, and back south down the eastern coast of Luzon before we can land our teams along the coast of the Sierra Madre." Gus pointed with his finger at the chart as he talked.

"What's your real top hullborne speed?" Semenkov asked. "Ten or eleven knots?"

"Eleven, in good weather."

"Then it's going to take you almost two days to get there. What would it take at foilborne speed, ten hours or so."

"If the seas hold calm, a little more than that," Gus answered. "But I don't dare risk it. Even with the extra fuel drums, we can't do more than seven hundred nauticals at foilborne speed. I would get there, but I wouldn't have any fuel for operations after I landed the troops. Even if I mix it up with part hullborne and part foilborne operations along the way, we would still end up with too little fuel to operate effectively for very long after we get there."

"At hull speed you get the full effect of the sea. Your intel teams are soldiers, not sailors. They'll be exhausted and seasick by the time you get them on shore, in no shape for the dangerous job they have to do."

"Are you just telling me about my problems, or are you going to propose a solution?"

"I told you before that what the North Koreans have done is not good news for my government either," Admiral Semenkov answered. "What if I could arrange a refueling at sea, say somewhere off this point?" He pointed his thick finger at Escarpada Point on the northeast tip of the island of Luzon.

"How would you propose to arrange this?" Gus asked, looking across the chart table at the Russian. "You would have to get some kind of government approval. What happens if you ask for the approval and it's not given?"

"I don't necessarily have to take this to Moscow," Semenkov answered. "We get regular tanker deliveries at Cam Ranh that come from Vladivostok. The schedule is such that there should be one somewhere along this line about right now." He pointed to the area of the map at the Luzon Strait between the northernmost part of the Philippines and Taiwan. "If I can contact either the ship, or my base in Cam Ranh, I can divert the tanker to here." He pointed at a spot to the north of Escarpada Point.

"What are you going to tell them?" Colonel Ziga demanded.

"I will tell them the truth, that I have managed to escape an extremely dangerous situation and that I require a pickup at sea so that I can get back to my command."

"They would send a warship, or a submarine, not a tanker, for such a job," Ziga pointed out.

140

"I will tell them that the people who brought me out insist that I not be picked up by a warship. I will try first to make direct contact with the tanker. I'll use our emergency channel. There are codes that will convince them I am who I say I am."

"Admiral Jones, you can't trust this man," Ziga interrupted. "The communists have taken over my homeland. The Russians claim they are no longer communists, but can we believe them. Can we believe this man agrees with what has happened in his country?"

"Colonel," Semenkov said, turning toward the Filipino. "If my navy wants to put this operation out of business, they do not need tricks from me to do it. If I am in . . . cahoots," he had to pause to remember the English word, ". . . with the North Koreans, every ship in our Pacific fleet will already be looking for you. Our passive sonars are good enough that any submarine within two hundred miles of here may already be picking up the tremendous racket this ship makes as it flies through the water. The North Koreans do not have the technology they need to find you in a hurry, but we do. And believe me, our weapons will be more difficult to fool than those missiles the Korean sub shot at us."

The Russian turned toward the American admiral. "What do you have to lose? Surely, someone on this ship will understand enough Russian to keep me honest. Let me in your radio room so I can give it a try."

Gus didn't speak Russian, and he didn't know any of the crew who did. He wouldn't expect any of the Filipinos on board to speak the language either. Then he saw the smile on Kathy Melendez's face. She gave him just enough of a wink to let him know she could keep the Russian honest.

"Admiral, we have to get an antenna fixed before anyone can use the radio," Jack Phillips said.

"Get it fixed, and let the admiral here know when he can use it," Gus said. He saw the frown on Colonel Ziga's face. "Look at it this way, Orlando," he said. "If the Russian is pull-

141

ing a trick on us, we can try out a couple of Harpoons on a Russian warship. Then we'll go save your country."

Two hours later, Gus was still in the darkened wheelhouse. He was sitting in one of the wheelhouse chairs that was bolted to the deck just to the left and behind the chair at the helm station. The helmsman was doing nothing but watching dials. When foilborne, the automatic control system provided continuous dynamic control, making adjustments with no attention from the crew. Course changes were made by keying a computer, not with the wheel which was only used during hullborne operation.

Gus got up out of his chair and walked around the pilothouse, checking the horizon for a full 360 degrees. Two crewmen were at work replacing the plexiglass that the explosion had blown out. The moon was up now, but Gus could see no shadows of ships nor any running lights. Radar was tracking what was probably a commercial jet flying high above and a couple of fishing boats working over the horizon to the east. Other than that, it looked like they were alone and that nothing that might be after them was close enough to shoot at them.

Kathy Melendez's head showed in the ladder hole and she climbed up to the deck. She saluted Gus, then stepped over to where he was standing.

"He made contact with something that appears to be a Russian oiler. We have to figure other Russian ships are listening, but he didn't say anything to give away our position. He arranged a rendezvous and told the story just like he said he would. It looks like it's all set up. He and Jack are plotting the rendezvous point on the computer right now."

"I hope I haven't just thrown the whole mission away."

"I think he's for real," Melendez answered. "I bet though that this oiler is not one that runs back and forth between Vladivostok and Cam Ranh. It's more likely on station in the area to service intelligence trawlers and any other traffic they have moving along the route."

"That's what I figured from the start."

"I'd let him tell you himself about it. I didn't tell him I speak Russian."

"He may have figured out you did anyway."

"I don't think so. He was watching Jack all the time he talked. That's whom he thought might speak Russian. As far as he's concerned, I'm the invisible woman, or the dumb greaser gal standing in the corner. Our navy is not the only navy that suffers from a heap of male pig *caca*."

She turned to head back for the ladder. Gus called her last name, using commander before it. She turned back to look at him.

"You have any more surprises for me, like maybe speaking Korean or something?"

She smiled. "I speak French and Spanish, of course, but I don't think we'll need them on this trip. But I might have a couple of more surprises for you one of these days." She spun and headed for the ladder.

Two minutes later, Admiral Semenkov came up through the well. He gave Gus the same information that Kathy had just given him. "Lt. Phillips tells me we will get to the rendezvous point in about seven hours. It will take the *Erkut* at least twelve hours to get to the point."

"I'll go look at the charts with Jack then," Gus said. "We should be able to find an island where we can hide and sit out part of the daylight."

Chapter Fifteen

The Pentagon

"What the fuck is that man trying to do?"

Vice Admiral Greg Backlin, the Chief of the Office of Surface Warfare, looked up to see Admiral John Miller standing in the doorway to his office. Backlin jumped to his feet. It was the first time Admiral Miller had ever walked into his office. Always before, Backlin had been summoned to the senior admiral's office when Miller wanted to talk.

"I don't have any more information than you do, just the State Department's memo of conversation with their ambassador."

Admiral Miller walked into the office and sat down on a chair that faced Backlin's desk. Backlin sat back down in his own chair, not sure of the protocol of what to do when a senior officer walked into your office and flopped down in front of you.

The State Department's memo reported that Ambassador Black had been called at four o'clock in the morning by the NPA's Foreign Minister. The Foreign Minister had demanded that the ambassador immediately order the ship that had sailed out of Subic Bay back to port. The ambassador had then called Subic on the phone line that was suddenly working. Captain Reilly told the ambassador that Admiral

Jones was missing, along with the PHM 2 Hercules and part of her crew. Reilly claimed he had no idea why the facility commander had suddenly escaped.

"I've had three calls from the Chairman, two from Tabor Carol and one from the President in the last hour," Admiral Miller complained. "They are all hopping mad and screaming at the Navy. They think we set this up, either us or CINCPAC. The NPA has already released the information on this to the press, and they make it look like we're provoking them. They're claiming the hydrofoil came out of the bay, attacked a ship operated by the new government of the Philippines, and then fled."

"That's not the whole story," Backlin said. "A SIGINT satellite picked up a radio broadcast from what we think is a Korean sub about 1300 our time. It was in a code that NSA has broken. I just got a copy." Backlin looked up at the digital clock on his own desk. It read 1735 hours, 5:35 P.M. It would be 6:35 A.M. in the morning at Subic Bay.

"The sub claimed they fired two missiles at the hydrofoil, and then dived to avoid attack. They shot first."

The way Admiral Miller was listening without interrupting meant that he hadn't had a chance to read through his SIGINT take for the morning.

"The way I read the intercept, the *Hercules* came tearing out of the bay about 2330 at top speed," Backlin continued. "The sub tried to sink her with STS (surface-to-surface) missiles but didn't succeed, then the sub dived to avoid a counterattack. When she came back up the *Hercules* was gone."

"Who was the sub talking to?"

"Obviously, the NPA headquarters, wherever the Hell that is. I've matched the times. The NPA foreign minister was screaming at our ambassador an hour and a half after the sub sent out its report. The NPA called in the press even before they called our ambassador to complain about the attack on units of the NPA armed forces, which is so much bullshit.

145

That sub has to be North Korean, but we can't prove it. The message was sent in English text."

Greg Backlin didn't have to tell Admiral Miller that the NPA government had played the press well from the very beginning of their takeover of the Philippine government, even to giving the international press handouts on how they had constructed nuclear warheads in jungle laboratories. While any nuclear physicist could point out the fallacies in the claims of making weapons that way, no one in the international press corps had bothered to look up a scientist to get an opinion.

Although the new government officials were censoring outgoing reports about political developments and the damage reports from the nuclear explosion sites, they let the press wander around Manila without much supervision.

It was hard for the United States to argue its people were held hostage when the press kept reporting on plane loads of Americans leaving the Philippines as fast as the commercial airliners could carry them out. Another favorite press report were interviews with Americans still living in their luxury apartments and homes while they waited for confirmed reservations out of the country.

Most of the American government civilian personnel and their families had already left, and NPA officials kept telling the press that all the people at Subic Bay would be permitted to leave as soon as the facilities were surrendered. A number of the more liberal American newspapers, including the *Washington Dispatch,* were demanding that the facility be abandoned so the American personnel could immediately leave the Philippines. Even the conservative press was arguing that the U.S. should get its people out first, then take action against the new communist government.

"Do you think Captain Reilly really has no idea what Gus Jones is trying to do?" Admiral Miller asked.

"If he does know what Jones is doing, he's not going to admit it over an open, unsecure line, and that's all he's got right now," Backlin answered. "You want me to try and establish some kind of classified satellite communications channel so I can ask Reilly what the hell is going on?"

"I don't think we want to give the NPA another reason to claim provocation. The President made that very clear. He's scared that idiot admiral has given the NPA the excuse they need to nuke the base. The NPA is telling the international press exactly that. They're announcing that they intend to take over the base immediately in retaliation for the attack on their ship. If they meet armed resistance, they will use whatever weapons are necessary to defend their country. This makes us look like we've provoked a nuclear attack. How do we get this back on the talking track?"

"We announce Admiral Jones has gone outlaw," Backlin suggested. "We call the *Hercules* on an open channel, and we keep trying to call them. We invite the press in to listen to the communications, including any answer we get back. We send out search planes over international waters looking for the *Hercules,* and we ask the NPA government for permission to overfly their waters. They won't grant it, but we give big play to having asked for permission. We issue orders to all our ships and planes that they are to capture or kill the *Hercules* if they find it, and we make those orders public. We do that and we do it public enough, the NPA won't dare launch that attack against Subic. If they do, we'll have the necessary public support to respond like we want to respond."

"We don't actually go looking for the *Hercules,* because the NPA won't let us get near their water," Admiral Miller said, thinking out loud. "I like it. Put it in play!"

"Immediately."

"I'll clear it with Tabor Carol and have him call State. The ambassador out there can tell the NPA government what we're doing."

Admiral Miller got up from his chair and walked toward

the door. Almost there, he turned and looked back at Greg. "What do you think Jones is really trying to do? Did he chicken out, cut and run, trying to save his own hide?"

"I'd bet my life he didn't do that. He's got some kind of plan. The *Hercules* isn't just carrying the usual Harpoons. She's got four SLAMs on board. I'd guess that Gus either knows or thinks he can find out where the NPA is hiding and where any nukes they have left are stored."

"Is there any chance he's put nuclear warheads on any of those SLAMs?" Miller asked.

"None! There is no way he could use nukes without the Presidential codes. There is no way he could get those."

"Too bad," Miller said with half a smile. "If he could have used those, whatever he is trying might have worked."

"There's one other thing," Backlin said. "Whatever he's doing, he has to be pulling down satellite data, navigational information, if nothing else. He could still be collecting daily intel reports, all the general traffic on ship movements, that kind of thing, everything we put out for all our commands. He could also be planning to use tactical satellite communications links. It's all coded, but he has the codes. Do we want to change the codes? It's a hassle and we'll have some blank spaces when others won't be able to download. But if he can't get information, he can't try anything. Without the navigation satellite, he won't even be able to find his way back to port."

Admiral Miller stood thinking about it for a moment.

"You know," he said. "I didn't say that I didn't want Gus to succeed in whatever the hell he is trying to do. I just said I didn't think he had a chance in Hell of doing it. If I was asked, I'd say we have to leave Gus on-line because we can't afford the hassle of disconnecting him, not now, not with the NPA threatening to launch a nuclear attack on the base at noon their time. Besides, if he does use the satellite systems, we'll be able to keep track of what he's doing."

General Bae Bong-Soo had been waiting in the great hall outside the office of the Dear Leader for almost two hours. A half dozen times the woman major had stepped out to tell him that it would be just a few moments more. General Bae suspected her trips out to see him were timed to keep him on his feet. While the chairs where visitors sat were usually lined up right beside the door, someone had moved them twenty feet farther down the hall. General Bae had been up since 3:00 A.M. when the message from the *Kyong Ki* had come in. He turned and started walking toward the nearest chair. He was almost there when he heard the door open behind him again.

The woman major, who, rumors said, served the Dear Leader as more than a staff aide, stood by the door. She waited until General Bae walked back to where she stood, her face frowning like a schoolteacher waiting to scold a pupil.

"You may go in, General," she announced, stepping back to allow him to walk past her.

General Bae walked through her office to the door that led into the Dear Leader's office. He opened the door and walked in. The Dear Leader was at his desk, reading something. He didn't look up.

The Director of the Security Bureau walked the twenty feet across the office using the quick measured pace of a military parade. He snapped to attention as he arrived in front of the desk, and stated "Sir!," in his best command voice.

The Dear Leader neither looked up or gave any indication that he had heard the general speak. Bae stood for another full five minutes before the Dear Leader took off the half-frame reading glasses he wore. He laid them down on the sheets of paper he had been reading. He looked up and into the face of the general.

The Dear Leader made a face like he was surprised. As an

actor, he didn't come close to pulling it off. The fake surprise made him look more than a little bit stupid, but no one would ever tell him that. Like any royal prince scheduled to inherit a throne of absolute power, the Dear Leader had acquired a collection of strange facial gestures, mannerisms, body movements, and tics that no ordinary mortal would ever carry around. The Dear Leader had no friends, lovers, or even enemies who would dare suggest to him that the way he drank his tea, smiled at a joke, coughed, belched, or made love was anything less than perfect.

"Aahh! Bong-Soo, how nice of you to come by." The Dear Leader was using the familiar form of Korean that parents use when speaking to their children. "I did have a question I wanted to ask. Could you give me the date when you have scheduled the arrival of the shipment of the material we need so badly for the defense of the mother country?"

The general was still standing at attention. "Our plan for the collection of the material is proceeding on schedule," he said. "We strike today. At noon, Manila time, our Philippine allies will send a force which will march to the base and attempt to enter to take over control. If they meet armed resistance, the NPA force will retreat back away from the base area. We will use one of the remaining missiles, kill the defenders, and salvage the nuclear material at our leisure."

Kim Jung Il reached for his glasses and put them back on. As always they slipped down his flat nose bridge and came to rest at the fat tip of his nose. He picked up one of the papers he had been looking at when General Bae had entered the office.

"I do read your reports," he said. "I know what you plan for today. You mention briefly this ship that Captain Kang allowed to escape from the harbor by his incompetence and the stupidity of his crew? Tell me more about it."

"The incident has provided us a propaganda tool which we are putting to effective use," General Bae explained. "The cowardly departure of the commander of the base will steal the will to fight from the hearts of those whom the admiral left behind. I predict that base will surrender rather than risk annihilation. But if they don't, we will kill them, their whores, their brats, and their camp followers."

"Why are you so sure that was what the ship was, and nothing more?" the Dear Leader asked, his voice suddenly icy.

Something was wrong but General Bae had no choice but to plunge ahead. "It was nothing but a patrol boat," he assured the Dear Leader. "Its breakout represents no threat to our plan. The ship carried a few criminal deserters. We know from listening to the telephone call between the ambassador and the base that it is the commanding admiral who fled."

"I have been looking at a report that General Yoo has prepared for me," Kim Jung Il said, smiling like he was about to spring a trap. "The report is an excellent example of General Yoo's competent work. It provides a great deal of information about the *patrol boat* you think is so insignificant, and more information about the weapons she carries."

The Dear Leader reached a pudgy hand to a pile of papers lying face down on the desk in front of him. He turned them over and handed them to General Bae. "Perhaps you should look at this. I am pleasantly surprised to learn that General Yoo has developed such excellent sources within the American military that he is able to describe in such detail their ships and their weapon systems."

General Yoo Jae-Sin was the Director of the Intelligence Bureau. Both his rank and his position were equal to General Bae's in the Korean military hierarchy. Bae Bong-Soo had not only known Yoo Jae-Sin since they were students at the military academy, he considered Jae-Sin his most dangerous rival. Both men had arrived at a point in their careers where only one of them would take the next step up the career ladder.

The papers which the Dear Leader handed General Bae

described in considerable detail the *Pegasus*-class hydrofoil as well as the weaponry such a ship carried. While the documents were written in Korean, the pictures had been photocopied from some unnamed source with English captions. General Bae recognized the source of the intelligence, one of the books published by Jane's, a British company. The information probably came from either *Jane's Fighting Ships*, or *Jane's Surface Skimmers*. The Korean text was a direct translation from the same publication. Col. Cho had copies of both books on his own bookshelf.

"Obviously, this is no *patrol boat* but a highly sophisticated warship," Kim Jung Il announced, sarcasm dripping from his voice like hot honey from a spoon. "You will note that this ship carries not only surface-to-surface missiles, but that it could also carry both torpedoes and depth charges. The captain of the *Kyong Ki* has already learned a painful lesson about how difficult it will be to deal with this new threat to our victory. He was fortunate to have saved his ship, even if he will not be so fortunate when it comes to saving his political existence when he returns to his homeland."

Kim Jung Il held out his hand for the reports. Bae handed them back to the Dear Leader.

"The American admiral must suspect what our plans are," the Dear Leader announced. "He intends to frustrate them. He has not fled, he has taken the initiative away from us. While we do not know where he is, we can be sure he is standing near by, perhaps hiding in a small bay of some uninhabited island. If I were him, my plan would be to lie in wait until we have loaded our ships with the nuclear materials. Then he will strike out from wherever he is hiding, sink our ships, and deny us the victory. And most dangerous, he may collect the proof that will prove our role in this matter, something we can not permit to happen."

"Then we will find him and sink him," General Bae said, trying to appear to agree with the Dear Leader's analysis, even though he did not. General Bae had read the report from Captain Kang Ae Kyong. The *Kyong Ki* had escaped because the Americans had made no effort to sink her. That made no sense if the American ship intended to stay in nearby waters. The American admiral was either trying to get away and save his own life, or he had some other plan to use the missile weapons his ship carried.

"It is too bad that I have to point out such an obvious conclusion to a man whom I have entrusted with so much responsibility," Kim said. "You have no choice, you must delay your plan to take over Subic Bay while we search for this ship. I have already ordered the Navy to send all our submarines and every other ship in the waters around the Philippines into the area near Subic Bay to search for this admiral and his miracle craft. I have also ordered two additional submarines to sail immediately from our sub base at Cha-ho to join in the search. I have done this knowing that this puts our entire fleet at considerable risk, risk that could have been avoided if you had been more clever in anticipating what the enemy might do."

General Bae did not try to point out that he had originally suggested that three submarines be stationed in the waters near Subic Bay and that they be backed up with two frigates instead of one. The Dear Leader himself had decided that there was no need to risk so much of the Navy.

"When a true hero of the revolution makes a mistake, his only course is to confess his error and to learn from his mistake," General Bae said. "I do confess the error. I will correct the error, and we will find the ship and sink it."

"For your sake, I hope it is done in a hurry."

The Dear Leader spread the intelligence report out in front of him on the desk. He put the reading glasses back on and began studying the report. Five minutes later, he looked up and tried again to put on a face of surprise.

"I'm sorry," he said. "Didn't I tell you that you were dismissed?"

153

The USS Hercules *in the Luzon Strait.*

Gus stood in the pilothouse watching as Chief Wozniak and four crewmen worked at connecting the fuel line stretching across ten feet of open water to the Russian oiler, the *Erkut*. The sea that separated the Philippines from Taiwan was running rough and while the *Hercules* could move on its foils through such water with a smoothness of a skater on ice, she wasn't built to plow slowly through pitching seas at hull speed. She was rolling and bobbing so badly that the crewmen were having problems jerry rigging the connections between two different fueling systems.

Gus felt like a naked child standing in the middle of the Hollywood Freeway, but there had been no surprises, not yet. No one below him on the deck was showing a weapon, but a large tarp spread across the stern deck covered eight men all armed with automatic weapons. Every other man not required for the refueling operation was standing inside, close to a port or a hatch, his personal weapon loaded and locked.

The *Erkut* had appeared where Admiral Semenkov had said she would be. The deck crew had lowered a Zodiac into the water and two crewmen had taken the Russian admiral across the stretch of open water to the side of the *Erkut*. The next twenty minutes had been the tensest time of all. Gus figured his vessel would be most vulnerable immediately after the Russian boarded the oiler. Gus half expected that as soon as Admiral Semenkov stepped onto the deck of the Russian ship he would demand the surrender of the *Hercules*. If that happened Gus and his crew would take as many Russians to the deep with them as possible. He wasn't sure what he would do if the *Erkut* just sailed away. The extra fuel that had been used to travel north to the rendezvous point on the foils meant that the mission was already at an end if they didn't fill their fuel tanks.

154

But ten anxious minutes later, Semenkov appeared back on the deck of the oiler to announce over the American UHF short-range transceiver he had taken with him that the *Erkut* was ready to begin fuel transfer operations.

It took more than two hours for the fuel transfer to be completed.

"Black King! Black King!" came the call over the transceiver that Gus was holding in his hand.

"White King, this is Black King," Gus answered. He could see the Russian admiral standing on the deck of the oiler, looking in his direction.

"The captain tells me we will be ready to disconnect the fuel lines in about five minutes," Admiral Semenkov announced over the radio. "I must tell you that Captain Korobov passed the information of my request for a pickup to Cam Ranh. I had told him not to do that when I set up the rendezvous, but I can not blame him for covering his posterior."

Admiral Semenkov paused and gave Gus a chance to respond to make sure his transmission was being received.

"There were orders waiting for me demanding that I report immediately my status," the Russian admiral continued. "I have delayed obeying those orders until you refueled, but I have no choice but to contact my headquarters now. As much as I wish to rejoin you, I am afraid my doing so could jeopardize your whole mission. I don't want to give the Russian Navy an excuse to help the Americans hunt you down. If I can get back to Cam Ranh I might be able to convince someone in Moscow that we should help you even if your own navy has declared you an outlaw."

Along the way from Subic, the *Hercules* had picked up the satellite communication ordering the *Hercules* to return to Subic Bay and tell all American ships to be on the lookout for the *Hercules*. Any ship sighting the *Hercules* was to intercept her. If the *Hercules* refused to heave to, they were to fire on her and sink her.

The good news was that no ships had been ordered to leave their current duty stations to search for the *Hercules*. The orders had also specified that American ships and their planes were to continue to avoid all Philippine waters by a distance of at least three hundred miles. So far, the *Hercules* hadn't been more than eighty miles off the coast of Luzon.

"I enjoyed having you aboard," Gus answered back.

"It was the most fun I ever had on board a fighting ship," the Russian answered. "Winston Churchill was right. It is an exhilarating experience to be shot at and missed. I wish I could be in on the end of your venture. I have a bit of intelligence for you also. We have a report that the North Korean Navy is on the move. Our intercepts of their communications tell us that several subs and a frigate have been ordered to proceed to the Subic Bay area. Captain Korobov reports his sonars have picked up the noise of two submarines tearing holes and heading south in the last four hours. I assume that they are going to look for you where they last saw you."

If the *Erkut* carried passive sonars of that sensitivity, she was more than a simple oiler. But why would the Koreans think the *Hercules* was still back near Subic, Gus wondered. "I appreciate the information," he spoke into the transceiver. "Perhaps we'll meet again some day. We never did have that final rematch."

"I look forward to it," Admiral Semenkov said before signing off. The Russian waved at Gus and Gus waved back.

"Admiral, we have disconnected," Lt. Phillips announced. He had just climbed up to the pilothouse.

"Hightail it out of here," the admiral answered. "We want to get as far away from here as fast as we can. I want all weapon and defense systems on full alert. I like that son of a bitch, and I think he did us a favor, but I still don't trust him. If this is a trap, the best time to spring it would be when we think we're safe and while we're leaving the party he threw for us."

"Do you think that's true about the Korean Navy?"

"I hope so," Gus answered. "But it doesn't make sense, unless they've badly misjudged our reasons for breaking out of Subic. If they are looking for us around Subic, our chances of success have gone way up. What's our estimated ETA for our target area?"

"I estimate about five hours if we maintain full foilborne speed. Do we want to find an island and hide out during the daytime?"

"With all the high tech stuff that is looking for us, the night doesn't give us that much advantage except when we are in close to shore. Make a straight run. We can take advantage of the night when we land our teams. I want to land the first one as soon after dark tonight as possible. I've got a terrible feeling we are living on borrowed time. If we don't find where they keep those missiles in a hurry, they'll use them before we can stop them."

Chapter Sixteen

The Sierra Madre mountains, the Philippines.

Colonel Cho slammed the report he had just decoded down on the table in front of him. Too angry to stay seated, he jumped to his feet and began pacing back and forth across the small hut he used for his personal office. "The fools!" he said out loud, speaking Korean which his orders forbade him to do, even in his sleep.

Everything had been ready to execute. Sorreno had ordered a small band of his troops to form near the main gate leading into the Subic Bay Naval Base. They were waiting for the order to begin their advance into the base. Several representatives of the international press were with them so they could report back to the world that it had been the Americans who opened fire first.

If the Americans did not start shooting, the team would take over the base and call in more troops that waited on the other side of the mountains. All the Americans would be disarmed and the base would belong to the NPA.

But Cho Chae-Jin had not expected that to happen. The foolish Americans would shoot and Sorreno would have his provocation. Colonel Cho would order a SCUD launched as soon as the NPA team could retreat away from the base perimeter.

158

Colonel Cho had spent most of the morning at the site where the remaining two SCUDs were hidden. Major Kye and Major Estuar had programmed one of the SCUDs and the only thing to be done was the call from Colonel Cho giving them the unlocking code to key into the warhead. In less than two hours the issue would have been decided.

Instead Colonel Cho had a message ordering him to suspend the operation until further notice. And all because the idiot navy had failed in its job.

Cho walked back to his desk and picked up the message the *Kyong Ki* had sent the day before. Damn Captain Kang Ae Kyong! His message made it sound like all that had escaped from Subic was a small patrol boat that could not possibly endanger the operation. Now Pyongyang was telling him the escaped patrol boat was a dangerous warship that threatened the whole plan.

Cho tossed the decoded message on the table and stalked out of the hut. He crossed the small clearing to the communications hut. Inside, Aguila Sorreno was preparing to tape the speech announcing victory over the Americans. Sorreno had already stepped up to the podium in front of the red banner flag of the New People's Army when Colonel Cho walked in.

"You will have to rewrite your speech," Colonel Cho announced. "We have a problem that makes it impossible to launch our plan today." He described the intelligence report of the dangers that the escaped ship represented. Instead of explaining Pyongyang's fear that the small American warship would prevent them from taking anything from the base, Cho told Sorreno that the ship was an immediate threat to Sorreno's own continued existence.

"Your new speech must be more of the same thing you have been saying," Cho suggested. "Emphasize how your patience is growing thin, how you wish no harm to the Americans but how the Americans are provoking and threatening you. Demand that the American ship that has attacked the forces of the New People's Army must surrender immediately."

Cho saw the relief flood the face of Sorreno. Sorreno had lost his initial enthusiasm for attacking the American base. Increasingly, he believed that all he had to do was to let the Americans languish until he could starve them into surrendering the base. He still had no idea why it was that the North Koreans wanted the base seized as quickly as possible.

"The American ambassador told us that ship is nothing but an outlaw band who are running for their lives," Sorreno pointed out. "Two hours ago you were telling me that your intelligence was reporting that every American ship in the South China Sea is hunting down the criminals, that if they caught her they were either going to sink her, or make her return to Subic. Why are you suddenly telling me that this ship is dangerous?"

Colonel Cho wondered that himself about the most recent message from Pyongyang. How could just one small ship be so dangerous when an entire fleet of American ships might be on its way to the battle?

"Because we have new intelligence, and a better interpretation of the old intelligence," he explained, giving the only explanation he had.

"I still find it curious, Comrade, the way you can not make up your mind about what to do with the American base," Sorreno said, giving the infuriating snicker he occasionally let loose when he was feeling superior to everyone around him. "This is the second time we have been ready to destroy it and then backed away because you demanded we do so. This time, I'm glad you changed your mind. I see no reason why it is so important that we do anything about the base. The Americans are bargaining with us. My Foreign Minister tells me they have conceded all the base facilities and equipment and all the stores in the warehouses. They are still insisting on taking their ships and planes and weapons, but give us a few more days of negotiating and we will get some of those things, if not all of them."

"And your Foreign Minister lives in luxury in Manila which you dare not do, not until you totally defeat the Americans."

"I think you are wrong about that too," Sorreno said. "I have been giving it considerable thought. With each day, we gain more control in Manila. My people have taken over the government. We have even appointed a new Mayor of Manila. Most of the masses welcome what we have done. It is time that the new president of the Philippines talks directly to his people instead of through a television screen."

"As soon as you do that, the Americans will kill you. They will drop one of their smart bombs on you."

"I think not, not if I am careful and only appear when I am surrounded by my people. The Americans do not like to kill civilians. I would be much safer in Manila surrounded by thousands, than here, alone in the jungle."

What Sorreno was saying was actually the truth. But Cho had to collect the treasures of Subic Bay before he lost his control over Sorreno. It would be easier to keep that control if he could keep Sorreno isolated in the jungle. Even in the jungle the easy victory was feeding the megalomania taking over Sorreno's personality. Once Sorreno experienced the firsthand adulation of the crowd, he would start listening to only his own advice and refuse to listen to advice from anyone, especially from Colonel Cho. So Cho could not admit the truth. He must convince Sorreno he should stay in the jungle.

"I agree you might be safe for awhile in Manila," Cho said. "But what would we do with the missiles? You must have them near so that you can command them."

He was playing to Sorreno's megalomania. From the first day that they had fitted the warheads into the missiles, Sorreno had acted like a rich man behaves around racehorses or a gun nut who fondles his collection of automatic weapons.

"We worked hard and spent much money to put the two missiles I still command on mobile launchers," Sorreno pointed out. "The plan was that when we moved out of the jungle we would take the weapons with us. My people in Manila have spotted several warehouses where we can hide those two missiles. Estuar tells me that the missiles will be much easier to aim

161

at the American base from Manila, too."

"If you move the missiles, you risk the chance that some American satellite will spot them while they are on the road," Cho insisted. "Why take the risk? You have spent the last fifteen years in the jungle. Why risk it all to avoid a few more days of this hardship. Our ships are looking for the American admiral. They will find him and destroy him and his little boat. Then you can move against the base. Once you either capture or destroy Subic Bay, you can march into Manila like a hero instead of sneaking in like a thief at night."

One of the crewmen operating the camera stepped forward to tell Sorreno that all was ready to start taping his speech. A young woman in the jungle-green uniform of the NPA who did his makeup pulled out a powder puff and began dusting his cheeks.

"Okay, I agree that we stay here for a few more days," Sorreno announced. "But for no longer than that. If your navy does not find this ship within two or three days, then I think we can be sure that it represents no threat to us. It will be time that we move into Manila. I have already ordered my staff to find us quarters where we will be safe."

Colonel Cho hoped that the North Korean Navy did its job in a hurry. He didn't have a lot of faith that they would. All the North Korean Navy had anywhere near the Philippines was one frigate and a half dozen submarines. But if the intelligence analysis was correct, the American hydrofoil was hiding out somewhere near Subic Bay. There couldn't be that many places for it to hide. They should find it soon.

The USS Hercules *off the coast of Aurora.*

More than twelve hours had passed since Gus watched the *Erkut* sink below the horizon. He'd tried for some sleep during the daylight run south, but had found himself back in the pilot-house fifteen minutes later, wide awake and staring at the horizon. They had moved in close to shore two hours after dark and started landing the recon patrols, spreading them out along the coast line ten miles apart.

The fourth team was now loading into the Zodiac for the run into shore. This was the four man team. Captain Torres, the man who had lost his other two team members in the blast from the exploding missile, still looked shaky, but was insisting he would be okay. The four men were sitting in the bottom of the Zodiac, surrounded by their equipment. Like all the teams, they wore jungle camouflage fatigues, camouflage patterned greasepaint on their faces, but no insignia on their uniforms. None of them had any illusions about what their fate would be if they were captured. The NPA radio had made it clear that any member of the AFP caught with a weapon in his possession would be summarily shot. The Americans couldn't claim to be prisoners of war because their own government had declared them outlaws.

In additions to their weapons, communication equipment, and intelligence gathering equipment, each man carried a four-day supply of freeze-dried rations which were even less tasty then the infamous MREs (meals ready to eat), but much lighter to carry. The orders were that they were to live off the food they could carry and what they could gather in the jungle. They were to avoid all contact with the population except when it was necessary for gathering intelligence.

The crewman started the well muffled engine and the Zodiac pulled away. The shallow draft of the *Hercules,* even when hullborne, had allowed them to approach within three hundred yards of shore. There would be less than a thirty minute wait until the Zodiac's return.

Gus stood on the deck watching through his night scope as the Zodiac made it to the beach, unloaded the team and started back toward the *Hercules*.

As soon as the Zodiac was back on board, deflated, and stowed, Gus climbed into the pilothouse and took his usual seat near the helmsman. The *Hercules* headed back out to sea, creeping at hullborne speed for a couple of miles and then picking up to foilborne speed. Thirty minutes later, the hydrofoil slowed and settled back in the water. Gus climbed back down to the cramped interior cabin that served as a command, navigation, and fire control center. Lt. Phillips was on duty, watching the six crew members who were monitoring a variety of CRT screens.

"Everything clear?" Gus asked.

"So far," Phillips answered. "It looks like the new government still hasn't figure out how to handle the technical equipment they inherited from the AFP. Even the weather radar at Cape Encanto is off the air. It's a good thing it's not the hurricane season. There would be no warning if one came roaring out of the Pacific."

"When the AFP was operating them, their coastal defenses weren't that good," Gus answered. "Admiral Rimaldo took me on a tour of a few of them when I first arrived. Things were in a pretty sorry state. That's why the NPA was able to smuggle in those weapons without getting caught. It will take several weeks for the new government to get organized and get the equipment manned. Then they'll have the spare part problem."

"I'm more worried about their new allies," Phillips said. "About the only long-range ships the North Koreans have are diesel submarines, but they have at least nineteen of those. Some of them have got to be around here someplace. When we're moving on the hull, I'll keep a string of sonobuoys in the water, but it wouldn't be too hard for a smart skipper to sneak up on us."

"Let's hope that Russian intel report is correct, that they have all gone to the other side of the island to look for us."

Gus left Jack Phillips and the air conditioned interior of the command center to step out on to the forward deck.

Kathy Melendez was standing on the front deck where she and three crewmen were assembling the MRPV. Carrying a hundred pound payload of intel gathering equipment, the high tech drone aircraft had a dual fuselage and a sixteen foot wingspan. Two turboprop engines with a range of three hundred miles provided the power. The equipment pod that sat on the wing between the two fuselages looked almost like a smart bomb with the one big eye on the front. Launched by a small catapult mechanism, they would recover it by catching it in a net rigged over the fore deck. A half hour after Gus had walked out onto the deck, Kathy suggested that they both move into the command deckhouse where the MRPV's command center module was located.

Inside the deckhouse, one of the CRT screens showed an underlay map of the coast and mountain area where the four teams had landed. Four blinking amber lights on the screen marked the current position of each of the teams. A burst UHF transmission from the EPUU that each team carried updated their position on the monitor every fifteen minutes. The EPUU automatically took a reading from NAVSTAR satellites, computed the exact position on the ground, then relayed that information to a military communications satellite, which relayed the signal back to the *Hercules* where the computer in the ship's system decoded the signal and placed it on the computer screen.

One of the things that Kathy had done while the *Hercules* was making its run from Subic Bay was to recode the equipment of each of the EPUUs so that only the computers on board the *Hercules* could read the signals from the ground teams. The systems carried by the teams also allowed the team to key in messages which the EPUU transmitted in the same way.

Kathy sat down in front of the console that controlled the MRPV. The console looked like a video arcade game with a stick lever that steered the drone, two levers that controlled propeller pitch, and a panel of switches that turned the various systems the MRPV carried on and off.

The screen in front of Kathy came to life as the crew on the deck launched the drone into the air. The low light television camera showed the surface waves below the drone as she climbed, gaining altitude.

"I thought I'd keep her just above the waves until she hits the coast," Kathy explained. "That will keep her under any coastal radar, if the NPA has the old systems working yet. From there I'll take her up to eight thousand feet and start flying a grid pattern." Kathy put the drone into a bank that headed her back toward the coast. "Her engines are muffled, so nobody on the ground can hear her once she's up that high. I'll fly her straight to where the radio signals have been coming from. The transmitter is off the air, but the ECM (electronic counter measures) system on the MRPV is sensitive enough it can spot an antenna that's receiving as well as one transmitting."

Gus sat behind Kathy, watching the screens for the next hour and a half. As the little plane flew the grid pattern that Kathy had marked out, she switched continually from one system to another, looking at the ground with the low intensity light camera, then the same area with a thermo imaging system, then the forward infrared system, and back again to the video image.

She spotted a truck moving along roads, heat spots under jungle canopy, and rising smoke from cooking fires. Each time she announced something interesting, she'd pass it to Marine Tech Sergeant Amos Younce who was sitting beside her. Younce was the technician brought on board to operate the Net Control Station, (NCS) that collected all data and messages from each of the EPUUs.

"I think we've found the antenna field," Kathy announced a while later. "Take a look at this. This is thermo imaging I'm using here. These two bright spots are probably diesel generators. They're turned off now, but they were running during the day. The EMS system confirms passive reception so someone is monitoring a shortwave radio signal. But I don't think this is the headquarters. These two faint hot spots are probably old cook fires, and I'd bet this bright point here is a fire some guard built to heat his coffee or something."

"Mark the spot," Gus said. "When we find the headquarters and the weapons stash, we might take out the antennas, too."

Kathy began manipulating the controls of the MRPV. She

flew the drone in a spiral pattern that took it out away from the spot where the antenna field had been identified.

"It should be easy to find the headquarters," Kathy said as she kept her eyes on the video screen. "They'll have at least one generator and it should be operating at night. There will be more cook fires and maybe some trucks and stuff. People who think that hiding in the jungle is a safe way to go don't understand how much we can see from the sky. They would have been smarter if they'd hidden out in a big city."

"What about the launch sites? Can we find them?"

"We should, but the pads may have cooled back down by now. Frankly, even if I find what I think is the headquarters and the launch site, I want ground verifications."

"That's why we landed those teams." Gus looked at his watch. It was almost 5:00 A.M. "You better bring it back. It will be light in a while."

They caught the MRPV in a net strung across the bow deck as dawn broke. While Kathy and her team of crewmen quickly dismantled the MRPV for storage for the day, Gus climbed back up to the pilothouse. Jack Phillips had already set the course.

The *Hercules* would spend the daylight hours hiding out in a bay somewhere in the Polillo Islands. It meant a run of sixty nautical miles each way, but there was too much chance that someone would spot the *Hercules* if they anchored anywhere on the coast of Luzon. Right now, Gus was pretty sure that no one with the NPA knew where they were or what they were doing. The longer they could keep it that way, the better the chance of success.

Chapter Seventeen

The submarine Kimch'aek *in the Philippine Sea.*

Captain Third Rank Chung Ha's leg muscles ached. He had been squatting for hours in the cramped engine room as he watched Lt. Yang Jyun-kyu and the six crewmen work on the massive diesel engine of the *Kimch'aek*. Chung Ha knew little about machinery. Yang Jyun-kyu and the machinist mates would work as hard without his presence as with it. But if Chung Ha didn't stay watching the work, he would have to return to the conn where Captain Chang Ui-ung, the political officer, and Captain Kim Tae-woo would scream their obscenities at him, demanding to know why he had let the diesels break down again and why he was taking so long in getting them fixed.

The fault for sticking the *Kimch'aek* on the surface in broad daylight wasn't Chung Ha's, nor the fault of the crew who worked under him. The *Kimch'aek* had been plagued by breakdowns and bad luck since the first day she slid into the water from the construction docks at Mayang-do. On this cruise alone, this was the second time that the diesel engines had required major repairs, the kind of repairs better done in a shipyard rather than on the high seas in dangerous waters.

Lt. Yang started backing out of the cramped quarters. Chung Ha backed out first to let the lieutenant out.

"I think we've got it," Lt. Yang announced once both men

were again standing on their feet. "All they have to do is to put it back together and try it out."

"How long will that take?"

"At least an hour."

"Can't you hurry it?"

"Comrade, we're lucky we got it fixed at all. I don't guarantee it will stay fixed. They must hire Japanese monkeys at Mayang-do. We ought to sail straight back home. The next thing that breaks could sink this tub."

Chung Ha was glad that the political officer, Captain Chang Ui-ung, was not present to listen to Jyun-kyu's criticism of the people's workmanship. He needed Jyun-kyu to keep the sub afloat and moving, a talent he could not draw on if Jyun-kyu was doing punishment time in the *Kimch'aek's* brig.

Back in the conn, Chung Ha found the skipper of the ship, Captain Kim Tae-woo, listening to the political officer's complaints about the sub's failure to obey a critical order. Chung Ha stepped up and told the skipper that the mechanics had fixed the problem and that the ship could get underway in an hour. The Captain ordered him back to the machinery compartment to insist that they finish the job in thirty minutes. Chung Ha went back and stayed there, again squatting to watch the work done for the forty-five minutes it took to put the machinery back together.

In the conn, Captain First Rank Kim Tae-woo waited impatiently for the word he could start his engines. He worried about what he should do once his sub was again operational. His original assignment had been to cover the entire eastern side of the island of Luzon. He was to gather intelligence on American ship movements in those waters and monitor any ships of the AFP navy that might still be afloat. He had suddenly been ordered to sail around the Luzon to the other side of the island to search for a pirate American ship that was threatening the success of the entire operation.

He had been operating in the waters north of the Polillo Islands and had headed south around the Island of Luzon. He had been sailing on the surface before dawn, preparing to submerge for the day when his primary drive diesel engine broke down.

It was almost dawn again and he had lost twenty-four hours. By the time he reached the waters around Subic Bay, he would be too late to take part in the search and he would probably be ordered right back to the eastern side of Luzon. As the sun was up and his batteries low, he would have to sail submerged, using the snorkel gear. He didn't want to risk any more time on the surface, especially daytime, than was absolutely necessary.

Fifteen minutes after they began running submerged, the sonar operator excitedly reported a passive sonar contact.

"The ship is a long ways away, but moving fast, very fast, at least forty knots, maybe more."

"Is she coming at us?" the captain asked.

"I don't think so," the sonar operator answered. "But she will pass close by."

The captain ordered a speed and course change, slowing the sub to the minimum speed necessary to maintain steerage and set a course that would take them in the direction of the sonar sound.

"Captain Kim, what are you doing?" the political officer demanded. "Your orders were to proceed immediately to the South China Sea side of Luzon. Why are you diverting?"

"Captain Chang, my orders were to proceed to that area and to search for a high speed American surface vessel. We have a high-speed vessel approaching in this direction. I think it might be a good idea to check it out."

"The orders said the ship you were to search for would be somewhere near Subic Bay, waiting to prey on our ships. You are already twenty-four hours late. I suggest that you get on your way at full speed."

"Fine, if you insist on full speed, I will give you full speed, but that means we must sail on the surface. We are not one of those nuclear powered beasts that drills holes through the water. Before I surface, I must check out what kind of vessel is coming in this direction in such a hurry. When I know it is safe, I will surface, and we will go as fast as we can to where our orders tell us to go."

Five minutes later he ordered the *Kimch'aek* to periscope depth. He would not raise the radar antenna. If it was a warship moving so fast across the water, that would not only give the *Kimch'aek's* position away, it would provide a weapon beam for one of the American weapons to aim on.

"What's the estimated position of the target?" he asked his sonar man.

"Twenty-five degrees, at about eight thousand meters. She'll pass us at about that distance."

"Up periscope," Captain Kim ordered.

Two minutes later he was looking through the scope set at its highest magnification and watching a hydrofoil skimming along the water. He could see the launch tubes on the stern of the hydrofoil. There was no question in his mind. The ship he was looking at was exactly the kind of ship he should be hunting on the other side of Luzon. The orders had been to find it and sink it.

"Down periscope," he ordered. "Take her down to one hundred fifty meters. Order fire control to give me a resolution, order torpedo room to load torpedoes with proximity fuses."

"Ship appears to be turning away from us," sonar reported. "The Doppler says she's going away from us."

"They must have spotted the periscope on their radar," the captain muttered to his second in command, Captain Third Rank Chung Ha.

"Fire control reports no resolution possible," Chung Ha reported back to him. "Target is now moving away too fast."

"You should have fired your torpedoes before you came up,

Captain Chang announced. "You have let her get away."

Captain Kim considered again the possibility of running Chang Ui-ung through the sub's garbage grinder. Like so many of the political officers in the PRK Navy, Chang Ui-ung had little sea experience. He had worked his way up through the party cadre apparatus and had been transferred to the Navy only a year before. Because the subs were the only serious long-distance sea vessels that the People's Republic of Korea (PRK) had, they were considered to be good for the career of the political cadre. It was a ticket-punching post. None of the political officers wanted to stay below the water for more than two years, so sub commanders continually suffered political officers who had little idea what went into submarine operations.

"Their lookouts would have seen the torpedoes coming and they would have turned and run," the captain pointed out. "We must get much closer to them if we are to comply with our orders. Our problem is to figure out how we get closer to the target without letting the target know what we are doing."

"You are going after the target?" Captain Chang asked.

"Chasing after them makes little sense," Captain Kim answered. "It would be like chasing a fast car on a bicycle. Let's look at the chart and see if we can figure from where she was coming and where she is going. Maybe that will tell us if she was passing through, or if she will be coming back this way again."

The officers walked to the chart table where Chung Ha quickly located the approximate spots where the sonar had first picked up the target and where the periscope observation had taken place. The projection of the line extended back to the coast of north central Luzon. The line marked a straight path heading toward the Polillo Islands.

"That's near the area where Colonel Cho has his headquarters," Captain Chang whispered, pointing at the southern Sierra Madre range. "I wonder what that hydrofoil was doing

172

there."

"Whatever it was, it can't be good news for Colonel Cho," Chung Ha said. "Is it possible that they landed some kind of team or something to go after the headquarters?"

"That's what I would be guessing," Captain Kim said.

"What are you going to do about it?" the political officer demanded.

"First, I'm going to tell Colonel Cho and Pyongyang, as soon as it's safe to go to radio antenna depth. Then I'm going to find a quiet spot on the bottom near here." The captain put his finger on a spot just off the coast. "I'm going to wait there and see if the hydrofoil comes back to these waters."

The USS Hercules *in the Philippine Sea.*

Admiral Jones was in his bunk, trying unsuccessfully to get the first sleep he'd had since the *Hercules* rendezvoused with the *Erkut,* when a sailor woke him to tell him there had been a possible hostile radar sighting. Gus jumped quickly to his feet and walked into the command and control center.

"We can't be positive, but we think our radar spotted a periscope right about here," Lt. Phillips explained. "We didn't get any active radar signals from the target. I turned and ran, just in case it was a sub. Unless they fire a missile, we're already long out of range."

"Did you throw sonobuoys?"

"At this speed they wouldn't have done much good, too much interference from our own noise. If it is a sub, it's probably moving slow and quiet, or it's sitting on the bottom. A *Romeo* running on batteries doesn't make a lot of noise."

Gus turned and looked over to where Sergeant Amos Younce was monitoring the NCS that was reporting position information on the intel teams. Sergeant Younce saw the Admiral looking in his direction.

"They are all hiding for the day," Younce explained. "Baker team headed up in the direction where the MRPV found what we think is the antenna farm. They followed a dirt road that shows signs of heavy truck use up to here. They hid for the day right here." The sailor tapped a spot on the map on the screen. He touched his finger to the screen, and the computer magnified the image, giving greater detail on a map that showed the blinking amber light that represented Baker team in the middle of the screen.

He moved his finger down to the corner, pointing to the second amber light on the screen. "Delta is hunkered on a hill looking over a small village that doesn't show on the map. They report quite a bit of vehicle traffic around the village. As soon as it becomes dusk, they'll work their way up parallel to Baker team."

Sergeant Younce punched a button again and a second section of map expanded into view, showing another amber light that marked the location of Alpha team, the last team that had been dropped. Alpha team held the southern most point. They were north of a town called Dipaculao. They had bedded down for the day on a mountainside that gave them a view of both the town and the coastal road that ran North out of the town. They would follow the road into the mountains, heading in a direction that would intersect with Baker team on the other side of the ridge line.

The fourth team, Charlie team, was the first team the *Hercules* had dropped. They were almost forty miles to the north, just south of the next center of population big enough to be called a town, a fishing village named Dinalongan.

"Alpha reports some road traffic going north, but Charlie's only seen one truck pass their position since they set up," the marine said. "Captain Lee reports they'll work their way south for about five miles, then cut west into the mountains."

The American on Charlie Team was Marine Captain Harold Lee.

None of the teams were blindly thrashing through jungle and climbing mountainsides. Each team had a specific coordinate on the map they were to move toward and occupy until the MRPV collected enough information to give them a target to look over.

"Hopefully we'll have some better directions soon after we get the MRPV back in the air this evening," Gus said. "Let me know if anything interesting develops." Gus turned and stepped through the hatch that led to the crew quarters, hoping to get a couple of more hours of sleep. The Mekong Delta river system had taught him the value of grabbing sleep whenever he could find it.

Thirty minutes later, they woke Gus again, this time to tell him they had monitored a VHF radio signal from the direction where they had spotted the sub periscope. The signal was not a frequency used by American or allied submarines. The radio signal had to mean that the sub had spotted the *Hercules* and was telling others what they had seen.

The Sierra Madre mountains, the Philippines.

Colonel Cho Chae-Jin was worried. He read again carefully through the decoded message from the *Kimch'aek*. He put that down and read the original message from the *Kyong Ki* which had reported the escape of an ultra-fast surface skimmer out of Subic. Then, he again looked over the message from General Bae Bong-Soo ordering him to stand down and wait until they had destroyed the American naval craft before he made the final move against Subic.

Like all smart military bureaucrats, Chae-Jin had learned early in his career the importance that a patron could have for a bright young officer. Chae-Jin had found his patron through the fine art of bride selection. He had postponed marriage until he was a major. When he married, he had

175

picked a woman who was much younger than he, but age wasn't the reason he had picked Bae Hwang. It wasn't beauty either. Bae Hwang was fat and had an acne-marked face that reminded one of *Bulkoki*, the thin strips of beef broiled on a fire pot. Despite her young age, Bae Hwang had already given up the hope of marriage and was dedicating her life to the Party when Chae Jin asked her to be his bride. Chae-Jin braved the face, the folds of belly fat, the chronic sinus problems, and the high-pitched, complaining voice often enough in the dark of the night that he now had two children who called General Bae Bong-Soo, grandfather.

Cho Chae-Jin read through the message from his father-in-law once again, paying careful attention to each word. His eyes focused on a sentence that read:

"The intelligence community has determined at the highest level that the escape of the *Pegasus*-class hydrofoil represents a serious threat to the operation. Therefore, the first priority must be the elimination of the ship, and all resources are being directed to where the intelligence community has determined that the ship will be operating."

The wording was strange for a man like General Bae who prided himself on his straight talking. And why the reference to "the highest level"? Reading back over it once again, Cho decided that General Bae had been trying to tell him that he didn't necessarily agree with the conclusion about what the hydrofoil might be trying to do. Someone had overridden the general and the reference meant that either the Dear Leader or the Great Leader had done the overriding.

Cho now had the evidence that the general was right. The hydrofoil was not off Subic Bay, it was in his backyard. It could only be there for one reason. The hydrofoil was looking for him and the missiles he had. He had to inform Pyong-

176

yang, but reporting the information had to be done in a way that would not cast doubt on the strategic abilities of the two men who ruled his country.

He carefully wrote out a report suggesting that the brilliant move in launching an all-out search for the American ship had succeeded in flushing the ship to the other side of the island where it was now hiding. He added the recommendation since they knew where the hydrofoil was, and it was in no position to endanger the collection operation at Subic, they should not delay any further the implementation of the primary plan.

Colonel Cho smiled as he finished the final sentence. That would be the best way to deal with the strange vessel. Take over the base the American admiral had left behind . . . or destroy it.

As soon as Cho finished the report he headed for the radio shack. He had no doubt that the American hydrofoil was exactly where it intended to be, doing what the American admiral had intended from the very beginning. The American represented an immediate threat to Colonel Cho and his operation, a threat that had to be avoided until he could either capture or destroy Subic Bay.

Two minutes after he handed the message to the Korean radio operator, Cho walked into the hut Aguila Sorreno used for an office. He moved to a map pinned on one wall and began explaining to Aguila what he thought the American hydrofoil was trying to do.

"A small craft like that can't have aircraft, not even a helicopter," Cho told the Filipino. "They must have landed at least one and maybe more reconnaissance teams to try and locate where we are. We are fortunate that the *Kimch'aek* suffered a breakdown or we would think that damned ship was still on the other side of the island."

Sorreno seemed to physically shrink as Colonel Cho explained the problem, almost like he was getting ready to duck the missiles if they came flying through the door.

"I knew we were making a mistake staying here in the jungle," Aguila answered, suddenly angered to the point where he was nearly screaming. "We would be safer in Manila. We have to get away. We must leave immediately. We can't sit here and wait for them to come for us."

"I agree we may be safer in Manila," Cho answered. He had learned that the best way to deal with Sorreno was always to agree with him at first, and to lead him from there.

"We will make the move soon," he continued. "But we must do it wisely. We must go at night so no satellite can observe our presence and we must take the two SCUDs with us. We have much to prepare and your men will have to hurry. We must also try to find the men in the jungle looking for us. We can not permit ourselves to be ambushed nor lured into a trap."

"Why bother?" Sorreno demanded. "A few men wandering around the jungle can't hurt us, it's that damn speedboat we have to worry about. Let's shoot one of the SCUD missiles at it. We can save the other one for Subic Bay."

"We don't know where the hydrofoil is. That American admiral now enjoys the advantage we once enjoyed. Even if my sub sights him, he will be able to run to a new spot before we can reprogram a missile. Our best hope is that our sub can surprise him, but we can not count on that."

"Then let us destroy the base and do it right now. That ship is trying to kill me. That's all the international provocation I need."

It was exactly what Colonel Cho wanted to do, too. There was no good reason why they shouldn't do that, but his orders said he was to wait. Until those orders were changed, he would wait. He hoped it would be no more than a couple of hours before the answer to his message came back. It was still early enough in the day that they could set up the demand for the surrender of the base for the afternoon. But he couldn't

178

tell Sorreno that, not till he got his orders.

"We can't risk hitting the base yet," he argued, thinking quickly for an excuse to give Sorreno. "If we launch a missile at the naval base, the hydrofoil will see the launch trail. It will give them the perfect target to shoot at. We must assume the admiral's weapons are loaded with nuclear tips. We will kill all the Americans on the base, but the admiral will kill us. Without your leadership, how can the revolution of the Philippine people survive?"

The importance of his own life was all Sorreno needed as an argument. "So how do we survive?" he asked.

"We must find his recon teams before they find us. How many men can you put into the search and how quickly?"

"Give me twenty-four hours and I can have five thousand men combing the hills around here."

"We don't have twenty-four hours. We have to assume that the hydrofoil keyed in on our antenna field. If it was me, I would locate that first, then start searching out from there in a spiral pattern." Colonel Cho pointed to the map, putting his finger on the spot five miles from where they were standing. "That means any men the ship landed are probably moving up this valley. We need to move what troops we have right now to here." He pointed to a spot about two miles from the antenna field, down the mountain toward the coast.

"As more troops arrive, you spread them out along this ridge line that runs north and south. Any recon team running a search pattern will have to cross the ridge line. Pick the choke points, set up ambushes, and you'll catch them."

He thought a second, then asked, "What kind of planes can you get in the air?"

"We've got several planes, but pilots are a problem. The only pilots we have are Colonel Chuey Drilon and one more. You can't learn to fly a plane while you're hiding in the jungle."

"Get both of them up and looking for that damn hydrofoil.

You've got a jail full of pilots from the AFP. Separate the younger ones out and make them an offer. They either join the new NPA Air Force today, or they and their families die. If any of them sign up, get them in any plane they can fly and up in the air looking for that hydrofoil."

"I still think we should move to Manila immediately," Sorreno insisted.

"I agree we should do that as soon as possible, but we will be even more vulnerable on the move. We must wait for dark before we can start preparations, we can only move after dark. The Americans will have satellites overhead watching during the daytime. They may have another team hiding along the coast road, too. We will have to take the back road and that will take much longer."

Chapter Eighteen

The Sierra Madre Mountains, The Philippines.

Major Steve Wendle watched the mosquito exploring between the black hairs of his forearm. As the mosquito dipped to drill its beak into his flesh, Wendle recognized the steep bite angle of the Anopheles, the vector for malaria. He squashed the bug with his thumb before she could bite in. He had put on repellent three hours before but his sweat had already washed it off. He slowly eased the small stick of heavy-duty repellent from his pocket and redid both his arms, trying not to move too much while he worked.

He looked to his left and saw Sergeant Joe Estrada smiling at him. Estrada didn't bother carrying a repellent stick. Mosquitoes never bothered him. Estrada wore a set of black earphones connected by a wire to a camouflage-colored parabolic mike sitting in front of him. The sergeant had the earphones because he spoke Tagalog as well as one of the local dialects.

Assigned to the Marine Barracks at Subic, Major Wendle had won a spot on the team because he knew more about high tech reconnaissance patrolling than anyone else at Subic. He had served a tour in the highlands of Viet Nam as a seventeen-year-old Marine grunt. After Nam, he had gone back to college, gotten an NROTC commission in the Marine Corps, and had spent most of his career since in Japan and other parts of the Far East.

Wendle put his eye back to the spotting scope sitting on a small tripod in front of him. Both the scope and the parabolic mike looked through breaks in the foliage toward a village located about five hundred feet below the team. The current center of activity in the village was the small, dusty village square.

Four vehicles had driven up the primitive road into the village about eight o'clock that morning. The vehicles were late model cars — two luxury Toyotas, one Datsun, and a brand-new Mercedes. The men who piled out of the cars wore khaki uniforms. Through the twenty-power scope, Wendle could make out the small red stars on the front of each of the uniform caps.

The three men who stepped down from the Mercedes were in charge and giving orders to everyone else. The Datsun unloaded two prisoners, a man and a woman. Both the prisoners had their hands tied behind their backs. The man fell as he tried to get out of the car. Three soldiers who were acting as his guards made no effort to help him up, but screamed at him to get to his feet.

When the male prisoner was back on his feet, the guards led him and the woman into the center of the square and roughly forced them to kneel down in the dirt. As they hit the ground, small clouds of grey dust rose up around them and hung in the still morning air. The male prisoner wore dark grey slacks and a long sleeve, cream-colored barong Tagalog costume. The woman was wearing a terno, the traditional formal Philippine dress with its stiff butterfly shoulders. The dress was the same color as the man's shirt. Both the shirt and the dress were torn in several places and spotted with dirt and grease.

Wendle wondered if they had been arrested at some formal party and brought to the spot, or forced to dress up for the occasion. He could see cuts and bruises on the face of the man who looked to be in his late forties or early fifties. The woman was younger, perhaps no more than thirty-five or so.

As soon as the cars had arrived in the village, a dozen villagers, all carrying rifles, had immediately assembled in the square. The leader of the local militia saluted the arriving dignitaries, then he and his men spread out through the village and began gathering the population into the square. With the village lined up on three sides of the square, someone found a table and chairs for the three officials, and the trial began.

Sergeant Estrada made a motion with his hand, indicating that he wanted to look through the scope. Wendle backed away from it. Estrada crawled over to take his place. Estrada kept the earphones on. The wire was long enough to reach without having to move the parabolic mike. Estrada lay watching and listening for a good ten minutes.

When he had seen and heard enough, Sergeant Estrada took off the earphones, lay them on the ground beside the mike, and backed up through the weeds and bushes to where Major Wendle lay waiting. The third member of the team, Captain Juan Nazareno, was stretched out belly down on the ground a few feet behind Major Wendle. The Philippine captain held his M-16 cradled in his arms. Three backpacks lay together beside the captain. The team's hiding place was a small shelf on the edge of a steep grade that rose above the village.

"The man on trial is the landlord," Estrada said, his voice a whisper so low that both Wendle and Nazareno had to move forward a few inches to hear better. "I recognize him from pictures in the newspaper. He owns much land around my village, too. The woman is his wife."

Sergeant Estrada came from a village about fifty miles farther north up the coast. His familiarity with the geography, the people, and the local language was the primary reason why Colonel Ziga had picked him for one of the teams.

"What kind of landlord was he?" Wendle asked.

"Who knows? We never saw him in person. This is probably the first time he ever visited this village. Right now, the man who calls himself the judge, he is reading all the crimes that the landlord and his wife are accused of committing. The villagers will be the jury. I don't think the trial will last very long."

"They're going to haul them around to each one of the villages where they own land for a trial," Wendle asked.

"I doubt it," Captain Nazareno said. "They probably picked the village where the NPA has the most sympathizers. It's the opposite of what you Americans try to achieve with a change of venue. They want to make sure they get a guilty verdict."

"From the sound of the cheers down there, I don't think they are going to have any trouble getting it," Wendle said.

"I don't suppose we could do anything to help them out?" Captain Nazareno whispered. "We've got the firepower and the surprise factor."

"Too risky," Wendle answered. "Even if we did kill the NPA soldiers, we'd have to worry about the villagers. Before the day was out, we'd have several hundred troops pounding these mountains, looking for us. We've got a lot bigger fish to fry." He turned back to Sergeant Estrada. "Get back there and keep an eye on what's happening. We'll get some rest and spell you in a while."

An hour later, Estrada came crawling back through the bush. "Major, Captain," he whispered, "maybe, you come see. All of a sudden, they end trial. One of the guards, he came up and gave the judge a radio. He talk for a while, then get very excited."

Both the captain and the major crawled forward to take a look. The villagers were still standing around three sides of the square, the landlord and his wife were still kneeling in the

184

dust in the middle of the square, but the three officers who had been sitting at the table were all on their feet. The soldiers who had come with them were standing together facing the officials. The local village militia were standing in a separate line, looking only a bit more ragged than the uniformed NPA troops. The lead officer was shouting orders, waving his hands in the general direction behind him.

Almost immediately, the entire uniformed force, except for the three leaders, broke ranks and began moving from the village toward the mountains. They stretched out into a scrimmage line, their weapons at the ready; their eyes alert, their heads scanning from side to side as they moved into the jungle undergrowth.

The head officer said something in a loud voice to the chief of the local militia. The man turned and walked toward the prisoners kneeling in the dust. He strolled around behind the man, holding the automatic rifle he carried in the ready position. He looked around at the crowd which screamed their encouragement even louder. He turned back to the prisoner, put the muzzle of his rifle up against the back of the prisoner's skull, looked up again at the NPA official, and got his nod of approval. He fired one round. The landlord sprawled forward in the dust, a pool of blood spread out from his head while urine soaked the ground around his crotch.

The woman prisoner started screaming, begging for mercy. She tried to get to her feet, lost her balance and fell headfirst into the dirt. The crowd roared with laughter. She struggled back to her knees, still begging for mercy, announcing with her screams that she had children who needed their mother and that she had been born in a village like theirs. She was almost to her feet when the executioner stepped up behind her and fired a three-round burst from two feet away into the back of her head.

The NPA land reform program in Aurora had officially begun.

Leaving the dead landlord and his wife sprawled in the dust, the village executor marched back to stand in front of the NPA officials. One of the officials called out an order and the crowd instantly broke up. A few minutes later, at least twenty village men were back in the square. They carried a collection of weapons that ranged from shotguns and muzzle loaders to bolo knives and sickles. Following the orders of the village chieftain, they and the rest of the militia began moving into the jungle, spreading out in their own search pattern.

"They're searching for us," Captain Nazareno whispered. "They've got to be looking for us."

"I don't think so," Wendle whispered back. "At least not specifically for us. From what Estrada saw, they got the order to start searching by radio. I don't think we've been spotted, but someone knows there is something dangerous in these mountains they want to find in a hurry."

Wendle crawled back to where the packs were and hauled out the tactical computer from his pack. Lying on his stomach, he turned it on, punched in the four digit code sequence then brought up a map graphic to the screen. "Look," he said to Nazareno who had crawled up behind him. "They're not coming up the hill straight toward us. I don't think they're trying to circle around us. They're heading up the mountain in a southwest direction. It looks like they are making a beeline straight to this point, where the message we got from the *Herk* says the antenna field is. Baker team is heading in that direction, too. Maybe Baker got spotted or something. The boys in uniform left the village exactly like they knew where they were going."

Wendle closed the TACCOM, and reached for the EPUU navigation and communication pack. Still lying on his stomach, he punched in a report on what they had observed and keyed the command to code the message and send it on a fifty thousand mile round trip through space to a satellite and back to the *Hercules*.

"What do we do now?" Captain Nazareno asked when Wendle had finished with the message.

"We sit tight until it's dark, hope none of the village militia get lucky, wait for orders, and then we move out. I suggested in my messages we move up the mountain, going straight west, then cut south on the other side of the ridge."

The Polillo Islands.

The *Hercules* lay at anchor and hugging the shoreline of a small, uninhabited island. Camouflage netting had been spread over the superstructure. Hopefully, the ship would look like one more small jungle-covered island from the air. One small plane had already flown overhead, but had shown no interest in the *Hercules*. Gus was sure, however, that the plane had been looking for them even if the pilot hadn't seen them.

Warrant Officer Craig Hanson, the communications officer, had been busy through the day. He had intercepted a series of radio messages from Sorreno to his commanders around the islands.

While parts of the messages had been spoken in code, the code was often nothing but a word substitute. The fishing expedition Sorreno kept referring to was obviously the search for the *Hercules*. Bushels of pineapples referred to either companies or platoons of NPA soldiers, and harvest operation referred to the ground search for the team of saboteurs that NPA radio was claiming that the Americans had landed along the coast of Aurora Province.

The *Hercules* crew had been watching NPA TV. There had been news reports that the United States Navy was launching an attack against the new government. The NPA promised that if the attacks didn't immediately stop and the "criminals" surrender, then all American military forces would pay the price of aggression. Public announcements offered hundreds of thousands of pesos for rewards for anyone who reported or captured a saboteur. Several statements by Sorreno himself had been directed at the "mad admiral," insisting he immediately return to Subic Bay.

Aguila Sorreno wasn't the only one trying to contact the *Hercules*. Every American military radio band that Craig Hanson had monitored during the day had made repeated calls to the *Hercules,* demanding that the ship either return to its base, or identify itself via its communications channel.

"They're getting pretty insistent," Jack Phillips said. "This is the first time in my career I've ever disobeyed a direct order from a four-star admiral."

"I'll swear at your court-martial that I ordered all the radios on board the *Hercules* turned off," Gus told the man.

"I don't expect to live to see a court-martial, Admiral. I knew what I was getting into when I signed on. I agree with your analysis. Most of the people at Subic are going to die if we don't get this done."

"What's the current status of the teams?" Gus asked Sergeant Younce who was sitting at the Network Control Station.

"Three teams are still reporting sightings of NPA or militia units moving through their areas in a search mode. Charlie team up north is the only unit that hasn't seen anyone. The NPA units are all moving in a pattern focusing around the area where we spotted that antenna farm. They may be getting into position to try and block or ambush our teams when they move into the area."

"That's going to make it difficult for the teams to sneak through to check things out once we identify a possible target."

Lt. JG Bryan Bradley walked through a hatch and into the command center. "Admiral, I'm working up a course for this evening. Do we want to go back to about where we were last night?"

Gus stepped over to a chart table and both Bradley and Phillips followed. "That sub has tipped off the NPA that we are here," Gus said. "It's obvious they figured out what we are trying to do. That's why the troops are combing the jungle looking for the teams we landed."

"They may be thinking we'll go back to the coast," Jack Phillips suggested. "The sub could be hiding someplace waiting for us to do that."

"I'm assuming the sub is doing exactly that. We're going to have to stay out at sea quite a ways. That means we'll have to fly the drone farther to get it to the target area. Let's do this. We run out to sea for about thirty miles, then cut north for about twenty miles up the coast. We'll work our way back down from the northeast, drop a line of sonobuoys right along here, then swing around so that the sonobuoys are five miles inland from us. That should give us some warning if that sub tries to sneak up on us. What do think, Jack?"

"I agree we have to do something like that, but we can't do that for too many nights. Sooner or later we start running low on fuel and we don't have that Russian along to make another appointment with an oiler."

Gus turned from the chart table and looked at the two men. "We don't have several more days. I've got a feeling that we had better get this done tonight. If they are going to blow up the base, they will do it soon. They can't afford to let us run around for another day. A bluff will only work for so long. If they are not bluffing, they have to prove it."

The Sierra Madre mountains, the Philippines.

Col. Cho read again the message that he had just been handed by the Korean communications officer. He felt the anger mixing with growing fear in his gut. Pyongyang was putting him into an impossible situation. The words of the message jumped out from the page.

> The analyses of the intelligence committee at the highest level is that the American hydrofoil which the *Kimch'aek* spotted is not the same vessel spotted by the *Kyong Ki* coming out of Subic Bay. It must instead be a second vessel, perhaps one already on patrol at the time the NPA launched the attack on the Philippine government. This conclusion is based on intelligence information that the *Pegasus*-class hydrofoil can not carry enough fuel to travel the distance at the speed necessary to take it to the other side of Luzon without refueling along the way. As our submarines report no American ships in the waters around the Philippines, the hydrofoil which sailed out of Subic Bay could not have refueled along the way.

There were those damn words "at the highest level" again. The message also ordered that as the hydrofoil off the east coast was not a threat to the operational success of *Team Strike,* the KPR naval forces were to continue an all-out search for the hydrofoil operating in the waters near Subic Bay. The NPA air assets that had been committed to search for the second hydrofoil were to be redirected to the west coast of Luzon to search for the hydrofoil which did threaten the success of *Team Strike.* The message repeated the instruction that the final strike against Subic Bay continue to be postponed until they could find and neutralize the first hydrofoil.

The only concession to Col. Cho's fears that the hydrofoil operating on his side of the island threatened his position was the order for the *Kimch'aek* to remain on station in her current location and to find and destroy the hydrofoil on the eastern side of the island.

Col. Cho wasn't sure what to do next. Cho was positive that his father-in-law was trying to tell Cho that he agreed with Cho's own analysis that there was only one hydrofoil and that it was after Col. Cho and the weapons he commanded. But to convince anyone above General Bae of that, Col. Cho would have to explain how the American hydrofoil could have refueled along the way.

The only other way to prove he was right was to capture one of the sabotage teams that Cho was sure the hydrofoil had landed. Cho got up and went looking for Aguila Sorreno.

As he strolled across the clearing toward Aguila's hut, he found himself looking up, wondering when a missile would come slamming in. The lonely jungle was not the place to keep hiding with the new situation. Fortunately the message from Pyongyang had not given him any orders about what he should do to insure his own safety and the safety of the weapons he controlled. Now, Manila would be a much safer place to hide. The trip would be dangerous, but not as dangerous as staying put. Once they were safe and well hidden inside the city, he could give the Korean Navy all the time it wanted to find that damn American, or for him to convince the "highest intelligence authority" that there was no American hydrofoil on the loose on the west side of the island.

191

Chapter Nineteen

The USS Hercules *in the Philippine Sea.*

Admiral Jones stood behind Lt. Commander Melendes, watching the screen that displayed the signal from the MRPV. The small aircraft had been in the air for almost an hour and a half. It was time to bring the drone back to the *Hercules* for refueling. Gus turned his attention to the screen in front of Sgt. Younce which displayed a multicolored map of the area around the point where they had identified the NPA antenna farm. A string of small red dots stretched in a north/south line a bit to the west of the antenna farm. The dots represented thermo sightings by the MRPV of cook fires, burning cigarettes, and motor vehicles with engines which were either running or had recently been turned off. There had been no such activity through that area the night before.

"They've figured out what we are doing and that we would head for the antenna farm and start our search from that point," Gus said to Colonel Ziga who was standing behind him. "They didn't figure on us doing it from the air. I'd be they've set up a line of ambush positions between their antenna farm and their base headquarters. There will be a lot more of them than what shows up on the MRPV screen."

Through the course of the day, the *Hercules* had intercepted dozens of radio transmissions, most of them in the clear, from Sorreno or one of his aides ordering troops into the area to search for saboteurs.

"They probably expect that our teams will search out from the antenna farm and blunder into one of their ambushes," Gus added. "That suggests the headquarters is on the west side of the scrimmage line here."

Gus looked again at the map on the screen. Three of the blinking amber lights were on the east side of the line of red dots. Those three teams had been moving slowly since dark, using their night scopes and listening devices to scout ahead and avoid contact with unfriendlies. Baker team had identified so many unfriendlies along the road they had been following that they had moved into the jungle where they were making slow headway. Delta had made better time for a while, but now their amber dot was spotted along the line with the red dots. They were all advancing only a few yards at a time, using their sensor systems to spot the enemy in the dark, then sneak around him. Charlie team was moving faster, but they were so far to the northwest, they were out of the action for the rest of the night.

The only team on the east side of the dotted red line was Alpha team, the one with four men. Alpha was moving up a heavily used dirt road. They had successfully circled around three guard posts, but were still at least five miles from the point that marked the antenna farm.

"Tell Alpha to keep going in the same direction," Gus said. "We may be able to sneak them in the back door."

"Gus," Kathy called out suddenly, her excitement trapping her into using his first name again. "Look at this!"

Gus turned to look at the screen in front of Kathy. The screen was moving as the MRPV traveled. She used the guide stick to bring the drone back to what she had spotted. "This wasn't there the last time the MRPV flew over this sector. That looks like two trucks, big trucks. They just started their engines. And look at this." She punched a button and the screen converted to a still picture the computers had captured.

"This is another site, about five hundred yards away. Look at these heat spots. Now look at the image we got from the low light TV Camera. See these huts. They are spread out almost like a small village. This hut has a generator, and the heat spot here suggest this one has a cooking fire inside. We got some light spilling out of the huts, too. Look here, where nothing but jungle shows up with the visual camera."

She punched some keys again and a thermo image superimposed itself over the visual image. "This is a motor pool hidden under the canopy. There are four vehicles here that had their motors running today. The EMS is picking up a lot of passive electrical activity from here. This has got to be the headquarters."

She switched the screens again. "This is the visual image of the previous spot. Look how nothing shows up. Everything giving off the heat here is covered up. I'd bet this is the missile launch spot. They've just started two diesel engines that are under camouflage. Look how the spots grow brighter as the engines warm up. I say they're trucks, given the signature."

"You sure this is what we are looking for?" Gus asked.

"Not dead sure, but I would like to get one of those teams up to look these spots over as quick as we can."

"It will have to be Alpha team," Gus said. He turned to Sgt. Younce and dictated the orders to type in for Alpha team.

"Admiral, I'm going have to bring the MRPV back for refueling," Kathy said a moment later. "We're so far out, I can't keep her over target for very long."

"We don't dare take the *Hercules* in closer, not with that sub out there someplace. You have the coordinates you need if we get a verification those are our targets?"

"I can hit damn close to them. If I can get the MRPV back over the target before we shoot, I can guarantee a direct hit."

194

"I want to get a team up there and make a positive identification first. We can't afford to shoot at any wrong targets."

Gus turned to Lt. Phillips. "What about that sub?"

"I'm not picking up anything on the sonobuoys we dropped," Jack answered. "No active sonar. Nobody is broadcasting an active radar signal either. And I haven't picked up anything on our radar."

"They may be lying on the bottom, waiting for us," Gus said.

The *Hercules* was moving slowly through the waters of the Philippine Sea. While it was riding on its hull, the foils were extended instead of raised into the hull wells. In that way, the ship could come up to foilborne speed faster than if they first had to lower the foils.

The Sierra Madre mountains.

Lt. Commander Wade Hernandez watched through the M-16's night vision scope as the man two hundred yards away sucked on his cigarette. The guard was wearing a uniform of sorts, jungle-green pants and a shirt with a military-style field cap.

The guard post had a single bamboo pole barrier across the road which the guard could raise or lower by pushing down or letting up on the counterbalance of three big rocks that hung on the short end of the bamboo pole. The guard shack that sat beside the barrier had sandbag walls four feet high and a bamboo roof. Except for the corner poles holding up the thatched roof, the small bunker was open on all four sides.

It was two o'clock in the morning and the man was on duty alone. A bamboo shack stood at the edge of the jungle, set back a ways from the guard post. If this post was like the first three that Alfa team had already snuck around, there would be a half dozen or more men sleeping in the hut.

The team had worked their way around the first three posts with no real problem, taking advantage of the ability to not just see in the dark, but to spot others who thought they were hiding under foliage or behind bushes. This post covered a section of the road that cut through a narrow canyon. The walls on both sides were steep and the underbrush thick. Wade and his Philippine counterpart, Hoppy Yarcia, had decided to take out the guard rather than waste more time trying to sneak around him.

The M-16, Wade held at his shoulder, was wearing not just the sophisticated sight, but a silencer as well. Silencers don't go *phutt* in real life like they do in the movies. Even silenced, the M-16 would make a noise almost as loud as a .22 short round, and the slug would leave a trail of supersonic cracks as it moved through the trees. No matter how well one aimed, there was always a chance that a target taking a lead slug would do a bit of screaming before dying. Wade was covering the single guard as a backup, in the event that more silent ways of killing didn't work.

Wade made two clicks with his tongue. The no-hands mike in front of his lips picked up the sound and transmitted it to the other three men on his team. His short-range, tactical UHF radio picked up the answering click confirmations that Hoppy Yarcia and Ramon Torres were in position to cover the entrance to the hut where the rest of the guard squad was sleeping.

Through his scope, Wade could see Sgt. Primo Mitra moving in behind the unsuspecting guard who was looking up at the sky like he was counting stars while he puffed on his cigarette. Mitra was wearing a set of night vision goggles and carrying in one hand a large rock that weighed seven or eight pounds. The weapon had been Mitra's personal choice for taking out the sentry, much more effective than the traditional knife which required that one first grab the victim from behind to cover his mouth to prevent screaming.

Mitra was only about three feet from the target when he either made a noise, or the target got tired of watching stars. The target turned and saw Mitra. Wade was about to squeeze his trigger when he saw Mitra throw the rock. The rock struck the sentry square in the forehead with a sound that Wade heard twice, first loudly through the earphone he wore in one ear and then faintly in his other ear as the sound crossed the two hundred yards that separated him from the sentry. The sentry dropped like a chopped cornstalk. Mitra bent over to check his victim as Wade moved up to the sentry post. He was almost to where Sgt. Mitra was still bending over the sentry when he heard the two-click all-clear sign from Major Yarcia.

The blow had killed the sentry. Mitra left Wade with the dead man while he went back to retrieve his backpack. Once he had that on, Wade and Mitra picked up the dead man and his weapon. Working together, they carried him up the road past the hut which Yarcia and Torres were still covering. They carried the dead sentry a hundred yards past the hut, and then Wade whispered a single-word command into the tactical radio mike telling the other two men to catch up with them. They dropped the body on the ground and Sgt. Mitra continued on up the road. Using his night vision scope, along with the sound and thermal detection equipment, he scouted ahead for evidence of human existence.

Once Yarcia and Torres had caught up with Wade, the three of them carried the dead sentry another two hundred yards up the road and hid the body in the brush alongside the road. Hopefully, the sentry's companions would assume the man had deserted during the night.

They moved the next four miles leapfrog-style, the lead man checking out the next two hundred yards with the so-phisticated detection systems, then covering the others while they moved up, took a new advance position and continued the process.

Hoppy Yarcia was on the point when his sound detection equipment picked up motor traffic coming from up above.

"It's heavy and it's big and it's coming this way," he whispered into his no-hands mike. "It sounds like trucks, and maybe some smaller vehicles, too. I'd estimate they're maybe five or six miles up the road and over on the other side of the ridge. But they are coming this way. I don't see any headlight flashes. They must be driving blind."

"Activate the EPUU voice link and connect me in," Wade whispered, the communication intended for Sgt. Mitra who carried the EPUU backpack.

"You're on," Mitra's reply came back in a few seconds.

"Skimmer, this is Delta, we've got something heavy coming down the road to our position, at least two big trucks, maybe more," Wade whispered, not bothering to get a confirmation that the *Hercules* was listening in.

"We copy," Sgt. Younce answered. "We've got the MRPV coming back in your direction, but it'll be another ten minutes before it's over target. We are directing it to your position."

"Given the condition of this road, it will probably take the convoy longer than that to get here," Wade answered.

"What do you think, Commander?" the voice of Admiral Jones broke into the conversation. "Is it possible that what's coming down the road is what we're looking for. Have we flushed them?"

"We'll get a good look at them when they pass by," Lt. Commander Hernandez answered. "Given the number of people beating these hills looking for something like us, we must have them scared. What should I do if the trucks coming down the road look like they are carrying missiles?"

"What's the chances of an ambush?"

"We're not in the best spot for it. That would have been back down the road about three miles. The canyon is pretty wide here, but if we pick the right vehicle to blow up we might stop them for a while."

"If we can get them sitting still for a while, we've got them," the admiral answered. "Set it up. Use the C-4. Don't take risks going for a sure kill. Just stop them and get you and your men back as far away from the road as you can. We'll target the SLAMs for your current coordinates. We'll put the MRPV over the target to guide the shots. Don't be heroes trying to stay too close to the action. I want you mopping up after we take the shots. I don't want the leaders getting away into the jungle after we take out their weapons."

"Aye!" Hernandez answered, cutting the communication so he could get to work. He ordered Captain Torres to find a spot with a view of the road while he and the other two men fixed an explosive charge.

The team only carried a small amount of C-4 in one of the packs. They would just get one chance. It took less than five minutes to bury the charge in the middle of the road.

"Ramon, can you see anything yet?" Wade asked. They were using first names as call signs to keep it simple.

"I can hear the truck sounds without amplification, but they are still a long way off, over on the other side of the ridge line. They're moving but they don't sound like they are getting any closer."

"The MRPV should be overhead in a few minutes. That can tell us what they are doing and whether or not we have a real target coming this way."

The USS Hercules.

Gus watched the scrolling screen as the MRPV covered ground. The scanner was on visual as the drone flew over Alpha team's position. Gus could make out the thin line of the road that Alpha team had been following. The MRPV was

199

climbing for more altitude as it followed the road up over the ridge line. On the other side of the ridge line, the video screen showed the road tying into another road that ran parallel along the ridge line. Melendez had to fly a circle before she spotted a convoy of vehicles moving slowly along the mountain road. The TV screen showed more than a dozen vehicles spread out. They could make out several small-and medium-sized trucks, a couple of jeeps and what looked like a bus. The last two vehicles were big trucks carrying covered loads on flatbed trailers. None of the vehicles in the convoy had their lights on.

"Shit!" Melendez swore. "Look at this. They passed the turn-off that would have taken them toward Alpha's ambush. They are heading down the other side of the mountain into central Luzon."

"Where are they going?" Gus asked, looking toward Colonel Ziga.

"There's not supposed to be a road there. It must head into the upper Cagayan Valley," Colonel Ziga said. "It will be slow, tough going until they get down to Maddela. But once they are on the highway, they can go any place on the island of Luzon they want. They got away from us." Ziga's voice carried a load of bitter defeat.

"Not yet," Gus said. "But let's make sure that convoy's got everything we want in it. Kathy, take the MRPV back to where we spotted what we thought was the headquarters. Let's check it out and see what's happened since we last looked at it."

Five minutes later the drone was circling over the site where they had thought the headquarters had been located.

"Take it down low," Gus said. "If they have all cleared out, no one will hear it. We have to know if they are still there."

"They're gone," Melendez said after a few minutes. "I can't see any signs that they left anyone behind. They've even taken the generators with them. The generators must have been mounted on trucks. Look at the site that we thought was the missiles launch area. Those trucks we spotted warming up on the first pass are gone. They must have moved out right after we pulled the MRPV back for refueling."

"Those trucks have to be mobile launch carriers," Gus said. "But is that all of them? If it is, they only have two missiles left. Kathy, take the MRPV back over the convoy. I want to get the best look we can."

A few minutes later, the MRPV was flying slow circles over the convoy still moving down the road.

"How low can you take it?" Gus asked.

"If I take it any lower, someone might hear it. I've got to be careful I don't get her below our line of sight too."

"Let's take the chance on someone hearing us," Gus answered. "That convoy will be putting out a lot of engine and road noise. Risk that, but don't risk the line of sight."

Another five minutes passed before Gus had the frozen frame showing one of the two larger trucks. The load on the flatbed was covered by tarps, but the tarp hid something long and narrow.

"It's definitely long enough," Kathy whispered. "It's got to be a mobile launcher with one SCUD missile loaded on her. It must be a real primitive launcher. It probably takes them hours to set up and aim it, but it will do the job."

"Get the drone out of there before someone does hear it. Kathy, what's the chances of hitting a moving target with those SLAMs?"

"It's high risk. We have to hit right on target to take them out, and we can't do that if they're moving too fast. It will take me some time to program the target data and set up the target navigation codes. We'd have to take the shots in tandem. The MRPV system can direct only one missile at a time. Our best hope would be if we could stop the convoy. That's why that ambush we had planned would have worked. I had the location and Alpha would have stopped them."

"If they get off that mountain, we're not going to get another chance at them," Orlando whispered.

"I know," Gus admitted. He turned to Melendez. "Can we do this. We use the MRPV to scout the road ahead of them. We find a spot a ways out in front of them, maybe a place with a switchback or something that we know will slow them way down. We mark it and get the coordinates from the MRPV. You feed the data into the guidance systems, and we launch when the convoy hits the spot you set for the target. The MRPV will be overhead to guide each SLAM in. We put the first one in on top of the lead missile truck. We look at the damage and then take the second shot. Maybe one of our teams can get in position up on top so you can shoot those second two SLAMs with laser beam guidance."

"It could work, but no guarantees. We can't leave the MRPV out there while I program the missiles. We can only keep her over the target for about forty minutes, and we've spent twenty-five of those already. By the time we get her back here, refueled, and back over the target, we're talking about a good two hours. It's going to be hard to figure where they are in exactly two hours with only a forty minute target time for the MRPV."

"We can give her more than forty minutes over target," Gus said. "We don't have to bring the drone back home if we get the hits we want. If we don't get those hits, we're out of business anyway."

Kathy had been flying the drone as she talked, directing it forward of the convoy, looking for the spot to aim at. "I've got a target spot," she said, after a few minutes. "Look at those series of switchbacks. The road doesn't look wide enough for those trucks to make the turns without backing up. They'll be on that stretch for an hour at least."

She turned and looked behind her "Jack, can you fly this thing back? I want to start programming the SLAMs."

Kathy slid out of the seat in front of the CRT, and Jack

Phillips took her place.

Gus turned to Sgt. Younce who was still operating the NCS. "Pass a message to Alpha and the other teams. Tell them to move up over the ridge line and see if they can get into position to watch what's happening. They may be able to see the road up from the top of the ridge."

The submarine Kimch'aek.

Captain First Rank Kim Tae-Woo looked carefully over the data sheet his electronic intelligence surveillance officer had just handed him. The officer and the crew he commanded had been monitoring the electronic communications of the American hydrofoil since she had reappeared offshore.

Captain Kim Tae-Woo had his ship exactly where he wanted it. The boat was resting on the bottom in water shallow enough to allow the *Kimch'aek's* periscope antenna to peek above the water. The captain was almost positive that what peeped out of the water was not enough to register on the American ship's radar screen. The antenna housing had been specifically designed to absorb rather than reflect radar signals.

Hiding on the bottom and gathering signal intelligence, was an activity that the crew of the *Kimch'aek* had lots of experience doing. One of the major responsibilities of the North Korean submarine fleet was signal intelligence collection. Every North Korean sub captain had spent long hours sneaking through the waters off South Korea attempting to learn what aggressions the South Koreans were planning next.

Captain Kim's ship was resting on a shallow bar about four miles off the coast. His hope had been that the American ship would move back close to the beach to either unload intel teams or pick men up who had been previously dropped. If he could get the American ship inside a semicircle that stretched

203

for ten miles in either direction, he would be able to set up a salvo of torpedo resolutions with angles that the American ship would not be able to escape, if he could catch the hydrofoil while she was on her hull. His plan was to fire the torpedoes, then surface, elevate his missile tubes and fire his surface-to-surface missiles.

Captain Kim had begun the night prepared for the possibility that the American would not show up and ready to wait for a dozen nights if required. But the American had come. The *Kimch'aek's* passive sonar ears had picked up the hydrofoil's sounds while she was still more than forty nautical miles away. His sonar crew had tracked the ship as she made the run up the coast and then doubled back. They picked up the sounds of the sonobuoys as they dropped in the water.

Instead of heading into shore like he hoped, the American hydrofoil had slowed down to hull speed and had been doing figure eights at such a slow speed that the sonars were picking up the sound only occasionally. She was too far away for a torpedo shot, and Captain Kim didn't dare try and move closer.

Disappointed, Captain Kim had gone back to doing what he knew best, collecting signal intelligence. That is how he had learned that the American hydrofoil was using a drone.

The most serious problem with command controlled drone aircraft is that the controller must be in constant communication with the drone. The problem becomes even more complex with a data collection drone because the communications channel must transmit in both directions on more than one frequency. For the drone operator, there is the dual risk that an enemy will capture the aircraft itself by taking over or jamming the frequency with a stronger signal, or he will intercept and decode the data collected. The MRPV communication system used high tech security countermeasures that included hardening again jamming, synchronized frequency-hopping, the use of UHF line-of-sight frequencies, and sophisticated coding procedures.

Those systems presented the signal intelligence team on board the *Kimch'aek* with enough problems that it had taken them three hours to figure out what the *Hercules* was doing. But once they had it figured out, they had been able to pick up and follow the drone as it has passed over them on its way back from its second mission. The evidence was all summarized in the sheet of figures that Captain Kim was now looking at.

"The Americans are clever," the captain said to the signal intelligence officer, Captain Third Rank Park Hyong-sop. "They didn't land teams like we thought they did. They have been using the drone aircraft to search for Colonel Cho and his weapons. The Filipinos have been searching for ghosts while that spy in the sky must be watching every move they make."

"Shall we raise the transmit antenna?" Captain Park Hyong-sop asked. "We must let Colonel Cho know what the Americans are doing."

"It may be too late for that. If the drone found what it was looking for, the American will launch his weapons before we can do anything," Captain Kim said. "But if it is not too late, I think Colonel Cho will appreciate much more our telling him how we have resolved his problem rather than if we do nothing but scare the American away. Let's hope they launch their toy aircraft one more time."

Captain Kim shouted a detailed list of orders for his crew to follow. The political officer smiled as he listened to the captain's orders. A successful mission was always good for careers.

Chapter Twenty

The USS Hercules.

Everything was ready to go. Kathy had the two SLAMs programmed and the MRPV was fueled up and waiting for launch on the forward deck. Gus was standing on the outside deck, watching three crewmen put the MRPV in position on the small catapult ramp. It was almost five o'clock in the morning. The long line of dawn was showing in the east. No one on board the *Hercules* was complaining about having been up all night.

For the last thirty minutes the *Hercules* had been moving toward the distant shoreline, still at hullborne speed. It was risky, but Gus wanted to cut the distance the MRPV would have to fly as much as possible to extend the over target time.

"Launch the MRPV," Gus ordered. Kathy Melendez was already inside sitting at the control console. Gus stood on the deck watching as the crew started the twin motors on the MRPV and launched the small plane into the early morning air. He watched the drone climb, the wings catching the first rays of the morning sun as the drone gained altitude. He turned and walked toward the hatch leading into the control center. As he stepped through the door the sonar operator called out a warning.

"I've got the sub! She's moving . . . she's blowing water. She's coming up."

"Shit!" Gus exploded. "What's her position?"

"She's between us and the shore, maybe six miles from us."

"Prepare to launch a Harpoon as soon as you have radar lock," Gus called out. "Bring ship to bearing 275."

"I've got her on the MRPV screen," Kathy called out. "The sub is surfacing."

"We've got active radar from her," a man on another monitor in the crowded control room called out. "It's in the antiaircraft bands."

"Get the MRPV away from her," Gus ordered. "That sub will have SAM missiles mounted on the deck that don't have to be manned. They can fire the SAMs as soon as she clears the surface. Do we have a weapon lock?"

"We have a lock!"

"Torpedoes in the water!" sonar shouted. "One . . . two . . . three . . ." He counted all the way to six. "They're all coming at us."

"Pilothouse!" Lt. Phillips barked into the communications mike he was wearing in front of his lips. "Give us hull speed immediately. As soon as we fire the Harpoon, put her into a sharp 180 degree turn and take her out to sea."

"Unfriendly weapons radar!"

"Radar jamming on!"

"SAMS in the air after the bird!" Melendez called out.

"Fire Harpoon!"

The ship shook with the roar of the rocket engine as the Harpoon was launched.

"Harpoon away!"

"I've lost signal from MRPV! One of the SAMS got her," Kathy cried out.

"Torpedoes closing in."

"We have a hit. The Harpoon got her. Holy Jesus!" The words came in over the communications network from Lt. JG Bradley in the pilothouse. "We've got a major and secondary explosions at target."

The *Hercules* went into a tight turn as the wheel man in the pilothouse punched in the computer commands that controlled the hydrofoil steering. The *Hercules* was already flying on her foils, but not yet up to enough speed to outrun the torpedoes.

"She's blowing sky-high and burning. It looks like she's going right back to the bottom," Lt. JG Bradley reported.

"What about torpedoes?" Gus asked the sonar man.

"The sonobuoys are reporting they're crossing the buoy line right now. That puts them about three thousand yards behind us."

The *Hercules* was heading toward open water and still picking up speed.

"We'll outrun them," Jack Phillips whispered, his voice calm. "At least we will if they're Russian 533s. Their maximum speed is 46 knots and they can only run for twelve nauticals. The sub skipper knew he wouldn't get us with the torpedoes when he shot them. He was hoping that if he gave us enough different kinds of troubles, something would get through. He was probably going to shoot his whole load of surface-to-surface missiles as soon as he got his launch tubes elevated. If he had gotten them away at that close range, he might have gotten us, too."

"She's under," the pilothouse announced. "I see no evidence of survivors in the water. We sunk the bastard."

Gus looked around. No one was cheering. They were all looking at the screen full of static on the CRT in front of Kathy.

"He sunk us too," Gus said, feeling very tired. "Without the MRPV, we're out of business."

"What should I tell the teams?" Sgt. Younce asked.

Gus had to think about it for a bit. "Tell them what happened. Tell Alpha to go ahead and check out where we thought the headquarters was. We want to make sure we flushed out Sorreno and his weapons systems. Tell the other three teams to pull back to the coast. We'll pick them up as soon as they can get back to the coast. We had better go find a place to hide until then."

He turned and looked at Jack Phillips. "Are we safe from those torpedoes yet?"

"We should run for at least forty nautical miles in case the Russians sold them the new 65 660s."

"Let's not assume they didn't. I just blew this whole operation by assuming that sub commander wouldn't risk his ship to shoot down a drone aircraft."

"He wasn't just trying to get the drone, he tried damn hard to get us," Phillips pointed out. "He might have made it if he'd had antiship missiles that could have been launched through his torpedo tubes."

"Admiral," Sgt. Younce called out a few moments later. "Look at this message from Alpha Team. Commander Hernandez suggests that we send Delta or Baker to check out the headquarters site. Alpha wants to keep on the tail of that convoy."

Gus stepped over to read the message on the CRT screen in front of Sgt. Younce. The message suggested that the convoy, especially the heavy trucks, would have to move at a crawl down the mountainside, given the condition of the mountain roads. There was a slim chance that if Alpha hotfooted it, they might catch up with the convoy if it got stuck somewhere. Even if they didn't, they could keep following them, maybe find out where they were going.

"That would keep this alive," Melendez said from behind Gus. "All it would take is one breakdown and we could have them. We have the two SLAMs that will ride a laser beam. We don't need the MRPV if we've got a team on the ground with a laser sight."

Gus turned back to Sgt. Younce. "Tell Alpha they have a go. Send Delta in to check out where the headquarters was. Tell them to be *damn* careful."

He turned back to Jack Phillips. "We have to stay handy during daylight hours in case we get a chance for a shot. Once you're sure we don't have any torpedoes chasing us, let's head for this coast along here." He walked over to the chart table and pointed to the coast south of Baler Bay. "It looks pretty wild along here. We should be able to find a bay to hide out in. Keep the radar on. Somebody else has got to be looking for us. Do we know if the sub sent any radio messages before we sunk her?"

"I've looked over the signal monitoring tapes," WO Hanson reported. "She did. It fits the pattern of a coded burst transmission. She got it off a couple of seconds before the Harpoon hit her."

The upper Cagayan Valley.

Colonel Cho wiped sweat off his forehead again. Sweat soaked the jungle-green shirt he wore, sticking it to his skin. The tropical sun climbing into the sky promised even hotter weather within the hour.

At least it wasn't raining. They were moving slow enough as it was, mud would make it almost impossible. Still, they were alive and the operation was still intact. Cho Chae-Jin had no doubt that his decision to abandon the jungle headquarters was responsible for that. The shortwave radio discussion he'd just finished with the Captain of the *Kyong Ki* was the proof. Captain Kang Ae Kyong had passed on to Cho the last radio transmission from the *Kimch'aek*.

The *Kimch'aek* had reported the existence of a drone aircraft and the intent of the *Kimch'aek's* skipper to shoot the aircraft down. Other reports from NPA teams operating along the coast had confirmed the *Kimch'aek's* success in destroying the drone, but the crew had paid the ultimate price for doing so.

Not knowing that the *Hercules* might have a drone aircraft

had been a major intelligence failure. The message from Pyongyang with the description of how dangerous the American ship could be should have also warned Colonel Cho about the possibility of a drone aircraft. The *Kimch'aek* and her crew existed no more, but the American hydrofoil was still out there, even if she no longer had her eyes.

Because of the bravery of a submarine captain and his crew, and Colonel Cho's own foresight, *Strike Back* was still alive, but the idiots in Pyongyang could not take any credit for that. If they had given him the authority to move against the American base when he wanted to, the base would have been destroyed before the sacrifice of the *Kimch'aek* and the prize would already be in their hands.

Now Pyongyang would have to give him the approval to go ahead with the plan, but they would have to wait for a day or so. It would take time to move the missile launchers into a safe place and reprogram them. And while they did that, who could know what the admiral on the American hydrofoil might be scheming to do?

Colonel Cho hung the mike on the hook of the shortwave radio and stood back away from the jeep in which he and Sorreno had been riding. He looked up the hill above him as the second of the two missile launchers backed slowly down a stretch of steep grade about five hundred yards long. The first truck was already at the bottom of that grade and had backed onto the extension that would allow the driver to pull forward onto the next stretch of downgrade that would take him to where Colonel Cho stood beside the jeep waiting.

The two trucks were backing down every other switchback because they were too long to make a switchback U-turn. The road was an engineering marvel that had been built by NPA hand laborers during the three years of the preparation phase of Operation *Strike Back*. At one point, the ash from Mt. Pinatubo had delayed the work for several weeks. The NPA labor force had not only constructed the road in secret, they had

211

disguised it to look like nothing but a jungle mountain trail from the air.

It was no superhighway and the going was slow. The convoy had averaged no more than five or six miles an hour. Luckily there had been no serious delays, but for the whole day they were going to be exposed. The American satellites were sure to spot them in the open. They would have to keep moving and hoping that the American government was not smart enough to do what their outlaw admiral had tried to do.

"Colonel Primero!" Aguila Sorreno called out as he came walking up from where he had been talking to some of his men riding in another vehicle. Primero was Cho's code name in the Philippines. "You can stay standing here in the sun watching those trucks crawl like caterpillars on a hot rock if you prefer, but I'm going to Manila as fast as I can get there. I do not intend to spend one more night on this hillside. Antonio Estuar and Comrade Jose can stay with the missiles and make sure they get to their destination. Tonight, I sleep in the luxury a great leader deserves. Tomorrow I address my people in person, not from a television set."

"I agree that you and I do not have to guard the weapons, and I would like a bath as much as you," Colonel Cho answered. "But I suggest you stay with television appearances for a while. That American admiral is still out there and the missiles he carries will reach into Manila if he knows where you are standing. His missiles are so accurate that he can take out the podium you are standing on and leave the first rows of your crowd unhurt."

"The American admiral will not bother us for much longer. You were wrong in insisting that I send my planes to look for the admiral near Subic Bay. I have already directed them to fly back to where he sunk your submarine. Colonel Drilon tells me that six more AFP pilots have joined our side including one who can fly an F-5. Chuey is putting them all in the

212

air with promises of promotion and a place in the new order for the one who sinks that damn ship."

"I thought we destroyed all the F-5s at Sangley Point," Cho said.

"One was on a training flight to Nicolas when we bombed Sangley field. The Cessna is flying the pilot up there right now. By mid-afternoon, he should be hunting the American admiral."

Colonel Cho walked around and climbed into the back-seat of the jeep. "So, if we are going to Manila today, let's go."

As he settled into his seat, he kept his anger hidden. It was already starting to happen. Now that they were leaving the jungle hideout, Sorreno was showing his independence. Ordering his planes back to the eastern side of Luzon was exactly what should be done. But it would have been better if Colonel Cho had first gotten the okay from Pyongyang. All would be okay, though, if the F-5 took care of the damned admiral and his strange ship.

Lt. Commander Wade Hernandez watched the men climb into the back of the jeep and head down the road. Wade was looking through ten-power binoculars but the distance was so far that he couldn't make out the details or even be sure if the taller of the two men was Aguila Sorreno. As he watched them pull out and drive on down the road, it looked like the men in the first jeep and in the two jeeps trailing behind were leaving the missiles to follow behind them.

Hernandez watched as the second missile truck finished backing down the switchback and started forward again. Hernandez had climbed out on the overview twenty minutes too late. If he could have gotten there when the first truck was still backing down the stretch of mountain road, it would have been the perfect chance to set up a SLAM shot. Now the trucks were moving again, and as he watched, they moved out of his view around a curve.

Wade and his team were not catching up, they were falling behind. Most of the time, the missile trucks were not in view. When they were, it was never long enough to set up a shot with a line-of-sight laser guidance beam.

Swearing silently, Wade pulled back off the rock he had been lying on, and slid on his belly toward the road until he was sure they couldn't see him from below. As he stood up, he heard the voice of Hoppy Yarcia on the tactical no-hands radio set he was wearing.

"There's a guard post around the next corner," Hoppy reported in a whisper. "It's like that one we hit last night. I see only a couple of men on duty."

"Can we work around them?"

"Probably, but you may not want to do that. Guess what's parked right beside their little guard post."

"A car?"

"We're not that lucky. Will you settle for a motorcycle?"

"Does it look like it will run?"

"I don't think they carried it up here. If we had a motorcycle, a couple of us might be able to keep up with that convoy."

"Can we take them without a lot of noise?"

"I think so. Torres and Mitra are working their way up the hill from this side. They'll cross the little ridge above us. If they can get into position where they have a view, maybe they can take them with a couple of shots."

"Let's try it," Lt. Commander Hernandez agreed. "Where are you?"

"Up in front of you. I've got a view on them, but not a shot at both of them."

Hernandez moved forward, taking it slow, trying not to make any noise. He was almost to the bend in the road when he heard two bangs; they were loud, but not too loud. Someone had fired one of the silenced M-16s.

214

"That was me," Yarcia's voice came in through the earplug. "One of them walked out of the post to take a piss and the other guy was watching him. Both were looking away from me. It was too good a chance to miss."

Wade hurried around the corner. Hoppy Yarcia stood half-way between the bodies lying in the dirt by the little guard station. This guard post didn't have a bamboo rail blocking the road, just a small guard shack.

Both men had been shot in the head; one from behind, the second from the front. The frontally assaulted man must have been twisting around to see where the first shot had come from. His fly was open and his cock exposed. He had been dressed in a light blue denim jacket and blue jeans. The second corpse wore crudely sewn pants and a shirt made out of jungle-green, cotton cloth. The were both wearing heavy ammo belts held up with shoulder harnesses, and they both had white sneakers on their feet. The sneakers on the corpse in jungle green looked almost new. Those on the other man were coming apart at the sole lines.

Hoppy saw Wade. He smiled a greeting, then turned and walked toward the motorcycle that stood leaning on its kick-stand. The motorcycle was a Yamaha Trail bike, one of the smaller models with a 250cc engine.

Hoppy slung his rifle over his shoulder. He wasn't wearing his pack. He grabbed the handlebars of the motorcycle, threw his leg over the machine so he straddled the seat, then dropped one hand to turn on the ignition key. He put his hand back on the throttle handle, twisted it a couple of times, and kicked down on the starter. The engine caught on the third try. Yarcia turned around and smiled a wide grin at Wade as Captain Torres and Sgt. Mitra came walking down off the hillside.

"We can't all ride it," Wade pointed out.

"We break up the team for awhile," Hoppy said. "We've got no choice. Let me and Ramon ride the cycle. Once we get to

215

Maddela, we're on familiar ground. We can follow those missiles to wherever they go. We'll dump most of our gear and live off the land if we have to."

"You've got to take the EPUU," Wade said. "It won't do any good if you find out where they are taking those missiles if you can't tell the *Herk* the coordinates."

"What about we take the little radios and relay through you?"

"Those are only good for line of sight," Wade said. "I'm high enough that maybe you'll never get out of line of sight, but we can't count on it. You have to take the laser beam generator, too."

"I think you better come," Hoppy said. "I'm not that good with that high tech equipment and neither is Ramon."

It was exactly what Lt. Commander Hernandez wanted, and he'd been ready to insist on it if Major Yarcia hadn't suggested it first.

"You'll stick out like a neon light on a whorehouse, carrying that thing on your back," Torres said.

"Maybe we can fit it into that backpack," Wade said, pointing to a pack that one of the dead NPA soldiers had set beside the trail bike.

"We'll take the C-4 too," Hoppy added.

"That's going to be a lot to carry. You're going to get spotted immediately," Ramon said. He wasn't ready to give up his position on the two man team.

"If we can get off this mountain, I don't think so," Hoppy said. "These bastards haven't had time to take every motorcycle in Luzon away from the owners. We'll stay back, just close enough to keep our eyes on those trucks. As long as we can keep everything in just one pack we'll look like two more men going to town. Maybe we can pass for NPA."

Hoppy got off the machine, turned the switch off and walked over to where one of the dead NPA soldiers was laying. He stooped and started to strip the body of its clothing.

"We'll last longer if we don't look so much like AFP," he said, looking up. "That's why I took the head shots. We can wear their clothes. We'll blend in with the crowd. Maybe we can pass as NPA. Things have to be real confused down there."

"I'll wear my own pants," Wade said as he bent over the second corpse. "This one shit in his and they're too small for me anyway."

"Change shoes with them, too," Sgt. Mitra suggested. "And put on those ammo belts."

"We can carry the M-16s, but without those fancy scopes," Hoppy suggested. "This one already had an M-16, but I'd rather take my own. It's in better condition."

The second guard, the one dressed civilian, had been armed with an old World War II, M-1 rifle. Most of the weapons the NPA carried had been taken away from the Philippine Army or the Constabulary. The NPA had received almost nothing in the way of arms shipments from any of the bloc countries, until someone had decided to give them nuclear weapons.

Hoppy stuck his hand in the back pocket of the pants he had stolen and pulled out a small leather folder. He opened the folder, then turned it up for the others to see. "Look at this," he announced. "I even have ID. I'm Sergeant Ramulo of the NPA."

Wade found similar ID in the pants pocket of the other corpse. He had to wipe blood and fecal material off it before he put it in his pocket.

The two men said goodbye and drove down the road; Wade Hernandez riding tandem behind Hoppy Yarcia.

Ramon Torres and Primo Mitra watched until the men on the motorcycle disappeared around a curve. Then they hauled both the naked bodies into the bush to hide them. That done, they carried the extra equipment that the other two had left behind another three hundred yards deeper into a canyon where they buried it under rocks and bush. After

217

that, they headed down the road hoping they would find their own motorcycles.

The USS Hercules.

"We have a radar contact! Incoming aircraft at 348 degrees. Sixty miles out at fifteen thousand feet." The voice came over the intercom from the radar operator in the control center. Gus was standing on the deck of the pilothouse. He looked quickly around but could see nothing.

"It's coming fast. About five hundred knots. It's got us on radar."

"Take her up to foil speed," Gus ordered. "Set course at 90 degrees."

He felt the thrust of power under his feet as the GE gas turbine engine took over the drive from the diesel that drove at hull speed.

"Is it one of ours?" Gus demanded, speaking into his communications intercom mike.

"Not unless they've changed the identification codes on us since we went outlaw," the radar operator answered.

"Fire control, lock the Mk 75mm on her, but don't fire unless she fires at us. I don't want to shoot down one of our own aircraft."

Orlando Ziga climbed into the pilothouse through the ladder hole. "The Philippine Air Force has some F-5s," he said.

"Then it's not going to be friendly. One of your pilots must have joined up with the new Air Force. You know what she might be carrying in the way of ship killers?"

"I don't think anything special. You talked us out of buying Harpoons and you wouldn't sell us the SLAMs. She may have old-fashioned ballistic rockets, but nothing more."

"Thank God for that."

"She's at ten miles and ten thousand feet," radar announced. "She's coming straight at us. I don't have any weapons radar locks coming from her."

"I have a visual", one of the crewmen standing watch announced. "It's an F-5."

Gus raised his binoculars to his eyes. He watched as the plane crossed directly over the *Hercules* and then pulled into a wide turn that took it in a circle around the ship. Gus could make out a red star insignia on the wings. The tail still had the old Philippine flag painted on it.

"He's talking on the radio," the radio operator reported. "He's reporting our position and asking for orders. He sounds damned excited and very young."

"Can you pick up the other station?"

"Negative!"

The plane above them suddenly broke out of the circle it had been flying. It flew toward the southwest, heading into the afternoon sun that had already started to sink toward the horizon. Gus could no longer see him because of the sun.

It was almost two minutes before radar announced that the plane was making a turn.

"He's coming back our way. He's at eight thousand feet and dropping altitude fast."

"The stupid kid is going to try a strafing attack out of the sun," Gus blurted into the hot mike in front of his lips. "He's been watching too many old war movies."

"He's five miles out at five thousand feet and coming fast," radar announced.

"Open fire!" Gus ordered, almost reluctantly.

The Mk 75mm, already pointed toward the sun, started barking, the muzzle flashing. At almost the same instant a brace of four rockets tore across the sky above the pilothouse and splashed into the ocean off the starboard bow, the explosions sending columns of water harmlessly in the air. Because of the sun, no one saw the explosion as the diving airplane blew up, but they heard the sound rolling in shortly after radar confirmed they had a hit. Pieces of airplane floated out of the sunlight as they fell toward the water.

"Fucking dumb kid," Gus muttered. "Keep her on course and at hull speed," he ordered the helmsman before he climbed down the ladder to the command center below. Orlando Ziga followed him.

"There will be others coming after him," he told Jack Phillips. "Some of them may not be so young and dumb. We've got no way of knowing how many planes they have."

"I'm surprised they had any F-5s," Ziga said. "I thought all of them had been destroyed at Sangley Point."

"Obviously at least one of them wasn't," Gus said. "That's why we don't want to assume anything. Our best bet for now is to take her to open sea on a straight run. Maybe we can convince them we're giving it up and running for the American fleet out there. Then we can sneak back at night."

"What do we do if Alpha team gets a spot on those missiles?" Kathy Melendez asked. "If we go much farther out to sea, we'll be out of range for the SLAMs."

"If we get the word the missiles are sitting still, we make a run back in at full speed while you program the guidance systems. We'll launch as soon as we are in range."

"We do much more running back and forth, we're going to have a major fuel problem," Jack Phillips said. "We're down to less than half of what we had when we left that sub."

"I know," Gus answered. "I hope to Hell those missile launchers stop somewhere for the night. What do we hear from Alpha?"

"Commander Hernandez and Major Yarcia are still following behind the launch trucks on the motorcycle," Sgt. Younce reported. "They just passed through a small town named Abbag. The trucks are moving slowly, but they are moving. Sometimes, they stop for something, but never more than five or ten minutes. Commander Hernandez reports that the chief heffy has left the convoy and gone on ahead."

220

"Where do you think Sorreno went?" Lt. Phillips asked.

"I'd bet he's heading right for Manila," Gus answered. "He's supposed to be the new head of state. He must have finally figured out he's safer in Manila than he is in the jungle."

"Remember, the plan was to take him out, as well as his weapons," Ziga said.

"I know, but the weapons are first priority," Gus answered. "Now that we know how many weapons they have, we can't miss an opportunity to defang the bastard."

"Can we be sure those two missiles on those trucks are the only weapons he has?" Ziga asked.

"Not positive," Gus answered. "But I've got one good reason to make that assumption. We've sunk a sub and we shot down a plane. That's all the provocation they needed to destroy Subic Bay. If they had a missile ready to fire, they would have already shot it. But they can't shoot those missiles while the launchers are driving down the road. They have to park them, program them, and elevate them before they shoot them. That's going to take them awhile. If Wade and Hoppy can stay with them, as soon as they park them, we take them out."

Chapter Twenty-one

Santiago, the Philippines.

Hoppy and Wade sat on metal stools on opposite sides of a rusty metal table with a battered Formica top. The sun went down as both worked on dishes of *Pancit Guisado,* baked Chinese noodles mixed with pieces of shrimp, pork, and vegetables. Almost as hungry as they were tired, they ate without talking to each other.

From where Hoppy sat, he could see the two trucks they were following. The trucks and the other vehicles in the convoy were parked on the side of the main road that ran through the city of Santiago. The convoy had been parked there for almost twenty minutes, but Hoppy and Wade didn't expect they would be there much longer.

Wade had thought about trying to set up a shoot while the drivers ate dinner, but had decided against it for two reasons. First they were in the middle of a city, and second, Wade couldn't spot a good high point from where they could throw a laser guide beam.

Looking around the streets of Santiago, the two men could initially see little visible impact of the sudden change in government.

Groups of noisy people still clogged a street or two as they celebrated their sudden victory over the central government, but the celebration was losing steam. Except for the streets where the crowds were marching, about the same number of people were out and about in the early evening hours as would have been in ordinary times. The restaurants were still serving, most of the Chinese merchants were still in their shops, and brightly decorated pedi-cabs still carried passengers. An occasional jeepney moved along the street, picking up and letting passengers off every few hundred feet.

There were lots of bicycles, about half as many motorcycles as more normal times, a smattering of trucks and buses, an occasional jalopy, and almost no new cars. The new cars that did come down the street always carried well armed men dressed in the same kind of clothing and battle gear that Hoppy and Wade wore.

There were some observed differences. Every gas station was closed. Posters displayed around the city announced the gas stations would soon be open and gave directions where people were to register for ration cards for gasoline. Other posters demanded that all private firearms be immediately turned in, instructed citizens on how to obtain one of the new ID cards that the new government was issuing, and offered big rewards for turning in any official or officer of the previous government or its military forces.

The two men had seen no policemen in uniform, but gangs of men and women wearing the colors of NPA were trying to act like policemen. None of them demonstrated any evidence of strict discipline and most seemed to be doing anything they wanted, including settling old grudges. The two men had seen several bodies lying in front of a wall that had served as a bullet stop for a firing squad. A block away from the sidewalk café where they were eating noodles, a man dressed in a blue, pin-striped business suit hung from a lamppost.

Hoppy and Wade had found it easier to move through the countryside and the rural towns on a stolen motorcycle than would have been the case when the old national constabulary or the AFP was manning road checkpoints. They had only been stopped twice and asked to explain who they were and what they were doing. Both times Hoppy had flashed the stolen ID card and announced in an officious voice that they were on important business for the new president of the Republic. In each instance, the checkpoint guard had waved them through with salutes.

Using the pretense that they were on the NPA side had worked so well that when they had run low on gas coming into Santiago, they had stopped one of the jeepneys and demanded in the name of the president of the New People's Republic that the driver allow them to siphon off a tank full of gas. They used a plastic tube they found under the seat of the motorcycle to do the job.

For now, the country didn't have a new government; it had *no* government. That wouldn't last long and the TV set in the café where they had bought the noodles was spouting a continuing blast of propaganda about what the NPA government was going to do. But, as long as the disorder lasted, Hoppy and Wade felt safe following behind the convoy. However, they would be in trouble if they ran into some NPA officer with the smarts to ask a few questions about what provincial NPA unit they belonged to.

"It looks like they're saddling up again," Hoppy said.

"Shit!" Wade swore. "I keep hoping they're going to stop for the night."

"My bet is they'll drive straight down Highway 5, heading for Manila. That's about three hundred kilometers. They'll have plenty of time to get there and hide the missiles under cover someplace before the sun comes up again. They're driving at night because they don't want the American satellites to know where they've gone."

"Won't they be surprised at what happens as soon as they think they're safe," Wade said with a smile as he stood up from the stool. "It's your turn to drive."

Thirty miles south of Santiago, the two men pulled off the road for a few minutes while Commander Hernandez raised the antenna on the EPUU and relayed a quick position and situation report to the *Hercules*.

The USS Hercules.

The *Hercules* was sailing on her hull with just enough speed to maintain steerage. They were over a hundred miles off the coast in what Gus hoped would be a no-man's sea-lane, not too close to the three hundred mile line that the American fleet was respecting, but closer than any NPA controlled planes would want to fly. The ship was keeping a low radar profile, not using any active radar. They were relying instead on passive radar monitoring and a screen of sonobuoys to warn them of approaching trouble.

While there were lots of radar and sonar static coming from the east where units of the American fleet were operating, they were getting only an occasional signal from the direction of the Philippine coast.

Jones, Ziga, Melendez, and Phillips were sitting around the table in the mess room when Sgt. Younce brought in the report from Hernandez and Yarcia. He also had the latest info on the other three teams. The four officers had finished eating, and each of them had a cup of coffee in front of them. They had spread a map of Luzon on the table in front of them.

"It's still alive," Gus said after reading through the Hernandez report.

"If those two men stay free, we'll have them in the morning," Orlando Ziga added.

"If we can get back into shore close enough to launch," Gus said. "And if we can get a reasonable accurate set of coordinates on their location."

Gus looked next at the latest situation report on the other two teams. Delta had located the NPA headquarters area and confirmed that was what it had been. The site had been abandoned. Baker team was at the site where the MRPV had spotted the trucks. They had located the fixed-launch sites of three weapons used against the AFP. Delta and Baker team both reported large numbers of militia were still beating the bushes looking for saboteurs. Baker Team had made one contact with a small group and exchanged fire. Since that clash, the search activity had intensified.

While the original plan called for the teams to retreat to the coast where the *Hercules* could pick them up, Delta team was proposing that they instead cross the ridge and head down the same road that the missile trucks had taken. They would try to join forces with Captain Torres and Sergeant Mitra. They were already talking to them on the tact radio.

Gus looked at the map for a few moments. "Let's not concentrate the forces like Delta suggests," he said speaking slowly. "I'm going with the bet that both Sorreno and the missile launchers are heading for Manila. Tell Delta to head southwest along the ridge. It will be a long walk before they cross a road, but when they do, it will take them in the direction of Manila. That leaves Charlie and Baker to pick up."

"Instead of picking them up, why don't we tell Baker and Charlie teams to try to make it to Manila on their own," Orlando Ziga suggested. "Going in to pick them up puts the ship at risk and we add nothing to the mission. But if they can get into Manila, they may be able to locate where Sorreno is hiding out. Maybe we can still take out both the missiles and the leadership."

Ziga pointed to the map of Luzon spread on the table. "Yarcia and Hernandez are taking the long way into Manila," he said. "Charlie team is already down the coast road, here. If they can find transportation and head south to Baler, they can cut across to Cabanatuan City. That ties into Route 5 and it'll take them right into Manila. It'll take more time for Baker team to get back to the coast road, but they can do the same thing. That will give us two backup teams right where we need them."

226

Pyongyang, North Korea.

Long after dark, General Bae Bong-Soo sat working in his office in the massive grey building that housed the Defense Ministry. Today, he hadn't been called to the office of the Dear Leader, not even to explain the loss of the *Kimch'aek*. Because Kim Jung Il was never wrong about anything, the Dear Leader had no need to call in those who had been right about something. History would record that Kim Jung Il had supported General Bae's and Colonel Cho's interpretation of what the American hydrofoil was or was not trying to do.

Two sets of orders personally dictated by Kim Jung Il sat on the desk in front of General Bae. The first set directed that the two submarines that the Dear Leader had previously ordered from the North Korea sub base at Cha-ho to the Subic Bay area instead divert to the east coast of Luzon. As the two subs were already in the Luzon Strait, they would be able to arrive on station to start searching for the hydrofoil in only a few hours. The order also directed two of the subs on the west coast of Luzon to sail around the northern tip of the island and join in the search for the American admiral's hydrofoil as fast as possible.

General Bae was sure that the change of tactics had come too late to have any input on the final outcome. The most that either of the subs would be able to do would be to avenge the men of the *Kimch'aek*. General Bae smiled as he looked again at the report received from Colonel Cho earlier in the day. Colonel Cho, with his brilliant decision to move his headquarters and his weapons in a nighttime flight, had saved the operation, even though it had exposed the missiles to possible satellite sightings. Now, thanks to the heroes of the *Kimch'aek*, the American hydrofoil had lost its eyes and would have no way to locate either the missiles or Colonel Cho's new headquarters.

Unfortunately, the commander and the crew of the submarine would get no public credit for their success. Kim Jung Il had decided that his government would not announce nor protest the loss of the *Kimch'aek*. To do so would draw attention to the North Korean support of the NPA, a support that must remain secret in order to avoid American retaliation directed against the homeland.

General Bae picked up the second of the two orders that the Dear Leader had signed late in the afternoon. This was a one paragraph note stating that, effective immediately, General Bae Bong-Soo would be serving as both the Director of Security and as the Director of Intelligence. The order made no mention of General Yoo Jae-Sin. Bae knew he would never see Yoo Jae-Sin's name in print again. General Bae had learned from his own spies where General Yoo was at this very moment. For the last six hours, General Yoo had been waiting outside the Dear Leader's office for the Dear Leader's pet major to come out and tell him the Dear Leader was finally ready to meet with him. When the day had started, General Bae had expected that he would be the one waiting for the Dear Leader's whore to come out and tell him it was time for the axe.

General Bae reached for a pen. The Dear Leader's order had not only given him a second command, it named him as the officer solely responsible for all operational aspects of Operation *Strike Back*. Bae began writing out the orders to be sent to the submarines that would soon be searching for the American hydrofoil. The submarines would learn from both the failures and the successes of the commander of the *Kimch'aek*. Instead of staying in close to shore, they would circle far out to sea and try to catch the American admiral between them and the shore. If they did, they were to wait until the American got as close to shore as possible, then bracket him so that they could fire their torpedoes at angles that would make it impossible for the American to escape.

Of course, the American admiral might be long gone like

the reports from the Philippine search planes were suggesting, but General Bae didn't think so. It was always a mistake to underestimate a clever and committed enemy. The American admiral impressed General Bae as the kind of man who would keep fighting, even after he had been blinded.

The general had one more order to write out, this one directed to his favorite son-in-law. This order instructed Colonel Cho to implement immediately the final phase of *Strike Back*. It was too bad that "immediately" meant a wait of twelve or more hours while they transported the missiles to new positions, set them up, and reprogrammed the guidance systems. But as soon as that was done, one of the weapons would be fired at Subic Bay. That would be the revenge for the *Kimch'aek* and for everything the Americans had done to frustrate the will of the people of North Korea. And they would still have one more weapon to use against whatever force the Americans eventually sent against them, a weapon that could be easily hidden in a shed or a barn to wait until the best target came near.

Aurora Province, the Philippines.

Marine Captain Harold Lee felt a cramp building up in his leg. He flexed his foot, lifting his toes up against the top of his jungle boot, hoping the tension would keep the cramp away. He wasn't that unhappy with the pain he felt. It kept him awake. He'd had been lying on his stomach for almost two hours. His position was a rock outcrop that hung on the side of a hill about twenty feet about the gravel road that wove along the line where the Sierra Madre met the sea.

Captain Joe Pimental and Lt. Wigberto Babijes, the two other members of his team, were both hiding on opposite sides of the road below him, waiting for his signal.

The waiting for a ride to come along was worse than hitchhiking, something he had tried only one time. That was back in his Annapolis days when he had tried to hitchhike down to Falls Church, Virginia, for a weekend with a girl willing to give him no-hassle loving. Dumped at a crossroad outside the Washington, D.C. beltway, he'd spent a cold January night waving his thumb at cars that didn't stop.

Sunday morning, he had no choice but to turn around and start hitching back the way he had come. He had been picked up by a Maryland cop outside of Annapolis, charged with hitchhiking and fined two hundred dollars. The cop and the justice of the peace had accepted his watch, his camera, a silver belt buckle, and his Sony Walkman in lieu of cash. It was the last time he tried to catch a free ride to anywhere.

The position he held gave him a view up the road for about a mile and in the opposite direction for maybe half a mile. As soon as he spotted something coming that looked like it might be worth capturing, he would signal Joe and Wiggie, then cover them when the driver stopped in front of the log laying across the highway.

The coast road of Aurora wasn't a busy highway. Only two sets of vehicles had driven by since Harold had climbed out onto the ledge, the first a four truck convoy that they didn't dare tackle, and the second, a couple of old pickup trucks filled with armed men. Both times, three or four men had jumped down and rolled the log out of the way before driving around it.

As soon as the vehicles had driven out of sight, Joe and Wiggie had rolled the log back across the road and faded back into the bushes. Captain Lee was wondering again if maybe they shouldn't walk the ten miles into Dinalongan and try to steal something parked on the street when he heard another vehicle coming.

The car was driving with the bright lights on. It drove almost to the log before Harold could get a good view inside the vehicle through the night scope. The car looked like a new model Toyota Corolla.

The road was bad enough that the driver was moving at

about twenty miles an hour. He saw the log and screeched to a stop, recognizing it for the danger it was. He backed up, spinning his front wheels to the left, then pulled forward, and saw he wasn't going to make it. He spun the steering wheel back to the right and backed up again. He would have made it on this try except he got panicky and backed two feet too far into the ditch. He was spinning a back wheel that was spitting rock and mud as Joe Pimental and Wiggie Babijes walked up on each side of the road, their M-16s pointed at the vehicle. Wiggie shouted for everyone to get out of the car.

Harold watched through his night scope sight as four people stepped out of the car. The two men who had been in the front seat both carried pistols in leather belt holsters, but neither made a move for the weapons. The old man and old lady who were riding in the backseat did not appear to be armed. As soon as they were out of the car, the old man and the woman fell on their knees and started pleading with the two Philippine members of his team.

When he was sure his men had everything under control, Harold climbed down from his perch and walked up the road. Joe and Wiggie lined the four people up with their hands on top of the car. The old folks were still begging for mercy.

"The driver told us the old man and his wife own a rice mill in Casiguran," Joe whispered to Captain Lee. "They've been hiding out since the country fell and they were trying to sneak south to Cabanatuan City. They all think we're NPA. The driver and the guard claim they were planning on turning the old folks over to the first NPA soldiers they found. The old folks think we're going to shoot them right now."

"So we surprise them and just steal their car. Are they going to be able to survive on foot?"

"They'll be safer than if we took them with us, and a lot safer than if we had let them drive through. The two bodyguards are fools and criminals. I'd do the old folks a favor if I shot the two thugs they hired as bodyguards."

"Don't. They're going to help us push the car out of the

231

ditch. Take their pistols away and give them back to the old man and his wife when we're out of the ditch. Let the old folks decide what happens to the bodyguards."

Ten minutes later, Charlie team was on its way south. Lee was in the backseat, Wiggie was driving, and Joe riding shotgun. The car lights were off and all three men wore their night vision goggles.

The USS Hercules.

Gus stood on the forward deck of the blacked-out *Hercules,* looking out to sea. There was no moon, and all he could see in any direction were stars. It was a little past 2200 hours. The ship was moving on its hull heading back toward the coast, using the darkness to get close enough to make a shot if the chance came.

"Can't sleep?" a feminine voice asked from behind him.

"I tried," he answered, turning to make out the shape of Commander Melendez in the faint starlight. "I keep thinking about this morning, wondering what I did wrong. I should have anticipated that the sub would pop up and shoot down our MRPV. I didn't even consider that possibility."

"I should have thought of it, too," she said, moving to stand beside him at the rail. "I'm the expert in technology. I fell into the same trap you did. You get so used to having all the technology advantage, you forget that the other side can pull technology tricks, too."

"That sub skipper's timing was perfect," Gus said. "He came up at exactly the right moment."

"I'm sure it was the drone radio control frequencies that did us in," Kathy said. "He was monitoring our radio transmissions. He figured out what we were doing, spotted the channels we were using to control the MRPV, waited until we turned on the system when we launched her the last time, and popped up with his surprise. I wasn't so surprised at what he

232

was trying as I was surprised when his missile hit the drone. We thought the infrared signature of the MRPV engines wasn't bright enough for SAM targetting. Either we were wrong, or they improved their guidance technology."

Gus didn't answer. Both stood silently for awhile, each staring into the night.

"You should get some sleep," she said after a while.

She wasn't the first one to tell him that. Both Phillips and Ziga had already done so. He must look like warmed-over shit. He wondered if they had sent her out on the deck to make another try at getting him into a bed. As he thought it, he smiled at the difference the gender made with that idiom. It was too dark for her to see the smile and ask about it.

"I told you, I already tried sleeping," he said. "I guess I've enjoyed the perks of command for too long. I'm not used to sleeping in a bunk with four other men snoring around me."

"That's my fault. You must think it was a terrible mistake to bring me along."

"I do, but not because you're sleeping in a bed I'd be using if you weren't here. I'm going to get you killed. That bothers me a lot."

"Does it bother you anymore that you may get *me* killed than that you may get Jack Phillips or Orlando Ziga killed, or that Howard Sharps did die, and poor Lt. Moleta will die if he doesn't get serious medical attention in the next day or two?"

"I know what you're saying," he answered. "And I know what you women in uniform say about it, that gender shouldn't make a difference in combat, but there is something different that makes me wish I didn't bring you."

"Do you regret coming yourself?"

"Hell no! I even think we still have a chance of making it work. If we do succeed, you're the one who will deserve the credit."

"So you're glad I came, but you wish I hadn't come."

He turned and looked at her, wishing there was enough

233

light to show him the smile she would be wearing.

"I guess that's it," he admitted. "I'm damn glad I brought Lt. Commander Melendez along, but I wish I could have left Kathy Melendez behind."

"Both the Lt. Commander and Kathy are glad we did come," she said, her voice tinkling with a suggestion of a giggle. "The Lt. Commander is glad because she's working with the finest commanding officer she knows," she added, her voice suddenly serious.

He started to say something, but she raised her hand, almost like she was going to touch his lips. "Let me say it. Admiral, you wear command easily. It fits you like an old pair of shoes. You don't have to tell the people you're the boss, you don't have to bark orders, or watch to make sure they salute. You listen when you should and you act without worrying too much about the decision when it's made. You complain about your mistakes, but that's because you admit you have them. It took you less than thirty seconds after we lost the MRPV to come up with alternatives for action."

"You ought to write my next evaluation," he said, trying to make it a joke.

"I'm just telling you why Lt. Commander Melendez is happy she's standing on this deck. You want to know why Kathy Melendez is glad she's here?"

"Tell me."

"Kathy knows she's going to die, sometime for sure, but probably within the next twenty-four hours. She happens to believe that you are right, that everyone at Subic has a very high probability of dying, and maybe sooner than we will. Kathy likes the idea of not just sitting there waiting for it to happen, but trying to stop it from happening with a man like you."

Gus wasn't sure what to say. He wanted to grab her and hold her, and he was half sure she wanted that, too. But admirals don't grab lieutenant commanders and make love on the foredeck. He was honest enough with himself to admit that

234

was what he wanted, to make love to her; to put it crudely, to lay down with her and fuck them both into exhausted sleep.

It had been a long time, years, since he'd wanted to make love to a specific woman like he wanted Kathy. It had been there building with each new crisis. He had tried to analyze and explain it away with Freudian explanations of the stress of battle, mid-life regrets, fear of aging, all the pop arguments used to explain desires that society didn't stamp with approval.

"I guess you're right," he said. "I'll go in and give sleep another try. There's not much that can happen before morning, anyway, not as long as those missiles are rolling down Route 1."

"Can I make a suggestion?" she asked. "Why don't you use the bunk in the CO's cabin. Then you won't have to listen to others snoring. I did get some sleep during the run out to sea. I'll sit up in the mess room while you sleep. I want to work on some firing equations anyway. I want to know how far off I can be if we have to make a snap shot without EPUU position accuracy."

He took her up on the offer. He did need the sleep. They both walked inside and he saw her to the mess room before he let himself into the CO cabin. He stripped to his shorts and crawled into the bunk. Inside the sheets, he could smell her presence. She had worn no perfume, it was the smell of her sweat with the faint, lingering odor of sex.

When he slept, she came to him in his sleep. When he finally woke, he had to think about it to make sure the visit had only been a dream.

Chapter Twenty-two

Aurora Province, the Philippines.

Charlie team drove all the way to the seaside town of Dipaculao and on through the town before they hit the first checkpoint manned by NPA troops. They were moving across a flat valley when they saw the checkpoint about two hundred yards in front of them. Wiggie cut the engine and braked to a stop.

The checkpoint stood on the other side of a bridge that crossed a river. A set of neon lights hung over the entrance to the guardhouse. The sound of a diesel generator revealed the source of the electricity for the lights. At least six men manned the checkpoint and the barrier gate that stretched across the road. A truck and the jeep parked next to the checkpoint suggested more men somewhere nearby.

"I don't think they heard us," Wiggie whispered. "That generator is making too much noise. Shall we try to bluff it through?"

"Not a good idea, not in this sedan," Captain Pimenta whispered.

"Can we dump the car and sneak around them?" Captain Lee asked. "Baler can't be too far, we can steal another car there."

"I think this is the only bridge," Wiggie answered. "If we sneak around we'll have to swim the river."

236

"That's too risky for the equipment, especially the EPUU," Lee answered. "We have to take them. Lieutenant, Joe and I sneak up on them, then you drive the car up like you had the right. We'll take out the guards while they're focusing on you."

"Let's go," Pimental answered.

"Don't open the door," Lee warned. "That'll turn on the interior light. Go through the window."

Both men slithered through windows. On the ground each took one side of the road and started moving up. The last fifty yards, they went on their bellies. It took thirty minutes before Harold Lee was in a position he liked. Almost to the bridge, he had a good view of the two men who were manning the gate on the far side of the bridge. He could see four more men inside the open-sided guard shack. A radio or tape recorder was blasting out a Philippine pop song while the four men played cards.

"You in position?" Lee whispered into the needle mike in front of his lips.

"I've got a good view of the shack, but the bridge cuts off my view of the two men on duty."

"I've got them covered. You take the shack. We do it this way. Wiggie starts his engine, turns on his lights, and heads this way. We wait until he gets almost to the bridge, and we both open up on targets. When Wiggie gets here, we pile into the backseat of the car and keep going."

"Got it," two voices came back.

With the neon lights giving him all the light he needed for iron sights, Captain Lee slipped the complicated night scope off the rifle, put it in a pouch that hung from his webbing, and thumbed the select lever to make sure he was on full auto.

"Okay, Wiggie, now!" he whispered

The lights of the Toyota lit up and the engine roared into

237

life. Both the guards on duty heard the car and saw its lights. Each instantly stripped his weapon from off his shoulder to point it at the oncoming car. One shouted to the men inside the open-sided guard shack. Those four jumped to their feet and moved to the door of the shack.

"On three," Captain Lee whispered as he sighted on the guard standing to his left. "One . . . two . . . three!"

Lee squeezed the trigger for a three-shot burst, saw the target take the hit, and swung to the right. The second target was already swinging the rifle barrel toward him when he squeezed the trigger again. He missed. He'd hurried with the shot. The target dove to the ground, disappearing behind the slope of the bridge. Lee ran forward to the road and ran part way across the bridge. He could hear the sound of the car coming up behind him. He saw the target scrambling across the ground, trying to find cover. Lee raised, aimed, checked himself to make sure he had the target in the sights, and fired.

He turned to the guardhouse. No targets were up. He'd heard the pops of Pimental's silenced weapon. Either Pimental had taken out all four men or they were behind cover. Wiggie screeched to a halt beside him and Harold jumped into the backseat from the left side. He saw Captain Pimental coming from the right, still ten yards away at a run. He saw the flashes from the left and heard the explosive sounds as someone opened up from the guard hut with an unsilenced weapon. Harold fired, shooting across the backseat through the right front window which was down. He fired one burst into the wooden sides of the guard hut, then emptied the rest of the clip into the lights mounted above the guardhouse.

There was instant darkness as he popped the empty clip and shoved in a fresh one. Pimental clawed open the back door. Harold reached out to pull Joe into the car. He felt

238

warm, sticky blood on his hands where he grabbed the arm of Pimental. He could feel more arterial blood spurting onto his hands as he pulled the wounded man off his feet and onto the seat of the car.

"Hit it," he barked as Pimental slid into the car. The tires squealed and the car jumped forward, the back side door still open. They were across the bridge and had smashed through the barrier when more flashes started popping to the side of them. Harold felt the car shake as rounds pounded into it. The car swerved several times and for a moment Harold thought they were going to flip over. Instead it crashed off to the left side of the road.

Wiggie dove out from the front door. The opening door turned on the interior light which attracted an instant burst of automatic weapon fire which kept coming after Wiggie kicked the door shut and killed the light. Harold fell backward out through the back door which didn't activate the dome light. He rolled to his feet and ran fifteen yards to the side, fumbling with the case that held his night vision scope. He hit the ground, and fit the scope back on the rifle.

"Wiggie? You okay?" he whispered into the mike.

"Yo! I count four of them. They must have been sleeping under one of those trucks."

Harold secured the sight, set it for enhanced light, and lifted it to his eye. He had a view across the roadway. He swung slowly from left to right, caught the four soldiers in the green tinted night vision light and found a fifth, this one farther back, hiding behind a pile of rock. The man behind the rock was covering the other four who were moving cautiously toward the car, crouched, but on their feet. They were putting their trust in the night to keep them hidden.

"I've got a fifth one," Harold whispered into the tactical

radio. He flipped his selector lever to semi-automatic. "I'll take him first . . . Now!" He squeezed and saw the target shake with the force of the hit, then slip down the rock pile. He heard the snaps of Lt. Babijes's silenced weapon as he brought his own weapon back to where the four targets had been advancing. All four were on the ground. Two sprawled out in odd positions; the second two hugged the ground, but looked alive and well. They still trusted the night to keep them hidden. Harold aimed at one and fired, swung to the last, who was swinging to fire at Harold's flashes. Harold fired again.

"We've got them all, I think," he whispered. "Move up and check it out. I'll cover." He slipped on the night vision goggles that gave him a wider field of view than the rifle scope and watched as Wiggie moved across the road.

On the other side of the road, Wiggie checked the four soldiers lying on the ground, kicking each one. Not bothering with the fifth man lying by the rock pile, he moved toward the guardhouse. Arriving almost there, he stopped, raised his rifle and fired one burst into the guardhouse.

"All are down," Wiggie reported over the tactical radio.

Harold moved immediately back to the car to check on Captain Pimental. The captain lay sprawled on the backseat, his head hanging off the seat, his feet sticking out the still opened back door.

"Captain! The jeep here has the keys in the ignition. How's Captain Pimental?"

"He's dead. Help me carry our equipment to the jeep."

As he waited for Lt. Babijes to walk back, Harold took everything off Captain Pimental that might suggest who he was or what he had been doing.

Ten minutes later, Captain Lee and Lt. Babijes were driving through the back streets of Baler, the little town in the Philippines where *Apocalypse Now* was filmed. Wiggie drove while Harold operated the EPUU. Neither could think of anything to say about the man they had left behind.

San Jose City, the Philippines.

Hoppy was pretending to be the NPA again. He was driving with Hernandez riding behind when they stopped at a checkpoint on the outskirts of San Jose City. As he had done before, Hoppy flashed the ID card, talked loud with authority and a bit of anger, explained to the guard manning the drop gate that he and his comrade were providing rear guard security for the convoy of trucks that had just driven past the checkpoint, and demanded that the guard get out of the way.

The guard saluted and was stepping back when a second man stepped from the guard hut. The man looked like he had just woken up. He was stuffing his shirttail into his pants as he walked up, holding the waist of his pants out with a hand that cradled a rifle under the arm while he stuffed in the shirt with the other hand.

"What kind of shit is this?" the man asked. "First those goddamned trucks and now this." He was almost up to them, and Hoppy could see his face in the light of the Coleman lantern that hung from the front of the guard post.

"What the fuck . . .?" was all he said of the next sentence before Hoppy shot him, using the 9-mm pistol he'd been holding under his shirt.

He put the second two shots in the first guard, jammed his gun under his belt and twisted the throttle handle as he pushed off with the foot he had on the ground. The motorcycle jumped forward as a surprised Wade Hernandez grabbed hold of his back. Hoppy could see several men

241

pouring from a small house off to the side. They all carried rifles and were bringing them to aim. He'd gotten another twenty yards down the road when the firing started. He tried weaving and decided he was already going too fast for fancy work. He ducked his head low, gave the cycle a full twist of gas, and tore down the road.

He heard two loud whacks behind him and Wade groaned, but still hung on. Hoppy reached a corner and turned to the left. He drove down another hundred yards, killed the light on the cycle, and made a right hand turn. House lights were going on around him and he could hear the sounds of racing engines back by the guardhouse. Driving slower, and now in the dark, he fumbled for the kit that held his night vision goggles and fit them over his head with one hand. Able to see again, he sped up and rode the cycle through the residential streets. He turned corners a half dozen times before he killed the engine and let the cycle coast to a stop. He pulled the cycle into a vacant alley with the last bit of coast and parked in the shadows.

"How bad you hit?" he asked.

"I don't know," Wade answered. "My back hurts like a mule kicked me, but everything moves. I think they got my pack, not me."

Both men stepped off the cycle. Hoppy looked Wade over as he helped him take off the backpack. They found two holes, but the rounds hadn't gone all the way through the pack. The EPUU inside the pack had stopped them. Wade pulled the piece of equipment from the pack and examined it.

"How bad's it damaged?" Yarcia asked.

"It looks like it's had it. What the fuck did you open fire for?"

"That guy who stepped out and started walking toward us. I thought I recognized his voice. He got closer and I

242

saw his face. His name was Rusty Bernardo. He was in my freshman class at the military academy. The commandant caught him fucking his daughter. Rusty's family didn't have the class background to qualify as a husband for the slut."

"So he got kicked out and joined the NPA?"

"Not quite that way. The story on the grapevine was the commandant ordered him killed, but no one ever found the body. I guess he got away from the thugs the commandant hired. I was as surprised to see him as he was to see me."

"Seventeen thousand NPA soldiers and you had the dumb luck to run into one who knew you. So what the fuck do we do now? Where the hell are we?"

"I think I can find my way out of town. I used to have a girlfriend who lived here."

Wade pulled the small laptop computer from the pack. It was still working. He punched it on and brought up a map of the area. "Once we get out of town, how do we find out which way the convoy went? San Jose is a fucking cross-roads."

"Let's hope they are heading toward Manila and staying on Highway 5."

"Someone may figure out we're following the convoy," Wade pointed out. "They'll be putting up checkpoints on the highway looking for us."

"I know a route that will take us around the highway but bring us back onto it just north of Cabanatuan City," Hoppy explained. "It will be a fucking rough ride, but those trucks are moving slowly. Maybe we can get there before they do. If we find the missiles again, what do we do then? How we going to get the word to the *Herk* where we are?"

"As soon as we hit a high spot out of town, I'll try to use the tact radio. If either Delta or Baker are still up on the mountain, maybe one of them can pick us up."

Thirty minutes later and well out of the city, they pulled off the side of the road. Wade took another look at the EPUU. Satisfied it would never work again, he dumped it into a ditch and took out the tactical radio.

"This is Alpha, Alpha! Do you read? This is Alpha, Alpha! Do you read?" He tried it four more times.

"Shit!" he said, looking at Hoppy. "If we catch up with those missiles, we're going to have to take them out ourselves with the C-4."

As he reached his hand to shut off the transmitter, he heard the words through the earplug. "Alpha, Alpha, this is Delta. Alpha this is Delta. I have you two by three." The signal in Hoppy's earplug sounded as broken and weak as Delta was reporting theirs to be.

"Delta this is Alpha. Master mounts, I repeat Master mounts.

"His woman, I repeat, his woman," the countersign came back.

Wade quickly explained the situation and his plans to Major Wendle whose voice he recognized.

"We'll monitor every hour and the half hour on the mark," Wade explained after giving his report.

The USS Hercules.

"We lost the contact with Alpha team," Lt. JG Bradley announced as Admiral Jones entered the command center. Bradley had been the duty officer since midnight. Lt. Phillips and Colonel Ziga had entered before Gus walked in. Gus was feeling like a new man. He'd slept five hours without waking once. Lt. Phillips looked like he'd gotten some sleep, too. The clock read a little past 3:00 A.M.

"We got any idea what happened?" Gus asked.

Bradley described the report they had received from Delta team about the tactical radio contact with Alpha and the loss of the Alpha EPUU. "That one contact was the last contact," he added. "Hoppy and Wade may be out of range, or they could have run into more trouble."

"Let's hope it's distance," Gus said. "Right now Alpha team is our only hope. We've got to get someone close enough to them to pick up the tactical radio transmissions."

"Delta team is moving south and staying high," Bradley explained. "They're looking for a position where they can pick up the signal better."

"What about the other teams?"

"Charlie team had a shoot-out and lost one man — Captain Pimental. Captain Lee and the sergeant dumped the sedan they were driving and picked up a jeep. They've made it all the way past Bongabon since then. Baker team still hasn't reached the coast road. We don't know where Alpha's other half is. Delta lost contact with them a couple of hours ago."

"We've got to get one of those teams with an EPUU back into contact with Hoppy and Wade," Gus said. "Our best bet is to get what we can into the Manila area as quickly as possible."

"Right now, Charlie team is the only hope," Lt. Bradley answered. "They should be in Cabanatuan City in ten or twenty minutes. From there it's a pretty straight shot into Manila."

Gus turned and looked at Jack Phillips. "How far are we from the coast?"

"About forty nauticals."

"Let's try to pick up Baker team. They're totally out of it right now. Charlie team burned the bridges between Baker and Manila. The roads along the Aurora Coast must be crawling with NPA troops by now. But if we can pick Baker

245

up, we can bring them down to here." He touched Dinahican Point just below the Polillo Straits. "That will put them less than sixty miles from Manila and get them back in the action."

"That's going to be a long run and we'll have to do it on the foils," Jack pointed out. "When we finish, we won't have much left in the fuel tanks."

"I know, but we're getting desperate."

San Juan del Monte, the Philippines.

It was Sunday morning. Lt. Commander Wade Hernandez and Major Hoppy Yarcia were crouched in the bell tower of a church. They could hear the sounds of a 5:00 A.M. mass coming up the staircase they had climbed up. The two men had snuck into the church in the predawn hours without being seen. They had picked the church because the bell tower was the highest point in the neighborhood.

Hoppy cautiously moved to the side of the tower and raised up enough to take a look out. He was wearing his night goggles. As he hoped, from the height of the tower, he could see into the large copra storage shed five blocks from the church. The two trucks they had been following for so long were parked under the tin roof of the open-sided shed.

"Anything happening?" Hernandes asked.

"They've parked the trucks and surrounded them with guards. They haven't taken off the canvas covers or anything. There are a lot of soldiers walking in the street. They're going door to door. It looks like they are evacuating the whole area."

Hoppy ducked down and sat beside the American. He leaned back against the stone wall of the tower and stretched his legs across the wooden floor. Wade looked at his watch. Another ten minutes and he would try the tactical radio again.

The priest chanting the mass in the chapel below stopped in mid-sentence. There was a sudden argument, followed by the noise of people moving.

"I think they ordered the church cleared," Hernandez whispered. "Do you think they'll look up here?"

"It didn't look like they were searching any of the houses, just knocking on doors and ordering people to clear out."

Both men sat quietly for almost ten minutes. No sounds of footsteps on wooden stairs warned them of someone climbing up. The loud noises of argument died as both priests and parishioners left the building. Another ten minutes passed before either of the men could look at the other with a smile.

Chapter Twenty-three

The USS Hercules

Gus stood in the pilothouse looking at the Philippine coastline through binoculars. The sun was already breaking the dawn, making the night goggle useless. Sgt. Younce had contact with Baker team but they were a hundred yards above the coast road, and another thirty yards from the beach.

Baker team was battered and bloody. They had fought out of two ambushes, and one of the three men was wounded. They would break cover and make a dash for the beach only when they saw the Zodiac come near the shore.

No aircraft flew overhead, but Gus expected them to appear at any minute. The *Hercules* had made a run parallel to the coast about five miles out and dropped a line of sonobuoys then moved in closer. They were about a mile off the coast and moving on a northern course. While the ship was riding on the hull, they had the foils lowered so that they could get back to foilborne speed as quickly as possible. Gus planned to swing in with a 160 degree turn that would take them back toward the south and in closer to the beach for the pickup. The course would keep the *Hercules* behind the line of sonobuoys that had been dropped. They would raise the foils into the hull wells at the last moment to allow the *Hercules* to get as close to the beach as possible.

"Let's start the turn," Gus ordered. "Is the Zodiac ready to launch?"

"Aye!" the answer came back from the chief, with the crew out on the deck.

"Admiral, this is sonar," another voice on the headset interrupted. "The sonobuoys are picking up a screw. It sounds like a sub. Estimated bearing is 110 degrees, distance five miles."

"Shit!" Gus swore, forgetting he had a hot mike. "Belay the turn! Take her to foil speed! Radar! You have anything?"

"Nothing, sir. . . . Wait, I'm picking up an active radar signal. Bearing 112 degrees at six thousand yards."

The sub was positioned in a line with the *Hercules* that was perpendicular to the shoreline. The *Hercules* was in the worst possible position. The shore was too close to run away from the sub, and the sub had an angle where the sub skipper might get a fire resolution before the *Hercules* could get up to speed.

"Torpedoes in the water! Torpedoes in the water!" the sonar operator called out.

Gus moved to the other side of the pilothouse and used his binoculars. It took him a few seconds, but he located the torpedo trails. He counted four of them. They were fanning out. It looked like all four were aiming at a spot somewhere ahead of where the *Hercules* was headed. The *Hercules* was picking up speed. The gas turbine had taken over from the diesel and the ship was riding on its foils but still moving slowly, the foils lifting it higher out of the water with every knot of additional speed.

Jack Phillips climbed up to the pilot deck from the command center down below. While the *Hercules* was a few knots faster than the reported speed of the torpedoes, the

Hercules was in the same position as a speedy running back racing along the sideline of a football field who slows to catch a pass while four slower defensive players come running in at an angle. He may be faster but he might not get up to speed before the defenders pin him against the sideline.

Gus painted in his mind where the corner of the angles were going to intersect. The four torpedo trails were still fanning out farther apart from each other. Gus was sure he was going to get past the first two, the third maybe, but the fourth had a chance to be the winner.

"Take her in closer to the shore!" Gus ordered.

"We're not going to make it!" Commander Phillips whispered. "We can't get closer to the beach. We'll run her aground."

"We have to risk beaching her," Gus barked. "The charts show an even drop-off line along here."

"We hit a sandbar at foil speed and we're history. Our bottom finder doesn't function at foil speed to give us a warning."

"We may be history anyway."

They were flying along now, the speed building up, the hull rising higher in the water. Inside the air conditioned pilothouse they had no sense of wind, and the smooth ride of the *Hercules* gave no real sense of speed over the water. To Gus, it felt almost like the ship was standing still. It was only when he looked to his left at the beach which was flashing by no more than thirty yards away that he felt the sense of speed.

The first of the torpedoes crossed behind them and ran up on the beach. The second torpedo did the same thing fifteen seconds later. The third torpedo must have been running lower than the depth that it had been set for, because it ran into the bottom or hit a submerged rock and exploded with a shower of water that fell on the passing hydrofoil.

Gus watched with fascination the trail of the fourth torpedo as it closed, now almost at right angles with the line that marked the future forward progress of the ship. It looked like both the torpedo and the ship each had exactly the same distance to travel to that point, less than a hundred yards in front of the *Hercules*. Then Gus saw a deviation in the torpedo's trail. The torpedo was no longer under wire guidance but was on its own, following its computer instructions based on its homing sonar. The torpedo's computer brain had made a mistake. It had turned the torpedo toward the sound and lost the perfect angle.

The proximity fuse still blew, but the torpedo was more than five yards from the *Hercules* when it exploded. The *Hercules* had no hull in the water for the shock wave to crush, but the force pushed both foils up. For a single instant the rear foil was out of the water.

"We fucking made it," Phillips whispered as the rear foil slammed back against the water surface with a jar that shook the ship.

"Sonar! Where's the sub?"

"I can't tell. Our noise is washing out what the sonobuoys are picking up from the sub."

"The skipper blew it," Lt. Commander Phillips said. "He got too anxious. If he'd waited five more minutes, we'd had the foils up and we would have never made it to speed in time."

"Let's go down and look at the charts," Gus said. "We're going to have to tell Baker to hide out and hold. We don't dare try another daytime pickup."

"What about course?" Phillips asked. The *Hercules* was still moving at full speed parallel along the coast going north.

251

"Set it at ninety degrees and take us out a ways. Put on lookouts and watch for more torpedo trails. Whoever owns those subs has figured out the way to hunt us: hide, stay put, and wait until we wander by sailing on our hull. We've got to decide what to do next."

Manila, the Philippines.

It had been a long time since Colonel Cho had slept until seven o'clock. Even after he was awake, he lay in bed for awhile, enjoying the luxury of clean sheets, a soft mattress and air conditioned temperature. The only thing he didn't have was a woman. But that would come . . . and soon. Maybe even this very night. He got out of bed, walked to the window, and looked out across the city. The view was as luxurious as the room.

The Makati International was the newest and best of all the hotels of Manila. No wonder Sorreno had insisted they use it as his headquarters. Colonel Cho had agreed with the decision to make the Makati the new government headquarters even though he had insisted on some changes before they moved in. After their secret arrival through the hotel parking garage, they had not taken over the two top floors of the hotel that the NPA staff had prepared for them. Instead, at Colonel Cho's insistence, they occupied the ninth floor, with only NPA officials permitted on the tenth and the eight floors.

He had instructed the NPA officials to move the members of the international press corps who were staying in the hotel to the fourteenth and fifteenth floor. With the international press on the floors above him and the international diplomats and businessmen on the floors below him, he had no worries about a surprise attack. Even if the American should discover where the NPA leadership was hiding, they would not risk killing so many innocent people.

Someone knocked on the door. The colonel grabbed a robe that the hotel furnished to its guests, slipped it on, walked over and opened the door. A young woman wearing the jungle-green uniform of the NPA cadre came in carrying a tray with his breakfast. Cho recognized the woman. Sorreno had introduced her to him the evening before as they were settling in. Her name was Juanita. She was young, no more than twenty-two or three. Her hair was long and black, her features fine, her skin a light cream color showing more Chinese ancestry than Malayan. He stepped back to let her come in.

"Comrade Cesar," she greeted him, using the given name of his code name, Cesar Primero. "I hope you had a pleasant night," she added as she walked by him and into the room. She set the tray on the table and turned to him as he walked toward her.

"Comrade Sorreno asked me to make sure you are comfortable and that everything is exactly as you desire it. I will clean your room. Comrade Sorreno thought it would be better if we not trust the hotel staff until we have a chance to check them out."

"That's wise," the colonel said as he sat down in front of the breakfast.

She lifted the shining stainless steel cover off the plate, exposing an American-style breakfast of scrambled eggs, toast, ham, and what looked like fried potatoes. It wasn't the breakfast he would have preferred, but he did not complain.

"While you eat your breakfast would you like me to prepare a bath for you?" she asked. "I can give you a very good massage afterward, too."

He was tempted, but he had important things to do

soon. He would win victory, then he would take the time to enjoy the luxury and decadence that Manila and girls like Juanita offered.

"I bathed last night," he told her, "and I must meet with Comrade Sorreno as soon as possible. Is he in the office or in his room?"

"He is in the television studio. He plans on speaking to the people at noon."

Colonel Cho began eating the breakfast. The food was much better than the jungle fare he had been eating. While he ate, the woman laid out the clothes he would be wearing for the day. There was a brand new jungle-green uniform, one like the one she was wearing. There were new combat jungle boots and even new underwear. As he finished his breakfast and stood up, Juanita stood waiting to help him get dressed, her smile suggesting that she would have no embarrassment for what she might see in the process.

A few minute later, Colonel Cho walked out of the room and down the hall to the suite that was now the office of the new president of the Philippines. General Sorreno, as he was now calling himself, was in the suite's adjoining room that had been converted into a small television studio. Sorreno looked up, surprised to see Colonel Cho. He must have expected that Cho would take immediate advantage of what had been sent in with his breakfast.

"Are the missiles in place and ready to fire?" Cho demanded.

"I talked with Comrade Estuar a few minutes ago," Sorreno assured the Korean, a smile on his face. "They hid them under cover before sunrise, so we have nothing to worry about as far as the American satellites are concerned."

"Are they aimed and ready to fire?" Cho asked, his voice getting angry. "Your men were supposed to do that as soon

254

as they were in place."

"Antonio tells me that will take only a short while. But Antonio and all the other men are tired. They have been up for more than twenty-four hours. Even your Major Kye agreed that it would be better for them to take a rest before working on the missiles."

"Fool! We want those missiles ready to fire immediately. It is time that we settle the issue of Subic Bay."

"Why? What's the hurry? We are not under attack. That boat and the American admiral have fled. My foreign minster tells me he has almost concluded his negotiations with the American ambassador. The Americans will leave us everything, if we will only let them take the ships that are anchored in the harbor. We have no need for those ships, so why not do it that way?"

"If you agree to that, they will think you are weak," Colonel Cho argued. "They may even think that you have no more weapons. That American admiral and his boat are a test of your will. If you fail the test, the Americans will come, and they will not send just a single patrol boat. You must do what we planned. You must demonstrate how strong you are, how you have no fear of them. That American admiral has given you all the provocation you need. You must give them one last warning this morning. They either surrender the Subic Bay base or we destroy it. We should wait no longer. You must make the Americans fear and respect you."

"Then I will make them fear me tomorrow," Sorreno insisted. "Today, I am here in Manila, the capital. It will be a day of celebration. I am holding my first meeting with the international press, and I will speak live to my people, not by tape. I have decided, I will let them live at Subic one more day. Tomorrow my troops will move in and seize Subic Bay. We will have no need to use those bombs. The

Americans will know that they have no choice."

"Even if we wait until tomorrow to settle the issue, the missiles must be prepared today. We must be ready for any emergency."

"I will send the order, then," Sorreno conceded.

Colonel Cho left Sorreno with his makeup girl and angrily walked through the connecting door into the office that had been prepared for his use and his small staff. The office, which also had a door that opened into Sorreno's suite, had been converted from bedroom to office by moving out the bed and moving in two desks, typewriters, extra phones, a photocopy machine, and a file cabinet. A young Korean communications officer, wearing the jungle green of the NPA, snapped to attention as the colonel entered.

"Colonel Cho," the young officer announced. "We have a communication from the *Taedong*." He spoke English so badly that Colonel Cho had difficulty understanding even the single sentence. The Taedong was one of the major rivers of North Korea, and also the name given to one of the subs that was now stationed off the east coast of Luzon.

Colonel Cho reached his hand out and took the message from the young officer. It was a single-sheet report of the *Taedong*'s encounter with the American hydrofoil. The *Taedong*'s captain claimed that he had failed in destroying the hydrofoil only because the guidance system of one of his torpedoes had malfunctioned at the last moment.

Cho Chae-Jin smiled as he read the report. As an adversary, the American admiral was a worthy opponent. He had not fled as Sorreno was so sure he had done. He was still trying desperately to fight back, even though he would have no idea where the targets were.

Cho wondered if the American suspected that the base he had fled from was going to be destroyed. Cho hoped so. It made a much more interesting game thinking that the

256

American was running around desperately trying to save his base and his people. Maybe it wasn't such a bad idea to wait one more night before achieving the final solution of the Subic problem.

It would be best if the American understood how desperate the next twenty-four hours would be for him. Cho would make sure that Sorreno's television speech spelled out that if the American did not immediately present himself at the nearest port to surrender to the NPA then all American facilities would be attacked at dawn the next morning.

Colonel Cho looked again at the report from the *Taedong*. There was still a good chance that the American admiral would not survive even twenty-four hours. The *Taedong's* skipper reported that the hydrofoil had turned to a course that would take it close to the position that had been staked out by the *Che Ju*, the second of the two subs that had come down from the Luzon Strait on a search and destroy mission.

The USS Hercules.

The *Hercules* was still moving away from shore on it's foils.

Gus was back in the control center.

"What's the radar situation?" he asked.

"Some aircraft are looking at us," the radar operator answered. "But they are standing way off."

"They're scared of our antiaircraft gun after what happened to the F-5," Col. Ziga suggested.

"A good pilot could get in close enough to fire his missiles," Gus said. "Maybe the good AFP pilots haven't defected. But they can keep the subs informed of where we are and which way we are going. We have to do what we did yesterday. We head out to sea, drop sonobuoys, and sit it out until we find out where those missiles are, then we come back in on the run to take the shot."

"We had better come back in from another direction," Lt. Commander Melendes suggested.

"Let's swing out to here," Gus said, pointing his finger to a spot on the chart about fifty miles off the coast. He moved his finger to another spot on the map. "Coming back, we circle the Polillos so we can make a run north up through Polillo Strait. That puts us in good position, if we can reestablish contact with Hernandez and Yarcia."

"We don't have the fuel to make that kind of run out and back, not on the foils," Phillips said. "We're down to our last hundred miles on the foils, and maybe not that much."

"Can we do it at hull speed?"

"Easy, provided we don't run into another sub. But at hull speed we're sitting ducks. I hate to get in close without the reserves to run on the foils."

"What's your suggestion?" Gus asked.

"We hope there is only one sub looking for us. We drop down to hull speed right now. We drop the sonobuoys we have left. We wait it out until we get a position on the missiles. If we get that position, we make a run straight in until we are in range and we fire the SLAMs."

"That has a lot of *ifs*," Gus said. "Let's go back to hullborne while we talk about it. We must have left that sub way behind us."

Phillips gave the order to slow her down.

"The only other choice is to find us a gas station," Phillips said to Gus, stretching for a bit of humor.

Gus thought about it a second. "Maybe that's an idea. What if we hit a fishing village, one big enough to have

258

boats with diesel engines? Could we get fuel you could use?"

"I'm not sure," Jack answered. "Let me check with the chief." He picked up a phone, punched a number, and got the chief in the engine room on the line. He asked the question and got his response.

"Chief Horton says it depends," Jack explained. "What the Russians gave us isn't up to the quality the engine specs call for. We couldn't run for very long on bad fuel. The chief is already working overtime keeping the injectors clean, but it could work for a while, if we can find a fishing village big enough to have quantities of diesel fuel and small enough not to have an NPA unit guarding it. It's a pretty desperate choice."

"We're pretty desperate," Gus answered. "Orlando, where would you suggest we go looking for it?"

Orlando Ziga took his turn at studying the charts for a few moments.

"I'd suggest Umiray, here on the south side of Dingalan Bay. That's such a remote area, they may not even know they have a new government. But I can't guarantee we'll find fuel and that we won't find NPA troops."

"Okay, we'll try for that," Gus agreed. "It puts us in range of Manila, too. Maybe we'll get lucky and reconnect with Alpha before we get there."

"Torpedoes!" The call came from one of the two men who had been posted on top of the pilothouse, the highest point on the ship to watch for such things. "Off the port bow."

"Hard right!" Phillips called out. "Full battle speed!"

Gus ran up the ladder to the pilot deck, put his binoculars to his eyes and spotted the trails immediately. He counted four trails, running parallel to each other but strung out in tandem forming a chain that the *Hercules* would have crossed at her current speed. As the *Hercules*

259

made the sharp turn that would put her on the same course as the torpedoes, he could see two of the trails adjust to bring the weapons in toward the ship. The other two trails still under the wire guidance of the sub that had fired them continued on a parallel course.

For a few moments, the distance between the leading trails of the torpedoes that had turned into the *Hercules* drew closer, all the way down to no more than fifty yards. By then, the *Hercules* had made its turn and the trails were following along in the wake of the *Hercules*. For a few more moments, they still gained until they were no more than twenty-five yards off the stern. But the *Hercules* was reaching for full battle speed, and the distance began to increase.

Phillips came up to the pilot deck, surveyed the situation and announced, "They are not even going to come close. As long as we can maintain foilborne speed, torpedoes are no problem. The bad news is that we are reaching a critical fuel situation. If we don't go to hull speed soon, we won't have enough fuel to make it to that fishing village or even get close enough to fire the SLAMs if we do get a target."

"We can't risk slowing down yet, not until those torpedoes chasing us run out of fuel," the admiral said.

"If we keep running in this direction we head back to where that other sub might be," Phillips warned.

"I know. As soon as those torpedoes are far enough behind us, we have to cut across them and head out to sea for a ways. We'll have to circle around and approach that fishing village from the southeast."

Both officers walked to the chart table and stood studying it a minute. Jack played with a small hand calculator for a few moments.

"We can only make it, if we can cut to hullborne speed about right here." He pointed at the map coordinates. "But from here on, it will have to be hull speed the rest of the way in or we're out of fuel."

"I wish to hell we'd brought an ASROC (antisubmarine rocket) launcher along," Gus whispered, referring to the anisubmarine depth charge that was missile launched and carried a small nuclear warhead.

It was another twenty minutes before they reach the map point where they had to go back to hullborne speed. They were so low on fuel that they couldn't afford the luxury of keeping the foils extended below the ship. They had to be raised into the wells to cut down on drag.

"That's the last of the sonobuoys," Jack remarked as they dropped a set off the starboard bow. The *Hercules* was headed back toward the coast. Polillo Island was off the port side, about ten miles in the distance.

"Let's hope those two subs think we'll try to go back and pick up our team," Gus said, "and that they are waiting for a chance to ambush us up north, not down here. What's the word from Baker team?"

"They report they're pinned down and surrounded by at least fifty men," Col. Ziga reported. "They don't have much chance. They're destroying their high tech equipment so the enemy can't use it. We won't hear from them again."

"Damn that sub," Gus whispered. "What about the other teams?"

"Delta is still working south along the Sierra Madre ridge line and Charlie is still alive. They're on the way to Cabanatuan City. But neither Delta or Charlie has re-established contact with Alpha team."

"Admiral, I've got sub screw sounds off the port side, maybe halfway between here and the island," the sonar operator monitoring the sonobuoys announced over the intercom. "It's not a *Romeo* either."

"Is it one of ours?" Gus asked, sure he wouldn't be that lucky.

"No, I think it's a Russian *Alpha*. There! She's started active sonar. It sounds like target acquisition sonar."

"Go to hull speed!" Phillips shouted. "Fast!"

Phillips turned and looked at the admiral, his face a helpless mask. "That tears it," Phillips mouthed. He reached a hand up and turned off the transmit button on his mike. "All we can do is run until we run out of fuel," he said when he was sure the whole crew of the *Hercules* wouldn't hear him. "Then we drift and hope we get a target acquisition before someone sneaks up and sinks us."

"So much for the friendly Russians, the bastards," Gus snorted bitterly. "I'll bet that fucking admiral was playing with us from the beginning."

"Torpedoes in the water!" the sonar operator called. "Two. They're big and they are coming this way."

The *Hercules* was still on its hull and only beginning to pick up speed. The hydraulic system was still lowering the foils.

"They must be the new Russian 65 660," Phillips said.

"Torpedoes!" the call came from one of the lookouts on top of the pilothouse.

"Can we outrun them?" Gus asked Lt. Commander Phillips.

"Maybe, but we'll use so much fuel we'll be drifting at the end of the run. That sub can follow us and sink us at leisure."

The *Hercules* was leaning into a sharp turn away from the coming torpedoes and was starting to rise on its foils, but the hull was still in the water.

Gus couldn't resist the temptation to look at oncoming death. He didn't need the binoculars to locate the two trails in the water coming in from the port side. The torpedoes were less than five hundred meters away. Gus watched them like a chicken watching a snake, unable to do anything

They weren't going to get up to speed in enough time. The torpedoes were still closing.

He thought about Kathy Melendez who was down in the command center, still manning the weapons control system that was of no use against a submerged sub. He looked toward the ladder well and fought the temptation to go below, to see her face one more time.

He looked back at the torpedoes and saw that they were not quite on target. He expected to see them turn in as the guidance system sought out the sounds of the *Hercules*. But they didn't turn, they held to the same straight line. They weren't going to hit the *Hercules*, they weren't even going to come close. He watched as they shot past the *Hercules* almost two hundred yards out. Then they did start to turn, not back toward the *Hercules* but in toward the coast of Luzon.

"They've malfunctioned," Orlando who who was standing beside the admiral whispered. "They missed us."

The *Hercules*'s hull was out of the water and she was picking up speed.

Gus watched as the trails extended for another thousand yards heading in toward the distant shoreline and then they did hit something. Giant gushes of water shot up, followed by an instant oil slick. Debris started floating to the surface.

"What the fuck!" Phillips, who was also now in the pilot-house, swore. "That sub sunk another sub."

"She sunk the Korean sub," Gus whispered. "It must be the first one who shot at us awhile ago. Look where it was. Right where we were heading. We would have been ambushed at close range and while we were riding on the hull."

"Those torpedoes must have homed in on the wrong signal," Orlando said. "They sunk their own sub."

"I have a periscope on the radar," the radar operator reported. "It's the sub that fired the torpedoes. It looks like she's coming up."

"Get a Harpoon lock on her," Phillips ordered.

"Don't fire until we can check it out," Gus warned. "She just did us a favor. Maybe she's friendly."

"We have a signal light blinking on the periscope," the lookout above called. "It looks like Morse code. Does anyone read Morse code?"

"Chief Wozniak does," someone shouted.

A half minute later, the chief was on the deck, looking through binoculars at the periscope growing smaller in the distance as the *Hercules* pulled away from the area. "It's a repeating signal," he said. "KT TO KB3, then it repeats."

"KT TO KB3, that makes no sense," Phillips said. "What's she trying to tell us?"

"It makes a lot of sense," Gus said. "It's a chess move. Knight to the King's Bishop three. It was a foolish move made in a chess game. Helmsman! Bring us about. Take her down to helm speed, and set a course for that periscope. Wozniak, signal an invitation for that sub to come to the surface."

Forty-five minutes later, Admiral Yegorov Semenkov was again standing on the deck of the *Hercules*. Chief Wozniak and his men were working on the deck with hoses making the connections for a diesel fuel transfer from the sub.

"We can't fill your tanks," Admiral Semenkov explained. "We only carry fuel for auxiliary engines. But we can give you another day or so of running."

"You here legally, or did you go outlaw, too?" Gus asked.

"I'm not sure. I have some rather strange orders telling me that it is not in the interest of Mother Russia that the North Koreans take anything dangerous out of Subic Bay. I am ordered to do anything I can to prevent the Korean

264

from obtaining illegal supplies of weapon grade nuclear material. I think they meant that I am to take this sub to the Subic Bay area and sink any ships the Koreans loaded up and sailed out of the bay. But you know how it is, an admiral is supposed to show initiative in achieving his objectives. The best way to make sure the Kims don't get more nuclear material is to make sure they don't take Subic Bay."

"How much do you know about what has happened so far?" Gus asked.

"We taught the North Koreans their code system. Of course, we taught them one that we can read, even though they don't know that. I know that you have flushed the game and that they think they have escaped your wrath. I also know that if we had not flown the coop, Subic would already be a cinder. They were going to destroy the base, even if you surrendered, the next morning, the same day you escaped. They were not bluffing."

"I knew something was up," Gus said. "All the Philippine employees had left the base. Why didn't they do it?"

"They thought you were going to sink the ships they have waiting to move into Subic as soon as it is surrendered or destroyed. Someone in Korea decided it would be better to destroy you first. So they postponed the destruction of the base for a few days."

"But they still intend to either force the base to surrender, or to destroy it?"

"It's now scheduled for tomorrow morning. Your Captain Reilly will either surrender the base, or he and everyone on the base will die. You will be blamed, of course."

"I figured I would take the blame," Gus said.

"Can you stop it?" the Russian asked. "I know you've lost your toy plane. What other plans do you have?"

"I don't know, and I am not sure I should be telling you, even if you are giving me fuel."

"Smart man. A good adage. Never trust an old enemy, even when he claims to be a new friend. I could have come here to help the Koreans. I discover what you intend to do and as soon as I get back to the sub, we frustrate your plans. That wasn't really a sub I just sunk, but some old derelict wreck we found sitting on the bottom."

Gus didn't have to confirm those were his exact suspicions.

"So let's do it this way, we will wait until we have transferred all the diesel fuel the sub can spare. When the sub has disconnected and sailed away, then you can tell me the plan."

"You want to stay on board?" Gus asked.

"Of course, but even if I didn't, I have little choice. I can either join you or I will be put ashore someplace so that I can claim that I escaped you by jumping overboard."

"I don't understand."

"The international press knows that I was visiting your base. They are asking my government what happened to me. The press thinks you are holding me prisoner on the base. It would be inconvenient for me to turn up someplace else, especially if the base is destroyed in a nuclear holocaust. It might make people think that my government knew about it and that I deliberately escaped after I helped set it up. So I will stay on board and pretend that I never left you. If we survive, which I doubt we will, I will deny helping you. I will never be the one to explain how you could sail this ship so fast and so far on one tank of gas."

Gus laughed, the first time he had laughed since sailing out of Subic Bay. "Warriors should never play politics," Gus muttered. "It is a much more complicated game than war is."

"Perhaps that is why people win at war, but never at politics," the Russian said with his own laugh.

Chapter Twenty-four

Cabanatuan City, the Philippines.

Captain Lee and Lt. Babijes ran out of gas five miles outside Cabanatuan City. They had watched for some place to steal or buy gas for the last fifty miles. No gas stations were open and no one was leaving empty cars parked unguarded along the highways and streets.

"We'll have to hoof it into Cabanatuan City," Harold said as they climbed out of the jeep.

While it was past seven o'clock in the morning, no traffic was coming from either direction even though the highway was the main artery from Manila through central Luzon. The sun was already hot. The stretch of road where they had run out of gas cut through dry, sunbaked rice paddies.

"Maybe we can find a car parked in a garage or something, if we can make it into the city," Lee added.

"We're going to stick out like whores on a street corner," Lt. Babijes said.

"We'd better cut across country and stay off the main highway until we find more wheels."

"We'd be safer if we could find a place to hide out until dark," Wiggie argued.

"I know, but we don't have time. Someone has to make contact with Alpha."

267

The two men left the highway and walked through a rice paddy. With the dry season just ending, no farmers were working the dusty brown fields.

Twice, they stopped and tried the tactical radio, but they couldn't raise any of the other teams. They didn't use the EPUU. They didn't dare take it out of its pack in the open in broad daylight. A little past 9:00 A.M., they finally reached the outskirts of the city. There were not many people walking the streets. Those who were, hurried on their way, looking from side to side like frightened deer as they moved along.

As they walked along a dirt street, they saw four men talking to each other under the shade of a banyan tree. The men were all sitting on the ground. As Harold and Wiggie walked closer, they could hear the subject of the conversation—the nuclear explosion about thirty miles to the west of Cabanatuan City. Survivors were pouring into Cabanatuan City. One man described to the others how the city hospitals were filled with burned, blinded, and crippled victims.

Engrossed in their own conversation, none of the men noticed Harold and Wiggie approaching until they were less than ten yards away. Then one of the men looked up and immediately whispered something to the other three. All conversation instantly stopped. The four men looked nervous and scared as Harold and Wiggie walked past them. Once the two men walked farther down the street, they heard the conversation behind them pick up again. Now it had angry tones that hadn't been there before.

"They think we're NPA," Wiggie said.

"Let's hope we can find someone with a car with a tank full of gas who thinks that," Lee answered.

"Fuck the car, let's find a place where we can rest for a while," Barbijes said. "I'm fucking A-1 exhausted."

Captain Lee felt the same way. It had been thirty-six hours since he had slept and the last time he had lain down was while he waited on a rock for the car that old couple and their bodyguards had been driving. "Maybe we had better rest for a couple of hours," Captain Lee conceded.

They found a school, a two-story cement building. There were four classrooms on each floor, plus a smaller room on the bottom floor with a sign on the door announcing it was the teachers' lounge. The school had no interior halls. Each classroom's door opened onto a covered walkway. Although it should have been a school day, no children or teachers were around, the classrooms stood empty, and the doors were locked. They looked around, made sure no one was watching, then broke into the teachers' lounge, popping the lock with a K-Bar knife that Wiggie wore on his belt.

They found two well-worn couches in the lounge. They closed the doors behind them, locked it and flipped a coin to see who would take the first watch. Captain Lee won. He told Wiggie to wake him up in a half hour, then Wiggie could take a nap.

Captain Lee felt something hitting him on his foot. For a moment, he thought it was his wife. He remembered he wasn't married anymore. He hadn't been for two years. He woke with a sudden start and looked at the barrel of his own M-16 pointed at his face.

The man holding the M-16 was a Filipino. He was middle-aged and growing bald on top. A smile spread across his fat face, showing two gold teeth. Lee looked to his side. Lt. Babijes wasn't on the couch, but on the floor. He lay stretched out on his stomach. Another man dressed in civilian clothes stood above him, the point of an M-16 rifle pressed against the back of Babijes's head.

Lee wondered if Wiggie had gone to sleep, or what? He recognized the face of the man who had taken him prisoner. He was one of the four men who had been sitting under the banyan tree.

269

"On the floor, bastard," the man ordered.

Harold rolled to the floor, stretched out, and felt the point of the rifle barrel hit the back of his head hard enough to send sharp needles of pain through his brain.

"Hey, look what I found!" a third man called out.

Captain Lee could hear him going through the two packs he and Wiggie carried.

"I think these two are very important men," the third man said. "Maybe this radio will let us listen to the secrets they are telling each other."

"Take it all," a fourth voice called out. "Let's get out of here."

"Do we shoot these two?"

"Don't waste bullets. Bash their heads in, and slit their throats to make sure they die. Let them be a warning to others."

Lee felt the pressure of the gun barrel against his head release as the man holding him down pulled it away so he could switch it around to use the butt end. Figuring he was dead anyway, Lee rolled, kicking out his feet as he did so. He caught the man above him by the legs, catching him off guard and tumbling him to the floor. Lee got up as far as his knees and was about to dive for the rifle when he felt a hard blow against the side of his head.

The blow didn't knock him out, but it did knock him down. He tried to move, but he couldn't. Numb from the blow, he could hardly feel it as someone kicked him three or four times in the ribs. A hand grabbed his left hand. The man had seen the gold ring he was wearing. Two hands roughly pulled it off his hand and let his hand drop back to the floor. He felt the weight as someone straddled him and sat on top of his back, the stranger's knees on each side of his ribs. A hand grabbed his hair and jerked his head up. More waves of pain bounced around inside his skull as his eyes tried to focus on the knife that suddenly flashed into view.

"Wait! Don't! Not yet! Let me see that ring."

270

The hand holding his hair let loose and his face pounded back against the floor. The man still straddled him, his knees pressing against Lee's ribs. Harold could roll his aching head enough to watch through blurred vision as the man on top of him handed his Naval Academy ring to the other man. The other man took the ring and looked carefully at it.

The pain of his own stupidity hurt more than his pounding head. He shouldn't have worn the ring on the operation, but it had always been more than a ring to him. It had been the symbol of his climb out of the sweatshop work of a family restaurant in Tucson, Arizona into a new world of adventure and honor. It had been his good luck charm. Now it would tell these idiots that he was an American. It would be all the proof they would need to justify their destruction of Subic Bay.

"You American?" the man holding the ring demanded.

Harold said nothing. His head hurt so bad, he wasn't sure he could say anything if he tried to talk.

"You American Naval Officer?" the man demanded again. "You know Lieutenant George Stout?" He babbled a long string of sentences in one of the Philippine dialects. The man on top of Captain Lee suddenly got off him.

Puzzled, Lee raised up, bringing his knees under his body so he could sit on them. He looked across the floor at Lt. Babijes who was also sitting up. It looked like Wiggie had taken a blow to the head, too, but his throat hadn't been slit yet.

"Do you know Lieutenant Stout?" the Filipino insisted again.

Lee couldn't think of any Lieutenant Stout he knew.

"Lieutenant Stout, he wear ring like this one. I always remember that ring. It was the first thing I see when Lieutenant Stout help pull my school off of me. I was a teacher at Christian College."

"He's talking about the earthquake relief program," Wiggie said. Wiggie sounded like he was talking with a mouth full of mush. He didn't look alert, but he had understood the Tagalog the man had been speaking to his friends. "They had a big earthquake here in July 1990. A lot of American military came in and helped pull out survivors. I think we just met the resistance."

"The resistance," Lee muttered. "Then why the fuck are they trying to kill us?"

"We thought you were NPA," the Filipino still holding his ring said. "We were going to steal your weapons so we could use them to get more weapons. You act like NPA, swaggering down our street like you fear no one and we see your weapons. We follow you. We need weapons if we are going to fight these bastards. You know Lieutenant Stout?"

"I'm afraid not," Lee answered. "But if I ever get out of this, I'm going to hunt him down so I can thank him for saving my life."

"If you are American, why are you here, and with a Filipino?"

"We're working together. We're trying to put the people who nuked your country out of business."

"Then many Filipinos will help you. Most are afraid, but we do not want this Sorreno. He will be even worse than the Japanese. I am Rafael Batac. These are the few men I lead today. Tomorrow we will be twice as many. The day after that, twice as many again. How can we help you?"

"Can you help us get to Manila?" Lt. Babijes asked. "If we can get into Manila, we might help take that bastard off the throne he's sitting on."

An hour later, Captain Lee and Lt. Babijes were riding in the back of a truck carrying coconuts to Manila. They and their equipment were hidden under the coconuts in a make-shift box. It was hotter than the center of Hell, and Captain Lee's head still felt like a cage full of fighting cats, but they were moving at highway speed. Twice Lt. Babijes had tried to apologize for going to sleep while he was on guard duty. Both times Lee told him to shut up and forget it.

"Admiral!"

Gus turned to see Kathy's face looking at him from the ladder well. He and Admiral Semenkov had been sitting in the pilothouse. It had been an hour since they had cut loose from the Russian submarine.

"We've got contact with Hernandez and Yarcia. Captain Lee made the hookup."

Gus jumped out of his seat and moved to the ladder. He followed Kathy down to the main deck, Admiral Semenkov following him.

Kathy pointed to the net control station's CRT. The message from Captain Lee was still on the screen.

"Harold Lee picked up Captain Hernandez on the UHF tactical radio," Kathy reported. "Wade and Hoppy did catch up with the missiles. They followed them off Highway 5 and into a small village north of San Juan Del Monte. They parked the missile launchers in a big, open-sided, copra storage shed. The launchers can't be spotted from the air or by satellites, but Hoppy and Wade have them under surveillance. They're hiding in a church tower a few blocks away."

"What's the chances for a shot?" Gus asked.

"We've got them cold," she answered, her face a broad smile. "The church tower is high enough they can see directly into the shed. They say that the launchers sat there most of the morning with the canvas covers still over the missiles. NPA soldiers cleared out the population around the area, but they didn't find our men hiding in the tower. Hernandez thinks they will have to haul the missiles out from under the roof to fire them. He says there's a school football field about half a block away where they could launch them from."

"What about map coordinates" the admiral asked.

"They still have a Trimble navigator. I've got the data I

need to program the guidance systems, and Hernandez has got the angle for good laser guide. But we're going to have to get a lot closer in. We're still too far off the coast."

Gus turned to Lt. Phillips. "Let's get it done. I'm going to assume that if they have any planes or another sub looking for us then, they'll be looking where they saw us last. So let's swing south of the Polillo Islands and approach Luzon through Limon Bay. Then we can turn to starboard and head north through the Polillo Strait. That will put us on a parallel run up the coast that will keep us well within the SLAM range."

"Admiral, you do it this way, you save the Americans who live on the base, but you don't save the people of the Philippines," Orlando Ziga said, his voice suddenly demanding. "I agree that if they start getting the missiles ready to fire, you take them out. But those missiles are just sitting there right now. Let us use the time we have to find the monsters who command them and take them out, too. If you only destroy the missiles, they still hold my country. They will tell the people that they have more weapons and the people will believe them. Sooner or later, the same criminals who gave them missiles will give them more. But if you take the leader out, then my people can rise up and take back their country."

"Colonel Ziga," Admiral Jones answered, "I would like to do that. But Manila is a big city. We have no idea where Sorreno may have his new headquarters."

"I have watched this monster on the TV." Orlando pointed with one hand toward the small Sony portable TV that they used to monitor the TV broadcast from the Philippines. The set was on, although the sound was down. Some NPA official was explaining one of the new regulations they were imposing on the Philippine nation.

"He is a madman who wants the crowd to adore him," Ziga continued. "Now that he is in Manila, he won't want to speak just from the tube. He will want to appear in front of the crowds. If we watch that TV set we can see where he is speaking from. When he does, we take both his missiles and him out."

"Admiral," Melendez interjected, "it's going to take them awhile to get those missiles ready to fire, and they do have to haul them back out of the shed. They can't shoot them through a tin roof."

"That last intercept we picked up suggested that they've scheduled the attack on Subic Bay for tomorrow morning," Admiral Semenkov added.

"That means you have the time to take out Sorreno, if you can find him."

"The tube announced a while ago that Sorreno is scheduled to speak live at 2:00 P.M.," Jack Phillips said. "It's going to take us that long to swing around the Polillos and get into position."

"Can you make a shot into the city with the data we can pick up off the television?" Gus asked, looking at Kathy.

"If he picks a public place, a park or a stadium that we can identify, I can get almost as accurate coordinates off a map as I can from an EPUU or one of the Trimbles."

"What about a laser guide beam?" Gus asked.

"For that kind of shot, we don't need doorway accuracy. We'll risk killing some of the crowd, maybe a lot of the crowd, and he might live through it, but not with his macho pride intact."

"Those two men from Charlie team are already in Manila," Ziga pointed out. "They might get into position to put a laser beam on the target."

"That'll cut down crowd casualties, too," Melendez added.

Gus looked at the men and the one woman in the compartment. He knew how the call would go if he asked for a vote.

"Okay, we'll go for it, but the first evidence we see of them getting ready for a launch we take the missiles out. We also do that if Wade and Hoppy attract any attention while they are

275

hiding in that church tower."

All the officers were standing in the command center
watching the small Sony TV set at 2:00 P.M. sharp. Once
again, the face of Aguila Sorreno filled the screen.

"People of the Philippines!" he began. "Today, for the first
time, I speak to you live from here in the great city of Manila."

He might be speaking in Manila but he wasn't speaking to
a crowd. He was speaking from inside a studio or a room of
some kind. After he had talked for a few moments, the TV
camera panned around the room, showing the members of
his new government sitting at stiff attention in a group of
lined up chairs. They were his only live audience.

"Shit!" Col. Ziga swore. "He's not going to make a public
appearance."

As Ziga made his complaint, Aguila Sorreno mentioned
the subject on his own, explaining why he was still speaking
from private headquarters. He promised he would soon
speak at a massive public rally, but that he would not be able
to do so until he could be sure that the members of his new
government, "the servants of the Philippine people," were safe
from attack by the American "imperialists."

"Even as we speak, the imperialists are not only planning
the destruction of the People's government and the murder of
their leaders, their ships and submarines are patrolling off
our waters, and saboteurs have landed on our lands. These
despicable acts have been launched from the treacherous base
that occupies our own territory."

He demanded the immediate surrender of all American
forces in the Philippines and threatened that if the Americans
did not surrender that they would not survive for another
twenty-four hours.

"That's it!" Gus said. "There is no way we can locate where

276

he is staying, not before tomorrow morning. I don't want to leave those two men stuck in that bell tower all night long unless we have a good reason. Let's take out those missiles right now. Maybe we can get it done before he finishes his speech. I'd like to watch how he handles it when they hand him a note telling him his teeth have been pulled."

"Admiral," Kathy said suddenly, her eyes still on the screen. "I know where he is."

"How?"

"The camera panned across one wall. I recognize the wallpaper. It's very distinctive. I stayed in a hotel with that wallpaper, the Makati International."

"You sure?" Gus asked.

"Positive! There can't be another place using that kind of paper. The management was very proud of the hotel's individual character."

"Knowing he's there doesn't do a thing for us," Gus said. "The TV says the international press and the diplomatic community is staying there. There is no way we dare hit it. He's a smart bastard."

"Admiral," Orlando Ziga said. "We have to make him pay. If we don't take him out, he'll never pay for what he's done."

"I'd love to get the bastard, but that's why he's in that hotel, so I can't get him without killing a lot of other people."

"Not necessarily so," Kathy Melendez interjected. "If we can find out which floor he's on, and if we can get someone with a laser beam in the right position, I can put a SLAM right through the window."

"Delta team is still alive," Ziga pointed out. "If we can get them into Manila, they may be able to find out what floor the headquarters is on."

"Charlie team has tied up with some kind of underground," Phillips pointed out. "Maybe they've got some contacts with the hotel staff or something."

"There was a tall apartment I could see out of my hotel

window," Kathy pointed out. "If we could get someone into that building, or another one close to the hotel, they could use that laser listening system to pick up sounds in the Makati International. We might locate the headquarters' floor that way."

"I know the building you are talking about," Ziga said. "The Gardenia Apartments. It's a condominium where mostly rich businessmen live. Most of them will be gone by now."

"Okay, we'll do it this way," Gus said. "I don't want to risk losing our link with Alpha team. Charlie sits tight and keeps that channel open. We tell Delta to move as fast as they can south. If they get close enough to talk tactical with the two Alpha men in the church tower, then Charlie cuts loose and tries to get in position in that apartment building. But if we see one plane over our heads, if anybody gets near that church, or if they start moving those missiles out from under cover, we give up on the leadership and go for the missiles by themselves. We can't let those missiles survive."

Chapter Twenty-five

Manila, the Philippines.

Captain Lee looked through the front door into the apartment. It must have once been the ultimate in luxury, but no more. Now it looked like it had been trashed by the Charles Manson family working in cahoots with a hurricane. What looked like a mixture of human shit, chile sauce, and ordinary mud covered large portions of the white marble tile floor. The ruins of vases, dishes, pottery, and glass were sprinkled here and there. The broken glass of empty whisky bottles surrounded a bar made from carved teak. Someone had thrown a chair or a piece of furniture through the plate glass picture window of the dining room. A white, cordovan leather couch was a bloodstained testimony to the violence it had witnessed.

The walls of the apartment looked no better than the floor. The vandals had used what looked like dried human blood to write political slogans across the walls announcing, "The NPA forever," "Kill The American Bosses," and "We Belong To Marx, Not To Christ."

Captain Lee took a couple of deep breaths before he followed his two Philippine guides into the apartment. They had climbed fourteen stories to reach the apartment. While the city had electricity, the building had none for some reason.

Lt. Babijes and two more Filipinos followed him. The two Filipinos following behind Babijes were carrying the packs of Charlie team.

"What happened here?" Harold asked.

"The NPA took trucks out to Smoky Mountain the day of the explosion." The young Philippine girl who was one of the guides offered the explanation. She spoke the words in short gasps. The climb up the stairs had almost done her in.

The girl's name was Concepciòn. She'd told Harold and Wiggie to call her Concha. She was tall for a Filipina, and wore her shiny black hair shorter than most Philippine girls. The color and the features of her face showed more Spanish and European blood than Asian. She was wearing dirty jeans and a man's white shirt several sizes too big for her. She didn't wear the clothes like she belonged in them. She looked like she belonged in silk and high heels.

"The NPA dumped the people from Smoky Mountain in front of the building and told them it all belonged to them," she continued, breathing a bit easier. "They moved in, threw out or killed the owners and had a grand time for a few days. When they could find no more food to eat or liquor to drink they took everything they could carry and left. Now all of Manila is like Smoky Mountain."

Smoky Mountain was the popular name given to the Manila garbage dump. Thousands of the poorest people in the city lived on and around the dump, feeding off the garbage and selling what they could salvage and clean up or repair.

"Let's see what kind of view we can get of that hotel from here," Captain Lee said. He picked his way around the trash over to where the late afternoon breeze was blowing through the broken window. The view from the apartment window was to the east, away from the bay side of the city. From the window he could see the Inter-Continental, the Peninsula and the Makati International hotels. The new Makati stood the closest, less than a city block away.

"Will this do?" Rafael Batac asked. Batac had ridden with Lee and Babijes into Manila. He had stuck with them while they made radio contact with Hoppy Yarcia and Wade Hernandez and watched in fascination while Harold used the EPUU to report back to the *Hercules*. When Wiggie explained to him what they wanted to do, he had disappeared for a while. He had come back riding in a jeepney that was so old it must have been constructed from one of the original jeeps left in the Philippines at the end of the war. The three other men and Concha had come with him.

By that time, Harold had already made tactical contact with Delta team who was also talking to Hoppy and Wade on the tactical radio. With Delta handling the chore of linking Alpha with the *Hercules,* Lee and Babijes and their new allies had snuck through the streets of the Manila suburbs to the apartment house that stood so close to the Makati International.

"This is perfect," Lee told Batac.

"So let's set up the equipment and hope our friends in the hotel picked an ocean view," Wiggie suggested.

The two Filipinos who had carried the heavy packs up the stairs had already taken them off and laid them on the floor. Harold opened one of the packs, pulled out the EPUU, and set it up so he could notify the *Hercules* that they were in position. While he did that, Wiggie pulled out the laser beam listening device from the other pack and set it up so that it pointed across the open space toward the Makati International. He positioned it back away from the window so they couldn't be easily seen from outside.

Lee made the final adjustment on the equipment and turned on the laser generator.

"We'll start with the top floors and work down," he said as he fit the earpiece in.

"Is that a ray gun of some kind?" Concha asked. "Are you going to shoot them with that?"

"No, I'm going to try and listen to them talking. This little red beam reads the vibrations off a windowpane. The computer chips in this thing convert those vibrations into the same sound patterns coming from the other side of the window."

As he talked, he played with the adjustments, looking through a sighting scope as he swung the beam across the row of windows on the top floor of the hotel. At the third window, he stopped, adjusted the sound, and listened.

Concha brought up a dining room chair for him to sit on. She used a piece of dirty cloth to wipe what looked like strawberry jam off the seat before he sat down.

"What do you have?" Wiggie asked. "Is that the floor?"

"I've got a conversation. There are at least three people in the room." He listened a while longer. "I think they are press people," he said. "They're complaining about how the new government won't let them anywhere near the sites of the nuclear explosions."

The unit had a small external speaker and Harold turned it on so that they could all listen. The three men in the hotel room across the way drifted from complaints about how every word they reported was censored to a discussion of one of their colleagues named Susan Trencher, whom two of the three men bragged they had bedded.

Captain Lee readjusted the laser beam and moved it to the next window in line. He listened there for awhile, picking up the sound of a shower, then moved to the next window. The loud voice of Aguila Sorreno exploded in his ears. He turned down the volume and hit the switch that turned on the recorder.

"I think I've got him," he whispered. "It sounds like he's giving a speech."

He listened for another ten minutes, wondering how long the speech would last. The sound suddenly cut off in mid-sentence. He was reaching for the adjustment dial, wondering what had happened to the sound when another voice broke in.

"The fucker has been talking for four hours already. He's repeating himself for the sixth time or so." The voice was loud, deep, and masculine. It was an Australian accent. "Do you think he's really going to nuke Subic Bay tomorrow unless they all surrender?"

"Hell no! He's too damn smart." The second voice was feminine. "If he was planning that, he wouldn't have invited a bunch of us to witness the NPA accepting the surrender of Subic."

"Come on, Susan, look how he picked the reporters going to that shindig, anyone who ever said a nice thing about the NPA, or bought his line about benign agrarian reform. He's counting on you liberals to report it like he wants it reported when they don't let him on the base and he blows them up."

"No way that's going to happen. The foreign minister told me this morning he's convinced Sorreno not to destroy the American base, that they'll be able eventually to talk the Americans into surrendering like they should have done a long time ago."

"Let's not fucking argue about it. Come on back and get into the fucking bed."

"Gee," she said. "I think that's the first time I've ever heard you use that adjective in its proper meaning."

Embarrassed and very much aware that Concha was standing right behind him, Capt. Lee quickly moved on before the speaker could broadcast the noise of afternoon lovemaking.

Three windows down, Lee picked up the TV sound of Sorreno's speech again. From the sound of it, the speaker was winding down.

Lee moved on, stopping at each window. Most of the time he picked up no conversation. When he got below the floors where the press was residing, no one had the TV on. He heard complaints about personal belongings left in houses people would never go back to, worries about whether or not someone was going to get out of the city, children crying, hotel maids gossiping as they worked, and guests demanding hotel room service.

On the tenth floor he picked up the sounds of Sorreno's TV speech again, this time off every single window on the floor. The same was true of most of the windows on the ninth floor, and again, almost every window on the eighth floor. Below the eighth floor, again, only an occasional room was listening to Aguila Sorreno.

"We've got them located," Lee said, looking at the people in the room around him. "The NPA is occupying the eighth, ninth, and tenth floors. They're the floors that have every television set tuned into that clown."

"Which floor do we aim at?" Lt. Babijes asked.

"I'm not sure," Lee answered. "We'll keep playing with this damn thing. Maybe we can pick up some real conversations once he stops the serenade."

"So let's eat while we wait," Concha suggested. She and the other guide, a young man no older than she was, had carried backpacks filled with packages of food up the flights of stairs. Harold left Wiggie monitoring the laser listening device and followed Concha and the young Filipino man into the kitchen. Neither objected to his presence as he stood watching. While there was no electricity, the kitchen stove used gas from a tank.

As Concha worked at the stove, the young Filipino talked to Lee, asking questions about the United States and the American Marine Corps. As the two of them talked, Harold learned the man and the woman were not husband or wife, or even lovers like he had thought. They were brother and sister, and the apartment they were in was the place that they had called home. They had both been at a local country club playing tennis when the bombs had gone off. Today was the first time they had been able to sneak back into their own home.

284

Neither had any idea what had happened to their father and mother who had been at home when the Philippines fell. Both were sure, however, that the bloodstains in the front room must be the blood of either, or both of their parents.

Harold was asking how the two of them had tied up with the small resistance movement when Lt. Babijes called him back to the front room.

"The speech is over," Wiggie announced. "But I'm still listening to Sorreno, and I don't think he's speaking on the TV."

The Makati International Hotel

The idiot had deliberately defied him. Colonel Cho had been tempted to march in and interrupt the stupid television broadcast. Instead he had waited, sitting alone in the office, watching the idiot on the tube who was promising a socialist paradise to the people of the Philippines without telling them how much hard work, sacrifice and time they would have to spend to build such a paradise.

The idiot speech was finally done and Sorreno was back in his own office next door to Colonel Cho's. Cho could hear his loud voice as he accepted the compliments and adulation of the growing band of sycophants gathering around the man who claimed to be so powerful. But he wasn't the power, Colonel Cho was the power; Colonel Cho and the nation he represented. Only, that stupid bastard was trying to take away the control of the power and hold it in his own hands.

Cho picked up the message that had been sitting on his desk since shortly after Sorreno had begun to speak on the TV. The message had been written in a code that required Cho to decode it personally using a onetime pad he carried. The message came from General Bae Bong-Soo. It informed Colonel Cho of the destruction of another North Korean submarine, apparently by an American submarine that had moved in to support the mad American admiral. The message put the blame on Colonel Cho for not having already carried out the destruction of the American base, and it directed Colonel Cho to launch the missiles immediately. There was to be no offer of a chance to surrender, no warning, just total destruction.

Cho, seeing no reason to interrupt Sorreno's speech, had immediately gone to the communications center on the eighth floor and called Major Kye Dae Jung who was with the two SCUDS. He had given Major Kye the special weapons codes and instructed him to launch the two missiles as soon as they were programmed and aimed.

Ten minutes later, he was working on the message reporting his compliance with his orders when he had been called back to the communications center.

"Have the pigeons left the roost?" Cho asked, surprised at the speed with which the deed had been done.

"No sir! I find that I cannot get near the pigeon roost. Antonio Estuar informs me that he has orders that he is not to launch the missiles except on the direct orders of the president of the Philippines."

"The president is occupied! He's giving his speech. My order is all that you need. Launch those missiles immediately!"

"They will not obey my orders! Antonio is watching me right now. He has prohibited me from approaching the missiles. He has armed men standing by. He has given them the order to shoot me if I walk toward the missiles. I would gladly die for our revolution, but it makes no sense if I die without complying with my orders."

"Your orders remain the same, if you get the opportunity do it. I will do what is necessary to make sure you have that opportunity." He angrily slapped the mike back on the hook and walked out, leaving his Korean communicator staring at his back.

Since the conversation, Cho's anger had continued to

build, but he would have to control it. As much as he wanted to march into the office and shoot the idiot between the eyes, it would be smarter to manipulate him. The solution would be to find the right ego wire and feed the right jolt to it, but he needed to have Sorreno alone. That was why he hadn't gone into the office next door. As soon as the crowd left, Cho would have his confrontation.

He had to wait another hour before the sounds of conversation in the next office died down. When it was finally quiet in the other office, Colonel Cho got up and walked through the open door that connected the two rooms. Sorreno was still not alone. There was one woman in the office with him. She was sitting on Sorreno's lap and kissing him hard, her arms around him. Sorreno had one hand under her jungle-green blouse. He was fondling her young breast.

Sorreno saw Cho standing in front of his desk and broke the kiss, but kept his hand on the girl's breast. She twisted, looking back at who had come in. She made no effort to jump off her perch.

"Comrade," Sorreno announced, his face smiling. "Have you come to tell me how much you liked my speech?"

"Get rid of the whore. We have important matters to discuss."

"I am no whore," the woman proclaimed as she slid off Sorreno's lap. "I am a comrade in the revolution, just like Comrade Juanita."

Cho wondered what the woman Juanita had told the others about her services to him in the morning. Sorreno waved with his hand and the woman left.

"What is so important that it must interrupt a bit of celebration?" Sorreno demanded.

"While you talked and made love, the Americans attacked. They have sunk another of our submarines. Now you have not just that patrol boat to worry about but a submarine as well. Soon the whole American Navy will be attacking you.

287

We must launch against the Americans immediately. Only then will you be safe."

"You overestimate the Americans. That hydrofoil was only trying to pick up the team of saboteurs they had landed. They failed in that. My men have the team surrounded and we will soon have their heads stuck on poles. We would have the hydrofoil, too, if it was not for the incompetence of your submarine captain. My men were lying in wait for the hydrofoil to get a bit closer to shore when your submarine foolishly fired its torpedoes and scared the admiral away from the beach."

Cho ignored the accusation. "The attack on your coast, the shooting down of your plane, the destruction of the submarines of your ally are all the justification you need. It is time to destroy the Americans."

"I wanted to destroy the Americans several days ago," Sorreno answered. "You talked me out of it. Now I know that was wise advice. I have listened to my foreign minister, Comrade Peralta, who is meeting with the American ambassador every day. They will soon give us what we want. Why do you sneak around my back and try to launch those missiles without my order?"

Sorreno smiled as he looked up from his seat at Colonel Cho who was standing in front of him. "Yes, I have talked to Comrade Antonio," he added. "He told me how your man Major Kye tried to launch the missiles without my order." Sorreno paused as he said Major Kye, letting the colonel know he was deliberately not using the code name *Jose* assigned to the major.

"Doing that behind my back was very foolish," Sorreno continued. "This is the Philippines and I will be the one who will decide when and where we use the weapons of the NPA. We appreciate the gifts of the people of Korea, but gifts become the property of those who receive them. We will use them as best fits the needs of our revolution."

"Those gifts are worthless without the codes that only

know," Colonel Cho pointed out. "If you do not use them as we suggest, you will not use them at all, and you will receive no more of them. If you do not destroy the American bases as I insist that you do, the Americans will destroy you. And when they come, you will have nothing to shoot at them."

"I have those two missiles and they will be enough. You are not the only one now who has the codes. You gave them to Major Kye and soon Major Kye will tell them to us."

"You have arrested Major Kye?"

"Of course not," Sorreno answered, his voice shifting to a tone of a used car salesman. "But we have collected his cyanide pills." He grinned, watching the effect that announcement made on Colonel Cho.

"We want the peace, friendship, and cooperation of the Korean people," he continued, his voice as smooth as a cobra's skin. "But that must be mutual cooperation. I would prefer that we work together. That means that we will use the weapons when we both agree on the target. But I must let you know that you will play the game by my rules or I will play it alone."

"That American in his patrol ship has some kind of plan. If you do not destroy the base, he will destroy you," Cho argued.

"If the American patrol boat shows up again, we will sink it. Colonel Drilon has made much progress in getting our new Air Force organized and flying. He now has ten planes ready to fly and the pilots to fly them. We have four T-28s, a C-130, and two Navy sea planes. They will be in the air the first thing in the morning, covering the whole east coast of Luzon. They will carry bombs and rockets. I have promised that the man who sinks that patrol boat will be a general in our new Air Force."

"Even if you do sink the patrol boat, the Americans will never surrender their bases and you will eventually have to fight them. Better to do it now, while their fleet is still far from our coast."

"Comrade Peralta tells me the Americans will only fight if I kill many of them. He tells me that the Americans will surrender and soon. Peralta assures me that he almost has an agreement that they will leave Subic, taking only the ships in the harbor and what those ships can carry. Everything else will be left for us, all the weapons, all the supplies, everything."

"You are a fool. They will leave you nothing. What they do leave will be worthless or booby trapped."

"We will inspect everything first. Let them carry away what they can load on the ships and we will keep the rest."

What the Americans would carry away on the ships was exactly what Colonel Cho and his superiors wanted. Cho's orders were clear. If they could not get that, then all the Americans were to die. But what he had feared had happened. Sorreno was no longer listening to his advice, but to the advice of others. If Colonel Cho were going to take back that control, it would be better to let Sorreno think he had won the contest of wills for awhile. If one is to force a dog into good behavior, one must first find a whip.

"As you say, it is your country," Cho slyly said. "I think you are making a mistake, but I will agree. We only fire the nuclear missiles when we both agree on the time and the target."

Sorreno smiled. "You must learn to enjoy life more," Sorreno said, suddenly shifting the conversation. "Forget about the Americans and their little patrol boat for awhile. They represent no threat to us. Enjoy the victory we have. I have talked to Comrade Juanita. She is a beautiful woman and you have impressed her. It is nice that we have some comrades who are so young and beautiful. When we were in the jungle they did much to make life bearable. In a luxury hotel like this, a comrade like Juanita can be even more of a joy."

Colonel Cho turned on his heel and stalked back into his own office. He sat there for only a few moments, before leaving the office and going directly to his room. In his room,

ook him two minutes to open the secret compartment in the
ottom of the briefcase he carried. He pulled out what looked
ike a small Sony shortwave radio.

Sorreno was a double fool. He thought he knew the names
f every North Korean who had entered the Philippines to
vork with his revolution. But General Bae and his protégé
vere old foxes who always prepared for unexpected events in
var. For every North Korean that Sorreno knew about, three
nore he didn't know about waited for orders to serve the
vorkers' revolution.

Colonel Cho turned on the radio, pulled out the antenna,
nd punched what looked like the band selection buttons in a
equence of six punches. He moved closer to the window to
nake sure the building structure would not interfere with the
ignal. Speaking Korean, he barked into the hidden micro-
hone speaker on the face of the radio. Fifteen seconds later, a
oice answered, giving a code phrase. Cho repeated his own
ountersign, and dictated a short list of orders. He ended his
ecitation with a precise description of the spot in San Juan
el Monte where the missiles sat waiting on their launchers.

When he finished, he listened as the Korean comrade on
ne other end of the transmission repeated the orders and
riefly described how they would be implemented. It would
ake most of the night to get everyone in position. By morn-
ng, a hundred well armed men would be in San Juan del
Monte, and Major Kye would be back in command of the
veapons.

Colonel Cho shoved the antenna back down, turned off the
wo-way radio, and put it back in its hiding place.

He would have to spend the rest of the evening pretending
aat he was accepting Aguila Sorreno's usurping of leadership
vithout challenge.

Someone knocked on the door. He opened it to find Com-
ade Juanita standing there. She wasn't dressed in jungle
reen but wore a dark red cocktail dress that she must have

expropriated from one of the shops in the hotel lobby. She had also expropriated a bottle of expensive perfume. Colonel Cho had no idea what brand it was, but it smelled as nice as the woman looked.

"I've come to get your dinner order. We've found a cook who can prepare some Korean dishes. I thought that perhaps you would prefer to eat in your room this evening."

"I would, if you will join me."

"I was expecting that you would ask," she said. She smiled and entered, as he stepped back to let her by.

He was doing his duty. What better way to keep the idiot Sorreno off guard than by acting like he was enjoying the hospitality Sorreno was offering. But that wasn't quite the truth. He wouldn't be acting. He was going to enjoy it very much.

Chapter Twenty-six

The USS Hercules.

"It sounds like the base might not be in as much danger as we thought," Jack Phillips said as he looked at a hard copy of the most recent message from Charlie team.

"I'd believe that if we didn't know about that damn Korean," Gus answered. "I wonder who in the Hell he is. I wish I knew who he was talking to in Korean."

"We know he was talking on a radio," Lt. Commander Melendez pointed out. "Captain Lee could see him through the windows."

"Whoever the Korean is, he must work for General Bae Jong-Soo," Admiral Semenkov said. "Bae's the Director of the North Korean Security Bureau. He's intelligent and he's dangerous. Anyone on a mission like this is his handpicked choice. You've been thinking that Aguila Sorreno was the enemy you had to take out. You were wrong. That Korean is the man that you must kill."

"We know where he is right now," Kathy said. "Do we take him out before he beds that woman or while he's doing it?"

"No!" Col. Ziga insisted. "We want to get him and Sorreno together. We don't know where Sorreno is right now. He left the office with that woman and he could be anywhere in the hotel. He might be on another floor, or even down in the restaurant. Let's wait until they are back together. Then we take them both out."

"That may not be until tomorrow morning," Gus said. "Can we afford to wait?"

"If we hadn't heard Sorreno say he didn't want to nuke you Americans, I would agree we couldn't wait," Ziga said. "But now I think we should. I want the puppet as well as the puppeteer."

"Charlie team seems secure, but what about those two men in the church tower? Can they last another night?" Gus asked.

"They're low on food and water, but they are catching up on some rest," Lt. Phillips said. "I'll check, but I'll bet they will be okay."

"And what about us?" Gus asked. "We'll be a lot safer making the run in close to shore at night. Come morning the planes will be back in the air looking for us. We know there is another sub out there, too."

"Don't worry about the sub," Admiral Semenkov assured him. "You've got ASW now. That's what my sub is doing."

Gus looked around at the men and the woman. The decision he was about to announce was the decision he had decided on before the conversation had started. "Okay, we find a place to hide for the night in one of the bays in the Polillo Islands. We monitor developments over night. If there is any movement at all around those missiles, we take the shot and get what we can get at the hotel. If not, we wait until morning and catch Sorreno and the Korean when they are in the office together."

The Gardenia Apartments.

Captain Lee opened his eyes, suddenly wide awake. He

as lying on the floor in one of the apartment bedrooms. The Smoky Mountain hoard had stolen the mattresses. He was sleeping on the pad from his pack. Harold looked at the luminous face on his wristwatch. It was only 11:30 P.M. He could see nothing in the dark room. He fumbled around, found a match, and lit the small candle he had carried into the room when he went looking for a place to sleep.

Then he saw the girl. She was sitting on the floor, leaning her back against the wall. It looked like she had been crying.

"I didn't know you were in here," she said, a frightened look on her face. "It was dark when I came in. I didn't light a candle. I knew the way."

"I picked the first room I came to. How many bedrooms does this place have, anyway?"

"Five, and a den. This apartment takes up the whole floor. This was my bedroom."

"I'll go find another place to sleep," he said. "I didn't know it was yours." He started to get up.

"Don't bother. It's okay. I like the idea that the man who is going to avenge my parents is spending the night in my room. You are going to kill them all, aren't you?"

Instead of getting to his feet, he sat on his rump, his knees crossed in front of him Indian-style. "I'm not going to kill them," he said. "A missile is going to do that. I'll guide the missile."

"But they will die, especially Aguila Sorreno. That's what counts. I thought it would take me a lot longer to see him dead. When I heard what had happened here, in my home, I swore I would personally kill him. I thought it would take me years to do that. I want to be standing right beside you when you aim that magic dot at his window tomorrow. I want to be listening to the last words he says."

"That's fine with me." He looked at his watch again. "Who's on guard?" he asked.

"My brother and Rafael Batac. They are listening to the Korean make love to his Philippine whore. My presence embarrassed them. My brother told me to go to my room and get some sleep. He didn't know you were here." She giggled.

"Maybe I had better go. I don't want him to get angry."

"No! Please stay. I like talking to you. And my brother won't be angry, not like my father would have been. My father was very old-fashioned. He thought it was funny when my brother got one of our maids pregnant. He paid her off and sent her back to her village and bragged to his friends about his virile young son. But he was sure that I was still an innocent virgin. Are American men such fools?"

"I guess sometimes the fathers are."

"My father would not have been pleased at the plans I made to avenge him," she said. "I was going to use my body to get close to Sorreno. I had it all planned out. I was going to become a girl like Juanita, the one who is sharing the bed with the Korean. I think I could have done it very well. People tell me I am pretty. My boyfriend told me I was good in bed. I joined with the underground so I could become a spy and an assassin. I think I would have been a good one."

"Where's your boyfriend?" Harold asked, deciding he wanted to take the conversation in a different direction.

"He was a captain in the Air Force. He was stationed at Sangley Point. He was on duty when Aguila blew his whole base off the map. At first, he was the reason I hated Sorreno so much. Then someone told me what happened here."

"You've got reason to hate," Harold admitted.

"I hated them so much I was willing to fuck them so I could kill them."

The use of the Marine Corp's favorite swear word jarred him. Hearing her say it in such a context meant the word would never sound the same to him again.

"Are you married?" she suddenly asked. "Do you have a wife on the base, or back in America?"

"No," he answered, not adding he was divorced.

"When we have killed them, I would like to go visit America again. I've been there already. My parents took me. We visited San Francisco and Disney Land. Where do you live in America?"

"I'm from Tucson, Arizona. My family owns a restaurant here."

"What's its name?"

"The Chungking Garden. It's a Chinese restaurant."

"Will you take me to your restaurant some time?"

"I'm not sure my father would give you the welcome I would want you to have. We don't speak to each other any more. We haven't for several years. He was proud when I got the appointment to the Academy. But he thought I was doing it to get a free education, that I would serve the required years and then go back to the restaurant. He got angry when I told him I was going to stay in the Marines, make the Corps my career. We had a fight, and we haven't talked since."

"Then I have a duty to go see him. I must tell him of the great good that you have done, how you have saved many lives, and how you have punished those who took many lives."

She smiled at him and he believed what she was telling him. He closed his eyes for a moment and enjoyed the mental image of it. She would be talking to his father and mother. They would both be standing together in the

297

kitchen, his mother wearing the apron, his father the tall white hat he wore while he worked at the stoves. His two sisters would be there, too, dressed in their waitress uniforms.

He had been thinking for a long time that he should try to make peace with his father. He kept putting it off. For the last three days, he had been sure he would never get the chance to make that peace. Now he had the chance again and he would take it, whether the Philippine woman went with him or not.

"Okay, I'll take you to the Chungking Garden," he said. "If you'll go."

She stood up and walked across the room toward him. She sat on the floor beside him. Neither of them said anything. She reached her hand out, touching the side of his head. They leaned toward each other and they were kissing. He broke it.

"You don't have to do this," he said.

"I know, but I want to. I was ready to fuck the enemy. Because of you, I don't have to do that. So I want to make love to a friend. I thought I would never get to do that again."

She leaned back in and they kissed again for a long time. This time she broke it. She stood up and started unbuttoning her blouse. The flickering candlelight played across her beauty as she slipped the blouse from off her shoulders and dropped it to the floor. She was wearing no bra. Her breasts were large and full, but with no droop; her nipples were small buttons on top of flat, round areolas. She dropped her hands to her waist, unbuttoned the jeans and pulled the zipper down.

Harold got quickly to his own feet and started to remove his own clothes.

He heard her walk across the deck behind him. He'd een hoping she would follow him out when he had stepped nto the night air. He walked back aft and stood beside the tarboard missile launcher. She came up to stand beside im. The *Hercules* was anchored up close to shore in the mall bay and Gus could smell the land and the tropical orest. The temperature was in the low eighties. It felt almost cool after the hot, tropical day.

"Still having problems sleeping?" she asked as she walked p to him. With no moon, it was so dark, that all he could aake out was her shadow.

"There is no way I can sleep tonight," he answered. "I eep worrying that I'm making a mistake by waiting until norning. Maybe I should have taken the shots at the misles this evening. I could have taken out the command cener in the hotel, too. Those are the classical military ojectives. But I'm putting it all at risk so I can go after one aan and his foreign advisor."

"I was surprised you are doing it this way. I know that rlando hates Sorreno, but he's just a figurehead. The ussian is right, it's the Korean who's the villain. You uld have gotten both the Korean and the missiles. You ill can, right now."

"I don't agree that the Korean is the primary villain," Gus id. "The Koreans couldn't have done this if they hadn't und someone like Sorreno. I know the argument. If they adn't found him, they would have found another. There ill always be a quisling, but that doesn't excuse the man ho plays the role. I'm old-fashioned. I believe in the imortance of the individual. One human does make a differace, sometimes for good, sometimes for evil."

"You think Sorreno is that important?"

299

"When someone takes power and shows utter contempt for human life, we have to call him to account and make him pay. We made a serious mistake in Iraq. Saddam was the only reason we went to war. He was an international outlaw and someone had to stop him. We claim we won that war, but we didn't. We lost it because we never took the objective we were fighting for. We didn't put him out of business. We walked away and left him in place. He kept on killing. That's why I'm waiting until tomorrow to take our shots, even if I am risking it all. I can destroy the nuclear weapons that Sorreno holds, but if I leave him alive, he'll still keep on killing," Gus avowed.

"You won't stop the killing. Someone will take his place."

"I know. That's not the point. The point is that someone must make him pay. Then we must make those who take his place pay. The cycle will keep rolling on as long as humans exist. It can never stop, unless we want people like Saddam and Sorreno to take over forever."

"Are you a warrior or a philosopher?"

"I think every philosopher who believes in his own philosophy has to be a warrior. Ideas never win, unless someone is willing to fight for them."

She had moved closer to him. He could feel her presence. As the boat rolled, their arms would sometimes touch. He wanted to turn and take her in his arms. The uniforms they wore got in the way.

"What happens after we shoot the missiles tomorrow?" she asked.

"I give myself up, if we're still afloat. I'll sail east and radio to the nearest American ship. We won't have enough fuel to run all the way out to the fleet. Someone will have to come in and pick us up. Funny, that's the first time I ever thought about that question."

"Will they put us in the brig, or what?" she asked.

300

"They may put me there. I hope they don't put you, or ack, or any of the others in the brig. I've tried to set it up) make it look like none of you had any choice, that you ere following what you thought were legitimate orders. m afraid it won't do your career any good, but you should ay out of jail."

"Screw the career. I'm glad I didn't miss this. If they let te stay in uniform, I'll stay in for twenty and collect the ension, but that's all. After this excitement, what I've been oing looks kind of dull. It's going to be hard to go back to te old rut."

He held his watch up to look at it. It was not quite one clock. "I guess we had better go in," he said. "We both tould try and get some sleep."

"You want to sleep in my bunk again?" she asked.

He coughed a quick, embarrassed laugh at the way the uestion sounded. He wanted to sleep in her bunk, but not y himself. "You need the sleep as much as I do," he said. 'll be okay."

"We could share the bunk for a while," she whispered.

Again, her sudden bluntness caught him by surprise. He dn't say anything. He wasn't sure what to say. He hadn't xpected to have to deal with it because he wasn't going to aggest it.

"That's what I want," she added. "I think that's what you ant, too. I saw you look my way before you stepped out r some air. The look said you wanted me to follow you d I did."

"It won't work, not like that," he finally whispered. "I ad-it I want to make love to you, and not just for tonight. I ant to learn everything I can about Kathy Melendez. But hat I want is too personal a thing to do while we're wear-g our uniforms."

"I thought we'd take off our uniforms before we climbed

301

into the bunk," she said, her voice carrying a light giggle.

"We'd still have the ship wrapped around us. The ship'[s] the real navy uniform, not the clothes we wear. If we're going to put men and women on the same ships, the Navy has to treat loving like it treats liquor. It can't be something we do while at sea."

She stood silently for a moment before asking, "What happens when we leave the ship?"

"If I'm not in jail, I'll be on your doorstep."

"If you are in jail, I'll wait until they let you out."

They walked back inside. They hadn't kissed. They hadn't even touched hands.

Chapter Twenty-seven

an Juan Del Monte.

Major Yarcia was holding the watch and Lt. Commander Hernandez was sleeping when the shooting started. Wade woke up with a start, reached for his weapon and scrambled into position beside Hoppy. Hoppy was looking through a sight scope in the direction of the copra shed. Wade fitted his own scope into view. He picked out a couple of muzzle blasts and saw several men running through the deserted streets toward the copra shed. Several more shots rang through the early morning darkness and then suddenly everything was quiet. Whoever had attacked the position was rounding up and disarming the troops who had been guarding the missiles. The whole attack had taken less than three minutes.

"What the fuck happened?" Wade asked. "Is that the new resistance or what?"

"I don't know," Hoppy answered. "Whoever they are, they're good. I didn't see any of them moving up."

The attacking soldiers who now held control of the copra shed started lining up the men who had been on guard. Two dead men lay on the ground in full view and several wounded men were calling for help. The casualties were all defenders.

Three of the attackers brought someone out from inside the shed's small office space. The man was walking like someone who had just been freed. He greeted the man who appeared to be in charge of the attacking force with a salute.

Harold and Hoppy recognized the newly freed man. He had been with the missiles ever since Alpha team had started following the truck. He looked like Chinese or North Asian, not Filipino. For most of the time they had followed the trucks, he had appeared to be the man in charge. Sometime during the previous afternoon he had disappeared, now he looked very happy to see the men who had just attacked the position and freed him.

"Can you pick up anything with the parabolic?" Harold asked.

"Just a bit, but I don't understand it. It sounds like they are talking Chinese or something."

"It must be Korean. I think the Koreans have just taken back possession of their toys," Captain Hernandez whispered. "I'll notify Delta so they can call the *Herk*. Now we know what kind of orders that Korean in Manila was giving." The two men on Alpha team had been passed a quick summary via the Delta team about the conversations that Charlie team had picked up off the windows of the Makati International.

"You had better hurry," Hoppy whispered. "They're stripping the covers off the missiles."

Captain Hernandez reached for his tactical radio. "Delta, Delta!" he called. "This is Alpha."

"Alpha, Delta here!"

Delta gave the sign of the day, Wade responded with a countersign and briefed Major Wendle on the new developments.

The Makati International Hotel.

Col. Cho stood beside the bed in his hotel room. He looked down at the still sleeping woman. She was naked and lying on er side, one arm hugging the pillow. Her legs were split apart, giving the colonel a full view of the pink slit that glistened with drops of the semen that the colonel had deposited in the woman through the night. Cho Chae-Jin enjoyed the moment. It had been a night that he would long remember. Comrade Juanita was not only pretty, an adjective that could never be used to describe the wife who waited for him in Pyongyang, but the girl acted like sex was fun, not a duty for the revolution.

Chae-Jin felt himself getting hard again and he turned quickly away. He wanted more nights with Juanita, many more nights. But if he was to enjoy them, he had his duty to do first.

Already dressed in his jungle-green uniform, he walked to the briefcase and pulled out the miniature transceiver. Carrying it to the window so he could get the best reception possible, he pulled out the antenna, hit the on button, and made the call. The answer was instantaneous, the report was short and quickly given.

As he put the radio back away, he saw that the sound of his voice and the answering transmission had awoken the woman. She was sitting up, staring at him, a puzzled look on her face. She made no effort to cover her pert breasts nor hide the thick, black pubic patch.

"Get dressed. Immediately!" he ordered. "Go find Aguila Sorreno. Tell him I want to see him in his office."

The puzzled look on her face turned to a pout. She glanced toward the window. The morning light was taking charge of the day.

"What time is it?" she demanded. "Comrade Sorreno will not like it if I bother him so early. He will be angry with me, and with you too."

"Tell the dear comrade that if he is not in his office in ten minutes that he will no longer be the one who commands the New Philippines."

The fire in his eyes frightened the woman. She jumped off the bed and searched around for her clothes. She found the dress, put it on over her head without bothering with underwear, and hurried out the hotel room door.

The only piece of his uniform that the colonel had not yet put on was his pistol, another secret he had kept hidden from the new president of the Philippines. Unlike Sorreno, he didn't wear a heavy piece of iron strapped to his waist like some American cowboy gunfighter. The pistol he carried was no bigger than the palm of his hand. He carefully tucked it inside his belt and under his shirt. It was an American make, one his father-in-law had taken off a dead American during the Korean war. It shot .22 caliber long rifle cartridges which were not available in his own country, but the six-shot clip was full and Chŏ was deadly accurate at close range.

The USS Hercules.

The *Hercules* had already moved out from the small bay where they had hidden during the night when Delta team passed the message from the church tower.

"It will take us about twenty minutes to get into a good firing position," Lt. Phillips reported.

"If the girl does what the Korean told her to do, that'll make it absolutely perfect," Gus said. "He and Sorreno will be in the same office. If they are not, we still fire at the missiles."

"I'm set to fire the two SLAMs as soon as we reach right here," Melendez said, pointing to a spot on the chart. "That gives us the best firing angle over the mountain."

"Radar is picking up aircraft, at least four planes," the radar operator announced. "Two of them are coming this way. They are out looking for us early."

Gus turned to Admiral Semenkov. "You want to watch the video games down here or go up to the pilothouse?"

"I came to see the battle."

"Commence firing with the deck gun as soon as you have a target lock," Gus told the WO on the console that controlled the Mk 75-mm antiaircraft gun. He turned and followed the Russian admiral up to the pilot deck. Like the Russian admiral, he was already wearing a helmet and a flak vest.

It was now full daylight outside, but the mountain peaks of Polillo Island still covered the rising sun.

"Full battle speed!" Lt. Phillips gave the order.

The *Hercules* was soon moving across the surface of the water at more than fifty knots as the gas turbine engine pumped 41,000 gallons of water per minute through the water jet nozzle.

"Aircraft closing from the stern at eight thousand feet," the radar operator announced over the intercom.

"Take her forty-five degrees to port," Lt. Phillips's voice called out.

The helmsman sitting at the control console punched in the computer commands and the ship responded, turning toward the island of Luzon to give the antiaircraft gun on the front deck a better angle of fire at the attacking aircraft. The unmanned deck gun, commanded by computers and radar, swung around, the barrel elevated and commenced firing.

Gus could see the attacking aircraft through his binoculars. There were two of them. They looked like T-28s. Both had started their dives at the *Hercules*. The lead aircraft was showing muzzle blasts as it opened up with its cannon.

"Evasive maneuvers!" Phillips ordered.

The deck shifted just a bit and the *Hercules* turned farther to port. Gus watched as two bombs on the first aircraft detached from the wings. He saw the splashes of the aircraft cannon's fire off the starboard bow, marching across the water toward the deck as the first plane blew up. The bombs were still dropping. For an instant Gus thought they were going to hit, but both struck the water about thirty yards off the starboard side

of the forward bow. Geysers of water rose high in the air as th
Hercules's progress carried them through a torrent of fallin;
water.

The antiaircraft gun swiveled, the radar guided muzzl
sought out the second attack aircraft and barked angrily. Sev
eral cannon slugs plowed through the aluminum alloy hull o
the *Hercules* before the pilot broke off his attack. He put hi
plane in a tight turning, trying to escape the antiaircraft fire

The plane never pulled out of its tight turn, but slid into
dive that carried it straight into the ocean. It disappeared in
stantly beneath the waves.

"Can we fire the SLAMs yet?" Gus asked over the inter
com.

"We are just in range," Kathy's voice came back to him
"Give me five miles more and I'll guarantee perfection."

"What about those other two planes?" Gus asked.

"They're circling out about ten miles," radar answered
"They've got friends on the way, at least four more."

"That could be too many for one gun to handle," Gus said
"Especially if they get smart and come in from four differer
directions. Fire control, when those planes start the attack
launch immediately. Don't wait for a perfect shot."

"Aye, sir!"

"We have a message from Charlie," Sgt. Younce's voic
came in over the intercom. "The sheep are in the shearin
pen."

The Makati International Hotel.

"How dare you send your whore to wake me up?" Aguil
Sorreno demanded as he walked through the door into his o
fice. Sorreno's shirttail was hanging out, the three top butto
were undone. He hadn't combed his hair, and he was wearin
the shower sandals the hotel laid out for guests. He had, hov

308

ver, taken the time to strap on the fancy leather belt that car-ied his favorite Beretta 9-mm automatic.

"And what the fuck are you doing sitting in my chair? You've got your own damned office. Get out of mine."

"Don't snarl at me when I am doing you a favor," Colonel Cho answered, his voice icy calm. "I have news that will make you look very foolish if others learn of it before you do."

"If you're going to tell me that my planes are attacking the American patrol boat, you're too late. I was informed of that ten minutes ago. They have the boat surrounded. In a few minutes, that admiral and his crew will be dead."

"The American admiral has no meaning for the historic events of today," Cho snarled. "Today will be a momentous day in history, even more important than the day you seized power. The question is, do you want to appear to your people as the man who controlled the events, or do you want to look like the fool you are. A puppet in the hands of a smarter and more intelligent mind."

"What are you talking about?" Sorreno demanded.

"If you wish to appear to be in charge, you will do exactly as I tell you to do. You will put on your best uniform and you will gather the press. You will turn on your TV cameras and you will announce that the American Navy has launched an attack against your country and that you have retaliated. You will tell them that you have destroyed Subic Bay in self-de-nse."

"I told you we were not going to do it that way. What makes you think I would change my mind?"

"I am giving you thirty minutes to do as I command," Colonel Cho said, ignoring the question. "If you do not immedi-tely agree to do so, I will not wait thirty minutes. I will order the missiles launched immediately. We will kill all of the Americans, and the world will think it was an unjustified and unprovoked attack. The Americans will come for you with their own bombs and you will be defenseless."

"You can't launch the missiles. Comrade Estuar will only launch them on my command."

Colonel Cho reached his hand out to the little transceiver that sat on the desk in front of him. He punched the button and spoke into the radio, "Jose! This is Primero."

Major Kye answered immediately. Colonel Cho suggested that Kye call Major Estuar to the radio. It took a few moments for Estuar to arrive. While he waited, Cho Chae-Jin took his pleasure in watching the sudden fear play across the face of Aguila Sorreno.

"Estuar here." The voice sounded like the voice of an old man, one in much pain and very tired.

"Major Estuar," Colonel Cho spoke into the radio. "I have a friend of yours here. Would you tell him who controls the pigeons that you have in your roost?"

"Major Kye and his men are in charge." The words were spoken in a harsh whisper.

Colonel Cho flipped off the switch and looked up at the stricken Sorreno.

"So what is your choice?" Cho asked. "Do I call back Major Rye and tell him to launch the missiles now, or do I wait for you to play your charade with the international press?"

"I will tell the press, but I do not think it will save us. We kill those Americans and the fleet will come and kill us. I cannot understand what your government hopes to achieve."

"I have no time to explain it to you," Cho told him. "Go and get yourself ready."

"Can I be sure that Major Kye will not launch the weapons until I have a chance to explain this to the press?"

"Of course. We prefer to make it look like you were defending yourself from aggression. But have no delusions. All Kye needs is one word from me and he will launch."

Sorreno had the information he wanted. He started to turn toward the door, but suddenly swung back to face the Korean colonel. His hand dropped to the pistol grip on his waist as he

310

arted what he thought would be a classic Western draw. Colonel Cho expected the move. His hand was already on the .22 caliber automatic. Before Sorreno had come in, he had taken the little pistol out of the hidden holster under his shirt and placed it carefully on his lap where it was hidden from view by the desk.

Cho had his small pistol in position, aimed, and fired, before Sorreno could clear his holster. Cho, knowing Sorreno had taken to wearing a Kevlar vest since moving into Manila, went for a head shot. He fired four quick shots into the face of Sorreno. None of the .22 caliber slugs hit with the power to knock a man down. But the four slugs burrowed through eye and skull and cheekbone, and plowed through brain cells.

Cho had the impression he was watching it happen in slow motion. After Cho fired the four shots, Sorreno's arm kept rising, the Beretta pulled free from the holster, the finger fitting into the trigger guard. Cho got another shot off before the Beretta was pointed at his chest. He aimed for the other eye, but missed, hitting instead the cheek below the eye.

Sorreno would have put at least one shot into the chest of Cho, if he had been carrying a single action pistol, but the Beretta was double action. On the first shot, the trigger pull had to cock the pistol first, then drop the hammer. The already brain dead man did fire the pistol, but he was dropping to the floor when the hammer hit the firing pin. The slug tore through the desk and buried itself in the floor behind Colonel Cho.

His ears ringing from the sound of the shots, Cho couldn't hear people running in the halls on their way to investigate the noise, but he knew they would be coming. But he had time to give the order before they got there. He reached out to punch the button on the transmitter.

"Jose! This is Primero. Release pigeons! I repeat. Release pigeons."

He waited a moment, then hit the transmit button again.

"Jose! Acknowledge receipt of order."

He waited a moment and tried again. "Jose! Acknowledge receipt of orders. Release pigeons immediately."

Something was wrong. Why wasn't Major Kye answering? He looked up. Three NPA soldiers had come running in. They stood staring at the body of Aguila Sorreno sprawled on the floor.

"Jose! Answer me!"

Neither he nor the three soldiers saw the needle beam of red light shining through the window behind him. The beam of light crossed the room and stopped at the far wall.

High above the city, lost in the rising sun, the computer chips guiding the second SLAM missile fired by the *Hercules* decided they had cleared the mountains and it was safe to start the descent into the city below. The optic scanner in the missile's nose pivoted on its swivel, searching for a specific band of the light spectrum. As the missile dropped from the sky at nearly the speed of sound, the computer eye found what it was looking for and sent the commands to the guide vanes. The missile changed course and headed straight to the point of red light shining on the ninth floor window of the Makati International.

"Jo . . ." was the last thing that Colonel Cho said before the glass exploded behind him. The missile passed by him, missing him by only a foot, but killing him with its shock wave before it tore through the body of one of the NPA soldiers and exploded as it hit the doorjamb across the hall.

The exploding five hundred pound warhead left no survivors on the ninth floor and only a few on either the tenth or eighth floors. Three innocent people died on the next lower floor and four on the eleventh floor. Nobody below the sixth floor was injured, and the international press corps on the upper two floors took no casualties either.

"They're coming in from all four sides," radar called out.

Gus scanned the skies. He could spot two of the planes as tiny dots. The third was bigger. It looked like a C-130. It was flying the highest. Designed to carry cargo, the aircraft would have no electronic defense systems. The deck gun was already tracking and firing at it. Before it blew up in air, Gus saw a collection of small dots fly out from the rear end of the cargo plane. At first he wondered if they were jumpers, then realized that the crew had shoved a whole load of bombs out the open ramp door of the plane before the antiaircraft had connected.

The antiaircraft deck gun was firing a steady stream of shells, the barrel moving up and down and the housing swinging from left to right as the fire guidance system sought out new targets.

The *Hercules* was still moving at full battle speed. As soon as the second of the two SLAMs had been fired, the ship had put into a sharp turn and was now heading straight out to sea making irregular *s*-shaped course changes in an effort to spoil the aim of the attacking aircraft.

"Those fucking bombs are going to come close," Admiral Semenkov whispered.

Suddenly the water all around the *Hercules* was boiling in anger as the bombs from the C-130 hit and exploded. The whole ship shivered with the shock waves racing through the water. Pieces of the C-130, which had dropped the bombs, were falling out of the morning sky. There was one parachute in the air, a sole survivor drifting down.

"We've got one coming in from starboard and one from port," radar called out.

Gus swung his binoculars to starboard. It was a T-28. He could see the muzzle flashes as the aircraft's cannon opened up. The plane blew apart as the shells from the Mk 75 connected. Gus swung his binoculars to the port side where a sec ond T-28 was closing in.

"Get down," someone shouted. Gus and the Russian admi ral dove to the deck as lead slugs ripped through the super structure of the *Hercules*. Someone started screaming in pain Gus raised up off the deck and looked up out through th front port to see the underbelly of the T-28 pass directly ove the bow of the *Hercules*. The pilot was pulling up when wingtip blew off. The plane headed down as the pilot fough for control. He hit the water at a flat angle and bounce across the surface, pieces of the plane breaking off the fuse lage each time it smacked against the ocean surface. Wha was left of the fuselage finally stopped and slowly sank. Th pilot made no attempt to climb out of the cockpit before i sank beneath the water.

Gus was back on his feet and moving to the aid of the sailo sitting in the helmsman's chair. He had been the one scream ing, now he wasn't. His whole right shoulder had been blow away. His blood covered the control panel and splattere much of the deck. He had already bled to death. He was sti sitting in his chair, his eyes staring up through the broke glass of the pilothouse ports. Another crewman, wounded bu not badly, helped Gus take the dead man out of his position.

"We've got a ship on radar," the radar operator announce "Thirty-three miles out at 63 degrees. I'm sure it's a sub."

"Is that your sub?" Gus asked the Russian who was als back on his feet.

"My sub has orders to stay under the water."

"I've got the ship zeroed in with the Harpoon system Kathy Melendez's voice came over the speaker.

"Incoming missiles," radar called out. "Two on the way."

"Send her a Harpoon," Gus ordered. Ten seconds later, on of the Harpoons tore away from the launch tube. It rose int the air, then dropped back down and leveled off a few fe above the water as it accelerated toward the sub more tha

314

irty miles away. It would take less than three minutes for the issiles to cover the thirty miles. In the same time, the missiles that the sub had launched would come calling.

Everything that could be done to make sure they didn't find the *Hercules* was already being done. Large clouds of chaff filled the air behind the *Hercules* and the EMS systems were blanking out radar and sending false signals. As soon as the incoming missiles got within range, the Mk 75mm would automatically open fire.

"Give me a damage report," Gus demanded into his needle mouth mike. "We've got one KIA up here."

"Lieutenant JG Bradley, Sergeant Younce, and two others are hit down here," Phillips reported. "Bradley's dead. The PUU network control station is out of order."

"Shit!" Gus swore. "We won't know if we hit the targets."

"Here they come!" the radar operator called over the intercom.

Gus could see the incoming missiles flying across the waves. Neither one looked like it knew where it was going. They both missed the *Hercules* by a hundred yards, their electronic brains confused by chaff and false radar signals.

Thirty seconds later, radar reported that the *Hercules*'s Harpoon had exploded before reaching the target, probably shot down by a SAM missile.

"Shall I fire another one?" Kathy asked.

"Not unless they shoot at us again," Gus answered.

"She's going back under," radar reported. "I think she's running away."

"Can we talk to Subic?" Gus asked.

"I have Subic on the line."

"Then that SLAM must have hit the missile launchers," Gus shouted. "Pass a message to Admiral Rimaldo. Tell him the country is his, if he can take it back."

Gus looked around at the damage in the pilothouse. The dead man was laid out and someone had covered his face with

315

a cloth.

"Radar report," he barked.

"There is one aircraft in the air, but standing way off, more than twenty miles."

Gus stepped to the ladder and climbed down to the deck below. The command center was a shambles. Kathy Melendez was on her knees by the side of one of the wounded, her hands and arms covered to the elbows with the arterial blood of the young sailor. Her efforts had failed. The man was dead. Others were taking care of the other wounded.

Kathy looked up at him. "We did it," she said, her voice a quiet whisper. "I know we did it." There was no joy in the words. She was arguing with herself that the boy, whose head she was holding on her lap, had not died for nothing.

"We've got five more wounded and another dead in the engine room and other compartments," Jack Phillips reported. "A couple of the wounded need quick medical attention. We're losing fuel, too. We've got so many holes in the hull that we may sink if we go to hullborne condition."

"Head her out to sea and keep her on the foils until we run the tanks dry. Get on the radio and contact the nearest American ship. It's time for me to surrender. Ask for helicopters to pick up our wounded."

Chapter Twenty-eight

White House.

t wasn't the first time he'd been in the White House. There
been a picture-taking session in the Oval Office when he
come home from Nam to accept the medal. This time he
n't in the Oval Office, he was sitting in a small office off
Sit Room. Instead of a dress uniform, he was wearing a
k gray business suit.

I advised the President this meeting wasn't a good idea,"
or Carol, the National Security Advisor, said. Carol had
Gus at the employee entrance to the White House and
him into the room where they now sat.

He insisted he wanted to meet you, but we must keep it
et," Carol continued. "If the press ever gets hold of the real
ry, it will embarrass us all."

And you would have to court-martial the men and the
man who fought with me," Gus said. "I understand the
eement. I'll stick to it, as long as all the survivors of my
n can stay in the military, if that's what they want."

We've fixed it so none of this will show on their records. It's
portant that the public continue to believe that Philippine
istance fighters planted a bomb that killed Sorreno and
st of his cabinet."

I don't have any problems letting the Filipinos take the

317

credit," Gus answered. "They deserve it. They're the ones wh[o] made it possible. They're the ones still doing the dying."

Admiral Rimaldo had led an attack on Manila after bo[th] the SLAMs landed on target. He had taken the prison whe[re] the NPA had been holding the President and most of his cab[i]net. The old government was now back in place at Malacaña[n] Palace. But the remnants of the NPA were putting up a v[i]cious fight for survival, and they had captured heavy weapo[ns] that they never had before. Some commentators were pr[e]dicting the NPA might still win the civil war raging across t[he] island of Luzon. It was a civil war fought with convention[al] weapons. None of the fighting threatened any American pe[r]sonnel at Subic Bay.

The news stories of the fighting and the destruction of t[he] remaining nuclear weapons by resistance forces had push[ed] off the front page the story of an admiral who had deserted h[is] post.

A side door to the office opened and the President of t[he] United States walked into the room. Gus jumped to his fe[et] snapping to attention, then relaxing when he remember[ed] that kind of courtesy wasn't demanded of civilians.

The President held out his hand and Gus took it for [a] shake.

The President announced he was glad to shake Gus's ha[nd] and suggested they both sit down.

"I'm sorry I can't make this a public occasion," the Pre[si]dent said.

"Frankly, I'm glad it's not a public execution," Gus a[n]swered. "That's what I expected to get, or at least a long st[ay] in Fort Leavenworth."

"I've still got people telling me I should order you cou[rt] martialed. They're telling me you not only deserted yo[ur] post, you put the people you deserted in imminent danger."

"I thought what I did was the only way I could get them [out] of imminent danger."

"My Russian friends have passed me some intelligence

North Koreans that suggest you did exactly that. I ought I was doing the right thing when I decided that Subic y would be safe if I kept talking. I didn't realize the Kims re as crazy as Saddam. They really must have it in for the ited States."

"What are you going to do about them?" Gus asked.

"I can't do a whole lot. You blew up all the evidence. We 't prove any of the corpses in that hotel are North Koreans. e same at the missile site. We'll put diplomatic pressure on m, demand they comply with the nonproliferation treaty, ist on verification, and look for the hard evidence that uld justify a preemptive strike if they keep producing apon material. But I didn't bring you here to talk politics d foreign policy. I want to hear the story . . . the whole ry."

Gus told it. It took him an hour. Four times, someone led on the phone to tell the President he had other appoint- nts. Each time, the President told Tabor Carol to tell the ler he was still busy.

"I assume you understand the politics dictating that we 't decorate you with the medals you deserve," the President d when Gus finished.

"I've already got medals," Gus answered. "I know the U.S. 't go around killing heads of state, that we are not sup- ed to interfere in the affairs of other countries, and that we er hit first."

"And you did all three. I like to think that if I had been in ur place, I would have done the same thing."

"I'm not sorry I did what I did."

"I did look for ways for us to keep you in uniform. The only ig anyone could suggest is that we fit you out with a whole v identity and a fake career history."

"I like the name I have. Jones may sound common, but I it to keep wearing it. It's time for me to retire anyway. I ght one last battle from the deck of a ship. I can't repeat t again, so why stay around for less?"

319

"What are your plans?" the President asked.

"I'm going to take on a new job. I had a wife once who told me I couldn't imagine what a difficult job it was. I'm looking forward to finding out if it is."

"What kind of job?"

"I'm going to become a naval spouse. I'm marrying a lieutenant commander."

"The woman on the *Hercules?*" the President asked.

"The woman on the *Hercules.*" Gus answered.